MADAM MULDOON'S GARDEN

THOSE RESILIENT MULDOONS
BOOK TWO

E.V. SPARROW

To my resilient family members who made tough choices to live in freedom. Their unknown descendants thank them for it.

To all families who embrace hope. Those who must uproot from their loved ones and go far away for an improved way of life.

INTRODUCTION AND GLOSSARY
OF TERMS

Unfamiliar words or terms written by the author and explained for readers. This glossary is intended to be helpful, although not perfectly accurate nor exhaustive.

*Irish Gaelic Words, Historical References, or Catholic Terms:

Adhlacóir. Undertaker.

aingeal dubh
black angel

aye
Affirmative, ever, forever, always.

bàn
White.

banshee [**ban**-shee] (*bean sí*)
(In Irish legend) a female spirit whose wailing warns of an impending death in a house.

bhainne
Milk cow.

bùird-luinge. Ship deck.

boyo
Boy or man (used chiefly as a form of address).

Castle Barracks
Where local British soldiers were housed in King John's Castle, (in Limerick).

claddagh [**klah**-d*uh*]
A ring in the form of two hands clasping a crowned heart, given in friendship or love. First recorded in 1880–85; named after Claddagh, a fishing village near Galway, Ireland, where the ring was supposedly first designed and made

cobs
A powerfully built, short-legged horse.

coffin ships
Any of the ships that carried Irish immigrants escaping the Great Irish Famine and Highlanders displaced by the Highland Clearances. Coffin ships were crowded and disease-ridden, had poor access to food and water, resulting in many deaths as they crossed the Atlantic. Although it was the cheapest way to cross the Atlantic, it had a 30% mortality rate.

colaimbín
Columbine.

Cù a' gabhail a' chuthaich
Dog going wild, barking madly.

cupán tae
Cup of tea.

dearg súile
Red, bloodshot eyes.

draganta
dragon-like
or draig
Dragon, fire.

eolchaire
Sadness, grief, lamentation.

fáilte
Reception, welcome, hospitality.

fascicle [**fas**-i-k*uh*l]
A section of a book or set of books being published in installments as separate pamphlets or volumes.

Fearbán féir
Meadow-buttercup.

Fenián [**feen**-yuhn]
A member of a 19th-century revolutionary nationalist organization among the Irish in the US and Ireland. The Fenians staged an unsuccessful revolt in Ireland in 1867 and were responsible for isolated revolutionary acts against the British until the early 20th century, when gradually eclipsed by the IRA.
1810–20; < Irish *féinne* (genitive of *fiann* band of Fenians) + -ian; influenced by Old Irish *féne* ancient inhabitant of Ireland

fraochán

Bilberry, whortleberry.

gabhair bainne
Goat's milk.

gall-luch
A rat.

gealtlann
lunatic asylum, or madhouse

hooligan
A violent young troublemaker, typically one of a gang.

Land Rights
The inheritance method in 1700-1800 Ireland was the "stem family system." The Irish Catholic could not "own" the land. One child inherited control of the family holding renting a parcel of land from an English overlord. Occasionally the oldest son didn't inherit "the farm." Most Irish Catholic families were large, and the plots of land were too small for dividing among all male offspring, or the businesses too small to support many. Other children were forced to live a celibate life at home helping on the family property, take a menial job with very little hope of ever getting a piece of land, or they immigrated.

Lios Tuathail
Modern town of Listowel, which translates to "Tuathal's ringfort" or "the fort of Tuathal," and also means the earthen fort.

lucifer
Early Matches:
The first commercially produced matches, developed in the 1820s and 1830s, were known as "lucifers." The term "lucifer" was chosen

because it means "light-bringer," reflecting the matches' function of providing a quick and convenient source of fire.

macushla
Literally, my pulse (mo + cuisle), used as an affectionate form of address, like "darling."

minseach
Nanny goat, she-goat.

moors, or *moorland*
A tract of open uncultivated upland; a heath.

mummers
Performer, actor in pantomime.

Oíche na Gaoithe Mire
The Night of the Big Wind, a powerful European windstorm that swept across Ireland beginning in the afternoon of January 6, 1839, causing severe damage to property and several hundred deaths before moving across northern England. The worst storm to hit Ireland in 300 years.

ollphéist ghráiniúil
Fearful monster.

reticule
Women's small handbag originally netted and typically having a drawstring and decorated with embroidery or beading.

scraith
A strip of sod, or straw and sod.

shillelee [shuh-**ley**-lee]

A stout stick or cudgel of blackthorn or oak used in Ireland, typically as a weapon (club).

slíbín (sle-veen)
An untrustworthy or cunning person.
-
snug
Small, private room or compartment in a pub.

tam o'shanter, (tam)
Round woolen or cloth cap of Scottish origin, with a tight headband, wide, flat circular crown, often with a pom-pom on top.

Teach na mbocht
Poorhouse, or workhouse.

The Crown
The government of England (and therefore any countries ruled by England).

tuama leac
A tomb or grave.

*Roman Catholic Terms:

absolution
Roman Catholic Theology: a remission of sin or of the punishment for sin, made by a priest in the sacrament of penance on the ground of authority received from Christ.

catechism
A summary of the principles of Christian religion in the form of questions and answers, used for the instruction of Christians.

Confession

A formal statement of admission of guilt.

confessional, or booth
An enclosed stall in a church divided by a screen or curtain in which a priest sits to hear people confess their sins.

crossed themselves
Making the Sign of the Cross over themselves. A Christian (Catholic) sign made in blessing or prayer by tracing a cross from the forehead to the chest and to each shoulder, or in the air.

crucifix or crucifixes
A representation of a cross with a figure of Jesus Christ on it.

First Communion
(Especially in the Roman Catholic Church) the occasion on which a person receives the Eucharist (a Catholic Mass including the Holy Communion) for the first time, often celebrated as a religious ceremony for children of about 7 or 8 years of age.

Hail Mary

Last Rites
(In Catholic and Orthodox Churches) rites (prayers and ministrations) administered to a person who is about to die.

nun, or Sister
A member of a religious community of women, especially a cloistered (living in a convent) one, living under vows of poverty, chastity, and obedience.

Our Father (prayer)
Also called The Lord's Prayer.

penance

Voluntary self-punishment inflicted as an outward expression of repentance for having done wrong.

priest, or Father

An ordained minister of the Catholic, Orthodox, or Anglican Church having the authority to perform certain rites and administer certain sacraments.

Purgatory

(In Roman Catholic doctrine) a place or state of suffering inhabited by the souls of sinners who are expiating (atoning for) their sins before going to heaven.

rosary (worry pearls)

Prayer beads. In the Roman Catholic Church, a form of devotion in which five (or fifteen) decades of Hail Mary are repeated, each decade preceded by an Our Father and followed by a Glory Be.

sacraments, and Sacrament of the Sick

(In the Christian Church) a religious ceremony or ritual regarded as imparting divine grace, such as baptism, communion or the Eucharist and (in the Roman Catholic and many Orthodox Churches) penance and the anointing of the sick.

Saint Christopher

The patron saint of travelers venerated in Roman Catholicism, Eastern Orthodoxy, Lutheranism, Oriental Orthodoxy, and Anglicanism.

saints

Verb: formally recognize as a saint; canonize: A person acknowledged as holy or virtuous and typically regarded as being in heaven after death.

thurible [**thoor**-*uh-buh*l]

a censer. Censer: a container, usually covered, in which incense is burned, especially during religious services; thurible.

*Definition and pronunciation when available:
https://www.teanglann.ie/en/fuaim/

*Definitions and descriptions:
https://en.wikipedia.org/wiki/Main_Page

GAELIC CHARACTER NAMES

Pronunciations and/or origins:

Aidan, *Aodhan,* 'little fire,' St. Aidan 651 AD.

Allana, *Aleanbh,* Gaelic 'a leanbh': 'O child'. Alana is a variant.

Brian, after Brian Boru, High King of Ireland 1014 AD.

Cathal, (CA-ol) for *Charles.*

Clodagh, (CLO-dah) a placename: a County Tipperary river.

Eoghan, (OH-wen) 'well-born,' used as a form of Eugene and Owen.

Fiona, *(FEW-nah)* '*Fionn*' meaning 'fair.'

Kathleen, *Caitlín* a Gaelic form of Catherine, Caitlin is a variant.

Maeve, (MAY-bh) *Meadhbh* is 'intoxicating one.'

Orla, (OR-lah) *Orfhlaith* Gaelic: 'golden lady.' Orlagh and Aurnia are variants.

Siobhan, (SHIV-awn) *Síobán,* a Gaelic form of Joan. Judith and Julia are variants.

Tarah, from *Teamhair,* a placename: the seat of the High Kings of Ireland.

Main source for or of names and definitions: https://www.ireland-information.com/heraldichall/

Pronunciation when available:

https://www.teanglann.ie/en/fuaim/

CHAPTER 1

Beauty Lies Within Her

Beauty's never been within the eye. I fear 'tis within the soul
Orla

ounty Kerry, Ireland
Summer, 1863

PURE AGONY PIERCED Orla Muldoon's dream. She jerked awake with a squeal, then clamped her palm over her mouth. Her right cheek and eyebrow throbbed. With her lungs heaving for breath, and her fingertips massaging the scars on her face, she waited for the nightmarish memory of self-injury to evaporate. Her heart thudded as hard as when she beat the cottage rugs on laundry day.

Gray shadows cloaked the shared bedroom with her younger

sister, disclosing the time as before sunrise. She turned and reached out beside her. *Empty.* Voices were raised in the scullery, then footfalls drew nearer.

"Saints preserve us! Thought someone was murdering me girl in her sleep." Mam's shrill voice seemed to be the force which opened the door. The hearth's light glowed behind her tiny silhouette inside Orla's doorframe, outlining her mam's arm raised above her head with her hand gripping a poker.

Orla swung her legs over the edge of the paltry mattress and shimmied her tattered nightgown down over her knees. "Apologies for giving you the frights, Mam. Was only another nightmare." Icy flagstone chilled Orla's feet, and she headed toward the shelf for her woolen stockings. Nausea from the blood in her nightmare fought with the gory images in her memory. She shuddered. *Wasn't a brilliant idea to change me looks, was it?*

The youngest Muldoon, Kathleen, peeked around Mam's shoulder. "Was it the one 'bout when you tried to stab your eye out?" She pulled a face. "'Tis the most terrible one. Or was it the one when Billy Murray burned your hair to make it darker and set his sleeve on fire? Or the one—"

"For heaven's sake, Kathleen," Mam huffed and hissed over her shoulder, "leave your sister be. Aye? 'Tis bad enough she's marred with the scars. Don't mention the nightmares. Orla, you're needed to cook the breakfast, you are."

"And you must be the one to cook your delightful sausages you brought home for us, sister." Kathleen gave Orla a pouty lipped smile.

Mam whipped around and fluffed her apron at Kathleen to direct her back to the hearth and followed her. "Orla's a strong one. And your brothers will arrive soon. Let's get on with our duties."

"Aye, I'm a strong one." Orla gulped down the bile in her throat. *But not beloved. Shunned.* She shook herself and breathed in deep a few times. Snatching her warmest shawl from the foot of the black iron bed, she wrapped it tightly around her shoulders and joined the food preparations.

Why had she thought the answer to her acceptance in the village was to gouge out her pale blue eyes? "Alter their superstitions? All for naught. And I'm no devil's spawn." Orla mumbled while she flipped the sizzling sausages in the iron skillet. Thank God Kathleen had caught her in the middle of the deed before she did more damage to herself. "Lamb, you're the best sister there ever was."

"Because I stopped you from your wicked plan? I heard your mumbling 'bout it." Kathleen twisted around from the table with utensils in her fists. "Thank heavens Mam shooed me outside. I saw enough blood at five-years-old, thank you. When Mam worked on your wound, your screams made me scamper and hide. It gave me the worst shivers, and I cried harder than ever. Or mayhap I cried that loud when Katie twisted her ankle and we thought 'twas broken, or—"

"Not from your sorrow for me, 'tis because of your love for me." Orla slid a peep at the cottage's deep-set window, to the golden sunrise highlighting the top of their stone wall and the emerald hills beyond. The pastoral view swam with her own tears of remembrance for the rash actions and abject loneliness of her seven-year-old self.

Kathleen pointed a spoon in her direction. "Your reason to injure yourself was all for naught. How could you do such a terrible thing, aye? Never understood—"

"You wouldn't. I've naught anything good 'bout me from God. You all possess beautiful auburn hair. He cruelly created me with peach-colored hair, and these odd eyes. He could've made them sapphire like the rest of yours—"

"Hush, now." Mam thrust up her arms and hands and shook them in the air. "Never be bringing a curse down upon us with your sacrilege. God loves you as well as the rest of us. He made you in His artistic way. He did. No more complaints 'bout it, girlie. We all have our burdens to bear."

"Aye, Mam." Orla shrugged and scooped a pile of eggs onto Mam's chipped serving platter. "Fixing me eyes seemed the best answer to me problem. I regret me choice terribly."

"As you should." Mam set the last of the plates from her green hutch onto the marred tabletop. "Haven't I told you beauty varies with people's sight? But did you heed me?"

3

"Couldn't."

"No, not her." Mam nudged Kathleen. "Your sister didn't accept herself and her lot, did she? Ah, be sure to set the delightful sausages out, Lamb."

Orla removed her apron, wiped her hands, and stood beside her chair at the table. She grumbled. "Beauty's never been within the eye. I fear 'tis within the soul." *Me own may match me face.*

"What did your da tell you 'bout what true beauty is?"

Low-pitched voices and shouts of laughter approached the Muldoon's cottage, and Mam and Kathleen hurriedly removed their patched aprons after they laid all the food in the center of the bumpy table.

"What Da said?" Orla clasped her hands in front of her. *Me lovely da.* "He said a brilliant mind is more winsome than beauty." How would he know? He was a handsome man. His normal blue eyes did not frighten people. *No one spit at him or told him he was evil.* Her heart contracted with longing to have him back with the family, but was God not selfish enough to take him to heaven? She would not mention this thought for fear of a curse.

Kathleen unlatched the front door and tugged it inward. "Morning to you, our charming men. So glad you all work on the farm." She bobbed a curtsy to one of her older brothers, Mick, as he entered ahead of the other Muldoon brothers, Ed, and Rory.

"As if we have a choice, aye? Where else could we work? Feeling spritely today, are you, Lamb?" Mick kissed the top of Kathleen's head.

"'Tis a good day to be so, as there's a cloudless sky above us."

Orla snorted. "Quick, someone should paint a painting as proof of Ireland's rare clear sky."

Kathleen grinned. "We can ask Rory. How is your *macushla* faring, Mick? Has Fiona's fever abated?"

Mick took a wobbly seat simultaneously with his three brothers, and they scooted closer to the table. He rubbed his eyes. "Nah, Lamb. She's still poorly. I'm fearing for her wellbeing. She was fast asleep when I left her, but Father Shanahan is to visit us later to perform the

Sacrament of the Sick and anoint her. 'Tis why I've come for breakfast. Then I'll away directly." He addressed Mam with a raised brow.

"Oh, aye. As always, you may take what's left of it home with you after you've had your fill." Mam sat, and the girls followed. She nodded at Orla. "Our Orla has given me the egg money and earned us more by going to market with our Tarah, aye. They must pay higher wages in Limerick, for we'd enough coin to purchase sausages this time."

"Am glad to do that for the family, Mam." Orla studied her plate and fumbled with her fingers on her lap under the table.

"Kathleen, now your brothers are seated, and 'tis your turn to give thanks. Add a prayer for God's mercy upon Mick's bride." Mam crossed herself and closed her eyes.

Everyone did the same but Orla. *Those sausages weren't from God's angels.* She had learned her destiny was to provide for each of the families, had she not? She studied each precious member as Kathleen blessed the repast.

"Bless us O Lord, for these Thy gifts, for which we are 'bout to receive from Your bounty through Jesus Christ our Lord. Christ, have mercy upon all the sick in our village, and especially Mick's bride, Fiona. Amen."

When had God ever answered her own prayers? Not when her da was ill. Not when Mick's first wife and both little sons were ill. They had all passed away. *Why pray for Fiona?*

Mick took two pieces of meat from the plate Mam handed to him, and passed it over to Ed, who passed it to Rory. Then Rory passed it to Mam. Around the table in a circle those expensive sausages went, with only Orla herself knowing the cost to herself to bring them home. Could she force herself to swallow a bite? She scrunched up her shoulders.

Kathleen leaned against her. "Orla, do you have a chill? Sally got ill with the typhus this time round, and then her brother and sister. 'Tis why we avoided Mick's home. You must be careful not to get ill."

"Who's getting a chill? Who's getting ill?" Mam's shrill voice almost cost Mick his sausage as it jerked on the tongs of his fork.

Ed scoffed. "All this family needs are more ill people. When will it ever end? The Crown starves us. It weakens us." He spat. "Ah, apologies Mam."

"You know how I detest anyone spitting upon me clean floors, Edward Muldoon." Mam's auburn eyebrows formed into one long "V" shape. *Glad I'm not the brunt of her ire.*

Orla turned her eyes to survey the stone floors. *Clean enough, they were, with only a bit of dust.* Thanks to Kathleen's chores, for certain.

Rory finished his last bite and dropped his fork onto his already cracked plate. *Rory.* Such a quiet man one can almost forget he exists. *Methinks, he prefers it that way. Whilst I'm forced into the shadows where I don't wish to be.*

"Orla." Kathleen tapped her sister's arm with her teaspoon. "Mam's been asking you a question."

"What was it, Mam? Was thinking of Da, and lost track of what you asked me whilst heeding the interruptions. He always made us wait to speak until after we'd eaten, aye?"

"Not I. Me preference is to speak whilst everyone is in one room altogether." *She means demand every detail of our lives.* She craved fodder for the village chinwag, Mrs. Gilhooley.

Wheels crunched on the path outside the cottage. Through the recessed rectangle window facing the front yard of the cottage, a cart pulled up near the front door. If only Kathleen had wiped the windowpanes during her other chores, they could identify the person approaching.

"Glory be. Now who would be arriving at this time of day, when all good Irish families are breaking their fast before work? If good fortune gave them a full cupboard, that is." Mam craned her neck to peer through the window. "And Kathleen, why haven't you wiped the glass?" *There 'tis. Poor Kathleen.*

Mick stood and clutched their mother's shoulder. "Let me see to it, Mam. Could be someone fetching me."

A thud at the door, and Mick swung it inward. "Ah, morning Aidan. What's the goings on to bring you here so early?"

"Aidan?" Kathleen perked up like a hen discovering bugs in the grass.

His own expression lit up when he spied Kathleen. "Morning, all. I've a question for Orla—"

Mam's tabby cat rushed in between the men's legs with something in her mouth and set it on the floor. It was a bird. Not yet dead.

"Holy heavens, she's done it again." Orla tipped her chair over as she stood, and the bird flew past her to the hearth.

Aidan crunched his tweed *Tam-o'-shanter* in his fists. "Me apologies, Mrs. Muldoon. I'd no intent—"

"Get the bird!" Mam shrieked. "No, get the cat."

The tiny bird hopped and settled onto the iron rods cooling the pans beside the lit hearth. *Catching its terrified breath, no doubt.*

Kathleen rushed toward the hearth with a bowl, and the sparrow fluttered to the ceiling's thatch and rafters. "Good heavens. 'Tis too high now."

"I'll do it." Orla dragged her chair over by Kathleen. "I'm taller. Give me the bowl."

"Make haste." Mam wrung her hands. "Pitiable thing, 'tis bleeding. Glad 'twasn't a lizard this time. Holy angels. Tabby's not full grown, yet she'd find a way to drag in an elephant by its toe if they lived in Ireland."

Ed huffed. "Just flap your hands at it, Orla, and 'twill fly out the open doorway."

A split second before Orla thumped the bowl over it, the sparrow regained its strength. It avoided the men near the door and glided above the table to land on Mrs. Muldoon's green hutch.

Tabby sprung into action and sprang four feet off the ground. She landed on the tabletop in the middle of the sausage plate, tracking the movement of her hunting trophy. Tabby knocked over teacups and stepped on the leftover eggs and toast.

"Our breakfast! Grab her before she jumps onto me dishes and breaks them." Mam clutched her head between her hands. "'Tis why I don't allow cats inside of me home."

Orla scrambled off the chair. "Doesn't bode well, does it? Tabby's not giving up her prey." She hurried to protect her mam's valuables on the shelves from the hunter, but the tiny bird launched from the hutch toward the ceiling above the hearth. It clutched the *scraith* between the open rafters, hanging on tightly while eyeing its predator.

Tabby scurried after it, and skittered onto Mrs. Muldoon's favorite chair, impaling the bird with her murderous scrutiny.

"None of us can snatch Tabby, Mam." Kathleen rubbed her neck. "She bites and scratches. She shan't catch the bird now, aye? But how do we coax it outside?"

Mick stepped away from the open door and stared at their trodden breakfast. "Mam, will you allow me to stand upon your table? I shall wave me cap at it to startle it away."

Mrs. Muldoon raised her hands. "Aye. What damage will boots do after Tabby? First, we must do something 'bout the mess."

Everyone cleared a spot on the tabletop and set the dishes in the sink, while Mick removed his boots. His big toe peeked out of one gray woolen sock.

Orla chuckled. "You need some darning, brother."

"When me *macushla* is well, she'll get after it." Mick scampered onto the highest piece of furniture, and Tabby did the same.

Tabby sat alongside his foot. He scooted her with his foot, but she bit it. "Ow. Someone, seize that wicked cat." She defended her position with her teeth and claws, focused intently on the sparrow.

"See, as I warned, aye? Tabby won't let us." Kathleen reached for the cat. It scurried beneath the table, across the seats, and returned to crouch by Mick's feet.

Orla snorted. "I learned the painful way. Never touching her again, the hell-born beastie."

Ed ran his hands over his hair. "Mam, since our breakfast is ruined. Might as well be done here." He headed to the back door. "Our donkey's waiting for his, and Rory must do the milking."

"Ah, 'bout that. Wait. Rory, Ed . . ." Aidan hurried after them, leaving the back door open.

Kathleen stared after Aidan and chewed her lip. "I wished to speak to him for a moment before he left."

"And he's left another door open. Mayhap it'll tempt the bird, aye?" Mick waved his *tam* in the air. "Go on, fly away. Now's your chance, little one."

The sparrow took flight. The predator cat clambered after it, and the two dashed outside into the golden sunrise.

Mam banged the door shut. "And that's as it should be. Such a hullaballoo to deal with first thing in the morning. What further unfortunate happenings lie before us this day?"

Muffled voices outside the cottage drifted in.

"Someone's out front." Kathleen rushed to the window. "'Tis our men with our *minseach*."

Orla swung the door open and leaned out. "They've untied our goat from Aidan's cart. Why was she tethered to it at all? We would've known she was missing if Rory would've milked her earlier."

"Shoo, Orla. Don't let the cat back inside." Mam jostled her outside and she and Kathleen followed her, closing the door. They gazed at Rory together and rubbed the chill of early morning from their hands while the sun hovered low above the green hills and trees.

Rory clenched the rope that had fastened the goat to Aidan's wagon. "Wondered who'd stolen her when I found the shed empty with the gate open. We all need our milk, but couldn't figure out which one of our good neighbors would do such a terrible thing, aye?" He led the goat down the hill back to the pen.

"Your nanny was happily eating grass beside the road as I was on me way to Limerick." Aidan pointed at his stack of crates. High pitched peeping emanated from them. "Me uncle wishes me to deliver his chicks in three days' time. Since I'd to return your goat home, I thought Orla might be needing a ride to the city? Mayhap she can help me with feeding the hatchlings and warming them on the journey, aye? What say you, Mrs. Muldoon?"

Orla turned to her mam with a smile and entwined her fingers behind her back. "I know I returned only last week from helping Aunt Clodagh, but she and Tarah are always in need of it."

Kathleen gasped. "Oh, Mam, may I go as well? She always goes, and I never have. We'll be of more help together, and we can return with haste. You know how good I am at doing chores and—"

"You may not. I can't spare both me girlies at the same time. It takes nearly six days to go back and forth, aye? Orla may stay to help. Don't pout Kathleen, you're nearing fourteen." Mrs. Muldoon glanced between Aidan and Orla. "Sure, and you'll be under your uncle's escort, and you'll also abide by society's rules of conduct for unmarried young people?"

They agreed.

"Then you may be away." A sudden shaft of sunlight beamed upon Adian's cart from behind the oak tree in the yard. Mam Muldoon shaded her eyes.

'Tis a grand sign I'm to go. Orla raised her hem and hurried into the cottage. Footfalls behind her in the soft mud alerted her that her younger sister was not willing to drop her request to accompany her on the journey. *What could be done 'bout it?* Mam happily ruled their lives with her decisions since their da went to heaven.

A soft sob from Kathleen, and Orla paused to embrace her. "I know, Lamb. I'd be sad to stay if I were you. Come with me whilst I pack up."

They entered together and headed for their room. Kathleen sat on their narrow bed and swiped at her cheek. "Why can I never leave, even for a few days? 'Tis all because you're the oldest daughter. Why did God make me the youngest? Mam depends upon me for everything—"

"Imagine how 'twould be to be Mam. Would you enjoy us both away?" Orla stuffed her other skirt and shirt into a tattered pillowcase.

Kathleen sniffed. "You know I wouldn't."

"Nor I." Orla grabbed her hairbrush from their dresser and her unmentionables to add to the stuffed pillowcase. She knotted the top closed and smoothed out the wrinkles on the red rose quilt Kathleen had pieced together for their birthdays. She sat on it and pulled her sister beside her.

"God must love you dearly, Orla, to give you time away from our Mam."

If she believed God cared for her welfare, would she not be convinced of God's love as well? *Has He ever even seen me?* Orla kissed Kathleen's cheek. "Being in Limerick gives me a way to earn some coin. Wishing to purchase a *bhainne* for Mick when I've enough coin saved. Will further add to the family coffers by selling her milk at market. 'Tis me plan anyway. And the mooing will add a musical sound to the barnyard, aye? One day, Lamb, I'll surely take you with me when the time is right." *How shall I ever explain our family's dire situation to our innocent lamb?*

As Orla did not believe God noticed anything about her, it was likely only destiny was behind what happened to her. Her family's welfare was her burden to bear, and she would do her utmost to carry it alone. She would accept any chance to feed them. Plus stash a portion in her hiding spot for her own secret plans.

CHAPTER 2

Fairy Garden

Well, if hair washing be the way to magic in our lives, I'll do it all the more
Orla

$\mathcal{L}$imerick, Outskirts
Summer, 1864

NEAR THE STONE wall's opening in front of Aunt Clodagh's home
Aidan coaxed his donkey and cart to a standstill. "Glad to be of help in
bringing you with me, Orla. 'Tis a fine and sunny day for Limerick.
Even the winds are calm."

"Aye. The drive was lovely as well. The wildflowers in bloom are
me favorites. *Fearbán féir* and *Colaimbín*. 'Tis the kind of day to
venture out and absorb the sun's rays."

Aidan's brows lifted. "Buttercups? Can surely imagine the Columbine but would've thought you to be a rose-lover, aye?"

"And who can argue with roses?" Orla climbed down with her sack and waved as Aidan departed for his uncle's home. She shut her eyes and raised her face to the sun for a moment. Her young cousins' shouting at something drifted from Tarah's small cottage garden in the rear yard. *Makes me heart glad to share Tarah's burdens.*

Three young women passed by Orla on the lane, loudly chattering and laughing. They carried their laden baskets from the market. The taller one furtively waved to her. *Siobhan and her sisters.*

She returned the greeting before she knocked on the chipped red door and swung it inward. It took a moment for her eyes to adjust from the sunshine to the shadowy interior. The only window was inset deeply into the wall beside the entry door, the same as her mam's cottage. The hedge here had overgrown most of Auntie Clodagh's window. *Many things within this home are in want of repair.* Orla whispered to herself, as usual. "Mayhap God will do something 'bout it one day."

Voices from the scullery area alerted her where to find her aunt's family.

"Hey ho, Tarah. Help has entered your home." Orla hurried to the scullery and clapped her hands. "So, what were the boys yelling 'bout outside?"

"Such a lovely surprise! Didn't expect you for another week. Me impish brothers are the guardians of our garden. Gives them space to play and an important task—shooing away the blackbirds." Tarah shrugged. "Shan't birds be birds now? They're after the *fraochán*. Berries entice their appetites, but not the herbs for alleviating Mam's pain. If the hungry creatures ate those, I'd throw stones at them meself, aye?"

"Aye." Orla stroked her Aunt Clodagh's head. "So, Auntie, 'tis bathing day? The sun is ready and willing to welcome you."

Tarah smiled at Orla while she removed her blue shawl covering the basket of herbs on the table in front of her mam. "Your arrival is timely, Orla. thinking to bathe her meself, I've readied the tub and

Mam is all situated. The lavender is steeping in her bath. Can you smell it? 'Tis lovely. Now you're here, I must be away to the market with me herbs. I'm taking the littles to help, although for them 'tis more 'bout wishing to see the beasties." She called over her shoulder. "Cathal. Brian. Let's get to market then."

The boys rammed into each other when they rushed through the rear door from the tiny garden. They embraced Orla with their dirty hands, leaving smudges on her skirt.

"Boyos, such a rude thing to do to our cousin Orla. Ah, your clothes." Tarah brushed at the dirt specks on Orla's dress.

Brian rubbed his nose, leaving a trail of soil above his upper lip. "Apologies, Cousin Orla. Did you bring us scones in your pockets?"

Tarah slapped at his outstretched hand and pointed at the sink. "Wash up. Make haste."

"Apologies for getting you dirty." Seven-year-old Cathal rushed to obey his sister.

"'Tis what brothers do. Hands washed first." Orla reached into her sack and handed each boy a flat potato scone wrapped in cloth. "But I shall tell you, 'twas cousin Kathleen, not I, who made these. Your Orla is not a good cook. We'd also no jam for me to bring you this time."

Cathal unwrapped his scone and inhaled its earthy aroma. "I shall imagine the currant jam. Let's spread butter on them—"

"We've no time for that. Eat them as we go." Tarah took her brothers by their shoulders, aimed them toward the doorway, and spoke over her shoulder. "Be careful not to slip on the floor when it's wet, ladies. We'll return shortly."

Aunt Clodagh grunted, and her mouth contorted with the effort to speak. Her gnarled hands swished in a farewell in front of her twisted body.

"Such a lovely sendoff, Auntie." Orla embraced her aunt's thin body. "We shan't miss them a bit. Twill be grand, won't it? Would you like a scone before your bath? We'll plump you up before they return, aye? Won't they be surprised?"

Clodagh heaved a graveled giggle and shakily nodded her head.

"Oh, so now you're a greedy gut since they've gone. You're wishing for both a treat and a bath? I'll keep your secrets safe." Orla winked at her and removed the last scone from her rucksack. She retrieved a small plate from the white cupboard, a spoon from the drawer, and unfolded the fabric covered treat at the table.

Her aunt snorted.

"In such a hurry, you are. Did our Tarah forget to feed you break-fast? For shame on her." Orla scooted her aunt closer to the table, careful not to pin her arms too tightly against it. "That one's distracted. Not me. I've come to your rescue."

Clodagh grinned lopsidedly.

Orla broke and crumbled the potato scone onto the dish and scooped up enough crumbs to halfway fill the spoon. "Open as wide as you can, Auntie. And after, you'll get a sip from the warm *cupán tae* Tarah luckily remembered to make for you. A lovely chamomile tisane. She didn't forget that one, aye?"

Her aunt hoarsely chortled.

"Holy heavens, was that a laugh? You must do more of that. Partake from a long sip of tea, aye. And a few bites more? Would be grand for you." Orla slid another bite of crumbs into her aunt's slightly open mouth. "There 'tis. You'd do better with a mouth as big as mine, aye? Always opening it when I shouldn't."

Auntie tipped her head back as she chewed and squinted at Orla.

"'Tis a mercy you're not speaking what you're thinking, aye? I'll take your frown to mean you agree. Can you not eat any more scone?"

Orla couldn't reach Clodagh's mouth with another bite when she turned her head away.

"What 'bout a bit more of your favorite tea, Auntie? Only a sip?" Orla held the cup to her lips. Tea dribbled down Clodagh's chin onto her neck and nightie. "Would you look at what a clumsy niece I am? Didn't wish to burn your mouth with hot tea but holy heavens, burning your neck would be a disaster as well, aye?" She dabbed at her aunt's face and neck with the wrap from the scone.

Clodagh bobbed her hands in front of her torso and mumbled.

"By all the saints. Didn't know you were so eager for a bath. Let's get to it then."

Orla dragged two chairs beside the tub, then undressed and readied her aunt for her weekly bath. She tested the water with her elbow. The hot water Tarah had filled the tub with had cooled to a warm temperature. She hoisted Clodagh's diminutive body by her armpits onto her own bent legs and strained to gently lower her aunt's stiff legs into the liquid. She straightened Clodagh and propped her up with a cloth to keep her tender skin from bruising against the metal rim.

"'Tis a blessing I'm as tall as a man with the strength of an ox, aye?"

Clodagh let out a long sigh and stared at Orla before she slowly closed her eyes.

"'Tis glad I am to make you happy, Auntie. Soothing to the bones, aye?" She fetched the soap from the floor next to the cup Tarah had set out for Orla's use. She lathered up a washcloth.

Her aunt lurched with a cry, and some water splashed over the tub's rim.

"There, there, Auntie, I've got you. You're grand. Relax and lean forward whilst I pour some water over your head. I believe you've a fairy garden growing in your hair since last week, don't you know? I swear I saw a magic light twinkling within it just now. Did you feel something tickling you?"

Another twisted smile and a hoarse giggle from her dear aunt delighted Orla's heart.

Such a miserable condition tormented Clodagh, yet her cheerful disposition helped to lighten her cousin's burden. What was this evil disease that had stricken her sweet aunt three-years back? Why did it have to come after her husband passed? No one knew, not even the priest. *No sense praying for answers.* It was up to her and Tarah to keep their families together and from starvation and lack.

"Well, if hair washing be the way to magic in our lives, I'll do it all the more, aye, Auntie?"

Soap dripped down Clodagh's thin and contorted body, and her spine was more pronounced than a few months ago. She shivered a little, so Orla dipped the cup into the warm liquid again and drizzled it onto her aunt's nearly transparent skin. Chill bumps arose on her arms.

Orla rose and quickly checked the kettle. "What say you to adding more heat to your bath? Aye? Tarah mayhap left us more to use."

Her aunt moaned. She shivered and coughed while Orla hastily returned to pour warmer water into the tub. She held Clodagh snug against the tub's wall and her own chest. "Precious Auntie, you're cold." She wiped Clodagh's face with the towel.

Clodagh caught her breath and stopped coughing. Her frail body shook. She stared at Orla with her head tilted cockeyed, then cackled. The low rumble vibrated against Orla's arm.

"Holy heavens. You were near to an iceberg, yet you find humor in it?" Orla tsked. "You're braver than I ever believed, then. What would Tarah have thought when she came home to find us both ice cubes in the scullery?"

Her aunt shifted with Orla's coaxing, and after a few moments of soaking, grunting and turning, she boosted her mam's dear sister out of the water, onto the wet flagstone, and finished drying her upper torso. "Oh, Auntie. The cloth slipped from the edge, and you've a bruise on your back. I fear Tarah shall accuse me of taking terrible care of you. Shall you forgive me?"

Clodagh nodded awkwardly and raised her most limber arm first for Orla to shimmy a nightie over it and then over her head.

Orla sopped up the damp floor with her own skirt, then maneuvered her aunt onto the chair she scooted up to the hearth earlier. "I'll stoke the fire for you, but I'm thinking the quickest way to dry us is in the garden's sunshine whilst the flames grow. I'll help you outside, aye? We'll go slow."

Her aunt squeaked.

"So, you're a dainty mouse now? Compared to me giant self, you are so." Orla looped her arms through Clodagh's from behind and wrapped her own snugly around her aunt's chest. Careful to line up her aunt's feet with her own supporting them, she methodically trod to the garden door, thankful the boys had left it open. "A few more steps, and we'll greet the sunshine."

Holy heavens. Forgot to bring a chair out first. She rested against the doorjamb to catch her breath, then finished getting them outside. *What now?*

All there was in the garden beside berry bushes were gray stone walls, a crooked wooden gate, soil, and Tarah's herbs. Vervain, rosemary, chamomile, a patch of lavender, but no seating for them. Herbs weren't all that useful at such a time as this.

She couldn't lay her aunt on the moist earth. *A shawl would do.* Tears swam in her eyes and a lump of frustration lodged in her throat. *Left that as well.* "I'm tired from sitting all that way from Listowel in the cart, Auntie. Let's stand together in the sun, shall we?" *I'll catch me breath. Then haul us back inside. Can you send us Your angels, God? Nah, You don't see us.*

A ruckus near the front of the cottage several moments later, and the boys' joyful banter announced the return of Clodagh's children. *Thank God in heaven. Me arms are stones.*

"Cousin Orla, are you out there? Look." Cathal and Brian burst through the scullery into the garden. Their excited expressions changed to concern when they saw her. "Mam? Is she well, Auntie?"

"We're enjoying the sunshine, boyos. What's there in your hands?"

Cathal raised his to show Orla. He clutched the clucking reason for his excitement. "Aidan's uncle bade him sell laying hens at the market, and he let Eoghan give us two. Eoghan paid for them. Can you believe it?"

"We each got one." Brian cooed to his little hen with her feathers poking out from between his fingers.

Orla grinned. "How grand and lovely for you both, aye?" *Well, God, You did a good deed with that.*

Tarah entered the garden and shaded her eyes. "Ah, Orla. Was thanking Eoghan, or I would've made haste had I known you needed me. How'd you bring mam outside without help? I'm stunned."

"God built me like a tree, that's how. Would you help me return her inside? She's tiny but grown heavy. Must be all the scone and tea she partook of before her bath. Aye, Auntie?" Orla propelled herself off the cottage wall, while Tarah reached around frail Clodagh to lend support to her other side.

The progress of the three women together worked smoother and quicker than earlier. They directed Clodagh to the chair before the hearth, and Tarah carefully strapped her onto it.

"There, Mam, how does it feel? Not too tight? We'll get you to your cot as soon as the heat dries your hair. Shan't be long, now."

Orla shook her arms to get the circulation going in the right direction. She massaged the inside junction of her burning elbows. Should she explain her incompetence?

Tarah peered out the garden doorway. "Boyos, set the hens down. They must explore their new home and earn their keep eating the bugs, aye? Stay with them until we bring them in for the night. Did you hear me? And you must still protect the berries from the wild birds as well."

Orla drew up a chair near her aunt. "'Tis fortunate Eoghan gifted you the hens. Eggs shall fetch you some coin, and mayhap the hens shall frighten away a few birds. But how shall you protect the hens themselves? Your wall is low, and foxes can climb it."

"Aye, 'twas a lovely blessing, the hens. Surely an answer to prayer. We'll build a small house for them. I'd been worrying 'bout how to feed everyone. 'Tis more difficult than I thought. I sold a few herb bunches from the garden." Tarah hung the leftover herbs on the low rafter above her.

"Enough to pay for a henhouse? I didn't bring any money with me. I planned to earn more whilst here. As we usually do." Orla fingered her aunt's hair to aid it in drying. *Ought to tell Tarah 'bout the mishap.* "Slightly damp. A few moments more, Auntie. Then you'll get your rest."

Clodagh sniffed.

Tarah dragged another chair to the hearth, stoked the peat's flame, and swung the kettle over the fire. "Well, the other blessing from the market was that Aidan and Eoghan agreed to build us a henhouse. With stone from Eoghan's home where one of their walls tumbled, added to what Aidan says he'll haul from his uncle's land, they'll have plenty to house two hens. And they'll cover the berries whilst they're here. They'll return shortly to begin. Isn't it grand?"

Orla grinned. "Aye, 'twill be perfect." *True blessing.* "Cousin, we'd a mishap in the bath. Your mam chilled quickly. I got her out, but me heart almost jumped from me chest. You may see the bruise on her back from when the cloth slipped."

"She's injured?" Tarah inspected her mam. "She seems grand, nevertheless. All me thanks for your help. I know 'tis difficult, her care."

The women drank their tea quietly for a moment. When Clodagh dozed off, Orla and her cousin shifted Clodagh to the cot in front of the fire. Tarah tucked her in and kissed her forehead. "Rest easy, Mam."

Orla and Tarah towed their chairs to the table and re-situated themselves with more tea. She raised her cup to her lips and paused. "Relieved you didn't think I'd abused your mam, don't you know? Wish we'd biscuits. Let's bake some tomorrow."

Tarah sat facing the scullery doorway and window. She gazed outside. "Aye. I'll need supplies first. Those hens ought to keep the boys busy whilst we chat and wait for the men." She leaned onto her elbow toward her cousin and lowered her voice. "One benefit of being short is hiding behind others with baskets on their heads at the market. Being not easily noticed, I overhear things. Several men discussed the *Feniáns* today."

"Are they at it again?"

"Aye, for we can never give up battling for our freedom from the Crown, can we?" Tarah blew on her second cup of tea before she partook of it.

"Nah, we mustn't. Look what happened to the poor Scots when they gave in." Orla shuddered.

Tarah smirked and knocked on the tabletop. "And look what happens to us if we don't give in? More starvation. More lack. Debtor's prison, or mam put in an asylum if they discover her. Well, the government could do so either way, nonetheless Orla, it makes me queasy to think of such things."

"Aye. So I turn me mind away from thinking 'bout it. We've mouths to feed, people that depend upon us, and you've the two littles. Those boys mustn't get dreams in their heads 'bout being freedom fighters, aye? I fear me brother Ed is a *Fenián*. Have I ever said?"

Tarah's eyes grew as wide as her mouth forming the word, 'No.' She frowned. "We need our fighters, aye, but I don't wish me little brothers to join them. I promised our da when he was dying that I'd care for everyone. I shan't break me promise."

The young women turned at the sound of the boys running outside beyond the scullery door. "There's one, Cathal. Get it!" Stones thumped against the garden walls.

"Sneaky blackbirds." Orla grinned.

Tarah squeezed Orla's hand. "And our hunger is why we sneak away to the garrison at night, aye? We ransom our own bodies and safety for food whilst our men sacrifice themselves for freedom. 'Tis one thing we can do, but I'd never wish me brothers to risk themselves."

"Nor I, Tarah. So, we'll go tonight, then? To the garrison?"

"Aye, for we're in dire need. Our cupboard is empty again, and the garrison is full of returning soldiers, I hear."

Orla groaned and set her empty cup into the saucer. *Mayhap God does note our hunger. But not all the other things I wish for Him to see.*

CHAPTER 3

Her Dragon's Lair

An Englishman's behavior mayhap be polite, but never to the Irish
Orla

𝓛*imerick, Ireland*
The Castle Barracks

ON DAY four of her recent trip, Orla rushed down the hill from her aunt's home because the summons from the garrison was crucial for her family's welfare. An officer typically paid women more than his soldiers did. Would he be uncouth? Or would he be a gentleman? "Mayhap kind, handsome, and rich as a prince." She chuckled.

The night was without moonlight, since the full moon was hidden behind the perpetual clouds covering the stars. The low clouds also aided as a gray cloak for the latecomers behind her on the stone bridge over the River Shannon. By now, most of the girls ought to be inside the garrison. *'Tis nearing eleven o'clock.*

"Orla. Orla, 'tis you, aye?"

She swung around. "Allana? You're late as well, then. What's happened?"

Allana hurried to catch up. "I'm grand, now. Everyone had to hide for a while from Bailey on patrol." She glanced behind her. "He's in one of his moods, and I didn't wish to be arrested, aye? Not sure where Siobhan went. Think she got away. Where's Tarah?"

"She's ill. Let's walk on. An officer summoned me for tonight. Don't wish to be late."

Allana softly whistled. "Glory be, now. Your pay is sure to be grand, then. Who gave him your name? Or don't you know? May he be the finest of gentleman, with the deepest of pockets."

They giggled together, then hushed each other, while they glanced around the surrounding area concealed in deeper shadows.

"Make haste." A wind gust disturbed Orla's shawl. It unveiled the scar she wanted kept hidden. Would her disfigurement repulse the stranger she was about to meet? Or was a young female form satisfactory enough?

"Our own Orla, stepping up in a manner of speaking. Don't you forget us underlings when he falls in love with you, aye?" Allana elbowed her ribs.

Orla paused to secure the shawls back in place with hasty tugs and tucks. Her heart thudded. She remembered to breathe when her lungs burned from holding her breath. "'Tis only getting through this evening which concerns me. You know we aren't allowed to break our status. We're born inferior and considered so by the Crown. And we must stay on the streets, or so the doxies say."

"Watch out tonight, aye?" Allana pointed ahead. "The law's on the pretense of vigilance for us. What's amiss? They mostly turn a blind eye and let us be."

"'Tis always the confusing part. Are we allowed to work or not?"

Allana shrugged. "Have you heard of the Magdalen Asylums? They wish to reform us. Doubt 'twill work out for the rescuers. They've foolish ideas on how not to starve. We could go there all the same, aye." She scoffed.

"Tarah told me 'bout them. Said the Sisters of Mercy newly opened a Magdalen in Tralee. Now, let's make haste. I fear 'tis getting late." Orla clenched Allana's arm and tugged her along as they bent low.

On the far side of the bridge nearest the garrison, another policeman whistled to himself at the junction of the bridge over the river and the river's bank. The girls huddled together there hurriedly scattered into the deeper shadows. He paid no attention and disappeared down a side street away from the castle garrison.

"All's well, then. We're safely on our way, and may we make it safely home after." Allana linked her arm through Orla's, and they shared their body heat against the chill of the evening.

Wish Tarah could've accompanied me. Her cousin protected her and had told her the law mostly looked the other way from the activities of women like them. From necessity, there were abundant night walkers in many of Ireland's towns. Tarah was overall more informed about this risky business than she was.

Orla and Allana parted with a hug at the entrance, and Orla snuck through the castle's military encampment in search of the officer's quarters.

When she found the right door, she scratched her nails on it.

A man, probably a batman, greeted her. He stepped through the opening and raised his chin. His haughty stare pierced what remained of her young, hopeful soul. He sniffed, instead of speaking to her, and waited.

"Me name's Orla Muldoon." She forced up the volume of her voice. "I received a message to come here—"

"Yes, Miss. I suppose we couldn't expect you to be discreet, could we?" The skeletal man dressed in black glanced back and forth, then stepped aside with his hand still holding the doorknob. His icy tone hadn't changed, only his countenance had softened.

"Hoped I was so."

"I am Burton. Lieutenant Farmington's man." He bowed and

averted his focus upward. Was there a spider she had not seen dangling above her head?

Orla gathered her brown, patched woolen skirt in her fist. "Burton, he bade me come, but he didn't explain in his message 'bout more than one entrance or how to announce me arrival. Would've used it, and done it, for me Irish mam taught her children manners. An Englishman's behavior mayhap be polite, but never to the Irish. 'Tis from their stony hearts."

"He did not bid you. I wrote the message for him. There is a side entrance to the officer's quarters that I will show you when you leave." Burton's green eyes glinted with something Orla couldn't discern.

'Twas this man who wrote me? She shrugged and stepped across the threshold.

Soft glowing light from several lanterns on tables lining the spacious perimeter provided the quarters with a welcoming mood. A fire flickered in the castle's ancient hearth.

"Ah." She remembered to close her mouth and secure the shawl over it in the light. The soldier's narrow tents she visited contained nothing but cots and one dresser, if they were fortunate enough to have one.

Burton backed away, swinging the door inward. "The young miss you summoned is here, sir." He waved her inside.

Orla bit her lip during the officer's pause with his back facing the entrance. She twisted her shaky fingers, then hid her hands in her skirt's deep folds. *Is he difficult of hearing?*

"Thank you, Burton. You may leave us." Lieutenant Farmington continued to scribble on something at his desk while Burton saluted, exited, and locked the door with a *clunk*.

Minutes dragged on. Orla shifted her weight from one foot to the other. After she surveyed more of her surroundings, noting a bookshelf, wardrobe, and maps on his wall, she studied the color of the officer's hair. Dark with silver streaks woven throughout. *So, he's an older fella.* Mayhap he would turn out to be a kind gentleman. She sighed.

"Are you in a hurry?" Farmington spoke while he kept his back to her.

"Nay, sir."

"Splendid. You came highly recommended to me. By whom is of no consequence. You are here at my request, and my first allegiance is to my duties for the Crown, as you see."

"Of course, sir."

"And I do not need you to comment on everything I tell you. Do I?"

She tucked in her lips to hold her tongue.

"Ah, you understand. You are a quick learner. I like astute, yet biddable women." Farmington shifted some papers into a stack, closed his book, and turned to study Orla.

His eyes contained a callousness. His dark gaze wandered over her loose, unruly hair and her form. He flicked his hand in her direction. "Remove that covering from your face. You remind me of a highwayman, and I dislike highwaymen."

The chill in his tone hardened to a hoarfrost level. Orla's body quivered, and her fright angered her. Lieutenant Farmington was a man. *That's all.* She loosened her scarf from her face, drooping it beneath her chin, and stared at her bare feet.

"You are a bit of a Long Meg, are you not? And too thin by my standards. Step into the lantern light beside me."

She did and held her breath.

He scowled. "Is that a fake scar? Attempting to get pity from me is not possible, and what is more, it will not raise your pay. Make no mistake."

"'Tis real, sir. When I was seven—"

"Did I ask you to tell me how you received it?" He scoffed.

She slowly shook her head and concentrated upon the copper metal lantern.

He tapped his feather pen's tip on the wood surface. "It does not interest me to hear of anything that has happened to you."

Orla nodded and nearly curtsied. This fella was less human than he ought to be. She stared at the far side of his quarters into the shadows around its edge and concentrated on the nightly faint concert of frogs down at the river. *I'd give up me best shawl to join them.*

Farmington blew smoke from his pipe towards her.

It tickled her throat, so she held her breath to keep from coughing, without success.

He sniggered. "You still have a voice, then?"

She ground her teeth. Speak. Not speak. *Beastie. Draganta.*

"I requested a malleable young woman. You look to be about fifteen years. My youngest sister is that age. Although, she is never barefoot. Or alone with men. Beautiful Henrietta is exquisitely coiffed, indulged with any gowns she desires, plays the piano, and speaks French. Only God knows why it is important for the English to speak French."

When Farmington paused, Orla slid her gaze back to him. *Scorching words.*

His eyes narrowed to match his sneer. "I would shoot a man if he touched her. I suppose you have no brothers or father to keep you at home?" He lay his pipe on a metal tray beside his book.

Of course, he would defend his precious sister. She swallowed, hoping to moisten her mouth. "Me Da is dead. I've four brothers—"

"Do you imagine I care anything about your life? I know you are new to this occupation. Is this not how you avoid the poorhouse?"

Their laws oppress us to conquer us, then they mock us for our poverty. "Well—"

"That was not a question. At first, I thought you learned quickly. Now, I have my doubts."

Orla craved to retreat, but she instinctively knew revealing any emotion to this beastie human was something to prevent at all costs. And her family needed her earnings. She held her ground and stared at her feet again. Her skirt trembled, and she pushed the fabric against her legs.

He sniggered. "No use trying to hide your fear. I noticed. No matter. I have only two requirements for you to fulfill." He leaned closer to her onto his elbow. "Do not speak to me unless I desire it.

Your filthy accent irritates me. Follow my every command precisely how I give it. Have you questions for me?"

She shook her head at his obvious test and forced herself to relax with a slow exhale.

Farmington rose to her chin level and fondled her ringlets. "Odd color. Is it natural? I desire a drink. Do you? Of course you drink. All the Irish are drunkards in my experience. Unfortunately for you, I am selfish, and will keep my brandy for my own use. Much too expensive for your sort, is it not?"

She restrained a retort, and held still as he poured and drank, even when his fetid breath caressed her face. *I wonder how Tarah is faring. Is her fever yet spent?*

"You are either a master at this game, know your place, or you have brilliantly caught on to what I like. A compliant woman. Although you remain an unfortunate woman, indeed." Farmington reached for her, and the beastie's fingers distorted into the talons of a red dragon. Far worse than any *ollphéist ghráiniúil. This man is a draig with claws and scorching flames.*

But did his actions shock her? Had she not sensed he was inhuman? *Aye.* This British officer was a red dragon beastie come to life from a heraldic shield. He had ensnared her inside his lair with one locked exit and the promise of good pay. She closed her eyes to shield against his attack and fly away to a winsome place.

Auntie and the littles must be asleep by now. The cottage would be still and everyone at rest. Tarah would have given her mam her drink of warm milk to help her sleep.

Imagine the River Shannon. How it flows and creates mesmerizing swirls on its surface. Its depths continue down its well-worn, ancient path despite all the storms it survived and large stones in its way. Unfathomable, resilient, persistent on its course to the sea. Severe famines or droughts shall not dry up its rocky bed.

Freedom from any confines. Sunshine warmed her face while she rowed a yellow canoe on the river until it reached the sea, where she had never been. Gentle waves rocked her on her way, with yellow butterflies circling around her head like a golden crown. Clouds scuttled overhead, and black birds chased after them. Hidden obstacles marred the river's beautiful surface, for it was not a serene, motionless lake. There were hazards buried in its depths to the knowledgeable eye, and those experienced sailors avoided them. The unskilled would try to swim in it for pleasure, and because of their lack of experience with rivers, they would be in peril. Eternally lost.

Do the stones and boulders injure the lonely river? Nay. Because the river finds a way over and around them. Nothing stops it from reaching its destiny. Once it joins with the sea, it is forever freed.

A little later, Farmington stretched and yawned. "As for you, my greedy Irish girl, I am certain you will be more than agreeable to arrive at eleven o'clock every Saturday night for the same pay."

"Sir, I must explain. Limerick is not me home. I live in—"

He guffawed. "Do you imagine I care where you live? You must find your own lodgings. You arrived easily from my summons tonight. Do the same next Saturday. And do not expect to gain accommodation in the garrison's women's housing for the camp-followers. You will not visit other men."

Orla returned his steely stare with one she hoped was docile.

He pointed his claw at her face, then jabbed it into her forehead. "I pay very well, indeed. You can find a place. You belong to me, although I would not take you with me wherever they may send me. You are temporary. Understood?"

She nodded. Relief bathed her soul. For who would say nay to a dragon? He had graciously allowed her to live without scorching her alive. She ought to be thankful for that.

Tap, tap. "Sir? I am here to escort her to the wall." *Burton. Thank God in heaven.*

Farmington sat up when she stood. "Additionally, those worthless women in housing might sully you. Would you wish for that? I am certain you would not."

Beastie once more. That was as close to human as he could become. Keenness to be away from his reach flooded through her as the door lock unlatched, swinging it open. She suppressed the urge to sob by holding her breath and keeping her gaze averted from the *draig.*

Burton stood before her and dropped coins into her palm. He turned and led her down the chilly corridor from the officer's quarters to a heavy oak door, then across the courtyard. "Enter here from now on." He halted by the fortress wall without a glance at her, then turned away.

Somewhere in town, a rooster crowed. It must be nearing dawn, and she was never so glad to welcome the chill to experience it. Her feet beat against the earth. Orla hurried around the wall and wrapped herself snuggly with her shawls. One over her face, and two criss-crossed over her chest. She headed for the crossing bridge over the river she had sailed on. The water's gurgling and rushing echoes were a balm to her soul.

She must find a way to move to Limerick. *Mayhap Mam will agree to it. Holy heavens, if I go, Kathleen must take care of Mam altogether alone.* Orla could promise Mam she would help Tarah with Auntie and the littles. Women and children should never starve from lacking a man to feed them. Had not the village women said so many times?

"Hallo, there." Allana stepped up to her from behind a yew tree before she reached the stone bridge. "No patrol in sight. Fancy our timing. The others should be joining us soon. How did you fare? Was he a gentleman?"

"Nay. Nor would he be with the likes of me." A tear escaped, sliding down her cheek, and she wiped it with the back of her hand.

"That wicked beastie. Shall that surprise us? It shan't. Nevertheless, it saddens me that you were the brunt of his vile heart. Shall I untangle your hair, and you may smooth mine?" Allana removed a wooden comb from her pocket.

"Aye. For 'tis a lovely thing to help a chum." Orla slowly inhaled, and her soul reveled in the gentleness of a considerate friend volunteering to minister to her internal and external wounds with a kind touch. "I suppose we must come here forever, aye?"

Allana whispered near her ear. "And you're a rock of bravery and strength to your family. You are. They'd be in dire straits without your pay, aye? You endure cruelty on their behalf as a magnificent warrior ought."

But why must we endure such things for our families? "In such a way? Where is God, I'd like to know? I battle the *draig* alone. With one word He could break the iron rule of the Crown. He could stop more bloodshed, oppression, and suffering." Orla curled her fingers into fists. She would ask Him, if she ever found Him.

"Mayhap one day. We'll battle the Crown and take their coin until we win our freedom, aye? You know how stubborn and fierce we are. Look at me own da. Ten thousand more soldiers like him, and we'd be sure to defeat the Crown in one day."

"Or me own mam. Herself times ten thousand? That'd do the trick, 'tis sure."

They giggled together, as if it was Christmas morn, and they had discovered an everlasting feast magically served to them upon their plates.

When Allana finished her grooming, Orla wiped her moist cheeks and tucked her long, smoothed curls back inside her head covering. "Our choices are to be good and not sin, then starve and die, or do what we do with the enemy and live. For the first time, I understand why Mick and Ed spit when we speak of the British Crown."

"Aye. Our men battle as well so that our families may eat and live. The Crown won't ever come to our funerals and see their handiwork."

Orla patted the lump of coins in her skirt pocket and turned to face the east and Allana. "Nary a care for our welfare, have they?" *We're abused beasts of burden.* "One day, we'll have enough to pay for anything we need. That's me own plan."

The horizon had lightened to turquoise and gold. It shimmered with peach streaks close to her own hair color, highlighting the underbellies of several clouds. Sunrise's gentle colors reflected on the more tranquil spots of the river. Nighttime was ending with its stars fading away into morning, but her life would be the same tomorrow, and the next. The days' struggles would not end until God put a stop to them somehow.

Allana handed her the tiny comb. "Until that glorious day, we shall work to survive as best we can, friend."

"'Twas glad I was to see you safe and sound, although you've spoken nary a word 'bout your own evening."

"Aye, for I didn't escape from *draig* now, did I?" Allana turned around for her friend to untangle her hair, and Orla threaded her long, thin fingers through the dark locks to prepare them for combing. "Here come the other girlies. Everyone but Siobhan. Do you think she's safe?"

Orla glanced behind them and counted four, not five girls. She blew out a long breath. "Without swords and shields, how shall we ever be safe from the monsters, aye? Although, this *draganta* fella is willing to part with his mound of treasured gold pieces each time I risk meself to his control. I mustn't say nay to that. For are we safe in this world?" *Nevertheless, we Irish women shall never allow our families to famish.*

CHAPTER 4

Departing This Place

Departing should never be the way to benefit your family
Orla

*L*imerick, 1866
   Late Spring
   Clodagh McNeal's Cottage

TWO YEARS LATER, clouds shrouded any early morning sunshine that could have entered through the cottage window to lift Orla's downcast spirit. She gazed at the empty cot in front of the smoldering hearth while she listened to the hum of muted conversation between Tarah and her brothers at the far side of cottage. *Darling Auntie, how free and joyful you must be in Heaven.*

Orla rose and cleared the table of leftovers and crumbs left behind from neighbors who had attended the wake. She set Tarah's fresh soda bread in the center and scooted the chairs into a more orderly fashion around the table. Her mam and Kathleen should be arriving soon.

Brian dragged his feet as he rambled up to Orla, with Cathal following him. He stared at his mother's empty cot. "I want Mam. Can the *adhlacóir* bring her back to us, now? Shall God allow it before she gets to heaven? We need her more than He does."

"The undertaker takes them away, numbskull." Cathal sniffed. "He doesn't return people. And I'm sure God doesn't send them back. They say only Jesus did that. Then even He went back up to God again."

Brian's chin trembled, and he swung his fist at his brother. "What do you know? God can send her back. He can do anything!"

"But He doesn't do everything, now does He?" Cathal shoved Brian.

Orla caught Brian as he stumbled and pushed her palm against Cathal's chest. "Boyos. I know you're furious 'bout this, and battling amongst yourselves won't aid you in feeling any better for your terrible loss. Listen to your cousin, for I know this well, aye?"

Both boys wept and clutched at her skirt. She did not want to interfere with their sobs. "Your mam is with your da. Can you imagine what a glorious reunion they're having now?" When she slowly took a seat for stability's sake, she drew them with her. They leaned into her sides, then tumbled onto her lap and huddled together.

"What's all this?" Tarah scowled as she entered the scullery while she finished re-braiding her long auburn hair.

"Boys letting out their grief as we all must do. I'm leaving them to it." Orla stroked each tussled head. "*Eolchaire* for all of us, as our family has so many losses, aye? Except for me. The *bàn* and rejected one."

"Orla. Don't you believe that your light hair and eyes are a curse. I think you're striking." Tarah sighed and rubbed her reddened eyes. "*Eolchaire* with *dearg súile* from grief. I don't know what to say or do for the boyos. We spoke 'bout heaven earlier, and I thought I'd made some sense. Clearly not. Me own eyes sting from the crying."

"Aye, they're our soul's foggy windows which can't come to terms with what we're seeing before us. Me own eyes are blurry from heartbreak."

Door hinges creaked from the cottage entryway. "Hallo, we're here. We've brought some butter for you, and some milk."

Tarah grinned and twisted toward Kathleen's voice. "Cousin Kathleen. Aunt Martha. Welcome. The mourners have all left us, and we've been awaiting you."

Orla's mam and sister dropped their sacks and set the food on a chest, then hurried over to Tarah to embrace her with outstretched arms. Orla straightened the boy's shirts and smoothed their messy auburn hair. She gently guided them toward her women. "Go, and greet your family, boyos. They're here to comfort you."

At first, the boys reluctantly approached the two arrivals, but after their soothing words and attention, they allowed the women's loving embraces and condolences.

Mam Muldoon gingerly lowered herself onto the nearest chair in front of the fire in the hearth in the main room. She eyed her oldest daughter and leaned her *shillelee* against the chair's arm. "Orla, me girl, how're you faring?"

"I'm as well as you'd expect. Grand to see you, Mam." Orla kissed her soft cheek.

Tarah bent down to her brothers while Kathleen rubbed their backs. "See there, boyos? You've plenty of family to belong to, aye. There's a group over in Listowel. We're not alone."

"And what's more, we've God to watch over us, aye?" Kathleen smiled at Orla. "I've missed you, sister."

"And I you."

Mam Muldoon called the boys over to sit with her.

Tarah straightened and tipped her head toward the scullery. "Well, I'll add peat to the hearth and make us some tea. After you warm, and we break our fast, we'll go to the church all together, aye? Bring your gift of butter and milk with you please, for we've none left."

Kathleen lifted the butter and looped her arm through Orla's. "I'm that sad we couldn't come to the wake. We'd not received word in time, and Mam has been poorly as well." She glanced back at their mam. "She's doing grand now, but each day is not like the other."

Orla carried the milk and tugged her sister by her elbow into the scullery. "Let's chat by the fire, aye? I wish to hear any news from home, and more 'bout Mam away from her hearing."

"The day is oddly still. No wind to speak of. We'd also no rain for much of our trip. And before I forget it, I've a message for you and Tarah from your Allana. She waved us down as we entered Limerick and said to tell you this— 'Siobhan was found to be with The Good Shepherd nuns in a Magdalen Asylum in town. Then she sailed to America.' Is this message clear to you? Isn't to me." Kathleen released Orla's elbow and set the butter beside the bread, while Orla placed the milk on the table.

"Aye. We'd wondered what happened to her." *America. 'Tis a grand notion.*

Kathleen pulled a chair out from under the table. "That's all right, then. 'Twas nonsensical to me, and Allana refused to say more 'bout it. Said you'd know. Another thing you may know is that Aidan brought us with him on his way to see his uncle." Her expression brightened.

"Ah, yes. Your Aidan." Orla smiled.

"Go on with you." Kathleen flushed. "He's not mine exactly. Mayhap one day. Mam says I'm too young for all that. As if that's true. Mick was seventeen when he first married, aye?"

"And look how that all turned out." Orla grimaced, then glanced at Tarah taking a seat by the tea kettle awaiting the water to heat.

"Don't mind me presence." Tarah flicked her hand. "I'm enjoying listening to a sisterly chat, and I surely won't be telling Aidan any of what I hear."

"Hmm. If you promise." Kathleen leaned onto her elbows toward Orla. "The grief from our Auntie Clodagh's passing 'tis harsher than the news I've heard from Aidan. Yet, me heart shattered terribly. What do you think of this? He's planning to emigrate to America. Can't say more for the pain it causes me." She fisted her shawl covering her heart.

Orla and Tarah startled, then stared at each other.

"What? What do you know?"

"We know nothing, Kathleen. Aidan didn't share this news with us. He has a right to do as he pleases, but 'twill be a terrible injury for Tarah as well."

"Aye. Another loss. And isn't it the way of the world?" Tarah wagged her head.

Kathleen jumped up, knocking the chair sideways. She trembled. "Injury for Tarah? You want Aidan for yourself? How can that be true?"

"Nay, nay." Tarah stood, rushed to Kathleen, and patted her arm. "I assure you, Cousin. Aidan and his uncle have assisted me and the boys often, and 'tis all I meant. He gave us our hens and built a henhouse, and many other kindnesses since our da passed. We survived by their generosity. Me heart belongs to another."

Orla scooted back her chair and faced her two women with her hands gripping her hips. "What's this hullaballoo? I suspected 'bout Kathleen and Aidan, but you, Tarah? You never said. Who has your affections, I'd like to know. I'll not give me heart to anyone."

Her young women flushed and grinned. Orla huffed.

Tarah embraced Orla and whispered into her ear. "Eoghan."

Orla's mouth hung open. "Ah. Should've noticed that one, aye. You've known each other since childhood. 'Tis why you went to market though you'd only two sprigs of herbs."

"Hmm." Tarah blushed.

"Cousin, a man's got your heart. That's grand. Why didn't Orla know? Shall you marry him soon? Sally McCormick got married, and she already hates it. She told me so herself. Why, only the—"

"What does it take to get a *cupán tae* in this home?" Mrs. Muldoon squawked from the main room. "Kettle must be surely hot by now. Are you forgetting there's a guest awaiting her tea?"

"Mam." Orla and Kathleen chimed together, and the three young women giggled.

Kathleen sighed and arose. "'Tis on its way to you, Mam. I'll fetch it, cousin, for she'd want me to do it. I'm her housekeeper and maid and she'll not allow me to forget it. Remember Lord Richmond's maid, Colleen Finley, me chum from school? Well, she got engaged. To that mummer, Joe O'Malley. Why she'd ever marry him is beyond imagination. Mayhap to get free of Richmond's household. Joe's the one who got so drunk he mistook Father Donovan for—"

"Kathleen. Mam's awaiting her tea."

"Oh, aye."

Tarah bit her lip and set out the teacups with chipped saucers. "'Tis all we've got. Shall Aunt Martha notice the chipped edges?"

Orla raised her brow and spooned the herbs into a cup. "Mam? If her manners return, she won't speak of it. And her cups look much the same, I'll have you know."

Kathleen gripped the kettle's handle with a thick towel and finished pouring the steaming water. "Our mam notices everything. Why, only the other day she—"

"Make haste. Don't allow Mam to scream for it, Kathleen. She'll embarrass us all." Orla reached for the spoon Tarah handed to her.

"We're serving your mam the chamomile and lavender tisane to calm her nerves." Tarah twisted her fingers. "Does she enjoy it?"

Orla shrugged. "What we all would give for a fine cup of black tea. Shall she complain 'bout it? She's lost her younger sister, so mayhap she won't dare to pester her grieving niece. Who can know with Martha Muldoon?"

"Aye. Mam's one of God's own mysteries." Kathleen carried the tisane to her mam, and Cathal narrowly collided with her, rushing into scullery.

"May we please have our bread and milk now? We've got the rumbles." Cathal rubbed his middle and tugged on Tarah's shawl. "Aye?"

"Did you and your brother wash after handling the hens? Then, aye. And after, we'll all go together to Mam's grave with Aunt Martha and lay the lavender down, shan't we?"

Cathal shrugged. "Brian's asleep on her lap. Don't know how he did that. He barely fits with her on the seat."

"Grief fatigues most of us, me boyo." Orla sliced and served her mam's bread with butter onto each plate, while Tarah poured the *gabhair bainne*.

"Hope the milk hasn't cooled the tea, or I'll hear plenty 'bout that." Kathleen conveyed a tray of breakfast to her mam and sleeping young cousin.

When Kathleen returned to the gathering at the table, Cathal sat on her lap for lack of chairs in the tiny cottage. "You're a grand boyo, aren't you? You've grown so tall. Do you know who the tallest man in our village is? You'd never believe—"

"'Tis time for the blessing, me darlings." Tarah crossed herself and folded her hands along with her brothers. "Bless us, O Lord, for these Thy gifts for which we're 'bout to receive. Through Christ, our Lord. Amen."

Silence enveloped the home except for the clinking of cups in saucers as everyone settled to partake of their blessed food.

After Cathal finished, his eager expression replaced the dour one he had worn all morning. He leaned his head back against Kathleen's chest. "Cousin Kathleen, did God Himself truly give you the bread and milk to give us this day? Did you see Him? What does He look like?"

Orla and Kathleen choked on their bites of bread and butter. They swigged some milk, and Orla winked at her sister.

Tarah scrunched her face. "And what has you thinking that?"

"You said so in the blessing. You said 'twere His gifts He blessed us with this day." Cathal frowned at his sister.

"Brother, 'tis the same blessing I always say over the food."

Cathal made a face. "I mustn't always listen, then, for I only now heard it. Is it true?"

Orla raised her brows at Tarah. "I'd surely like to know that as well."

Mam Muldoon entered the scullery leaning on her shillelee with one hand and towing sleepy Brian sporting a milk mustache. "Girlies, shall we waste the day away with bantering and eating, or may we now be away to visit me dearly departed sister in her earthly *tuama leac*? 'Tis what I come for on that frightful, never-ending donkey cart ride. Got me all sore. But I always do what I must. No matter how agonizing or taxing." Her eyes flashed with an ugly glint Orla recognized as a temper fit or a martyrdom declaration rising to the surface.

"Aye, Mam.'Twas merely 'bout three days, I'm sure. Nonetheless, you're a veritable saint. Everyone knows that. We'll clean up afterwards." Orla widened her eyes at Tarah, and Kathleen rushed to her mam to support her elbow.

"Let's make haste, then." Tarah lifted Brian and situated him onto her hip. "We're ready, and I'll lead the way. Cathal, take hold of Cousin Orla's hand. Oh, Orla, snatch the bouquet of lavender."

On the way to the church's graveyard, the breeze tousled the family's hair and flung the women's skirts around their legs.

Orla gripped Cathal's hand tighter. "'Tis more like it. We can't expect the rain to hold off, can we now? Nonetheless, flowers for your mam are worth venturing out in a storm, aye boyo. 'Tis like me brother Mick always says. 'If we waited for the rain to stop, we'd never get anything done.' And he's right. Shall you wish to hold the lavender and lay it down for your mam?"

"More than that, I wish she wasn't gone at all, and I'd not need to lay it down."

"Aye, me boyo, I know."

Beneath the spreading branches of yew trees, the group entered the graveyard through the wrought iron gate and carefully tread along the path woven between the many headstones. Some markers leaned precariously, some were short or had Celtic crosses, and others had multiple names on them. What they sought was the fresh grave of their own Clodagh McNeal.

Tarah turned to face her family. "'Tis only a row further, I think. Aye, Orla?"

Raindrops splashed onto Orla's pale lashes. She blinked them off. "Aye. Be brave, Cathal. Your mam could be watching us from heaven. Take the lavender."

"Mam loved lavender." The bunch tied together with string quivered in his small hand.

The subdued group surrounded a darker mound of fresh earth with a cross marker made of sticks. Tarah choked on a sob, then nodded to Cathal. "Lay it, brother, and people will know she was loved. One day I'll pay for a carved stone marker. I know I'll soon have enough."

Cathal released the bouquet, and Brian fidgeted, then they both flicked their gaze around the burial plots with tombstones. *Too many ghost stories 'bout the graves, aye.*

Mam Muldoon, enveloped in Kathleen's arms wrapped across her shoulders, stared at the grave. "Me thanks for awaiting our arrival to lay the flowers, niece. I was aggrieved to miss the wake and the procession. Not to mention the burial itself."

"I know you tried, Aunt Martha. Some things aren't meant to be, aye?"

Mam's not one to be called 'auntie' nor is she anything near to Auntie Clodagh's sweetness.

Martha reached down with the aid of Kathleen, and tenderly fingered the lavender bouquet that Cathal dropped on top of the damp mound. "Well now, and her early death? 'Tis a blessing for you, Tarah."

The younger women gasped collectively. *Mam never could keep her thoughts to herself.*

Tarah's shocked expression must be from the rude comment coming from her own aunt and mother's only sister. It rendered her speechless. She eyed Kathleen and Orla. *Poor Tarah, she's not accustomed to Mam's peculiarities.*

"Departing should never be the way to benefit your family." Orla glowered at her mam.

"And speaking the truth shan't be avoided in me esteem. Come with me boyos, for the rain is falling in earnest. Help your frail, aged aunt return to your cottage, aye?" Mam Muldoon tapped her shillelee on the ground and the boys scrambled to escape with her.

Kathleen clutched Tarah's hand. "Me apologies for Mam. She far exceeds a truth teller's virtues. Let's speak 'bout your love. Tell us 'bout him, and any plans you've made. I've always been a nosy one, I have. Makes me life exciting to know things. Only God knows if I'll ever get married. Probably not—"

"Allow her to speak, by all the saints, Kathleen." Orla looped her arm through her cousin's. The women meandered toward the cottage clumped closely together in the light rain.

"Eoghan and I plan to marry soon. He's taking the boyos into his home as well. They all like each other. Me apologies, Orla. But there wasn't time to write 'bout it before you arrived again from your quick visit to . . ." She glanced at Kathleen.

Orla kissed her cousin's cheek. "Aye. Was quick last time. 'Tis the best thing to happen in our family for a very long time, cousin, your marriage." *Nah, I'm not envious.*

Kathleen tugged them to a halt. "Am I missing something here? Seems so. What is it?"

"Only that Tarah will be securely situated, and the boys taken care of, sister. I'll never be the focus of a man's affection. I've come to terms with that. So what'll I do? 'Tis time for a dire change. Mayhap I'll make escape plans of me own. Disappear where the *draig* can't find me."

"Dragon fire? You're making no sense." Kathleen clutched her sister's elbow.

Tarah gasped. "Orla. Would you go?"

"Being fanciful, yet nonetheless truthful. To escape a dragon's claws one must be invisible and leave Ireland forever. It'll take much coinage and secrecy." *His own treasure will pay for me escape. And me fresh start. Where I shall make me own rules.*

CHAPTER 5

Convincing Herself and Others

Telling the truth was the hardest and holiest thing to do
Orla

*L*istowel
Martha Muldoon's Cottage

HOME. *Where I couldn't return. Until I escaped the Dragon's lair.* Orla
thanked God in heaven, if He was listening, that her own dragon
never wanted to know about any details of her life. So, she could
safely hide from him. She lay on her side peering at the lightening
window. *It must be near sunrise.* Had the cock crowed? She twisted
slightly to find out if Kathleen was still asleep or already out of bed
helping their mother.

Kathleen's back was turned toward her. In the growing light, she raised her elbow as she brushed fine wisps of her curly auburn hair out of her face.

"You should wear a sleeping cap like Mam does."

"Holy angels, Orla. Me heart jumped in me chest." Kathleen flipped over to face her sister. "Me hair is so unruly I doubt a cap would help at all. Why're you awake with the dawn? You needn't be."

Orla stretched and yawned. "Don't wish to be either, nonetheless I am. Don't wish to be home at all. Seems I'm always on the run, escaping one thing or another and not wanting to be where I land. Hope that's not another bit of me lot in life."

"Could be too early to follow your thoughts. What're you escaping from now? I can't think of anything too dire. Unless it's something to do with—"

"Me entire life." Orla puffed out a breath. It nudged Kathleen's hair on her forehead.

Kathleen scrutinized her sister's face. "You've been dissatisfied with yourself for as long as I've known you, 'tis true. I don't fathom it because I love you. You're me only sister. We're outnumbered by men, aye? As lovely as our brothers are, nothing compares to a sister. Why, the other day, Molly was telling me that her da is beside himself wondering what he'll do with his seven daughters. He's thinking of selling them at the market like hens. Can you imagine them all packed into crates and buyers wanting them weighed and measured—"

"That's too close to the truth for many women in Ireland."

"What, buying women in crates?" Kathleen snorted. "Nevertheless, what shall he do with them all? Why, Cousin Tarah was lucky enough to find a man on her own who'd marry her without a da or mam to help her. And to take her brothers in as well, aye? Molly's da might marry his daughters all off, to be sure. Nonetheless, how many available men are there who'll take a bride with no dowery?"

"The best thing would be to send them away to America or to Canada. They'd live independently. Not relying on anyone or any man, aye? That would save him some coin in the long run."

Kathleen raised herself onto her elbow and pushed her long hair over her shoulder. "All by themselves? Across the vast sea? Without knowing where'd they go? 'Tis perilous enough for a man and worse for a woman alone."

Orla scooted herself upright, tugging the quilt, and leaned against the iron bed frame. "What 'bout if the sisters went all together, aye? Less peril. They could look out for each other and gather their resources together. Wouldn't it be grand then?" *We shall do it.* "Let's do it."

"What?" Kathleen jerked, dislodging the quilt. "Desert our home?"

Mam screeched from the other room. "If you two girlies are quite finished with your chitchat and disturbing me much needed rest, could you start me breakfast at last? Your voices are as loud as the cock crowing his cock-a-doodle-doos. The hearth is cold as the winter snow. Woe is me."

Kathleen pulled a face and grabbed her gray shawl from the foot of their bed.

"Thought Mam lost her hearing. Thinking she stays quiet to eavesdrop on everyone altogether more easily." Orla giggled softly.

"Oh no, Orla, do you think she heard us speaking 'bout leaving?" Kathleen paused donning her shawl.

"Nah. She would've screeched loud enough to awaken the village, if so." Orla wrapped herself up in her brown shawl and tugged her pair of wool stockings higher up on her legs. "Keep quiet 'bout it, Lamb. Nothing's carved in stone. We need more planning."

"And did you fall back asleep now?" Mam yelled louder this time.

"We're on our way, Mam." Orla stood and slid open the tattered curtains hanging over the small window since her childhood. Faint sunshine filtered into the bedroom.

Kathleen hurried off to help their impatient mother.

"I've done it. I've spoken aloud the notion to leave." Orla straightened the quilt over the bed and smoothed its wrinkles. "If only Kathleen can keep it secret from the family whilst we plan."

With the hearth hot, kettle boiling, and breakfast almost ready, their mother dozed off in her coziest chair. All was right in her small world. The knock on the door didn't disturb her.

Ed rushed in. "Orla. 'Tis a grand thing you've returned, at least for some. Mick's wife is very ill. The children are worse off as well. Shall you go see to their comfort?"

Mam Muldoon jerked awake. "What's this? Who's ill?"

Orla patted her shoulder. "Mick's family is faring worse. Ed says they need me—"

"No, they don't." Mam slapped the arm of her chair. "You've only recently arrived home. Take Kathleen, Ed. I wish time with our Orla."

Kathleen approached them and wiped her hands on her skirt. "Me? What are they ill with, Ed? Do you know?"

Ed frowned. "Looks to be typhus. It's striking again. Many in the village are suffering from it. If you go to them, be mindful not to get it, Lamb, aye?"

"As if being mindful works in avoiding it." Orla scoffed.

Mam Muldoon rapped the flagstone floor with her shillelee. "You must go at once, Kathleen. Leave Orla to the breakfast and cleanup. She won't pay it any mind, and she'll care for me needs. She knows what's good for her family, doesn't she? The brilliant one."

Orla pushed Kathleen by her shoulders toward the exit. "Won't mind it at all, Mam. See to Mick's family." She lowered her voice. "Don't spill our plans to him yet, aye? Not the time."

"Wait." Mother Muldoon pointed her shillelee at the herbs tied in bunches and hanging from the low rafters above them. "Take me herbs and the cloths. Kathleen, you know which ones for fevers. Be sure not to boil the water when you make any poultices. And check the heat for the babes. 'Twould be just like your scattered ways to allow your attention to wander and scald their tender skin."

"Mam, I would never." Kathleen's chin trembled.

Orla scowled at her mother and gave her sister a side hug. "Mam is in a mood. Let me help you, Lamb." She then collected the dried herbs and cloths to pack in a lidded basket. The stems and leaves crinkled and poked the inside of her palms. She took care when she stacked them.

Kathleen swiped at her eyes with the back of her hand and kept her voice low. "Why is Mam so prickly when she knows how hard I try, Orla?"

"She's a mystery to God Himself. You'll do well with your ministrations, Lamb." Orla raised her voice. "Mam, our Kathleen takes grand care of you, doesn't she?"

"*Hmph.* Give Mick and his family me love. May Christ have mercy upon their souls." Mother Muldoon crossed herself and wrinkled her nose. She turned her face toward the window.

"Make haste, sisters." Ed shifted his jacket to button it against the rain, headed to the door, started to tip his *tam* then returned to his mother. He bent and kissed her cheek. "See you, Mam."

After Ed and Kathleen bundled up and said their farewells, Orla gathered the breakfast dishes and flatware. She reached for her mother's teacup and received a *whap* on her hand with the shillelee. "*Ow,* Mam. What's that for?" She rubbed the sting.

Martha Muldoon narrowed her eyes and propped herself forward on her cane. "As if you didn't know, aye? You must ask a body if they'd wish for more tea before you take it away. I taught you manners, I did. Have you forgotten them since you went away on your larks to Limerick?"

Her mother's tone of voice and inflection warned this was a verbal trap of some sort. Orla massaged her hand and hesitated to answer. *Why had mam said 'larks' when I'd gone to help Tarah?* It was all serious business taking care of her invalid aunt and the young boys.

"Did you lose your tongue with your manners there in the wilds of Limerick?"

There it was again. The warning tone that she desired to pick a fight. Orla breathed in deep to slow her pounding heart. One misstep and this conversation could go badly indeed. Not at all in her favor. "First, may I pour you another tea? Aye? Then we shall have a chat."

"Your da insisted you have a brilliant mind. Must be so. 'Tis catching onto me intent at last." Mother Muldoon accepted the fresh tea, although annoyance still flashed in her blue eyes as Orla pulled up a chair.

Her ire bubbles beneath the surface. Speak carefully. Orla slowly sat in a chair away from her mother's reach and blew on her tea. She waited for a sign from of what was to come next.

Martha Muldoon scooted back in her cozy chair and situated her cane against the arm. "Now that you're home for good, I've some questions for you. What shall you say for yourself?"

"What do you wish to know, Mam?" The cup jittered inside the saucer, so Orla stirred her tea with a spoon she had grabbed although it was without milk or sugar. Her heart raced from the uncertainty of where this conversation might go.

Mother Muldoon studied her oldest daughter for a moment. "Well, now, you were a grand support for Tarah these past two years, I'm sure. Thinking of others more often than of yourself must've been a blow against your selfish ways, aye?"

Selfish. "Aye. Caring for an invalid? Wasn't at all easy, nevertheless, Auntie was altogether delightful. Had to think of the boys' needs as well—"

"Aye. Had to. 'Tis why I allowed it. Being a good thing helping me only sister and her family. For family's all we've got in this wicked world." Her mother smiled with hardly a wrinkle in her skin.

"Aye." Orla took a deep breath and relaxed. They slowly sipped their tea together as rain and wind pelted the thatched roof.

Mother Muldoon clicked her empty teacup into its saucer and lay the set in her lap. "What wasn't a good thing, me girl, were the rumors I'd heard 'bout your escapades at the garrison."

Orla spewed her last mouthful of tea over the flagstones. She swiped at the dribble of tea on her chin with the back of her hand.

Her mother's stony expression did not invite any comments. Martha Muldoon scowled and stared at her without blinking. That was the worst sign of warning for any of her children when they were on the verge of being reprimanded for an offense.

Rain and wind continued their deluge against the cottage walls and windows and on the tiny scullery garden. Orla focused her attention on the pattern of their watery music before she dared to speak. What safe answer could she give?

"Well?" Her mother's jaw clenched, and she reached for her shillelee.

Orla swallowed hard. The moisture in her mouth from the earlier swallow of tea had dried up. She chewed her lower lip. Ought she to be thankful her mother waited to ask this after everyone was gone? *Courage, Orla.* Telling the truth was the hardest and holiest thing to do. Speaking the truth was probably the holiest thing Orla had ever done in her life.

"Orla."

She should have moved her chair further away first. "Mam, I'm unsure what you've heard exactly, nevertheless mayhap some rumors were true." Still no blinking from her mother. "Well, Tarah's herbs, eggs, and then goat's milk altogether don't fetch enough coin to feed and care for a family of four or five, do they? And we didn't wish for Auntie Clodagh to be taken away and put into an *asylum* or Tarah and the boys taken to the *House of Industry*, aye? 'Tis why I helped. To keep them all at home." She held her breath.

"Aye, we did not wish for any of that. Tell me more." Martha Muldoon blinked.

Orla released a long sigh. "Tarah and I both visited *Castle Barracks*, 'tis true. I never knew all and sundry girls did such things." She slid her gaze back to her mother.

"I knew of sundry people." Martha Muldoon gave a slight nod.

"You did? Ah." *So she's not so astonished.* "Well then, we visited the garrison once a week. All that we earned from . . . we pooled together and got supplies for Auntie Clodagh's household, and everyone's needs. Then Tarah was given two hens, and more to eat sprung from that. What coin I had left over I brought home for you and Mick's family, don't you know? Well, and I've kept aside a portion for me own future." Orla's hands ached from clenching her knees.

"Mick's frightful losses. God rest their poor souls." She crossed herself, and Orla followed her mother's actions.

Orla stood and tightly clasped her hands together. "Mam, shall you forgive me? I'm not fully sorry because me earnings kept us from dreadful hunger."

Her mother's knuckles gripping her cane turned white. "Tell me this. Shall you cease these activities since you're now home? That wretched life isn't what I wish for me own girls."

Orla knelt before her mother. "I'm unsure, Mam. What else can I do? The family remains in want much of the time. The Crown keeps us this way with the Land Rights law, without opportunity for Catholics to purchase land and care for ourselves. None of that has changed. Don't you think they enjoy keeping us all subjected to them in hunger and lack?"

"Father O'Brien is teaching us we should abstain from immorality for the sake of our country. What's worse, our community and friends will label you an 'unfortunate girl' if they discover this. Destitute women have been Ireland's blight for many years, although brought on by the Crown's own oppression—"

"Mam." Orla stroked the scars on her own face. "The trouble, and why I don't care what people think, is the village has never accepted me. And what help does abstinence do in feeding our families? I must tell you this, I don't do the work for me own enjoyment."

Martha Muldoon released her cane. It bounced against the stone floor. She covered her face with her hands and sobbed.

Her tears were worse than anything Orla expected. "Mam. Please don't cry." She joined her with her own weeping against her mother's frail shoulder and clutched her until her mother ceased sobbing. They eventually quieted and wiped their eyes and noses with their shawls.

"Before you say anything further, Mam, I heard 'bout those Magdalen Asylums. Someone I know went to the nuns. You mayhap suggest I shall go, nonetheless I don't wish—"

The front door burst open, and raindrops spattered onto the floor. Ed entered dripping wet. He bent over and puffed from being short of breath. "Mam, Orla, the worst has happened. Mick's family all . . . passed into heaven." He crossed himself.

Orla scrambled to her feet. "What? Once more our Mick suffers terribly. Why would God allow such a terrible thing?"

Ed nodded. Water sprinkled from his wet tam and ran in rivulets down his neck and onto the stone floor. "And Kathleen is . . . beside herself."

"Hand me the shillelee. Help me stand." Mother Muldoon scooted forward with her hands outstretched.

He tugged her to her feet. "Mam, it's stormy outside. You shouldn't venture into it with the mud and the puddles and your footwork not being its sturdiest—"

"Edward Muldoon, why would you be thinking me judgement is that corrupt? Is there something askew in me mind that I'd go outside in that?" She poked her shillelee at the open doorway.

"Uh." Ed glanced at Orla with his jaw slackened.

Orla shook her head at him and pushed her finger against her lips.

"I'm wishing to get me rosary and to pray for our Mick and his family. And you, Ed, should fetch the *adhlacair*. I dare not send Orla, what with the story of her life she imparted to me. Nevertheless, she mayhap could convince him to part with his coin for her."

At Ed's puzzled expression, she closed her eyes and clutched at her throat to contain any retort. However, it did nothing to shield against her own mother's arrow shot into her unprotected heart.

CHAPTER 6

Setting Her Plans

As though it weeps for the loss of its precious occupants
Orla

*L*istowel
  Mick Muldoon's Cottage

TWO DAYS after Mick's second wife and children passed on to heaven, Orla readied to depart Martha Muldoon's cottage for his home. She must go to her grieving brother. This was not the kind of visit a person enjoys. It was the expected duty of family members to console the broken hearts of their own.

Orla spoke to Kathleen before she closed her mother's cottage door. "All me coins given to aid Mick's family were for naught." Was not death a horrible curse and an impeccable thief? She covered herself as snugly as possible against the damp and scurried in haste down the muddy lane.

The neighbor's dog charged at her up against their wood gate. He raised his hackles and bared his teeth in fury.

"*Cù a' gabhail a' chuthaich.* I almost took me final breath. What're you on 'bout? You've only known me for ten years." She clutched at her chest. No one else was out wandering the lane, so she lowered the shawl covering her face to below her chin. She breathed in blessed fresh air.

Her neighbor called to his vicious dog to cease his barking, and Orla dragged her fingertips along the mossy stone wall down the path to Mick's cottage. It helped to keep her balance as she sidestepped the puddles. *What shall I say?* Kathleen alleged their brother was irrational and inconsolable. Mother Muldoon urged her to take Kathleen's place and impart some sense to him. *What difference will it make if 'tis me speaking to him?* The poor man's heart was shattered, and no kindly spoken words could repair it, she was sure.

She turned down the lane at the opening in the wall and followed its mucky path toward her brother's front door. The low-hanging gray clouds parted for a moment during their scurry across the sky. She stopped and shaded her eyes against the abrupt brightness. With today's task, it seemed terribly wrong for the sun to shine on Mick's home. Its thatch dripped. *As though it weeps for the loss of its precious occupants.*

Orla collected herself and knocked on the cottage door. After no answer, she called out her greeting before turning the latch. Locked. "Mick, let me in."

Something scraped against the other side of the door, then muffled cursing. The door jerked inward. A disheveled Mick glared at her with bloodshot blue eyes. "Orla. All right then." He backed up as she entered.

It took a moment for her eyes to adjust to the switch from

sunshine to a barely lit room. The only window on the far wall was cracked. The room was chilly without a fire in the hearth. The powerful aroma of whiskey filled the small area. She reached for Mick too late, for he had turned his back to her and wandered to a chair near the table.

"Brother, where's your sweet family? Did Ed bring the undertaker in a timely manner? He never said. We've been wondering 'bout a burial—"

"No undertaker!" Mick threw himself forward onto his arms splayed on the table and buried his face against them. He sobbed uncontrollably.

She rushed to her brother and enveloped his head and shoulders. There was nothing she could say, so she made soothing sounds while she waited for him to spend his tears. She had lost loved ones herself, but never a husband and children. *Did it feel worse?*

Mick's sobs abated. He raised his moist face to her. "Mister Death overpowered God and stole the breath from me loved ones. What can you say to that, me sister?"

"Naught. His ways have always confused me. Take me to your family. I must see to their preparations." She attempted a smile.

Once they were inside the tiny bedroom, Orla's heart squeezed with sadness. Mick's wife was on the bed, and his babies were together in the crib. Kathleen had wrapped the bodies in sheets, but that no good Ed had done nothing to help. *He ought to have dragged the bed into the common room.*

Mick indicated the bed. "Kathleen was here to help, do you see?"

"Aye, I knew. Why didn't you and Ed take the bed to the common room? People may wish to pay their respects, and they cannot in this small space. Well, and to be fair to Ed, he and Rory took your place on the farm while your family grew direly ill."

He wagged his head. "I've turned all the people away when they came. Me family is only asleep. They'll awaken soon, sister. We must leave them to rest."

Orla turned back to face him and chewed her lip. This was the nonsense Kathleen spoke of. "You're not sober. Are you? They've been gone two days, brother."

"Has it been two? Lost track of time. I'd little to pay for *penance*, did you know? Spent all you'd given me. Nonetheless . . . they . . ." Mick slumped against the wall and slid down against it until he landed on the floor. He stared at nothing with a dazed expression.

"You know they're gone, don't you?" She crouched in front of him. "Brother, you're drunk, and you haven't slept, I'm sure. Stay there until I make you some strong tea. Close your eyes, now. I'm here with you."

He shut his eyelids. As soon as his head lolled sideways and he snored, she headed to the hearth. *This is far worse than I imagined.*

It took longer than usual to heat the kettle, since Mick and Kathleen had allowed the fire in the hearth to fizzle out. Was she the only one who could manage things? She collected more peat and lit a fire again, fetched some water, and finally found the tea. He was out of many supplies. *Why hadn't Kathleen kept up? Mayhap she was more concerned with Mick's mind.* It frightened herself.

"Sister." Mick leaned against the doorframe to his bedroom. "Thought I recalled you were here. I'm grateful to you."

Orla set the cup of tea on the table beside the whiskey bottle and arranged a rickety chair to face in his direction. "Come sit and drink, brother. Leave the whiskey aside for now. We've got work to do."

Mick studied the rafters, then grabbed his whiskey bottle from the table, ignoring the tea, and scuffled to the window.

"Brother—"

"You must love them, God. The church teaches this, aye. Why didn't You watch for Mister Death's trickery?" Her brother took a swig from the bottle.

Orla rushed to him. "Mister Death? *Sh.* Come rest a moment. Then, we must move the bed into this room . . . Mick?"

"Aye. Let's do it. Promise me you'll say a prayer for all me macushlas, sister?" He swaggered to the table and plopped the bottle down.

After much arduous discussion, they lifted and carried only the mattress with Mick's wife Fiona's body into the common room and laid it on the table. Orla and Mick panted from the dreadful task.

He fondled the sheet covering his wife's face.

Orla wiped her brow and took a sip of lukewarm tea while Mick drank a mouthful of whiskey. "Brother, drink the tea instead."

"Don't wish to." He lumbered back to the bedroom, and she followed him.

She was glad to help, although nausea swept through her when she lifted the tiniest body from the crib. Little James. *He'd not lived to see his first year.* Would she ever have any babes? *Unlikely.*

Mick silently carried his daughter, two-year-old Rosie, all wrapped in a sheet and slowly placed her beside her mother and baby brother.

He snatched his half empty bottle and drank. "Sister . . .'tis so hard to feel God's love ... we've only the crucifixes to affirm the rumors of it."

She stared at the one nailed to the wall beside Mick's hearth. "Aye, so they do."

"His love isn't strong enough against Mister Death."

She pressed her fingertip against Mick's lips. "You're making no sense, as Kathleen said—"

"God makes no sense." He wobbled sideways when he retreated from her. He shook his fist at the ceiling. "Starvation. Pestilence. Why does our God not break the grip of the English Crown—"

"Brother." She yanked away the whiskey bottle, and Mick wrenched it back from her. Droplets of alcohol splashed onto her hand. She shoved him, aiming for the chair. "Sit down, will you? You'll crash to the floor, soon."

Mick plopped onto it and nearly toppled over. He set the bottle before him on the table. "What's sinful 'bout us? Why doesn't God love us? He made me a cripple, and you . . . you're despised. Have you ever felt His love?"

Had she herself not always grappled with a loving God she ought to believe in? She crossed herself and slid a glance at the rafters.

"Mick don't bring more grief down upon us with that question. By all the holy saints, sit and rest."

"Am sitting. You pushed me. Is Mister Death yet here?" He breathed unevenly.

We're in dire need of the undertaker. "I must get something. Sit here whilst I'm away. Only for a few moments, brother."

He cupped his face and wept into his palms again.

Orla stroked his bowed head, then hastened to the cottage door and drew her layered shawls up over her head against the rain. She glanced back. "I shan't be away long."

Rain fell in earnest as she ran up the muddy hill to the lane. Her toes squished in the cold mud. The fresh air blew against her face, and she inhaled several deep breaths to erase the stench of death. She hastened ahead for several yards when the jingle of harness from beyond the curve warned her to slow down.

The undertaker's cart, hitched to two brown and white Cobs, trudged toward her on the muddy lane, and she flattened her back against the wet stone wall bordering the road. Its unforgiving resistance was an example of her own determination to see this appalling chore to its end.

Two men with their black hats tugged low on their brows hunched forward on the cart's wooden seat. They had not seen her yet because of their cap's brims. She recognized Undertaker Nolan's black and silver-streaked beard, for she often noticed him inside the pub. The younger man looked like he might be Timothy Reardon, a childhood classmate of Kathleen's. She would know when they drew closer to her.

Her own body's tension fled with the realization that her brother's ordeal was almost over. She must help her Mick to release his lost loves to heaven and God's arms. This one thing was within her power to do for him. Nothing else.

Undertaker Nolan glanced in her direction and tapped his brim. "Ah, Miss Orla Muldoon. What're you doing in the shadows? Almost didn't see you there."

She stepped away from the wall and wrung her fingers together.

"Apologies. Nevertheless, I've come out to look for you. Me brother Mick needs your services. Did you know of it? Had you heard the news of Fiona and their littles?"

The cobs stepped backward at the barking of another dog nearby, and the cart creaked with its burden. It was then that she noticed the various lumps wrapped in tarps stacked upon one another in the cart's bed. She gasped and jumped back, crossing herself quickly.

Nolan glanced behind him over his shoulder. "Aye, Miss Muldoon. We all know of the recent typhus deaths, don't we now? Your brother, Ed, had reported what's occurred at Mick's home. Was on me way to fetch them just now. I know the way."

Orla squashed herself against the wall again to allow the death cart to pass and follow it down the hill. The horse's hooves and her footsteps squelched out a slow dirge together. She could not discern if her wet face was from her tears or the raindrops. It was warm trickles, so it must be grief. She wiped off what she could and grit her teeth. Poor Mick. *Be strong for Mick.*

Imagine the summer sunshine and the climbing roses on the wall beside me, aye. The sweet aroma never failed to lift her spirits, had it? *What 'bout the black birds swooping into the hedgerows, their nestlings peeping a hungry tune? Or imagine the boys chasing their hens around the garden.*

The cart suddenly halted in front of Mick's home. She nearly collided into the back of it, and the stench from its human cargo assailed her nostrils. *Get to Mick before they do.*

Orla rushed ahead of the men to her brother's front door and tried wiggling the handle. She placed her mouth close to the crack. "Brother. Mick, open the door. 'Tis locked tight."

From the other side came scrapping, then footsteps shuffled toward the door. "No. I'll not let them be taken away from me. Do you hear?"

"Mick. 'Tis me. Open the door for your sister, aye?"

A *thud, clunk,* then a *click,* and the door swung open. Mick scowled at her and stared beyond her.

She twisted partly around. Undertaker Nolan and his assistant stood behind her. Her shawl and skirt's hem flapped against them in the wind and rain. She turned back to her brother. "'Tis time, Mick. Your mind says so to you, aye?"

Mick grabbed her shoulders. He yanked her through the doorway and up against his chest. His sobs added more heartbreak to her own.

"Hush, now. They've come to collect them. They must." Orla nudged Mick closer to the shrouded bodies and covered her face with her wet shawl. She held her breath to keep from sobbing as she gazed at the tiniest covered body. "Heaven awaits the innocents, aye? You know that."

"Aye." Mick's body slumped against the table his family lay on.

"Shall we return later?" Nolan's assistant, Reardon, remained on the stoop and peered inside.

Undertaker Nolan shook his head. "Nah. 'Tis beyond time to take them."

Mick spit. "The Crown lets us starve. Not a care has the English Crown for any of us. Not even the littlest and—"

"Fighting it all shan't help us." Orla stroked Mick's shoulder.

"Neither does me whiskey. Yet I keep hoping so." Mick wiped his mouth with his sleeve.

"I'll help you, me brother. Let them in?"

Mick rubbed his face and stepped aside. "Take them away, then."

The two men covered their faces with a black cloth tied behind their heads and approached the three bodies. Undertaker Nolan massaged his neck. "Been hauling away a third of our village for two days. We have."

Orla tsked and brushed Mick's hand with her cold one. "I'm with you, Mick. All the family are."

The sheet corner Nolan raised drooped from his fingertips. "Typhus fever, by the looks of it. Blotches of the red rash."

"Aye, 'twas." Mick shook his head in denial after he said so.

Nolan cleared his throat. "Mícheál Muldoon, you must give each legal name for me records. 'Tis sorry we are for your losses."

"Me losses do have their precious names." Mick peered past Nolan's hand with the lifted cover from the face of his wife. "Fiona Muldoon. Aged twenty-three."

Reardon scribbled out his notes.

Mick nodded at a smaller body. "'Tis Rosie. Two-years of age." His voice broke. "And the babe is James. All five littles lost to Mister Death, with both their mothers. Never me. He doesn't take me."

"Five?" Reardon froze his pencil in midair. "Two or five children? Two mothers? The count is all wrong—"

"He means he's lost others before these, man. Write it down." Nolan rolled his eyes skyward.

Mick growled. "One wife and two babes this time. Been married twice and lost too many too soon. No matter how you count them."

"Aye." Reardon blushed. "I've got it."

Orla drew her brother away as she stepped back from Mick's departed loved ones and wiped her damp nose. "I'm here for you."

"And they aren't. Why do we yet live, and the littles don't?" Mick sniffed and rubbed his eyes with his fist.

"Blame our Uncle Thomas for the long life. 'Tis a blessing, so they say. One-hundred and eleven years before God took him up. God has His ways, and I don't get most of them." She clung to Mick's arm to hold him steady.

Undertaker Nolan nodded to Reardon. "Ready. Let's lift them up." The men loaded the bodies onto a carrier shaped like a hammock and carried them outside to the parked wagon.

Orla followed them a few steps to where the Cobs hitched to the cart fidgeted and jingled their reins. She turned toward Mick, standing beneath his thatched overhang. "Those poor gentle horses don't want this task of towing the bodies away, me brother. None desire it."

"Aye. The terrible thing is coveted by Mister Death."

When she approached her brother, Mick yanked on her shawl tugging her beneath the cottage eves. "Will it never end, sister? Can you watch Mister Death steal our macushlas and our very hearts away again?"

"Nah, Mick. We've lost enough to hunger and illness. Poverty is not the way to live out our days." Orla grasped his sleeve. "Let's go in.

We've a plan to change things. We've been talking 'bout it. Me, Kathleen, and Ed."

He dug in his heels and frowned. "What're you saying?"

She cupped his face, then released him. "Are you listening? How to get away from all our troubles. Let's emigrate to America. 'Tis safer since America's war against slavery ended, aye?"

"War is forever horrible, and don't we know it? Nonetheless, 'tis one way to freedom." Mick blinked hard and shook his head. "Ireland knows 'bout wars and the cost of them."

"That we do. What do you say?"

Mick squinted at Orla, dragging his focus back to her. "I don't know. You say Kathleen's going? With Ed? Our Lamb will never survive a trip with him. Lamb's a gentle heart, God love her."

Orla huffed. "Am I not gentle? I'd like to know. Nevertheless, she's wishing to find Aidan. You shall be her guardian."

"Aidan's been in America for two years now. He could be anywhere."

"Lamb's heart's desire is to find him. Let's go inside." She took a few steps.

"Mam shall be brokenhearted. She's accustomed to us being nigh to her every day."

Orla sighed. "Rory and John are here. She'll be fine." She twisted her hands in her shawl. "When the church allows him the time, John shall visit Mam."

Mick entered his dim and dreary cottage. "Four of us going. Who's paying for passage?" He left his front door open, shuffled to his empty table, and slumped onto a chair.

"Give a listen to our plans." Orla maneuvered another chair beside him. "I've plenty for our vouchers. You've heard of cheap ships sailing over to America?"

Mick recoiled. "Ho, now. Cheap? You're talking 'bout risky transport in a coffin ship, aye?"

Orla chuckled. "Not in a coffin ship, brother. Our people often survive the trip across the sea nowadays. Haven't you heard? Are you in such a stupor you can't grasp this plan?"

"Head's clear enough now, and I can hear you fine. But you're daft if you'd think I'd go with you on a voyage of death. Had me fill of Mister Death."

She gripped his shoulder. "Would you come on the voyage for Kathleen? Our Lamb refuses to do it without you. Think, Mick. There's more to life than what we have, and 'tis found within that vast and promised land of America. I'm sure."

CHAPTER 7

Securing Her Dreams

God Himself doesn't see me, and they say He fashioned me
Orla

 *ueenstown Harbor (Cobh)*
Southwest Ireland

WITH EVERY SCREECH of the seagulls circling above her, two weeks later, and each deep breath of the briny Atlantic air, Orla's dream of freedom in America deepened. Waves slightly rocked the S.S. *Mona* in a mesmerizing motion. The view from the *bùird-luinge* encompassed most of Queenstown's harbor beyond the ships and boats. Colorful buildings lined together on the steep hills, magnificent St. Coleman's Cathedral, and the winding streets against the backdrop of blue-gray water capped with white foam further out to sea lay before her. *A masterpiece that beckons travelers.*

She checked the face scarf slung below her eyes, and the buttons on her shirt beneath its drape. "Glad the fog dispersed for a few moments. Look at this grand view."

The purser standing beside her earnestly checked his list, ignored her comment, and spoke to his assistant in their own language.

The mist quickly returned, swirled around the *Mona* once again, and sadly shrouded the sea. Waves splashed against the ship, and voices in the crowd below echoed eerily within the movement of the vapors.

Orla slid a glance at the purser's brown, stalwart face a few feet away from her side and slightly above her own.

He cleared his throat, flipped a page of his manifest, and his aide headed back inside the ship. Neither man had spared a glance in her direction once they stood at the railing.

So, now I'm back to being invisible. The battle between visibility, which often repelled people, and noticeability, which should give her value, created an endless cycle like the swirl of the mists nearby.

Well, her dragon's expert training unexpectedly aided her in dealing with men. She grinned from the ability to distance her soul during similar encounters as the one she experienced this morning with the purser. In childhood, she desired to be invisible, with the exceptions being her family and a few of the girls at the garrison. Then she discovered wretched loneliness was not a tolerable outcome of her hiding. *God Himself doesn't see me, and they say He fashioned me. Shall I be unseen in America?*

Orla coughed, yet the purser remained unresponsive. She sighed, and the stiff breeze parted the fog again as if it was from her own exasperated breath.

A vast crowd formed near the platform and docks since before dawn, and it increased during the past few minutes with the sunlight. Peoples' various sizes, shapes, and colored clothing mingled together as the clouds did in a Summer sunrise. The cacophony of their voices and the gulls overhead grew in volume until her ears ached. She tugged her thick woolen scarf snuggly over them and fluffed her sack. Then she switched its weight to balance between her arms and refocused on the gathering of passengers. *Where could they be?*

"Orla! Orla Muldoon."

She squinted and peered over the rail into the group nearest her. It sounded like Ed's voice. Of course, he would be the first to greet her. He had most surely been up to no good things in the dark, early hours. They were the most alike. "Ah, Ed. Where're the others? You've left them behind?"

"You know me. Wish to be away sooner than later. Come down." He waved her forward.

Orla did not speak to the silent purser and slid her fist along the rope for balance on the lengthy, unsteady plank to the dock. Face to face with Ed, she raised her brow. "What have you to say whilst leaving our family behind? Do they know not to await you at the boardinghouse?"

Ed guffawed. "Await them? Mick the limper and Kathleen the dawdler? Wasn't 'bout to allow them control over me own departure." He glanced behind himself and raised on his toes to scan the crowd.

The nearest people scowled and murmured at him, shifting to keep their places in line.

"Nonetheless, you look for them now. In your usual selfish manner, you make no sense. You're departing with us, aye?"

He swung back to her and smirked. "Departing at the same time. Not with. I secured me own passage, as you threatened me I should, when we were at the pub in Listowel making our plans. I did as you rudely encouraged."

"Ed." She grabbed his coat and shook him. "Your resolve was to punish us all from me own threat? You'll sail on another ship, and not with us. 'Tis your intent?"

He gripped her hands and tugged them off. "Brilliant mind, as Da always claimed. You and I've always had squabbles, haven't we? Too alike. What I've done is for me own comfort as much as yours. 'Tis best to go it alone."

"I disagree, Ed. This'll be a shock to Mick and Kathleen as well, aye?"

Ed guffawed. "A shock? Kathleen shall be elated. She'd drive me wild in a minute. And in an enclosed space, no less. Mick? He'd be constantly at me throat, for you know nothing'll change the likes of me." He squeezed her arms. "Nay, sister. Admit 'tis best this way."

He spoke enough truth to silence her objections. She groaned. "Nevertheless, they'll be heartbroken if you say naught of your parting from them."

"I promise I shall."

"Miss Muldoon."

Orla turned to stare up at the purser calling her from the deck. "Must see to what he needs."

"Of course you shall. Shan't you always see to what men ask of you?"

She glared back at her brother. "You're brilliant yourself, not to go with us. I'd surely strangle you in your sleep the first chance to come my way."

Ed laughed and embraced her tightly. "I'll miss you, I will, sister." He abruptly released her and disappeared into the midst of the crowd.

Unexpected tears choked her for a moment. She twisted around to head to the ship's official and bumped into him standing behind her. "Oh."

His dark eyes glared with an inner fire in them. "You. Gone."

"To speak to me brother."

"Agreement." He swished his hand between them. "Gone."

Her heart's erratic thudding squeezed her lungs and breathing. *I knew it.* Someone would try to stop her. There was no way she would allow this terrible man to interfere with her dreams. Orla released a screech comparable to her mother's that might bring the seagulls crashing to earth.

The purser nearly dropped his manifest into the swishing seawater below the steerage plank. His eyes and mouth rounded while he stepped backward. She must grab him then, or he could plop into the water.

He threw himself forward with her grip to correct his balance and knocked her into the curious people crowding around them.

Someone yelled. "Fight, fight, fight!" *Probably a boxer.*

Orla scowled at the ship's official who promised her safe passage to a new life, then stepped around him to block his way back onto the *Mona*. "Keep your word to me, as I kept me word to you. Unsure how much English you understand. Nonetheless, have you heard the words 'curse,' or 'ghosts,' or how 'bout 'murder?' By your expression, I see that one of those lit your brain. Should you not keep your promise to me, I'll further promise you those as well."

His Adam's apple bobbed, and his knuckles turned light brown. Then, his face reddened to mahogany. The official tipped his head back and glared at her.

She shrieked once more, and the crowd fell silent. She must thank her mother for her example sometime. Orla reminded the purser of her family's names. "I'll find you when we need a thing, or you find me."

"Me. I find you." He patted his chest, then cupped his hand around his mouth. "Mick and Kathleen Muldoon, come!"

She grinned and faced the massive crowd, jostling each other and murmuring together. Then there was a jiggle in the middle aimed toward the steerage plank. It narrowly parted a way through. The mass closed in again behind two people. Her own people. One limped terribly. She chuckled.

"Orla." Mick and Kathleen, clothing all tousled and a little out of breath, stood beside her.

"Your limp has worsened overnight, brother." She winked at him, then raised vouchers beneath the purser's prominent nose. "Here. These are me brother and sister. Owners of two of the vouchers. Remember me promise to you?"

"I do. Mister, your name. Your work?" He then addressed Kathleen and wrote something on his manifest. "Go, your kind, to ship's belly. Down to cargo." He turned away and addressed the crowd. "All aboard!"

Mick whispered into Orla's ear. "Did you see Ed? Did he tell you of his plans? He boarded a cursed coffin ship, Orla. To Canada."

Kathleen coughed.

"I know it. Lamb, are you feeling well enough? Or shall you go home?"

"Plenty well to stay with you. I wish to go."

"Then make haste, Muldoon family, and follow me into the cargo hold. It shall be our abode for a few weeks on the sea, aye?" She led them down the hatch into the dim and musty belly of the *Mona*. She swung to one side of the ladder when her feet hit the floor. In the dim light, they staked their places on the scarcity of bunks lining the walls, close to the hatch's opening above.

Kathleen sat on her filthy lower bunk with her sack. "There mustn't be enough beds for that crowd we passed amongst. The one above me is missing slats. Where shall they all sleep?"

"Orla, what have we done? I'm more concerned with lack of food and water." Mick laid his sack on his grimy bed and inspected the wobbly and broken bunk above him.

"'Tis why I arrived early. To secure first place in line. Amongst other help we'll need." She ran her finger over her bunk and cringed at the odd color of slime stuck to it.

Amid the stacked wooden crates in the center, distant squeaking and scuttling sounds scraped. "What I wouldn't give for Mam's eager tabby right now."

"Were those rats?" Kathleen ran to Mick and scrambled in behind him.

Orla peered into the shadows. "Your worst fear, Lamb. But we're here with you. We won't allow anything dreadful to happen to you. The ship should have a cat, I've heard. Mayhap something happened to it."

When the ship rolled slightly with the sound of many footsteps, she backed up to the foot of her shaky bed to be nearest to Mick and Kathleen. "Our journey to America now begins, me loves."

Mick stood and held onto his loose bunk post. "Sister, it seems they've hastily added bunks in this hole. Shall be a wonder if me bed shan't collapse with me upon it. This ship's belly isn't meant for passengers, is it?"

"Unsure. And your worries are mine. While the conditions on the ship are appalling, any country will take our coin from us, won't they? Sit. We're 'bout to be squished in. There're people's feet on the ladder's first rung." Orla settled herself on her worn, makeshift bunk and the slime stuck to her hand. She stifled a shriek. *How can I lie against that?*

Kathleen stared at her sister's hand and wiped her own together. "These beds are unfit for us. Nonetheless, 'tis a blessing. The floor is full of muck. Is the ship from France?"

Orla surveyed the steerage passengers now swarming the cargo hold. "Mediterranean of some sort. Merchant ships are cheaper than most, not as bad as—"

"By all that's holy, Orla. A coffin ship?" Mick gripped his bunk post.

"What do you take me for? We got a ship with sails and an engine. Single screw, they said. 'Tis where the 'S.S' in its name comes from. Our spot near the hatch? Got the lightest area, and we shall get out quickly when 'tis open." She eyed a group of four as they approached the Muldoon family. "No room here."

They scuttled into the deeper shadows, where indiscernible shapes shuffled in mass. The air inside the cargo hold had already thickened, and the aroma of unwashed bodies filled the space.

Kathleen coughed, sounding like a barking dog, and wiped her brow.

"Lamb, I'm asking you again. Do you wish to return home?" Orla patted her shoulder.

Kathleen's voice shook from behind her hand. "Me mind is set on going to America. And finding Aidan. Won't be so bad, shall it? And worth the trouble. May Christ have mercy upon us, and Saint Christopher as well."

"Let's hope they do, and we'll get through this journey to clean up grand in America." Orla ogled the wet floor, sloshing filth across it in slow circles. "Be mindful of John's warning to us. Watch for thieves.

Nevertheless, we've got the best light to guard our belongings. We've also got the crates to block ourselves with a wall. Let's try that, brother."

Mick rose and pushed and pulled, with Orla and Kathleen joining in. They huffed and sat back down while the hold filled with more people.

Orla quivered with a few qualms she had heard earlier from the purser. Should she tell them? *Aye.* She could not avoid sharing his warning. "One thing I'm told is that when storms arise, they'll lock us all in, keeping the seawater from coming in and sinking the ship. Sometimes for days on end."

Mick and Kathleen stared at her with slackened jaws and wide eyes. Mick wagged his head. "You're pulling one over us. Aren't you?"

"No. Wouldn't do that. Change your minds now or make the best of it." She clenched her hands over her knees. They had a right to know what they were in for. *Shall they stay with me?*

Kathleen's face turned pale green in the light from the open hatch, and Mick slumped. He stared at the wall high above them. "Right. Well, I'm glad for those windows up there."

Orla drew a long inhale and twisted her shawl's hem. "Those're ventilation slits. The sunlight shan't pierce through those. And the seawater will seep through them during storms. Notice the water on the floor? If you stay with me, get accustomed to the dark."

Kathleen leaned into Mick's side. He embraced her with his arm. "Mayhap our time spent in this hell will suffice for time spent in Purgatory after we pass on."

"One can hope." Orla scooted back against her bunk and studied the slits overhead. *I'd pray if I thought God would hear me.*

* * *

On the Atlantic Ocean
Day 3
Dreams of going to America had not included the S.S. *Mona's* hellish travel. What trouble had her dreams gotten them into? Orla

imagined sunny skies, vast blue water, possibly escorts of dolphins she had heard tales about all the way to her new life—not the sight of gray mist for two days. *Christ had mercy upon me, nonetheless.* Was it God who allowed her to not become seasick and reveal her fear of dark and enclosed spaces? *What good is it to think that?*

Wind off the sea battered her earlier and parted the fog. She shuddered and wrapped her shawl tighter. Today's view was spectacular with a glorious sunrise, a calm blue sea, and a quick glide across the surface. "How long will it last? I'd like to know." This was the stuff of her dreams. She stared at her sack of meager rations. The nightmare took place below. Right where she must go.

A family, the ones she remembered discouraging from taking the upper bunks near them, meandered past her on the deck. The father's face was pale green, and he glowered at her. Seasickness had cursed him, and she was glad to not witness it.

Orla approached the hatch's black opening. *Me loved ones need me.* They must drink and eat. Had she not searched for the purser's aid and paid for it? She must not waste that sacrifice. She shifted her sack, forced her thoughts to the ocean's beauty like she had often done with the Shannon River, and descended the ladder.

Mick lay shivering with his arms folded on Kathleen's bunk, exactly as she told him to do. Kathleen was still and pale between him and the ship's wall. *Christ, have mercy upon her.*

Orla bent down and shook her brother. "I'm here, Mick."

He rolled his eyes and focused on her face. "Orla. Where'd you go? We've needed you."

"I knew that. Grieved I was to leave you here. Had to get supplies. 'Twas more trouble than I shall tell you. Here I am. How's Kathleen?" Orla pulled a cask of water from her bag, sipped, and handed it to Mick. "Drink quietly, or the others may mob us."

Mick guzzled it with his shaky hands, and Orla glanced around the steerage compartment. "Now, hand it over to Lamb. She appears poorly. Her face is flushed. Is she feverish?" She caressed Kathleen's cheek.

Kathleen clamped her lips and turned her head away when Mick attempted to give her a drink. "She refuses it. What shall we do?"

"Don't know the answer to that." Orla removed two apples and a cheese wedge from her sack and divided it between them. "Hide the food and chew quietly."

A shadow blocked the sunshine from the hatch above. "Storm ahead. Batten hatches." A young, brown ship's mate slammed and sealed the lid. The clunk echoed around the gloom.

Orla's heartbeat raced in the sudden darkness. She reached out for her bunk. "Have slept little meself, Mick. There's naught else I can do for you two. Sleep now. It shall get rough in here soon."

"Get rough?" His voice jiggled with his chattering teeth. "Bad before. Now, 'tis a dungeon."

Holy heavens. He need not speak it aloud to remind her. *If only I drank whiskey.*

CHAPTER 8

On Her Dream Ship

He's nameless from me neediness
Orla

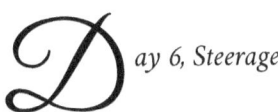 *ay 6, Steerage*

IT MIGHT BE EARLY SUNRISE, but with the hatch shut and in total darkness, it was anyone's guess for the time. *Thinking it's the sixth day.* The ship rocked and tipped. She preferred the fog she complained about over the churning seas. *Poor souls, retching with seasickness.* How many of the three-hundred or so passengers suffered like Mick and Kathleen?

Scarcity in Ireland did not compare to the lack of drinking water and food aboard the *Mona*. Orla tapped into her mental skills of escaping horrific situations around her and concentrated on the ventilation openings. Slightly gray and no longer black outside. *Sunrise is nearby.*

How does darkness feel oppressive? *'Tis merely a different color of air and light.* Orla wiggled her fingers in front of her without landing on any objects, so she tapped her face. No worries, her face and fingers were still there. She went from rejecting invisibility and despising hiding in the dark to embracing the ship's purser with her identity. Orla smirked at her perpetual back and forth in life.

A movement other than the churning ship wiggled her bunk, and her brother growled. "By all that's holy. Where is it?"

"Mick? What's wrong?" She sat up and knocked her head against the broken overhead slats before she slid off her bunk to calm him. She slowly tapped her fingers against the wood on her way to his bunk.

"Me cursed sack is missing. I can't see you. Hairy creatures are crawling upon me as well." His voice rasped and shook.

"Ah, Mick. Poor soul. I'm reaching out me hand for you. Here. Try to find me." She patted his thin, damp mattress trying not to think of the reasons for why, or what made it stink.

He seized her hand and tugged. She landed against his soggy and smelly jacket with her face. Mick trembled. "Did you move our sacks somewhere? Need me whiskey. Do you hear me?"

She wiped her face with her scarf. "Aye. Keep your voice low. Kathleen needs her rest. Remember, we put yours and Kathleen's behind her and the wall for safe keeping? But then—"

"Something's not right." He cursed. "Oh, aye. A thief took Kathleen's bread earlier when you were above. Where're me bottles?"

"Mick. Give a listen. Your whiskey was taken many days ago, remember?" Orla yanked him by his lapels. "Evil deeds surprise the innocent. We can't see. We can't accuse people, and we can't fight. There're more than Irish around us. We don't know them or if they've scruples 'bout killing. Don't go yelling and attracting attention. Be invisible. Sometimes 'tis the simplest way to survive. We must make it to America above all else. I've been amongst criminals and thieves. You've been a farmer. Aye?"

"Aye." Mick slid out of her grip, and a splash on the floor announced his landing. He leaned against her lower leg. "What's wrong with me? And Kathleen? Is it the typhus?"

"For you, 'tis the lack of drink, methinks. Pull yourself up out of the muck, brother." She waved her hands toward his voice to grab him again and help him rise.

"The creatures are circling above me. Need me whiskey. Can't live without it. Never been without it. The pain, sister." Mick whimpered.

She found her brother with her fingertips and stroked his grimy head now bowed against her bunk. "I know that well. 'Tis black in here. You can't see anything that's factual. Hold on, aye? We've mayhap four days more. I'll get another bottle for you, should I find one. Well, after they open the hatch."

"How'd we get trapped inside this pit?"

"I've told you a hundred times. They'll let us out soon."

"The demons?"

She huffed. *Patience, Orla. Mick's ill. His head is on crooked.*

Kathleen moaned. Her breath rattled in her chest amidst the waves crashing against the massive *Mona*, and others continued to retch and cry in the dark. *'Tis surely hell itself.*

Orla caressed Kathleen's face behind her with the backside of one hand while she stroked Mick's hair to her other side. "We must sleep in watches until we get above deck. Kathleen's breathing strangely. Pray for us, Mick."

"Pray? You pray. Only Mister Death hears me. God doesn't hear."

"Then we're out of luck if you can't pray because God hasn't heard me as well. Try Saint Christopher."

"You try Saint Christopher. Asked him for a safe voyage. He must be busy."

Orla sighed. Well, her dreams for a better life on America's shores were melting away. *Wonder if God thinks of me as often as I wonder 'bout Him?* "I'll go above for a doctor as soon as the hatch is unlocked." She crossed her chest. *Christ, have mercy upon our souls. 'Tis Orla Muldoon desperately asking for help. Nonetheless, You mightn't remember me from me miserable childhood.*

Her hand slid off Mick's head when he moved away. "Sleep, Mick. It shall help you feel better."

"Only whiskey does that." His voice grew distant, then his bunk creaked. "Where's me whiskey, Orla? I'm burning hot. 'Tis agony."

"As I've told you, your whiskey's gone. Stop asking for it." *Saint Christopher, Christ is busy. The Muldoon family are on a tormenting voyage here. Please do what you can.*

* * *

Day 9, *on the S.S. Mona*

Whatever day it was, Orla could not tell, but the calmer seas and *clunk* against metal burst forth a flower of hope within her heart. Silver, early daylight spilled down the ladder, fragmented the cargo holds blackness, and outlined her bunk. Her eyes ached while her spirit rejoiced. She squinted up at the perfect round circle fanning fresh, salty air onto her face, and drew in deep, cleansing breaths.

By the time she gathered her wits and inspected Kathleen thoroughly as possible in the growing daylight, able-bodied people climbed the ladder past her to the deck earlier. Orla prepared herself with a loose scarf over her scars to hide them from public view. She bent over Mick and shook his arm.

He groaned. "Mister Death? Don't. You grabbed me."

He's worse. Kathleen's worse. "I must find a doctor, Mick. Guard Kathleen. I'll be as quick as a shake of a lamb's tail." She had no choice but to leave them, did she? She must escape the horrible pit for a while.

After several hours of searching and inquiring from anyone who would speak to her about a doctor onboard, the sun hovered closer to the horizon line. She propped herself against the wall on the lower deck to relax a moment. *Must be late afternoon.* Chill wind and mist from the gray Atlantic's whitecaps slammed against her body and tore at her layered scarves to announce Mother Nature was still in control, and Orla had control over nothing. What should she do now? She could not return below without a doctor. Her sister and brother, whom she convinced to go on this journey with her, direly needed medical care. *I'm to blame for this tragedy. Help us, God in Heaven.*

A brown-skinned ship's mate sneered at her as he approached where she stood. He pinched his nostrils and shimmied sideways to avoid possible contact as he passed by.

She checked, and her scarf still covered her scars. *Get the purser.* Before she gave up, she would find him. They had that agreement. She gripped the wet rail as rough waves listed the ship to one side, then she hurried after the disdainful ship's mate as safely as possible on the slippery deck. He would know the whereabouts of the purser's lodging. Hopefully, he would tell her.

"Pardon me, sir."

The ship's mate halted and turned back to her. His dark brows lifted.

She clenched her purse strings inside her skirt pocket with one hand and gripped the rough rope running the length of the wall for balance with her other. "I must find the purser. Can you tell me where his lodgings are?"

"Purser? He not like . . . people to . . . bother." The mate grimaced and stared her up and down.

"He knows me. He would like to see me, 'tis sure." She raised her chin.

"Purser know you?" He pointed at her.

She nodded and smiled. "And he will thank you for telling me. Be happy."

The mate narrowed his dark eyes. He extended his palm between them.

Orla propped herself against the ship's side to avoid the dangerous waves and spray. *It always comes down to money.* The ship bumped her against its wall a few times while she drew out her purse and dumped some coins into his open hand.

He turned over the coins with his thumb and glanced up.

"Irish. Irish money. Money. Spend it or exchange it, aye? Um, yes? Purser will tell you how." She ground her teeth together.

The mate sniffed and shifted his position back in the direction he was heading. "Come. I take you." He unlocked and entered a door to their right and led her through dim narrow hallways until they came to a ladder going upward. They climbed it and arrived on the top deck. He glanced over his shoulder at her, then stepped ahead several yards to another locked door.

Although she was breathless and wet from the excursion, she welcomed the break from the splattering waves and knowing her day's ordeal was almost over. A doctor would be her prize.

"Here." The mate unlocked a narrow door, then held out his palm.

"More?" Orla frowned. "Is he in there?"

He grinned lopsidedly. "Purser."

She plopped two more coins into his hand. "That's all."

He pointed with his thumb and left her standing in front of the door.

"Rude fella." Orla pushed on the knob, it unlatched, and she pushed on the door. Another hallway with more doors? How was she supposed to find the exact room?

One door to her right opened and her purser stepped out. His jaw slackened when he spied her standing there. "Miss?"

"Nearly. Came to find you. Per our agreement."

He smiled. It was not exactly a friendly one, but he bowed and swung his arm toward the room he had exited. *He's nameless from me neediness.* He knew her name from the registration, so that was that.

She bypassed him into the tight space he lived in. Narrow bed. Tiny, metal washbasin. A small porthole. One table. Everything nailed to the floor or wall. "Thank you. What's your name, purser?"

"Abasi. I go work."

Orla stood beside the basin. "I need a doctor. For medicine. Please take me to one if there's one onboard."

"I go look. At paper. Must find for you." His gaze turned lascivious.

She fluttered her fingers. "I know. I know. When you return, yes?"

"Yes." Abasi gave her a stern expression before he exited. "Stay."

Orla quickly stripped, washed her undergarments, then herself. All she had to do after looping them over a short clothing line in the corner was wait. "Hope it shall be a short delay." Then she could bring aid to her ill loved ones.

She wiped a spot clear on the smudged porthole with her wet scarf to peer out at the gray sea with whitecaps. "Forgot to ask what day 'tis. America, I'm counting on your worthiness for the cost to get there."

Abasi returned a while later, after she wrapped herself in a towel and napped. "Found medicine. His room. Ross."

She released a long breath. This day was looking brighter. In a short time, she would triumph in her crucial goal. "'Tis kind of you, Abasi." That was the only way to describe his help.

* * *

THE SUN KISSED the horizon through the porthole's view before Abasi reopened his door. He led Orla, dressed in her nearly dry clothes, to the Salon Room section on the deck above them. She had never climbed so many ladders in her life. *Stairs would've been much easier.*

Abasi turned a corner within the wider hallways in First Class, then they passed a downward stairway. *What? Mayhap closed to the likes of me.* The classes observed their established distinction and separation, even on this horrid merchant ship. One day, she would be wealthy enough and be climbing the stairs to the upper class.

They stopped at a door labeled *Salon Room 3.* Abasi knocked. "Purser."

Footsteps approached, the latch clicked, and the door swung inward. The orange and red sunlight illuminated the space behind the man and highlighted the top of his silver hair. His surprised expression when he flicked his gaze over her nearly had Orla giggling. "Hello. What is it?"

Abasi bowed. "Woman. Need you." He rushed away.

Dr. Ross peered out the doorway down the hall after him, then blinked at Orla. "You need something from me?"

"Aye. The purser helped me to find you. Don't be angry with him. I

79

begged and such. Me name is Miss Orla Muldoon. Apologies for intruding upon your privacy. You see, me brother and sister are direly ill. Not with the seasickness, but something worse. I fear for their lives, I do. Please." She bit her lip and bounced on her toes.

Someone moaned inside the salon room. The glorious sunset shone its light onto a frail and wan woman's face framed against a pillow. She slumped over in a chair.

Dr. Ross stepped backward and aside. "Come in for a moment, and we can talk. I must see to Mrs. Ross." The Ross's rooms were spacious and had three portholes. All the furniture was nailed to the floor or wall, as in second class, where Abasi lived. Neither class had filth to deal with as steerage did. Fresh water in a pitcher waited to invigorate them. Condensed drops of moisture gathered on a pitcher atop the laden table beside fresh bread, hard cheese, apples, and a baked chicken.

Orla's mouth watered. She breathed in deeply of the tantalizing aromas and licked her dry lips. How many days had passed since she ate or drank anything? *And how shall I urge him to leave his languishing wife? He must come with me.* Lightheadedness overcame her, and she gripped the back of a wood chair nailed in place. "May I sit?"

"Please do." Dr. Ross straightened his wife's brightly patterned blanket of blue, orange, and yellow. He stroked her cheek.

"Does she have the seasickness?" *Hold on, Orla. Think of your errand.* She gripped her skirt to restrain herself from grabbing anything that tempted her beneath her nose.

Ross turned toward her. "No, thank God. She is, however, ill, and I am taking her home to America."

"I took care of me auntie back in Ireland. She'd been ill with something for three years and we'd no money for a doctor. She couldn't speak or walk or feed herself. 'Tis why I asked." Orla twisted her hands together. "And you must come with me below, to steerage. Shall your wife be safe alone?"

Dr. Ross took a seat across from Orla and frowned. "So, tell me what I will be facing. That will determine the time I must be away from Mrs. Ross. I always have my medical bag when I travel.

Although, I am a surgeon, not a general medical man. You appear drawn. May I pour you water?"

Orla almost fainted with relief. "Aye, please do." She gulped from the cup he handed to her, took a breath, and finished it. "I'm ever so grateful for that."

"You are undoubtedly hungry as well. Help yourself." He indicated the foodstuffs between them. "They give us much more than we can possibly eat."

What I always wanted. More than she could possibly eat or drink. And she would have it one day in America. She grabbed a roll, bit into it, and closed her eyes from the aroma. *Sweetbread.*

Mrs. Ross mumbled and stirred. She stretched her thin arms above her head to fully awaken. She focused on Orla. "Who is our visitor, darling?"

"May I present Miss Orla Muldoon? She needs my help. I will check my bag while you finish eating, Miss Muldoon." He headed to another room.

She said 'darling.' Like Mick called his wives and children. She may never have someone who calls her darling, but she would certainly have their luxuries one day. Plenty of money. Delicious food. Beautiful clothing. *This lovely soft bread is the start of it.*

Mrs. Ross smiled gently at Orla. *Her cheeks are as pale as me own, and her thin, white hair is near to the same color.* "So, Miss Muldoon, I must say it is nice to have a visitor. I have not been outside of our room for the entire nine days of our voyage. That is unusual for me. I enjoy the outdoors. I am Jeanette—dear me. I see you had an accident. I am sorry for that."

"Holy heavens." Orla dribbled a few crumbs and tapped her stuffed, scarred cheek. Her scarf hung below her chin, baring her ugly marks to these upper-class people. All she wanted to do was quench her thirst and gorge herself on the sweetbread. She shoved the covering over her face and gulped back her tears.

Mrs. Ross tittered. "Oh, do not be concerned, Miss Muldoon. You could never imagine what my husband and I have seen on our missionary trips to other countries. Why do you require help from my husband?"

"I'm that sorry to take him away from you. I am. We've been locked below in the cargo hold for three days, if this is day nine of our journey?" She turned to Dr. Ross as he reentered the room with his bag and stood to face him. "They've been ill mayhap six days, me brother and sister. Please come down with haste."

"You have yet to give me a description of their symptoms." He set his bag on a chair.

Orla jiggled her leg with impatience. So much time had already passed. 'Kathleen was ill before we left Ireland. She had a sore throat for months. Her breathing sounds terrible. And Mick? I'm uncertain. Could be the lack of his whiskey. A thief stole it. 'Twas his daily medicine for many years."

"And you have yet no symptoms?" He inspected her a little closer.

"I never get ill. Please make haste, if you can leave?" She slid a side glance at Mrs. Ross.

Mrs. Ross clasped her hands together. "Oh Daniel, please go help her and make her take some food for them. You know as well as I do, we will only throw it away. My appetite is not what it should be."

"You will be fine without me?" Ross went to her and caressed her wispy hair.

"Never that, darling. However, I will read my Bible here while you are away." She dug inside her covers and lifted a black book embossed with gold lettering on its spine and nodded to Orla. "I always have it for company."

"I'm that grateful to you, Mrs. Ross. Farewell." Tears from their mercy choked further words. Orla stashed the food in her outer skirt forming a sort of bag, then led the quiet, good doctor down the stairs with haste and boldness because of Ross's presence. The comical stares and expressions of other First-Class passengers as they passed nearly brought her to giggle, if not for her concern for her family's welfare. The sun was already disappearing beneath the clear horizon. As they descended, the engine noise increased. She almost turned back from returning to that horrible pit.

Concentrate. Escape me emotions. At least the *Mona* used its engine and sails both today, in the pleasant weather, and did not depend upon the engine only. That was for when it must forge ahead through storms. *As I am doing.*

"I have not been to steerage before, although we have sailed many times."

She stiffened and halted near the cargo hold entrance down to steerage. "Hold your breath, Dr. Ross, for as long as is doable."

"I have heard disgusting tales of steerage. Now, I shall see for myself what is true and exaggerated." He removed a kerchief from his pocket and tied it around his face. "I will follow you."

"Nevertheless, you mayhap never been in such a place as this hell-hole. Your kind wife mentioned some terrible things you've both seen during your travels. If you dare to continue below, this one shall make it onto your list of those memories." She breathed in deep of the fresh sea air and willed herself to climb downward into the darkness, stench, and despair. *Poor Kathleen and Mick await the good doctor's help.*

CHAPTER 9

Her Chum's Place

Nevertheless, Dr. Ross's opinion shan't interfere with me dreams of wealth
Orla

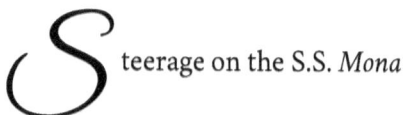teerage on the S.S. *Mona*

"HERE THEY ARE, DOCTOR." Orla paused at the base of the ladder to allow her eyes to adjust to the darker compartment, then scurried to Mick and Kathleen's bunks. They were both in blessed sleep.

Dr. Ross joined her, his eyes wide above his arm and elbow that covered his face kerchief. He scanned the crates nearby. "This is dreadful. The rumors are true. Someone must do something about this filthy hell for travelers. Regardless of what they can afford."

She sniffed. "The world has nary a care for the poor amongst them. Couldn't find anyone who cared to come down. Only you."

Ross bent down to Mick's berth to study his face. "Mr. Muldoon? I see you are awake now. I am a doctor. May I examine you?"

Mick released a long, shaky sigh, then a sob. "See to Kathleen first. Our Lamb is gone, Orla."

"Gone?" Her hope and stomach plummeted. "What do you mean? Lamb?" She shook Kathleen's bare arm. *Cold.* Orla's knees buckled. She sank into the muck on the floor. *No! No, God, You wouldn't. You took her away whilst I was gone. We failed her.*

Ross gripped her arm firmly. "Please, Miss Muldoon. Arise from the filth. I am sorry for your loss however I must examine her. Mr. Muldoon, can you shift yourself to the end of the bunk?"

Orla and Mick clung to each other and wept together while Dr. Ross examine their sister. "This can't be. I tried to find someone to help. None would. I couldn't."

Mick leaned his head against her waist and squeezed her hand on his shoulder while she sobbed.

Dr. Ross finished inspecting Kathleen's body using a *lucifer.* He dunked the tiny flame into the smelly, shallow water to stifle it, wiped down his instruments, then his hands on a rag, and repacked everything into his bag. "I know you searched for help, Miss Muldoon. It is sadly not always readily available. Especially onboard a ship. This one has no resident doctor, for it is a merchant vessel."

Orla wiped her face. "It took too much time to find you and bring you here."

"We should have already arrived in port, if not for the storms and getting off course. The captain kept some of us apprised of our progress you see."

The First-Class passengers of course. Orla clenched her fists as anger overrode her grief for a moment.

Ross lifted his bag and held it in front of himself. "Please unbutton your shirt for me, Mr. Muldoon. I must examine you. I will then arrange to take your sister above deck and list a reason for her . . . demise. Laws require it from an attending doctor, although we are at sea. I am so sorry for how terrible this must be for the both of you. So, your sister says you are having a rough time being without your whiskey since a thief stole it?"

Mick nodded. "Never been without it. Have nightmares. Me gut wrenches. Feel shaky."

"I see. It is understandable. Miss Muldoon, you may sit and ready the cask of water and food we gave to you. You are probably in need of it."

"I don't know if I shall eat more, but Mick shall and drink some water." She opened the outer skirt she tied into a pouch to carry their lavish feast. It gave her something to concentrate on. *But Kathleen.* Orla refused to glance at her again, her throat constricted with tears, and swallowing would not be easy. She removed the plug from the cask, stared at her lap, and waited a moment. Refreshing. Sweet as honey. *Water.* Tears trickled down her cheeks.

"Well." Dr. Ross stood and lifted his bag. "You all appear malnourished. Kathleen probably had scarlet fever. Malnourishment weakens the body's defenses against illnesses. Mr. Muldoon, you are nearly adapted to not having alcohol in your system. Give it a few more days. By then, we should be in port, and you will be stronger. Miss Muldoon, return to our room for more food and water tomorrow. I will leave instructions for the purser to escort you again. He will be paid by me."

Unbelievable. She would not need to secure his help again. Orla handed Mick the Ross's gift of freshwater in the cask. "Drink up. Sit by me. I've spread out the food the merciful Mrs. Ross insisted we take. Thank you as well, doctor, for your vast kindnesses to us." *A lovely gentleman, indeed.*

"It is the least we could do. But Miss Muldoon, please come with me. As next of kin, I will need you to sign the ship's documents as well. They require it before burial."

"Burial? Where would that be?"

Ross laid his gentle hand on her shoulder. "This will be a grievous event for you. You are Catholic, correct? I saw her rosary tucked beneath her bodice. Would you wish to have the Last Rites performed? There may be a priest onboard, although I am not hopeful."

"Aye." She swung her gaze to Mick, who nodded.

"One other thing. Do you wish to have your sister's rosary?"

Orla shot upright from the bunk. "No, 'tis hers. Our mam gave it to her for *First Communion*." Her voice and hands trembled. *He's truly taking her from us.* "She's gone and I should've done more to keep—"

"You are a dutiful sister. They locked the steerage for three days during the last storm. What could you do then?" Ross clasped her arm when the ship swayed.

Mick wagged his head. "And as for me? All messed up with me own travails. Couldn't protect her from Mister Death."

"Who?" Dr. Ross frowned and released Orla.

"Never mind him."

"Come, come. We cannot control all our circumstances or other people. Your sister is with God now because of her faith in Him. Take comfort in that fact."

Comfort in our faith? 'Tis a meager thing at best.

"Now, I must go above deck and report this to the captain. Please accompany me, Miss Muldoon, for the documents. Mr. Muldoon, drink and eat slowly. Small amounts at a time, or you will make yourself ill again. I will return tomorrow to see how you are faring."

Orla accompanied the doctor to the ladder, then paused halfway up the rungs to stare down at her only sister, laying lifeless. Lost at sea. *Tender and kind Lamb. Gentle. Unlike me.* She ground her teeth. *Should've made her go home. All me own fault, her death.*

That night, seawater engulfed her in a nightmare. Orla struggled and frantically flailed to reach the surface. She was out of breath. The waves continued to hold her down, and a shark circled with gray flashes below her feet. It drew closer. She jerked and sat up, hitting her head on the bunk. Drawing in deep inhales of putrid air, was far better than a shark on the attack.

"Orla?" Mick's low voice whispered in the dark. "You whimpered."

Her heart persisted in pounding fast. She pushed against her chest. "A shark was after me."

Mick scoffed. "Me with Mister Death and now you with a shark. Such an odd pair we make."

"Aye. Muldoon family, we are. Was like when they threw Lamb overboard. Truly horrifying. Was it also a nightmare that I screamed like a banshee at the whole of steerage? I recall being hysterical. Upset 'bout Kathleen. Or was it real?"

"You truly did so last night. I'll have me own nightmares from you shaming the thieves amongst us, and telling of Lamb's burial at sea, sister. I'm thinking the thieves will avoid us for the entirety of our voyage. Whenever it finally ends, this terrible experience."

"Kathleen's burial. The worst tragic happening ever by far. Dr. Ross assured me that God can find her soul in the water. Even in the depths of the sea." Her chin trembled, and tears filled her vision.

"Aye. A comforting belief to have. God has a powerful sight. 'Tis what we're told."

Warm tones overtook the gray light shining through the open hatch and lit the area around their bunks. Another day dawned and Orla did not know how near they were to America. The doctor said three more days, so it could be today. "Mick, aren't you forever grateful to Dr. Ross for sending the mattresses and blankets to us? I slept grand. When I did sleep."

"Aye. The facecloths are another miracle. Me breathing was shallow, partly because of the stink and putrid air. Don't notice it as much, now. A third miracle was that we didn't catch scarlet fever from our dear Lamb. Our macushla." He crossed himself.

Orla copied him and swallowed her tears. "Our gentle Lamb." She'd rather think about the doctor and her future than that tragedy. "Well, he's the kindest gentleman I've ever known."

Mick leaned closer to her in the gloom. "A kind doctor who says I shouldn't drink. Bah, he doesn't live me own life, does he?"

"Nay, but he cares. And him trying to find us a priest, well, that goes beyond a doctor's duties. Do you think he has a fondness for us? He gave me his card for when we're in America and if we find trouble. He's concerned. Says people in New York and other Americans rarely like Catholics. 'Detest,' was the word he used."

Mick flicked his wrist. "Let's worry 'bout that later and get through the peril first."

"We may yet encounter more. Nevertheless, he and his wife are lovely Americans. Mayhap he's wrong 'bout his people." *His opinions shan't interfere with me dreams of wealth.*

*   *   *

CASTLE GARDENS, New York City
September 13, 1866

ON THE DECK the following morning, Orla stood atop Mick's boots for a moment to get a better view of the dark spot on the horizon. The vessel tipped in a slight turn as wind filled its sails. Gulls swooped over the *Mona's* foremast. Other ships passed theirs, sailing in all directions, near and far.

She pressed her scarf over her face, squinted, and partially shaded her eyes against sun and the blowing mist from the waves. "Do you see it?"

"Think 'tis America." Mick craned his neck. He was taller than most, so everyone around them quieted to listen. "Ah. 'Tis a strange sort of castle."

"America's port is named Castle Gardens for good reason, then."

Cheers roared around the top deck, and people jostled each other for their first glimpse of their new home. America, the land of the free. The survivors from the terrible journey cried and hugged each other.

"'Tis a glorious day I'll never forget, sister."

"Nor I." *If only Lamb was here with us. God love her soul.*

A few hours after arriving in America, Orla raised her eyes from the map Maeve's boarding house to her new home of New York City. She turned to Mick. "'Tis grand that we're through that tangle of humanity. Have you ever seen such a commotion?" She did not expect that experience since departing the emigration depot at Castle Gardens.

"And me a farmer. I'd not choose this place." Mick scowled up at a two-story, dilapidated building.

"So, we turn left on Rose Street." She led her brother down a narrower lane than they earlier traveled upon. The horse and buggy traffic thinned. Disheveled and barefoot children played in a murky stream beside the lane. A bloated, dead horse lay nearby with flies buzzing around it. *Disgusting.*

She ignored Mick's dismayed comments and turned her gaze upward for any insignias on the rundown buildings. A hand-painted sign hung cockeyed above a shabby place with a cracked front window. Orla sighed. "We're here at last. Twenty-Two Rose Street." *Maeve, what've you brought us to?*

Mick shuffled his feet and turned in a circle. "Sister, I've me doubts 'bout this Maeve's home. Have you noticed this area—"

"Brother, you're 'bout to see and experience what you've never witnessed, aye? Remove your cap." Orla tapped her knuckles on the black, chipped door.

"Me tam covers a multitude of sins." He plopped it back on to cover his oily, stringy hair.

A few minutes passed, then the worn black door creaked inward, leaving a slight opening for a disheveled young woman.

Not much of a fiálteach. She expected a welcome from Maeve herself. This untidy person donned only with a flimsy camisole had the looks of Maeve. Could she be her daughter?

The messy brunette woman yawned. "Yes?"

"We're Orla and Mick Muldoon. Maeve expects us. Who are you?"

"Maeve's asleep. As we all were. I'm Annabelle, her, uh, helper. She mentioned chums from Ireland. By your speech, they must be you?" Annabelle smirked, stepped back and pushed the door open wider.

They stepped inside, but the heat did not abate. It increased.

Annabelle pinched her nostrils shut as they passed her. "What's that horrible stink?"

Mick gasped, and Orla huffed. "'Tis us. Fresh off the ship and desiring a bath."

"Never mind. I'll get used to it. Happens often enough." The young woman wiggled her shoulder and ogled Mick. She puckered her red-smeared mouth.

That does it. I know what we're amongst. "Back away from me brother, woman. He's not accustomed to such treatment, you creature." Orla glared at her until she stepped away. *Poor fella. Hope his shock shan't cause him to faint.*

"Hallo down there. Glory be, is that you? Me own Orla?" The husky voice above them coming from the upstairs could only be Maeve O'Donnell's. "Thought the ship had sunk or some such. But you made it across, so you did." Her long, unnaturally tinged yellow hair swung loose over the banister. Her buxom figure bounced, wrapped in a scanty pink robe. Purple outlined her eyes and red smudged her lips. But it was Maeve herself emphasized with all those odd colors.

"Me old chum, Maeve. You're such a loyal friend to help us in our need." Orla dropped her sack onto the dusty floor and reached out for her friend.

Maeve cringed away. "Aye." She opened her palm. "I'll be skipping me hug for now, till you've had your bath."

"Aye." Orla blinked, and squeezed Maeve's fingers, but her friend's hand remained flat and outstretched between them afterwards.

"Do you have the coin we agreed upon? We women must earn something one way or the other. I see only two of you. The price required is the same, nevertheless." She flipped her strange hair with her other hand and winked at Mick.

Orla reached inside her smelly bodice, removed her damp reticule, and dumped Irish coins into Maeve's outstretched palm. "Needs exchanging, aye?"

Maeve quickly counted her money. "I shall do that. Where's your sister?"

Orla and Mick crossed themselves, and Orla gave a shortened tale of the voyage and sweet Kathleen's departing.

Maeve and Annabelle *tsked*, crossed themselves, and murmured condolences. Maeve shook her head. "'Tis never been a safe journey. Tragedy happening to one's own loves is beyond wretched. Well, glad you could pay for three. I'll be expecting payment each month for your board, on account of your sister's passing not being me own fault."

Her friend's words stabbed her heart, and Orla winced with the pain.

"And you Mick, such a handsome fella you are. You were a younger man the last time I laid eyes upon you." Maeve leaned her bosom against him.

Mick recoiled and skittered behind Orla. The house's temperature had increased, and so did Orla's angst with her childhood friend. At least, the musty air would be an improvement from the stench in the *Mona's* cargo hold. She tugged the scarf off her face to speak to their irritating reception. "Maeve, we're weary and didn't expect such treatment."

Annabelle flinched and gasped. "Such gruesome—"

"Mind your manners, me girl." Maeve pinched her.

"As if flirting with me brother was good manners." Orla scowled at her chum.

The younger copy of Maeve rushed from the parlor entrance and ran up the creaking staircase. She called out to someone upstairs. Several footsteps thudded above.

"Annabelle often behaves how she wishes. Stubborn girl. Apologies. So, you're in need of baths, aye, Mick?" Maeve picked a damp lock of hair from her forehead.

He glanced at his sister. "Aye, and a long drink of water first."

"Let's away to the scullery, then." Maeve spoke over her shoulder. "We cook little here. Pick up supper at the market down the lane on the corner. Baths you can take in the tub outback by the outhouses."

"In public, Orla?" Mick crumpled his cap.

Maeve chuckled. "Behind a curtain on the rope. Or if you're shy of having an audience whilst you bathe, in the scullery 'tis." She collected an oval galvanized tub from a screened-in back room and clunked it onto the floor.

"Either will do for us, aye, Mick?" Orla nudged him.

"Let's go fetch your drinks, Muldoon family. Follow me." Maeve gathered two metal mugs from a grimy cupboard without doors. She led them through the screened porch, down three steps, and into an open area between the dingy tenements.

"Sister, 'tis nothing like me farm was back home. Where's the greenery?" Mick indicated the cramped buildings, the dirt all around them, and trash barrels lining a cockeyed fence.

"I'm noting that as well. Nevertheless, we should thank God for a roof, aye? Me hands are itching to sweep and polish everything inside and out." The dirt and grime gave her the shivers. "Much like the *Mona*." Nothing she could do about it now.

Maeve filled the two cups from the outdoor water pump and raised her brow. "And here you go. You two holy people think something's amiss with me home?"

Mayhap. "Ah, me chum, we're discussing the differences between our farm and the city life. Nonetheless, with yourself being so occupied with running your business, I'm offering meself as your housekeeper for part of our monthly payments."

Maeve snorted and headed back to the foul apartment. "Don't recall you behaving much like a joker. Always a serious one, you were. Why would I be needing a housekeeper? We're doing grand as is."

They reached the porch steps and Orla halted her chum. "Well, Maeve, noticed the dust, and general filthy condition of the place."

"We don't use the furniture. Or the downstairs." Maeve's wittiness had disappeared with a flash of anger in her eyes. "Here for nigh an hour and already conniving to slip out of paying me for your room? Should've known." She climbed more steps and turned around to face them.

"What's scrambled your brain?"

Mick had limped behind the women up the porch steps. He widened his eyes at his sister.

"I thought to only aid you in making your place more presentable to customers, aye, me friend?"

Maeve scoffed. "And why would I be wanting that? Business is grand. No one cares."

She mustn't pay attention to details. "'Tis grand for you, then. Me thought was to bring in wealthier customers with more funds for your business. The wealthy have more refined tastes."

"You think they'd come here? From where?" Maeve burst out laughing until tears ran down her cheeks and she clenched her waist. "Me stomach. Glory be. You are a jokester. Was wrong 'bout you."

And I was wrong 'bout her. Orla frowned. "Either I find some wealthier clients, Maeve O'Donnell, or you'll lose some faithful tenants. We can't keep paying the sum you expect month after month for three people."

Something shifted in her chum's eyes and manner, before she entered the back porch room off the scullery. "Ah, well, if you insist. We ought naught to let money come between us at our long-awaited reunion, aye? Two things before we go inside. Would be best to hide— uh, always keep your funds with you. And be quiet during the days. The girls sleep then, don't you know?"

"Annabelle and who else?"

"Aye, there're six of us, not counting you. Oh, and watch out for Digger. He's me fiancé, and he's not friendly to strangers. Especially to a handsome man like Mick. Jealousy and all." She tapped her chest.

Orla slid a quick glance at Mick leaning with his arms folded against the mudroom wall connected to the scullery. *He's got a tough time ahead.*

Something heavy crashed upstairs. "What're those silly creatures up to now? I'll knock some sense into them, and the fear of God, see if I don't. Where's me rod?"

Mick scuttled out of Maeve's way when she nearly jarred into him before she reached the scullery door.

Maeve raised the hem of her robe and rushed through the scullery. "Whomever caused that accident shall pay for anything broken! Do you hear?"

Orla turned to Mick. "When I establish me own business, I shan't rule with threats nor violence. Wouldn't go well at all for success."

CHAPTER 10

Her Two Gentlemen

I'm saving it so that I shan't do it
Orla

*M*aeve's Boarding House

ORLA COULD NOT TOLERATE this windowless, musty closet with unused mops, brooms, and buckets for the entirety of her life. *Miserable*. Freedom to provide for herself, riches, and luxury were her goals. "Me brother, 'twas not me notion of America's promises to be stifled in a cage."

"Aye. Nor mine to share a porch's back entrance with the vermin and neighbor's prying. No privacy at all. But took it for I can't abide these women in Maeve's home."

She huffed. "Was glad enough with her invitation to live here. Nevertheless, I can see how it distresses you in this house of ill repute. The more botheration to me is Digger's rage and jealousy with you regarding Maeve."

Mick twitched and rolled his shoulders. "As if I'd want her. Our cots she gave us don't quell me pain at night. So, shall we attempt to head downstairs?"

"Naught a shaft of outside light to tell the time of day in this horrible room. Was never intended to be a bedroom, this." She needed some fresh air and patted her sweaty neck.

"Glad your chum Maeve warned us of Digger's visit beforehand. Gave me time to hide up here."

"Happy times." Orla slid her hand into her skirt pocket, and fingered Kathleen's smooth rosary she decided to keep after all. The beads rubbed together and calmed her.

He snapped his fingers. "Ah, got Da's gift to check the time." He removed a tarnished timepiece from his pocket and flipped it open. "Nigh eleven o'clock."

She laid her ear against the storage room door and listened. "Quiet out there. Mayhap they've all settled in their beds. Don't hear Digger's voice. Nevertheless, don't wish him to catch us and attack you again. I'll knock that bully down, if so. Then allow me itchy fingers to somehow clench around his throat—"

"Never speak such terrible things, Orla." Mick stretched his arms high above his head and winced.

"I'm saying it, so that I shan't do it. Imagining it satisfies me ire a bit."

A door slammed somewhere along the hallway.

Mick froze mid-yawn and stared at her.

Voices and giggles from the direction of the stairway approached their closet room. "All's well, brother. 'Tis only the girls. Let's sneak down, aye? Go slow, boyo. Slide your feet, don't thud your steps."

She held her breath and glanced behind them every few steps. He closely followed her with stealth as she tiptoed toward the staircase. No one exited their rooms, and it remained soundless until someone guffawed.

Two different voices murmured in Maeve's room. A higher pitch mingled with a lower pitch, then both raised with curses.

"Make haste, Mick. Worry naught 'bout the sound of your boots. We must get outside." She rushed downstairs, past the entry and parlor into the scullery, headed for Mick's porch room. When a shout from Digger halted her, she swung around. Her heartbeat raced. *Where's Mick? Digger caught him.*

Heavy footfalls down the stairs alerted her to where the bully intended to go. *The scullery.* She skittered to the sink, slid her damp apron over her work dress, and hummed a tune from childhood while she stacked some soiled dishes in the basin.

"Where'd he get away to? I heard him. He's gotta pay for being here." The hulking, drunk Digger lowered his dark head and slid his bloodshot black gaze slowly around the room. He clenched and unclenched his fists.

"Am assuming you refer to me brother?" Orla clattered some dishes to warn Mick of her whereabouts, then raised her voice to caution him over the racket. "He's not with me, as you can see, aye? What's got you into the nettles? We're paid up with Maeve until next week."

Digger lunged at her, but she was ready for his violence. She pivoted and braced herself on the basin's edge, gripping a dirty knife from the sink between their two bodies.

He pulled to a standstill when he spotted the knife, then chuckled. "You thinking that butter knife is sharp enough to stop the likes of me? Dull as muddy water, that knife, and no good for—"

"Ah, this knife shall be piercing grand enough for me purposes." She scowled, then willed her fist not to tremble while she turned the grimy blade in the light from the bare bulb above them. "You know, I'm fortunately that skilled in using weaponry against people who try to harm me or me family. Are you wishing to challenge me?"

Digger's expression transformed from a dangerous, stalking

predator into daft, vague confusion. *May his dull mind grapple with me words and forget his plot.* She hoped God might hear this prayer of hers. The rosary was in her pocket, after all.

Someone knocked on Mick's wall at the back entry of the scullery. "Orla. Orla, me dear, I hear your sweet voice a speaking. 'Tis Brendan. Missed you yesterday. Let me in, aye?"

A coincidence or God's answer? Brendan was the only one who intimidated Digger. His hulk, yes, and because he won their boxing match and the money for it. She glowered at Digger. "What say you? Shall you leave Mick be? Or shall I bring in Brendan?"

Digger growled and stomped away. *Big bully. Cowardly lout.*

Orla blew out her breath, tossed the knife into the sink, and unlatched the rear door. Brendan insisted on using Mick's porch entry by way of the alley and the common area adjoining the tenements. He avoided the front door saying it was too far to walk.

Brendan grinned his lopsided, toothless smile at her. *Poor battered Brendan.*

He was not a handsome man with his smashed, crooked nose, and copper hair sticking out in tufts atop his head. Fellow boxers had slugged him one too many times, and his brain absorbed most of the damages—gloves being not enough cushion. Yet, he was a gentle natured type, and did not have Digger's rage. "Brendan, me boyo, glad to see you. Everyone's upstairs."

"That's why I'm here. Was me day yesterday, and I missed it." He tugged her into a firm embrace, squeezing her breath out of her lungs, then released her. "Apologies. Was that overly fierce?"

She massaged her ribs, inhaled deeply, and smiled at him. "Nah, I'm good. Forgot 'twas your day as well. I'll meet you after I finish those dishes, aye? Give me a few moments."

"Aye, Orla. I'll wait. But I heard Digger. Did he try anything? Don't trust him. He's bad news." Brendan bent down from his six-foot-six height to peer into her face and nearly toppled onto her.

Orla steadied him with her hands against his hard, muscled chest. "Well, now, your arrival was flawless timing, aye. He's frightened of you. As he should be."

"Aye. 'Tis all right then. I beat him and won, Orla." Brendan shuffled along, trailing his beefy hand on the walls for balance, and exited the scullery.

Such a terrible cost he paid for his fame and earnings. *Now, where's Mick?* She tugged off the apron and crept through the entry into the parlor. There was no other place he could be. One floorboard creaked above her and she halted to listen. Silence. As she bent down to search behind the tattered chaise, Mick's boot was barely visible. "Brother. Come out. Brendan's here now, and Digger shan't do anything out of his fear of him."

Mick moaned when he tried to uncoil himself into a standing position. "Help me, sister. Me back has a spasm." He reached over the back of the furniture piece, and she gripped his hand.

She grabbed his other hand and yanked him to the side of the chaise. "Thought you'd hidden yourself in here, knowing we never use this room."

"I'd go anywhere away from Digger. I can't live this way much longer, Orla. No work. Dependent upon your own coin. And the added hassle of dodging that ruffian. Not me dream of American life." Mick sat on the chaise's cushion and rubbed his hip and side. "This city is dirty, noisy, and gives me downright despair. What shall I do?"

"Don't know, Mick." Upstairs, floorboards creaked once more. "Brendan may be restless. Go out back and I'll join you soon. Mayhap we can make some plans away from eavesdropping ears, boyo."

A while later, Orla entered Mick's room and found it empty. No wonder. The day had been warm, and his room was without shade covering. She peeked out the screened windows and found him with his whiskey, sitting on a bucket in the shady corner between Maeve's place and the O'Leary's tenement. Another overturned bucket balanced a cup of water upon it. *Thoughtful brother.*

She tugged open the rickety door. A warm breeze tickled her forehead and blew a curly strand of her hair along her cheek. She did not wear her scarf at Maeve's place when everyone was asleep. It was the only piece of freedom she had.

Mick grinned at her when she approached. "Knew you'd find me.

Glad for the shade in this corner. Got you a drink, there. The house was quiet, so I snuck a cup for you."

"Knew you'd give me water since I don't touch that drink of yours." She indicated his whiskey bottle, raised her cup, and sat on the overturned bucket. Not ideal, with the rim digging into the back of her thighs. She re-situated herself into a more comfortable position.

He took a swig from his bottle and cringed. "Must tell you, sister, I'm 'bout to lose me mind living here. Even me searches for Aidan have turned up nothing. Seems he's been missing nigh to three years, from the rumors in our neighborhood. None knows what's happened to him. Looking for him gave me purpose. I'm without it now."

"'Tis glad I am that Kathleen never heard this. Her heart would shatter." She gulped her water in one breath. "Watching out for the children was another important purpose of yours. You've been their hero and guardian from the neighborhood bullies and villains, aye?"

Mick grinned, deepening his dimple. "The children give me much delight in me days. I imagined they're mine, or at least, like mine would've been. Some are similar ages. Nevertheless, Orla, 'tis terrible here. I desire greenery, a farm, and the open land." He clenched her arm. "It'll be the death of me staying here. And I've seen Mister Death creeping around."

Not again. Orla palmed his mouth closed and surveyed the area for listeners. Only pigeons cooed on the roof. "Never say that aloud. We don't know how people get put into the asylums around here. Mayhap you can get away from the city soon. I'll think on it."

He rubbed his lips after she removed her hand. "Aye. Newspaper advertisements haven't helped me to find work. Mayhap I can ask the priest at the cathedral? They must hear of opportunities. Look at me. I'm a cripple, as far as the bosses see. Nothing 'bout me has changed except I'm jobless. Back home, I had me own farm and me wretched body didn't matter."

"Hm." What else could she possibly do for him besides support him? If she believed God heard her prayers, she would ask Him for help. *Think.* Orla stared at her dusty boots. She made a design in the dirt with its heel. "Can you try again? Once more? I'll think of some-thing, I shall. Need a bit of time, aye?"

"Aye. I'll keep me hopes up for a bit longer." Mick stood and stretched. He picked up the whiskey bottle. "I'll dump this and go around the back way, out of sight, to search for a newspaper. Should Jimmy come looking for me to play stickball, tell him I shall this after-noon, aye?"

She nodded and slipped her hands into her skirt pockets. Her fingertips tapped an edge of the worn card she kept and treasured since the voyage. *Dr. Ross.* He said to contact him if they found any troubles. Mick's penniless situation was a terrible trouble. She grinned. *Grand idea, this.* She knew her way around New York City from working the streets and searching for Aidan.

A few hours later, the imposing, two-story brick building with a black wrought-iron fence and closed gate either welcomed her or rejected her. This tree-lined area of the city was one she never visited. Orla stared at the green painted door with a gleaming brass knocker. "Glad I wore me clean dress and best hat for this visit." Gloves would have been nice. One day, she would own a lovely, lacy pair.

A silver-haired man with a hat exited the arched green door with a leashed, large dog. The animal resembling a wolf with gold eyes barked at her, and the stylishly dressed man startled. He turned in her direction. *Dr. Ross.*

She could not restrain grinning, as relief rushed through her, and she relaxed her tense shoulders.

His eyes widened. "Why, Miss Muldoon?" He smiled and approached her, leading his pet. His dog wagged its tail, but Orla was not accustomed to being around friendly dogs. *Does it like me, then? Should she stay a safe distance from it? What exactly was a safe distance?*

Dr. Ross chuckled. "Goldie here is a friendly dog. She will lick you if she can. She has never met a person she does not like."

"Well, I've met a few." Orla eyed Goldie when Ross ordered the dog to sit.

"Pardon my rudeness in keeping you standing there, Miss

Muldoon. What brings you here?" Ross patted his dog's head but did not open the gate for Orla. Was it a mistake to come for his help?

She shifted her feet and bit her lip. Then she dug into her pocket and held out his card. "I remembered this. You gave it to me on the *Mona*. Do you recall warning us 'bout being Catholic, and that if we've any trouble, we should ask you for aid?"

"Yes, of course. So, you must require something from me, and that is why you have come to my home. Goldie is eager for her daily walk. Will you join us?" He unlocked the gate.

"I shall." Orla stepped back to the main walk area to allow man and dog room to maneuver. She focused on the friendly animal with the wagging tail. It did not lunge or growl at her. *'Tis a good sign, that.*

Ross guided Goldie to the street side of the walkway and offered his elbow to Orla. Her heart leaped. *A gentleman, 'tis true.*

"So, tell me of your troubles that I may help you."

"'Tis Mick. He can't find work, and despair is overtaking his heart. I pay for his needs, yet it humiliates him to be dependent upon me." She slid a glance at Ross's shadowed face.

A finely dressed couple faced them from a distance and ogled Orla and Ross. The woman with a white parasol and lacy gloves covered her mouth to whisper into the gentleman's ear. They both chuckled. "Good day, Dr. Ross," the man gave a slight bow.

Ross stopped and bowed. "Good day. This is my good friend, Miss Muldoon."

They smirked and murmured something.

"Enjoy your day." Ross tipped his hat and tugged Orla forward. "Snobs."

Orla giggled. "You know, I do like you even more than I thought."

Ross scoffed. "They do not impress me in any way. But continue. It sounds as if your brother requires employment. And what about you?"

She raised her gaze to follow the leafy trees they slowly passed beneath and shading them from the sun's heat while they strolled. "I've been earning me coin and planning for me future. Being a doctor, you must be astute. Do you know what me profession is?"

A moment passed while several horses and carriages drove by, with drivers tipping their caps and startling when they spied Orla. Was it her face covering, or was she so obvious in this section of town? "I believe you are a working girl, Miss Muldoon. Am I correct? Meaning no offense, if I am not."

"Aye. You're correct. 'Tis a story I won't bore you with. I can traverse the oceans and find work anywhere, but Mick? He's a farmer trapped in New York City. All's not well with his soul."

"I see." They stopped for Goldie to sniff a tree trunk. "Are you asking me if I have a job for him or for you?"

She shrugged. Would he want her? Scarred and used? Something close to a giggle escaped her. It was not an amused sound. It was more of a bitter, distressing sound. As if this gentleman would ever be interested in Orla Muldoon.

Ross squeezed her hand on his arm. "You do not know this, but my wife, Jeanette, passed several months ago. I have been somewhat lonely however, I do not want a mistress, and my household staff is already full. Otherwise, I would offer jobs to the two of you."

"Oh, 'tis wretched news 'bout your kind wife, Dr. Ross." Tears surprised her. Gentlemen and other good people should live forever. *There's a perpetual shortage of gentlemen.*

Ross turned back the way they had come. "Goldie, heel. What I can give to you, Miss Muldoon, is extra funds to help you with supporting your brother. I do not have a scarcity of income. God has blessed me for most of my life to the point where I do not experience lack."

Her utmost goal. Not experiencing lack ever again. Should she accept his money? *He wants to help us.* It was a fleeting fix, yet it could buy her and Mick time to find something more permanent.

"Once again, I thank you for your undeserved kindness to us." She was so close to knowing this gentleman better, and possibly his faith in God. Believing in the good people of the world drew her in. Her throat tightened at the loss of nearly being valued for herself and having her entire dream of riches with a good-hearted man to boot. She must force it out of her mind.

They arrived back at his beautiful home. He unlocked the gate, and

Goldie passed through. "Please, do not think me rude by not inviting you inside. My staff would not understand, and no one else needs to know about the cash. It is my gift to aid Mick in believing in God's provision, and that America is not all that bad to its emigrants. Please wait here. I will return momentarily."

In the evening, as the sun set in brilliant oranges and reds between buildings, Orla arrived at Maeve's home and entered through the front entrance. Her feet ached at the thought of several more steps to go around the back. Deep voices in the scullery drew her there before she could head upstairs and flop onto her cot. Was Digger waylaying Mick again?

"Ed. Oh, holy angels." She couldn't close her mouth. "How'd you find us?"

Amusement flitted across his expression. "Hung out at the pub. Watched for you in this area. 'Tis the Irish section, aye? Where else would you be?"

She glanced at Mick and shrieked. "What's happened? Who did this to you?"

He winced when she gripped his bruised jaw and brushed his split lip with her thumb. "Wasn't Digger. Some ruffians at the docks. Went there to find work, and they ambushed me. Ed, here, came to me rescue."

"That I did. 'Tis a good thing. Those fellas were planning on more than an ambush. Thinking they were 'bout to toss our Mick into the sea. I searched for our brother after I heard 'bout the Irish gangs. Bet for certain he'd end up entangled with those hooligans, aye? Came looking for him because I've won enough coin to fulfill me plans of purchasing us some cheap farmland together." Ed puffed out his chest.

Mick did a slow dance for joy—however painful it appeared. His dream. *Our bully brother is 'bout to make Mick's dream come true.*

Why did this news not cheer her? She shook off her fear from his injuries and his future absence. "When shall you two boyos depart?"

Ed nudged Mick's side. "Tomorrow. First thing. Our brother has little to pack, and he's not bringing his treasured cot along."

"Aye. Will be glad to never see it again. Never thought to see the day. Did you, sister?" Mick did another spin.

"I'd hoped this day for you. Prayed it on Sundays, nevertheless, I didn't believe." She attempted to swallow and squelch her thoughts of life without her Mick. *Think of something else.* It didn't work this time. Tears squeezed her throat.

Ed pointed to the table. "May we sit? That chair's empty, and I need a drink."

Orla dabbed at her eyes and turned to face Mick. "I'll be grand alone. I've plenty of money saved up for this eventuality. Always been a planner I have. 'Tis why I'm good at business. Good with numbers, as Da said." She studied Mick's handsome face with his sky-blue eyes and dark auburn beard. "I'll miss you, I will."

He embraced her for a long moment, then pushed her away, still grasping her shoulders. "We'll visit back and forth when the rails join up in the middle of the country, aye? Will be me one grand accomplishment by coming to America with you to own me own farm."

She would secretly give Mick some of Dr. Ross' cash before he left. *Not within that gambler Ed's notice.* There was nothing else she could do for Mick but say farewell. He could not stay in the tenements without shriveling up like an untended plant in a desert. She kissed his cheek, and he kissed her scarred, and damp one.

Three miraculous things happened today. Brendan's interruption of Digger's assault, Ed arrived for Mick, and the kindest gentleman in the world offered his willing aid. Maybe, once in a while on a Sunday, she shall continue to ask God for a few things after all.

CHAPTER 11

Acquiring Her Flower Garden

Money doesn't notice me scars
Orla

S̶ixteen Years Later
Lake Superior, Minnesota
Late Summer, 1882

SUNSHINE POURING through The White Feather's bedroom window introduced Orla's crucially important day as a possibly warm one for Lake Superior. It boosted her hopes. "A grand sign in me own imagination." She yawned and stretched, then unwrapped herself from the soft quilt. Swinging her legs over the lumpy mattress, she reached for her newest robe in the chilly, narrow room. Her thick stockings slid down to her knees as she slept, so she rolled them higher up her legs.

Voices outside invited Orla to satisfy her curiosity through the slightly clouded window. A few men hitched two horses to a loaded cart near the boardinghouse. "Cut lumber. More building, I suspect."

Footsteps passed her door, and a squealing child being hushed by its mama prompted Orla to get ready for breakfast. *A grand cup of tea, toast, and eggs to start the day right.* She splashed water over her face from the washbasin on its stand. As she contemplated what today meant to her dreams and ran a comb through her peach-colored tangles, the jitters took hold. "What happens to me if the building's sold before I get there? I dearly hope not. For heaven's sake, will God suddenly look me way and help? Nah, 'tis impossible." Her appetite vanished. "Yet, I must away to the dock with haste."

Dressed in her lucky purple velvet ensemble with the matching hat, Orla's newest boots tapped a pattern on the floorboards. Each step down the stairway echoed around her. *If the people don't hear me approaching, God surely can.* She straightened her posture when her soles planted in the hallway heading to the dining area.

Clinking of silverware against ceramic, and murmured conversation halted her. She checked the scarf wound over her face. Still in place.

"Good morning, Miss Muldoon." The boardinghouse owner, Mrs. Kincaid, carried a tray of soiled dishes. "I trust you slept well?"

"Aye."

Her brown eyes sparkled, and her rosy cheeks puffed with her smile. "I'm sure you'll find me cooking to your liking." She tipped her head toward the sound of customers enjoying their meal.

"Aye, 'tis sure that I would. 'Tis an important day for me, and well, may I have a cup of tea only? I'm in haste."

Mrs. Kincaid's sparkle disappeared. "But you've paid for breakfast with the fee. You surely don't expect a refund, aye?" Her rosy cheeks jiggled like jowls with the shake of her head. "There're no refunds."

"No, no. Not I." Orla tapped her middle. "'Tis only that I've a bit of a hollow, quivery feeling, is all. Thinking I'll skip the breakfast today."

"You're not ill, are you?" Mrs. Kincaid studied her from head to toe. "Don't wish illness closing down me business."

"Excitement's done it. 'Tis me nerves, aye? Never would I be interfering in another woman's business. Would be a shame, that."

""Aye. And I ought to tell you that I serve coffee, not tea here. American's do love a cup of coffee. Are you open to trying it?"

"Suppose so. A biscuit mixes well with it, aye?"

"Delightfully so. There's a table open for you by the window, as you enter to your right. You may sit there. I'll bring you coffee momentarily." Another inspection, from head to toe, then Mrs. Kincaid headed to the scullery with her full tray of empty dishes.

Orla proceeded through the wide entrance into the dining area. All sound stopped for a few seconds. People either gawked at her, glanced past her, or pretended to cover their reactions with overly loud conversation. *If they knew 'bout me scars, they'd be glad for the scarf.*

A handsome man fixed his gaze on her, as he sat alone at the table beside Orla's. His stare was not exactly rude, but uncomfortable. He was big, like a grizzly bear, and used his cup as a shield in front of his face. Those startling blue eyes above the cup's rim mesmerized her.

Dear me. Her heart thudded. *What in the world?* She never reacted this way to a man. She hesitated to sit while she decided which of the two chairs at her table would shield her from him the most to drink her coffee in peace.

"If you're alone, miss, you may share my table."

Orla startled at his deep voice and yanked out the chair furthest away from him. "No, thank you." Unfortunately, this chair faced him. "Oh, for heaven's sake."

"Here you are, Miss Muldoon." Mrs. Kincaid delivered a tray to Orla. It contained a delicate porcelain cup, matching saucer, and a small metal pot of steaming coffee. She pointed to a treat nesting on the saucer. "A landlady must serve biscuits with coffee as well, queasy or not, or it's not quite up to The White Feather's standards. Do you wish milk or sugar?"

"No, 'tis grand as is this time, thank you. Who told you 'bout me love for biscuits?" Orla shifted her position sideways. She fixed her eyes on the pretty cup and poured the coffee. Darker than tea. Not daring to glance at the bothersome man, she turned her head away and loosened her scarf from the wounded side of her face. Without taking the time for the drink to cool, she hurriedly took a sip.

Her shriek halted all commotion and conversation in the dining area, and the shocked patron's faces swirled into her view.

Orla spit the scalding coffee into the cup and replaced her scarf. Snatching the biscuit, she rushed outside with tears clouding her eyes. She could barely breathe. She knew better than to eat in public. How could she do business here? *'Twas always 'bout the people's reactions.*

After rounding the corner of the building, Orla propped herself against the wall and caught her breath. Crumbs wedged between her fingers. She opened her fist. Enough uncrushed biscuit remained for her to nibble on it even with her stinging tender tongue. She swiped at her tears. "I mustn't let a burnt mouth derail me from me dreams. Money is me saving grace. Money—'tis better than people. Money doesn't notice me scars."

A horse nickered nearby. Orla scanned the shadowed alley. Hitched to a cart, the Bay shook its dark mane. It stepped toward her until the tether tugged it to a stop.

"Aha, big boyo. You're a lovely horse. Did you smell me biscuit? So, you must be asking for me friendship, aye?" She approached with her palm upturned and caught a movement in her side view. She paused, then startled.

The big man from the dining room stood a few feet from the boarding house inside the shadowed gloom with his hands in his pockets. He dwarfed her own five-foot, eleven inches this near to him.

"Of course he'd be yours. You'd need a large horse like this." *Hush, now, Orla.*

"Irish. Thought so. Your light coppery hair color gave the first clue." He ambled toward her.

She backed away.

He halted. "Pardon me. My intent was not to alarm you. Name's Murphy."

Orla raised her chin. "You don't frighten me, sir. I've an appointment I mustn't be late for, and I don't wish to know you." She swung around and hurried toward the street. His chuckle echoed in the alley behind her.

Wind blowing off the vast lake rippled Orla's face scarf as she stood beside the dock. Relief flooded through her mind when she read the 'For Sale' sign still propped inside the building's front window. A spider's web remained attached to it and the window frame like yesterday. All her horrid fears it had sold overnight vanished.

She jiggled the doorknob. Although it was loose, the door unlatched and swung open. Was that house agent she was to meet with already inside waiting for her?

Something moved forward in the dim interior. "Miss Muldoon, I take it?" A thin, short man entered the light from the open door. His oily wisps of hair combed over his forehead, and his narrow, pinched nose twitched. He extended his limp hand.

She ignored it and curtsied like a lady. "Ferret. Uh, Mr. Flint?"

His piercing eyes flashed as he scrutinized her, and his lips pursed together.

He's a snake, not a ferret. "Recalled your name began with an 'F', didn't I? Glad to meet you here."

Mr. Flint gripped his jacket lapels and straightened his posture another quarter inch. "Yes, well, you are slightly early. A good sign. Look around. And do you have the money?" He ogled her ample chest.

Can't blame him, 'tis at his eye-level. Nah, blame him anyway. She dug into her skirt pocket for her mother's reticule she had brought with her from Ireland. The bulging material reassured Orla of its contents. She jingled the coins.

His avid gaze flicked to her face.

Now, we're in business.

He smoothed his wisps against his forehead and licked his lips. "You must be a very lucky woman because this just became available yesterday. Right before you inquired. Already four others have requested to view it. I have only a few moments to show you the rooms. Shall we go up to the bedrooms?" His stare returned to beneath her neck.

"No."

With Mr. Flint's attention returned to her face and their conversation, his brow furrowed.

"I'll take me chances and inspect them meself. I'm a clever woman, aye? You stay here and wait with the papers at the ready." She squinted down at him.

He swung away, and approached a dusty table, mumbling. "Hurry it up, then."

Orla kept him within view for a few moments, but he remained at the table with his back to her. A broom leaned against a corner, and she released it from wispy cobwebs.

"Well?" Mr. Flint called.

She twisted around. "This room'll do me grand. It has a scullery?"

"An adequate one. It was a family home originally. The owner was forced to leave due to illness, they say. It should suit your purposes if you want it." He sidled closer to her.

Orla retreated a step. "Don't rush me. I wish to count the rooms."

"There are three rooms downstairs and four rooms upstairs. I know if I lie to you, I surely won't get what I want for it." His tone sounded lewd.

"You'll get your listed price, and nothing more, aye?" She indicated the stairway with the broom handle. "I'll be checking the upstairs alone. I'd best mention I've four older brothers. None dared to cross me."

Apprehension replaced lust in his dark gaze, and the snake man recoiled and returned to the table. "As you wish."

Men. They see only what they wish to see. Orla stealthily climbed the stairway with the broom as she listened for footfalls behind her. The wooden steps were solidly constructed, for steps number three and seven were the only ones which creaked beneath her weight. She pushed against the rail. *Holding fast.* The fewer repair costs, the more for decorating. Dust and cobwebs were easy to remedy herself.

Reaching the top of the steep stairwell, she noted the tall, narrow window across from the landing. Tattered gold draperies hung in shreds on the rod, and a grubby settee sat beneath it. She turned to her left. Strips of dingy wallpaper clung to the first bedroom wall.

Someone had shoved a wrought iron bed without a mattress below the one window, and a small fireplace stood in the corner beside it. No other furniture, but there was space for a washstand and a wardrobe. *Small ones.* The floor did not slope. *Much.*

The next bedroom mirrored the first layout, but without wallpaper. She trekked past the landing to the far bedroom on the street side. It had two windows, one on both exterior walls, and a dilapidated washstand sat beside the black iron bed.

As she shifted the broom to check the washstand's stability, a stair creaked. Orla froze. "Don't you be thinking of following me up here, Mr. Flint."

Another creak.

"That best be the same step creaking beneath you, Mr. Flint." She held the broom like a sword and stood in the doorway to determine his whereabouts. "Best to speak up. Red-haired Irishwomen have some terrible tempers."

"Your hair is not exactly red, Miss Muldoon," said Mr. Flint. "I am back on the floor. Curiosity got the best of me."

She scoffed and leaned over the rail. The only things visible were the polished toes of his boots. "Don't let me hair color fool you. Peach is not a softer color of red. What's your haste? I've one room left to see."

Mr. Flint coughed and peered up at her from the base of the stairway. "As I explained I have another appointment."

"For this place?"

He glanced down to his left. "Well, as it—"

"Don't think to tell me lies to raise the price!" Orla pointed the broom at him. "Lies don't sit well with me temper."

His shoulders slumped. "Just get on with your inspection."

"That I will." She hurried to the lake side of the home, to the last bedroom, and stood in the doorway. This room had three windows, a larger fireplace, and a double white iron bed. She entered, and it surprised her to find a polished, newer wardrobe in the farthest corner beside a washstand with wilted, dried roses in a pitcher. "'Tis expecting me." *The Rose Room. Rose is me new name.*

Orla hastened to the stairs and descended with joy bubbling inside her. *'Tis happening.* Her dream of running her own business was a signature away from reality. The obstacle was the nasty viper downstairs.

Mr. Flint waited beside the table, spread with papers laid out in an organized fashion with an inkwell near them. He had even wiped the dusty tabletop with a red rag bunched up in a pile. *Willing to do business, then.*

She shook out her heavy skirts, faintly jingling the coins. "Aye, it'll do. Dirty as it is, and in need of care. More furnishings. It's a recent building, aye? At the price you've listed, it'll work."

"Recent enough." The viper tapped his lips with a feather pen and tipped his head down. "Let me see." He spun a paper to study it. "Ah, the quoted price here. This was last week's market price. Since then, more sales in the area have increased."

Orla pressed the end of the broom handle against his throat. "And?" She shoved the tip deeper into his skin as he stepped backward. "It remains fair today, aye?"

He nodded and massaged his throat when she lowered her weapon.

"'Tis never a good idea to change the cost of something mid-deal. People don't care for such slithery doings at all. Especially the Irish." She extended her hand. "Pen?"

Mr. Flint sniffed and carefully laid the pen on her upturned palm. He slunk backwards to the front door. "Be sure to sign each page."

She leaned the broom against the table. Her hand shook with anticipation, but her signature turned out near enough to her legal one. Orla kept the viper in her vision. She allowed each signed page to dry, then gathered and stacked them, before tugging her reticule from her pocket.

Mr. Flint drew closer. *Was that drool on his chin?*

Orla plunked the reticule on the table's surface and untied the drawstrings. "Will you be counting out our agreed upon sum? Mayhap we should do so at the bank, aye?" She grasped the wad of bills. "Or can you trust these kind townspeople as you hurry through the streets with your profits?"

His stare slid from her chest to the reticule. He shrugged. "You have been carrying around your earnings safely. Why should mine be any different?"

She grinned. "You don't have skirt pockets. And, as I'm not giving you me mother's reticule, you'll be carrying these bills in your fists, aye?"

"You, Miss Muldoon, are singularly observant and uncomfortably cautious."

"Survival."

Mr. Flint bent and retrieved a leather case from inside a battered cabinet underneath the window. "I always hide my case." He shrugged. "Thieves can deem it valuable if they enter a building I have unlocked and when I am busy showing a prospective buyer . . . around."

She ground her teeth and clutched the bills as he extended his hand for them. "I'll be handing over me earnings after you hand over me Receipt of Sale with the key." She stroked the broom handle.

His viper eyes glittered with malice. "My, oh my. I had forgotten about those, had I not?"

She pursed her lips together. *Serpent.* "Mr. Flint, you've yet to ask me what business I'll be doing in this building."

He unsnapped his case and shrugged. "Heard rumors." Without glancing her way, he said, "Once I sell a place, it is no longer my concern." He selected another document, signed it, and handed it to her. The key peeked out from under more papers inside the case.

Orla laughed. "You know, don't you now? 'Tis why you've been vulgar. Explains your behavior and your expectations of me today, doesn't it?" She snatched the key, the receipt, and dropped the bills into his open case. She gripped her broom again. "Count it elsewhere, Mr. Flint, for I'll be very busy."

After testing the key in the lock, Orla flapped her hand at the lascivious Mr. Flint and rushed toward The White Feather. Her stomach rumbled from missing breakfast, and her heart fluttered with each quick step. She squelched the impulse to shout for joy yet whispered to herself. "I've done it. Me first step to establish meself. I've gone and done it." *With the first knock on me front door, I'm in business.*

Three men dressed in overalls bumped into each other and gawked at her as she passed them. Two young women slid their startled gazes away from her. *Proper, married women, aye. How will I find some working girls?*

Orla glanced at a shop window, then froze. Her scarf had slipped down to reveal her horrid scars. "Merciful heavens." She tugged it over her nose to cover her cheek just under her left eye. The peoples' stares were not because they knew what business she was in. They were repulsed as usual by her odd appearance.

Satisfied she sufficiently covered her scars, Orla continued further down the street, past a saloon, a livery stable, and mercantile. There would be time to gather supplies later. She crossed to The White Feather in time to catch Mrs. Kincaid shaking a dusty rag over the porch rail.

The landlady smiled. "Hello, Miss Muldoon, don't you look joyful now?" She crumpled the rag. "There's a break in me tasks, so would you wish for a fresh cup of coffee?"

"That I would." Should she risk it? Could she confide in this woman? Orla cleared her throat, and her temple pulsed. She massaged it. *Courage.* "Ah, well, as you're the only woman I've met in town, I've a few questions. May we sit together a moment?" Orla shifted her gaze to her feet from the surprise or something else in the landlady's expression. *Eejit. Friends with me?*

"'Tis a grand time for that. Most tenants are out and 'bout." Mrs. Kincaid led the way into her home, her brown skirts swishing around her legs.

Orla's sight adjusted to the interior light. "'Tis much quieter than during breakfast." The dining area was completely clean and set for the evening meal. "And how did you ready the room so quickly? Wasn't away long."

Mrs. Kincaid laughed. "Me daughter, Janeen, and her friend set up." She waved her rag at the same chair Orla had occupied for a moment that morning. "Take a seat. The kettle's still warm. Shall be only a moment."

With the dining room empty, and no sounds from upstairs, Orla loosened her scarf. If she planned to divulge her secrets, best to begin with her scars. "If it doesn't do her in, we've got a budding friendship." She faced the window and studied the wide body of gray blue water in the distance. "Lake Superior. Aptly named, that."

"Here we are. Ready for . . ." Mrs. Kincaid halted her approach carrying the serving tray to the table. Battling with her shock nearly caused Orla to giggle.

Almost. One, two, three, four. . .

The landlady chewed her lower lip and continued toward Orla. She set the tray down, wiped her palms on her apron, slid the other chair out from under the table, and sat facing Orla. "Me apologies. It distressed me is all. Do you do that to people as a test, Miss Muldoon?"

"Rarely, but what's 'bout to happen in me life is important." Orla tensed her shoulders.

Mrs. Kincaid properly poured out the coffee. "And what's 'bout to happen?" She handed Orla a dainty cup like earlier at breakfast and stirred milk into her own drink.

Go ahead, girl. "You may call me Orla. Shall you be accepting a friendship from me?"

The landlady slowly returned her cup to its matching saucer. Her gaze flicked over Orla. "You may find me presumptuous with what I'm thinking, although if we're to be friends, I must know. There's a kinship between us, aye? Unmarried women from the Old Country, needing to earn our way in the world of men, we are." She raised her cup in salute, pausing it midair.

Orla breathed deep. *Conversation begun.* "I'm unsure who you are outside of being another woman near me own age. Here's me. I purchased a home today. At the dock. Plan to open a business in it. I've some education, saved me money, sailed across the sea, and I'm not searching for a husband. I'm searching for working girls to employ. Do you take me meaning?" She blew on her tea to fill in the terrifying silence. Was that too vague?

"Me name's Nuala, for starters." She fiddled with her spoon. "Are we promising to keep each other's details private?" At Orla's nod, she continued. "I believe I take your meaning. Before all this," Nuala fluttered her fingers above her, "I worked the street." She stared out the window. "Me husband changed things. He loved me. Was married a few years, then the Civil War . . . took away his precious life."

Orla murmured her condolences. Nuala's story didn't surprise her. "You're beautiful. Not like meself. Of course, he'd love you. " She fingered her puckered scar.

"He did." Nuala slid her stare from the lake back to Orla. "A man could love you as well. With time, and his devotion to me, I also came to believe in God's love for me. Your eyes tell me you don't believe in that either. Not surprising with what you've endured in your life. Nonetheless, I'll pray you'll find it. My husband had some investments, and there were some funds from those. As a widow with a very young daughter, a landlady was a good choice to care for us after his passing." She studied Orla over the rim of her coffee cup as she sipped.

Orla smirked. *She believes God loves herself. Why wouldn't He care for a beautiful woman? And a man could easily love her.*

"So, 'twas once you were in America that you began the profession?"

She wagged her head. "Nay. Began at the barracks in Limerick with me cousin. Her mother was an invalid widow, with four in the house to feed. I saved and shared me earnings with me own family as well."

"Aye, many girls did such work from necessity to stave off starvation." Nuala narrowed her eyes. "But here's a warning to beware. The military men there had a commander to discipline them, and the Law in Ireland was mostly intentionally blind to our doings. Not so in this country. Prostitution is a crime. You said you arrived in '66?"

"Me brother and I arrived in New York City. Was me home, and I detested it."

"Then, you ought to know by now you're no longer hidden

amongst the masses in the city. This town is small, yet wild and dangerous." Nuala stirred her tea.

"Aye. Lived in New York for nigh ten years, then St. Paul for six. Went there to be near me brother, Mick, who works for the railroad. Saved all of me money. Heard the rumors of Whiskey Row's opportunities for the enterprising, and when Mick couldn't talk me out of me profession, came here as soon as I stashed enough coin to purchase something. And I do know the law is different in America."

"I'm sure that you do, but there's more. These newer towns are lawless with freedom to do as you please, to be sure. But you'll be doing perilous work, nonetheless. Unknown men come in from far off with the ore barges. We aren't in a safe neighborhood." Nuala squeezed Orla's fingers. "'Tis worse for the girls alone on the streets. Never, ever lower your guard here, aye?"

A lump clogged her throat. "Mm." *Snake man.* Tears filled her eyes. *What's wrong with me?* Orla gulped her cooling tea. "'Tis glad I am for a friend. Now for a favor. Where shall I be finding working girls? I've three bedrooms to fill, aside from me own."

Nuala sighed. "I understand your life, too well. The trouble is how you see yourself. You'd best change your mind, or you've chosen a grim road, me friend."

Heat spread up Orla's chest to her face. She gripped her cup. "I know who I am."

"We're speaking frank with each other, aye? You've not Jesus to defend you as Mary Magdalene had, do you? Don't be shocked. We all know her story, don't we?" Nuala nodded and blew out a long breath. "Mayhap me daughter knows of some women. 'Tis much safer being cared for by a capable Madam with food and shelter. I'll speak to me own Janeen."

"She's not—is she?"

Nuala laughed. "No, no. Janeen would never do such a terrible, disgusting thing."

Orla blinked several times. This new friend confused her. *Does that remark portend badly for our blossoming friendship?*

CHAPTER 12

Her Favorite Eyes

No dog she'd ever known mumbled
Orla

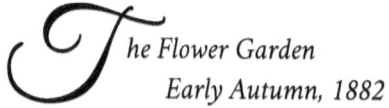*he Flower Garden*
Early Autumn, 1882

SCRATCHING noises at the front door alerted Orla to a visitor. She shuffled over to it in her slippers halfway from the scullery to the stairway, her candle flickering with the draft from her movement. *Could it be Janeen's friends at last?*

Yip.

She hesitated and shifted her blanket higher up over her shoulders. Could it be that filthy dog? It had followed her for five days whenever she ventured outside for supplies, food, or any other reason. Orla figured it would eventually go home. Yesterday, she threw it some scraps from her supper. *Mayhap that wasn't a sound idea.* "But such a sorry sight 'twas, poor creature."

Woof.

What should she do with it? Orla scanned the room. She'd just cleaned the floors today. She should not allow it inside. Her place was not beautified yet, but that dog was grubby. "Fleas." *Wouldn't be good for business, would it?*

Scuffling and mumbling broadcast something odd behind the door. No dog she'd ever known mumbled.

"Get! Get away from the door . . . you cur."

"That's done it." Orla set the candle on a small table beside the stairway. She rushed back to the door and turned the newly replaced doorknob. A wind gust pushed the door against her leg, followed by a flash of fur and two smelly, bundled bodies toppled into a heap onto her clean floor.

"Holy heavens." Orla pinched her nose and stood over the scrambling bundles of clothing. "Who are you, now? And is that your dog?"

A long brunette braid, and delicate hands poked out from one ratty bundle, as the lump positioned itself and stood. A waft of old food, hopefully, and a sour stench followed the movement. The candlelight behind Orla reached the wide violet eyes staring up at her. "We are Janeen's friends. She sent us over."

The other bundled figure stood beside her friend.

They're in desperate need of baths. In the shadows, both seemed younger than Orla expected. "Where's your dog? I never gave me permission to bring a dog along." She quickly turned in circles hunting for it. "Can't have it running through me place unattended."

'Violet eyes' said, "Oh, it is not ours. It was blocking the door when we got here."

'Blondie' nodded. "I shoved it away with my foot. But it growled and refused to leave. I can tell you it nearly nipped my foot off. I need my feet—"

"Where is it then?"

'Blondie' pointed toward the scullery. "It ran in there."

Orla hurried back to the table and snatched the candle. Guarding the flame with her cupped palm, she rushed to the scullery. "Me biscuits. You mangy cur. Was me breakfast."

The dog gulped the last bits of biscuits, licked up the crumbs, and left her floor spotless. It seemed pleased with itself, then backed into the corner and sat. Its amber eyes did not blink.

'Violet eyes' said, "It reminds me of a wolf. Do you think it is?"

Orla studied it closer in the candlelight. *It looks similar to Dr. Ross's Goldie.*

'Blondie' wagged her head. "My dad told me that wolves have silver eyes. He saw one once in Nebraska when he was out on the prairie hunting—"

"Hold on." Orla spoke over her shoulder while she intently monitored the wolf dog. "Can't keep calling you 'violet eyes,' and 'blondie' inside me mind. What're your names? 'Violet eyes' first."

"Aino."

"And I am Janna."

"Your true names aren't any better." Orla stepped back from inspecting the majestic black, tan, and white-chested animal. "Believes he's a king, that one."

He licked his chops.

Orla turned to the girls and scrunched up her nose. "Now that we've found the dog you allowed inside, we need a plan. Baths first." She lit the candle on the scullery table with her own.

The dog had scrambled up and scratched at the back door after the word "bath." The girls retreated with alarm in their demeanor as they stared at it.

Orla raised her hands and spilled some candle wax onto her hand. "Holy heavens. I won't use ice water on you, girlies. Why be afraid of cleanliness? You don't see me all grimy, do you?"

The girls did not speak, but they clasped each other's arms and ogled her.

"Bathing has you in a bother?"

Aino pointed at her. "Your face."

Orla tapped her scarred cheek with her free hand. In her haste to get to the door and the dog, she had forgotten to grab her scarf draped over the stair rail. Terror clutched her tight. Her knees shook. What should she do? *Run for it?*

"You poor thing. But it is not so bad." Aino turned to Janna. "I saw a man once with half his face and neck burnt. His skin was melted, and he did not care who saw it." She traced marks on her cheek and neck with her fingertips.

Janna snorted. "Well I saw a lady with her nose clean gone. It looked like someone bit it off. She still had her eyes, though." She crinkled her green eyes and blinked hard. "If I had to have something gone, I would rather it be my nose than my eyes, would you as well?"

"Why would we want anything to be gone? We would never get work again, silly thing."

Janna clasped her hands together. "I wish I had a scar. Everyone admires them, do you not agree? It means you are courageous, and people know they should not bother you. Or it might mean you are very dangerous and—"

"Or clumsy, or misfortunate, or a numbskull. After the war, there were men without their entire limbs."

"Well, I saw a lady with two heads once."

"I do not believe you. The injured men are worse."

"How do you know? I was the one who saw it . . ."

Unbelievable. Me face hasn't frightened them away. During the ensuing argument about who saw the goriest scars in their young lives, Orla slowly dragged a chair from under the dining table and sat. She placed the candle on the tabletop. "Makes no sense." Numbness replaced her fading trepidation. Everyone before these girls who had ever seen her scarred face recoiled with pity or bullied her in mockery.

The large mutt arose in the shadowed corner nearest the back door and approached Orla, keeping his amber gaze locked with hers. He did not appear timid, only curious, with his ears perked forward.

"Horses forward their ears when they're interested in something.

Well, if you're interested in me, you'll need a name. First one that came to mind is Perky."

His pointy, stiff ears twitched.

"Or Twitch." Orla reached her hand out, palm down for him to sniff at her knuckles.

"Watch out. He might bite you." The girls shuffled behind the table.

"Nah. He would've done it by now. What 'bout Sir Gallant?"

Woof! Sir Gallant sat like a knight, straight and tall.

Janna frowned. "If you are keeping him, he is not staying in my room. He will stink it up. And he probably has fleas. Fleabites itch. I had some once when—"

"You've made up your minds to stay with me, then girlies? Fetch yourselves the tub, aye?" Orla indicated the pantry and headed for the stove where a large pan sat. "I'll heat the water. Gallant can wait until tomorrow, but you two can't. There's no way you're getting into clean beds all smelly and grubby."

The girls sniffed each other and denied any stench.

"'Tis not the dog who's stinking up me scullery, for 'tis you, surely. I'll get you some nightgowns from upstairs whilst you take your baths." Orla retrieved her candle, then stopped within the doorway. "You do know how to take baths, aye? You add cold water to the hot, and you don't need much of it."

"We do know. Silly." Aino giggled.

Orla shook her head on her unhurried way to the staircase. "These two are the most confusing creatures to be sure. Thinking I understand dogs more than young women."

Soft clicking on the floor behind her startled Orla. She glanced over her shoulder. Gallant followed her, matching his pace to hers. He halted when she did.

"You seem like a very well-trained dog. Someone should be missing you, aye? How'd you end up here?" She chewed her lip. "Sure wish you could speak."

Woof!

She placed her foot on the bottom step. "There you go again. Acting like you can speak."

He barked again.

Orla raised her brow. "That's the oddest thing. Come on up, then." She steadied herself with the banister and climbed to the landing. "I'm guessing dogs are cleverer than we know."

Gallant passed her on the last two steps and paused at the top of the stairs. Turning his head back and forth, he appeared to be listening for something.

"Hey, boyo, you're giving me the crawlies. 'Tis naught but you and me up here." She entered the right hallway to her room overlooking the lake. Shadows bounced around the bedroom in the flickering candlelight. Her heart pounded with her chill bumps. She shook her herself. "Isn't a dog supposed to make one feel safer?"

Gallant waited in the doorframe while Orla lit the dresser candles with the flame she held. Once it grew lighter within the room, the bouncing shadows bothering her fled. "That's better." She smiled at Gallant. "I'm near to believing I'm like me brother. You'll never meet him, but he says he sees Mister Death in the shadows." She crossed herself. "Poor Mick."

Inside her wardrobe were a few more nightgowns, so she rummaged through it to fetch them for the girls. She clasped a hanger in each hand and studied the gowns. "Those girls are daintier than me, boyo. I feel like a horse. Come on in, Gallant. This is me room."

The dog obeyed and sniffed around where the walls and floor met.

"Hey, are you house-trained? And don't you be finding any rats or mice, boyo." She sat on the bed and stripped the gowns from the hangers. "Me plans to open business are coming together. 'Tis exactly what I wanted. But with these two? Makes me uneasy for some reason. Hadn't thought of needing to find clothing. Or feeding more mouths. Or—"

Ah, who-who!

Orla and Gallant jumped together. The wailing echoes encircled them, and the gowns she held slid to the floor. The dog rushed to the window, standing on his hind legs peering outside—his hackles raised.

"Is it outside, boyo, or inside?" The same haunting sound echoed from farther away. It wasn't as frightening as when it was nearby, but she still shivered.

Gallant turned his face to her, and quickly back to the window.

"Ah, outside. Did the banshees follow me, now? 'Tis sure it can't be the girls." Orla clapped her hand over her mouth. "Or can it? Let's make haste." She seized the gowns from the floor, the candle off her dresser, and hurried downstairs with Gallant.

Before entering the silent scullery, Orla slid to a stop. "Hallo, girls. Are you well?"

Water splashed, and someone said, "As much as we can be. We are waiting on you."

Orla covered her eyes, stepped through the doorway, and peeked between her fingers at whatever might be awaiting in the scene before her.

The two young women stood dripping on a blanket they had found from somewhere, and each had a large flour sack draped around them. They shivered, and their wet hair trickled water down their shoulders and arms.

Aino giggled. "Miss Muldoon, you seem afraid, or uncomfortable. Thank you, though, for your respectful entrance."

Orla peeked around the scullery doorframe and quickly scanned the area. "Wasn't that. Was more worried you'd murdered each other. Glad you didn't. Did you two hear that horrible howling?"

"Oh, you mean the loon?" Aino's eyebrows lifted. "It is a black water bird. Nothing to be afraid of. You will see."

"Ah, 'tis a *lúnadán*, as we have in Ireland? A water bird living in the lakes and waterways."

Janna cooed. "I like that name much better. Isn't it romantic sounding? 'Loon' sounds scary, but not your name for it. Can you teach us the Irish language? I always wanted to learn another language."

"Nah." Orla scrunched her nose. "Thanks to the English Crown, I speak better English. Know but a few words in the Gaelic."

Aino patted the flour sack covering her front. "These were not exactly clean. But we needed to wipe dry with something."

Orla stepped slowly into the room with Sir Gal beside her. He growled low.

Aino eyed the dog. "Oh, I see... you found clothes for us."

"How kind." Janna's teeth chattered and she extended one of her damp arms for the clothing without budging from behind the dining table.

"Gal will adapt to you, to be sure. Give him time." Orla laid the gowns out for the girls on the tabletop. "Can't promise these'll fit. Do either of you sew? Too much to hope for that we've a seamstress?" *Wouldn't that be grand?*

Janna laughed. "If we were seamstresses, do you not think we would be doing that?" She shook out a gown and held it against her. "Dear me. It is like a drapery. Whose is this? Did it come from a haunted mansion's window somewhere?"

Orla's face heated and she straightened. "Haunted curtains? Well, and we all can't be created dainty flowers now, can we? Some of us are majestic trees." She stared down her nose at the petite flaxen-haired girl.

"Dear me, I meant no offense. When I was a child, I always hung from tree branches to grow taller like you. It never worked. Then, I tried hanging upside down to make my legs longer, and all I got were scrapes and splinters behind my knees. I can tell you I decided then and there to just stay short. Besides, mama said—"

"You are pretty the way you are." Aino clasped the other gown. "Thank you for lending us your clothes, Miss Muldoon." She yawned. "Please do not be afraid of the loons on the lake. They are beautiful in their way."

"They only eat fish." Janna finished slipping the voluminous gown over her wet head. "Not humans. Can you imagine if they did? None of us would ever step a foot into lakes. I cannot reassure you about the other lake creatures."

"Are you not tired?" Aino nudged her. "I certainly am. Not to rush you, Miss Muldoon."

Thank heavens for Aino. She wanted to cry for how much Janna's chatty, confusing ways were like her lost sister Kathleen's. Orla crossed herself as a lump formed in her throat.

Janna squinted at her. "You do not need to do that, Miss Muldoon. The loons will not come inside." She tipped her head toward Gal. "I am more afraid of him. Is he going with us?"

"Aye, aye. Time to get upstairs and I'll take you to your rooms." Orla raised the candle, inspected the room's shadowed corners once more, and waited a moment while Aino and Janna draped the wet blanket and flour towels over the sink and woodstove. The empty shadows around the room did not ease her fears. Then she remembered Gallant.

His steady, amber gaze stuck to her like honey. *He'd never let anything terrible happen, would he?*

Orla and Gal led the way to the stairs. She climbed a few, before she heard a thump and a startling screech behind her, setting off Gal to barking. Her heart raced as she gripped the banister and whipped around.

"Dear me, woe is me." On the third step, Janna hopped precariously on one foot and held the other. "Will my toes survive this ordeal? I think they are broken this time."

"She stubbed her toes." Aino grabbed Janna's arm and flicked her gaze to Orla. "She does such things because she refuses to wear her spectacles. Right, vain girl?"

"Sacrifices for beauty." Janna grimaced and bit her lip. "I am fine. I will go slowly."

Orla breathed deep to calm her heartbeat and travel further up the staircase. "I know a bit 'bout vanity meself." Why did she not consider all the details of having strange and penniless women in her home? Could she figure out a way to fit these quirky girls into her business goals? *Unexpected worries need a strategy.*

She waited for the girls to arrive on the landing beside her and turned to her right down the hallway. "This'll be your room, Janna." *She takes up less space.* "It looks out over the street on this side, and the shore there." Orla used the candle to indicate the other yellow curtained window.

Janna limped to the black iron bed and bounced on it. The springs squeaked. She smoothed out the fresh quilt spread under her legs. "A real bed again. How I missed sleeping on a mattress." She bent and peered closely at the pattern. "It has daisies on it. I love daisies. Did you know that daisies are really weeds? You can also—"

"Let's discuss them in the morning." *Flowers. That's it.* "We'll all be flowers in a garden, and Daisy will be your new name." Orla turned away and called over her shoulder, "Aino needs her own bed and a new name as well."

Aino yawned loudly. "I do."

Orla traipsed across the room, met up with Gal outside the door, and glanced back to find Daisy there.

"It is cold in here." Daisy hugged herself. "Do you have wood for the fire?"

Do I? Orla pursed her lips. The hearth was empty. "I think Aino's room has extra. Or you can have a piece or two of me own, aye?" *Yet another supply problem.*

"Poor Miss Muldoon, you did not know when to expect us, right?" Aino's beautiful violet eyes sparkled in the candlelight. "She may be clever, but she cannot know everything."

"That I don't. I shall give you both a pair of stockings after we settle Aino."

Upon entering the back bedroom across the landing from her own, a faint howl floated through the window. Orla shivered again.

Gal's ears twitched but he was not alarmed this time.

"Girls, I've decided to name that loon when I see it sometime. Names make frightening things less so. I'll work hard to find it one day, and I'll name it Black Angel, or in the Gaelic, 'aingeal dubh.' Should make you glad for more words in the Gaelic, Daisy."

"Thank you, Miss Muldoon." Daisy grinned wide, revealing a dimple. "I will treasure every word. Do you know the word for horse? What about daisy, or dog? I should write all these down, so I do not forget. Do we have parchment to use? I noticed we need a lot of supplies."

Aino halted just inside her designated room and twirled in slow motion. She parted the lavender curtains to peek outside, but the windows were dark on the moonless night. Next, she sat on the black iron bed with the new quilt as Daisy had done. The covering in this room was in white, blues, and purples. "You are right, Jann—Daisy. It is lovely to have a bed again." Her face glowed when she spoke to Orla. "This is all so pretty."

"I'm that glad you like it. Thought so meself. The color suits your eyes, and so your new name is Violet." Orla raised her chin and studied her handiwork.

"I accept that name, Miss Muldoon. You have no idea what conditions we have been living in since we left Ma Brown's employ." Violet's calm voice cracked. "Although, her bawdy house was barely what I would call a house, and she treated us terribly."

"Stop that." Daisy rushed over and plopped beside her. "You said we were not to speak about that place to Miss Muldoon." She flicked a glance at Orla.

"And why not? 'Tis a secret? I'm good at keeping secrets. Like to have me own."

Violet and Daisy shared a look, then Violet shook her head. "Pardon my outburst, Miss Muldoon. I want to enjoy being grateful for a while. Maybe when we have known you longer, and the memories have faded some more. It was three years ago."

Daisy shivered. "Can we have fires in our rooms now?"

"Holy heavens, where're me manners? 'Tis grand to see I'd set some wood and lucifers in this room. Now 'tis when I wish we'd some peat to light, as we did back in Ireland." Orla bent and got to work on getting the fire going in Violet's room.

"Peat? Have you ever heard of that, Aino, I mean Violet? I know I have not. Is it a type of wood like oak or pine? Oh, get the dog, Miss Muldoon!"

Gallant drew too near the sparks with his sniffing. He shook his head, then pawed at his nose.

"Get back, Gal. Singed fur would stink up the entire place, which Daisy wouldn't appreciate, aye. She's a sensitive nose as well." She winked at her two young women wrapped in Violet's quilt. "There it goes, girlies. I'm away to light mine and Daisy's."

Violet smiled. "Thank you."

Orla's heart melted with the heat from her fire. "Thinking I'm already warming up to you, girlies." She tucked the lucifers behind the small stack of wood and wrapped a shawl over her shoulders. "Shall I give you each a shawl? I've two others."

Sitting in front of the newly lit fire on the hearth, Violet separated Daisy's damp strands with her fingertips to thoroughly dry it. The cozy sisterly interaction was something Orla had performed with Kathleen many times. *Another unexpected memory.* She sniffed back tears as she stood in the doorway cherishing her only sister.

Violet stood. "Let us leave Miss Muldoon to go to her own bed. We can discuss more details after sunup." She smiled at Orla and switched places with Daisy.

"I'll fetch your stockings and shawls." Orla returned to her room and dug through her undergarments in her dresser's top drawer. She had four pair, and now she would be down to one extra. *Wash day's getting complicated.* She flipped the stockings and shawls over her shoulder, retrieved two pieces of wood and more lucifers from her hearth, then ambled toward the chattering from Violet's room. "It might be crowded, Gal, but 'tis more cheerful than being alone, aye?"

Gal hesitated to get up then scrambled to his feet. He slowly followed her back down the hall, his nails clicking on the hardwood.

Violet gleefully accepted the stockings and slid them on. "Ah. My feet were getting numb."

"Speaking of getting numb." Daisy bent her leg and missed sticking her toes inside her stocking. She succeeded on her third try and dangled the next. "Do you know why we get pins and needles in our limbs sometimes? It is because—"

"Let me help you since you refuse to wear your spectacles, so we can all get some sleep." Violet worked the stocking over Daisy's foot, and they stood together.

Orla draped the shawls over the iron bed's foot post and handed Daisy the wood and lucifers for her hearth after being assured she could start her own fire without issue. The two women finally departed from Violet's bedroom, and Daisy tapped Orla's arm. She leaned close and whispered. "I just thought of something you should know. About the loons when you see one. Do not be too afraid, but God made them with red eyes for some unknown reason."

"What?" *Holy heavens, why would God do such a strange thing as that?*

CHAPTER 13

Her Flower Garden's Rules

Now's not the time for God to pay me any attention
Orla

$\mathcal{L}$*ake Superior, Minnesota*
Autumn

PEEKING OUTDOORS from the stair landing window three weeks after the girls' arrival, Madam Muldoon envisioned her brilliant idea to name her establishment, 'The Flower Garden.' It would fit perfectly on a sign from the overhang over the entrance. Her business must draw the wealthiest patrons.

Her new girl, Holly, also known as Hedda, filled the last position just a week ago. Her striking, dark beauty was sure to snag men's attentions. *The timing of her arrival was impeccable.* If she could ever believe God cared, this was one thing to cause it. The girls had already learned to call her by her official name, Madam Rose, and that was perfect. The old Orla was firmly in the past.

She bent to give Gal a rub behind his ears. "Whoever heard of an opening night without a sign to announce it, aye? I must ask Nuala how she got herself one. Well, and I suppose I must also make do for now with a hand-written notice posted inside the front window."

The 'German Shepherd' dog, as someone in town had told her his breed, cocked his head at her. His golden eyes bored into hers. Sometimes, his intense attention unnerved her.

Orla rubbed the chill bumps on her arms, then donned her favorite burgundy dress. She inspected her reflection. "Glad I didn't listen to that uppity dressmaker's advice in St. Paul to avoid wearing reds." She turned and faced the bedroom doorway while she adjusted the lacy collar pressing into her neck.

"Madam Rose." Violet's head and shoulders appeared between the stair rails above the middle steps and below the landing. *Like jailhouse bars.* "Will you be down for breakfast soon? Daisy somehow thinks her concoction is edible and sent me up to ask. I would hide if I were you."

"Since I must eat, I'll do it with strong tea and milk. We've some on the stove, aye?"

Violet winked. "Yes, to that. We also have the clothespins for our noses."

"I envy Gal, for he gobbles up anything despite the smell."

"And I am glad that Daisy is happy about the clothespins for they might reshape her nose. Vain thing."

After the women finished their tea, milk, and tasteless bowls of something resembling porridge, Orla dropped her clothespin onto the table and rose. "That's it for me. I'm away to visit Mrs. Kincaid."

"Your friend Nuala again?" Daisy pouted and gathered the clothespins. "Were you not just there? I am sure you were because it was the day Holly lost her hosiery and blamed me for taking—"

"I did no such thing." Holly knit her brow.

"You did. It was right after Violet spilled her tea on the tablecloth, or was that the day she forgot to do the dishes, and you scolded her?"

Holly slid a sideways glance at Orla. "Once again, you say such horrible things about me to make Madam—"

"Stop your squabbles." Orla pushed her palm toward the girls. "Was neither day. Was over a week ago. Me visit is to make a special request, and I'll not be sharing why. I hope to have surprises for you, don't you know. As I run me own business, do your household tasks as we agreed, and be done with them before I return. Or I'll be keeping the surprises for meself."

"Yes, Madam." Violet curtsied and smiled. "We are happy to do them. See our gleeful Holly there?"

Holly grunted.

After passing several boisterous businesses and a few homes on the same street as Nuala's home, Orla strolled through the pink rose arbor on the path into The White Feather's yard. "Like the roses back in the Old Country." She inhaled the delightful aroma. *Would be lovely to have fresh roses in The Flower Garden.*

After a brief tap on the door, Nuala opened it, and grinned. "Well, and aren't I that glad to see you this morning? Come in, come in. You must've known I was thinking 'bout you."

"You were?"

"Oh, aye. For I've a gift for you as I promised." Nuala untied her apron and led Orla to the enclosed back porch connected to the scullery.

Orla squealed. "You don't. What we discussed last week?"

Nuala turned back with glints in her eyes. "The very same. Me church donated it to me. You'll be glad, I'm sure."

They stopped beside a large, battered barrel, with rusty metal straps. "Here 'tis. Haven't yet opened it, as you can see." Nuala lifted a crowbar leaning beside the porch's exterior door.

"Doesn't look like it holds much of anything important, does it?" Orla fingered the lid.

"Aye, but the outside doesn't matter, 'tis the inside part that does. Step aside whilst I open it." Nuala inserted the crowbar and pried the barrel's lid loose, exposing its contents to the light from the porch windows. Colorful fabrics and objects sparkled and shimmered.

Orla eagerly reached inside with both hands and clutched a piece of royal blue velvet in one fist, and a sparkling diadem in the other. "Glory be. 'Tis more beautiful than I expected."

Nuala giggled. "You sound as if you've been awestruck by buried treasure, instead of a missionary donation barrel. I'm that glad you're delighted." She leaned closer, then dug around, tugging out a wreath of colorful feathers and ribbons. "Why in the world missionaries would wear these clothes or need these props, I'm sure I don't know."

"For playacting?" Orla sprawled silky garments onto a nearby chair and returned to the barrel. "These gowns will do grand for us, and mayhap we can use the headdresses. I'm confused 'bout the feathers though. You should keep any white ones for your business' name's sake. Are there any slippers or boots?"

"If we find a white feather, I shall. Let's tip it over and sort through." Nuala kicked the container with her foot, rolling it over until it collided with the wall and spilled its contents into a heap.

Orla frowned. "Your church gave you this? Where'd they get it? From a theatrical troupe, aye? No missionaries would want these." She fondled a long piece of black transparent lace.

"I'd say so." Nuala kneeled and spread out the various contents on the floorboards.

"Watch it. Don't snag the fabrics or get them dusty." Orla snatched up a piece of red silk and unfolded it into a bodice with black ties.

"Dusty? From me beautiful, clean floors? For shame." Nuala cocked her head. "'Tis a corset, aye? For the missionary wives."

They burst out laughing. Orla held her stomach. "If I believed God was interested in me, I'd say He knew I wanted these." She giggled.

Nuala stopped unfolding clothing with her eyes wide. "Oh, friend. I think you've hit it. He didn't want missionaries to get this. He made sure you did, so you know He does love you."

"God never has." Orla scowled. "As for dressing me? I asked Him for years to notice me and to help me. Now's not the time for God to pay me any attention. He waited overly long to convince me He loves me or to change me course in life."

"Well, 'tis never better than today to change our paths."

Orla flittered her fingers. "Hush, now. Must take these home and show the girlies. There'll be some quarrels over who gets what, aye? That part I'm not enthusiastic 'bout."

Nuala sighed. "Mayhap these will fit your girls without much fuss. Which one of you is good with a needle and thread?"

"Oh, holy heavens." Orla chewed her lip, then took a deep breath. "Another worry."

A few nights later at the grand opening of The Flower Garden, three men shifted uneasily in the chairs Madam Rose provided in her parlor. She would prize forever the expressions on their faces when she asked them to take their seats.

Mr. Cooley, with the long beard, raised his index finger. "Pardon me, but where are the girls? In all my times of visiting a, uh, a . . . home like yours, I was never asked to take a seat in the parlor first, Miss."

Madam Rose fingered her black lace veil, and slowly swished the single, slightly bent, peacock feather she had taken from a donated headdress. She aimed the luminous plume at him. "Madam Rose. And mayhap you've not visited a unique establishment before, aye? The Flower Garden is more marvelous than others."

Mr. Layton, the oldest gentleman next to Mr. Cooley, jiggled his leg and glanced at the men to his left. "It seems odd to be with a bunch of men. Where are they ... the ladies? You do have them?"

"To be sure, I do." Madam glided closer to him and lightly tickled his chin with the plume. "They're what's so marvelous."

All the men chuckled and hooted.

Madam Rose winked, and cleared her throat as she unrolled a piece of parchment. "Welcome to The Flower Garden, gentlemen, and may you enjoy everything we have to offer. It shall be a once in a life-time experience, to be sure. We aim to keep our patrons returning by delighting you in several ways. In exchange, we ask you to abide by a few House Rules—"

"Rules?" Mr. Fairbanks, the tall, lanky man with auburn curls stood, toppling his chair. "This cannot be right. Never heard of such a thing at a bordello."

"You meant to say, 'The Flower Garden,' aye?" Madam Rose called out above the grumbling. "Ah, but will be worth your troubles, Mr. Fairbanks, and you other fellas. Don't you wish for unusual adventures? Something beyond the common, aye?"

Mr. Fairbanks turned to the others on his right. "As long as we can still afford it."

The patrons heckled and guffawed, as Madam Rose curtsied. "You do recall that I mentioned upon your arrival 'tis our opening night with free entertainment? For you three only."

Mr. Cooley smiled. "That's right. Very generous of you, Madam Rose."

"Then, I suppose you have paid for my patience." Mr. Fairbanks settled on his seat. "You have five minutes before I leave. Are your girls ugly? Or do they have bad teeth?"

The other men sniggered at his sneer.

Mr. Layton tapped Mr. Cooley on the shoulder. "Maybe she is wasting our time to overcharge us on our next visits."

Madam's pulse pounded like a drum in her temples. She waved the feather at the door, nearly cracking the long shaft in half. "Gal, come."

Gallant rushed through the doorway, and the men's jeers stopped.

"This, dear patrons, is Sir Gallant. He makes me home a safe place, but he's not exactly safe himself. Get me meaning?"

The dog sniffed the air with his alert gaze pinned on Madam Rose.

Mr. Fairbanks appeared incredulous. "You are threatening us, your new patrons, with your intimidating dog?"

Murmurs from the group arose, Gal's ears twitched toward the men, and they quieted. Their trepidation of Gal helped tamp her impatience.

Madam Rose grinned, hopefully, at the group. "Not at tall, no. Wishing to explain this is his home, you know, and the House Rules are for his and your own safety as well. I don't run a willy-nilly business. I've a reputation to establish."

Mr. Fairbanks scowled. "What kind of reputation do you want? Can you not just put him outside for the evening? He is an animal." The fellas agreed as they eyed the alert shepherd.

She straightened her royal blue velvet gown's sleeve. "Well, now, you're visiting extraordinary women in me home, where me extraordinary dog lives. Shall I put them all outside as well?"

Mr. Cooley rubbed the back of his neck. "What else did you plan to do tonight, men? Can you not just cooperate and see what Madam Rose has for this evening? It is a free—"

Loud pounding on the front door interrupted him.

Madam Rose raised her skirt a few inches from the floor. "Pardon me a moment, gentlemen. I'll not be long. Gal stay." She left her guard dog on watch, and sashayed, as she had seen dance hall girls do, through the doorway to the locked door.

Another noisy knock, then a muffled deep voice spoke. "Hello? Anyone there?"

She spoke near the doorframe. "Come back another evening. We're full tonight."

"Miss Muldoon? Ma Brown told me this is your place and sent me to see how you are doing. It is Murphy. Do you remember me? We met at The White Feather last month."

"Aye." Her heartbeat's speed dried out her mouth, and she forgot how to speak. *Holy heavens.* She raised her veil and inserted the peacock plume's sheath between her teeth. She fumbled to unlock the door with her shaking hands, and stepped back as it swung inward.

Murphy grinned slow and wide, dragging his gorgeous blue eyes over Madam Rose's ensemble. "Is this the real Miss Muldoon before me?"

She tipped her head back to look down her nose, but he was a solid five inches taller than herself. His chuckle heated her face. *Confound the man.* She plucked the plume from her mouth and lowered the veil.

"May I enter, please?"

Madam Rose slowly wagged her head. *Those dimples.* It was unfair for a man to be so attractive. She fingered her veiled, scarred cheek.

Gallant barked, and a thump came from the parlor.

"Madam Rose," called Mr. Fairbanks, "is there some sort of trouble out there? Your menacing dog will not let me pass."

She cleared her throat and gulped. "No, no, Fairbanks, I shall be with you in a moment." At least she rediscovered her voice.

Murphy had stepped through the opening while her head was turned and shut the door behind him. "I'll latch it tight. Not to worry." He stared at the shoes and boots in the entry. "I will remove my boots."

This bear of a man must weigh 250 pounds and stand around 6 foot 6. What should she do with him? "You can't be here tonight, Mr. Murphy. There aren't enough girls."

"Ow! You pushed me into the rail, Daisy." Holly stood at the top of the staircase facing Daisy and Violet behind her in the hallway.

Violet craned her neck to peer down the stairs. "Stop fussing. Madam Rose has not sent Gal for us yet. But I think I heard Gal bark."

"I did, too." Daisy leaned around Holly. "Nothing else sounds like a dog when it barks. Well, maybe that is not true. I heard that seals sound like barking dogs, but we do not have any seals in Lake Superior—"

"Oh, give your tongue a rest, Daisy." Holly gripped Daisy's shoulder and shuffled her behind taller Violet. "For heaven's sake Violet, I think you left your pin in my gown. It is poking my narrow waist."

Exasperated, Madam Rose jerked her arms up, dropping the peacock feather. As she bent to retrieve it, her delicate crown clattered onto the floor.

A low chuckle from Murphy further irritated her. "By all that's holy." *Can nothing go as planned?* She re-pinned her crown to her piled hair and smoothed her ringlets.

"Is that you in the entry, Madam Rose?"

"Of course it is, Daisy." Holly tapped her nose. "You would know it if you would ever wear your spectacles."

Violet wrung her hands. "Dear me, did we miss our cue?"

Madam Rose huffed. "No. You did not. Never mind Gal's barking signal. Stay there, and count to one hundred, aye? Then you may enter." She slid her glance to Murphy and scowled. "If you won't politely depart, I suppose you must be me guest tonight."

"Very gracious of you, Madam." He bowed and indicated the parlor. "Please, lead the way."

"Lead? Pushy man." Madam arranged her skirts, tapped her crown, and headed past the staircase to the parlor.

At her entrance the men perked up, until they caught sight of Murphy. She almost burst out laughing at their expressions, if it was not for his intimidating presence filling the room.

Murphy collected a chair from the corner of the parlor and seated himself behind the others. The chair should hold his weight. She hoped.

"Fellas." Madam Rose handed her plume over to Cooley. "Please keep this safe for me, 'tis time to move forward with our evening." She unrolled her scroll to read aloud. "I've drawn up a document, 'tis a type of agreement between me establishment and you gentlemen."

Fairbanks raised his hands. "Here we go again. What kind of bawdy house is this?"

"As we discussed earlier, this is The Flower Garden, and I'll be thanking you for holding your tongue, aye?" *I'd pray, but God might finally hear.* "These're The Flower Garden's House Rules."

"Must we follow these?" Layton scanned the parlor as the other men scowled and complained.

Madam increased her volume. "Rule Number One—always be polite. Rule Number Two—take a bath before visiting us. We do."

The men moaned.

"Rule Number Three—no chewing tobacco. 'Tis disgusting. Rule Four—no spitting on the floor. 'Tis rude, and we'll make you clean it up. Rule Five—no petting the dog. He doesn't like it. Believe what I'm telling you, and you'll be grand."

"Who would want to pet your intimidating dog?" Fairbanks sniffed.

"Rule Number Six—no cursing or taking God's name in vain. No version of His name is acceptable to us ladies."

"Ladies?" Layton chuckled.

"Rule Seven—always remain clothed in public areas."

Murphy burst out laughing, and the others joined him.

"What's so hilarious? We agreed wholeheartedly on that one. Rule Eight—no running down the hallways. Slipping and falling results in injury."

"Running?" Layton scratched his head.

"After mopping the floors, they're slippery. Happened to me when I was in me stockings—never you mind."

Murphy leaned back. "Care to expound for us?"

Madam glared at him. "Rule Number Nine—no hitting, pushing, or kicking. Including each other. Rule Ten—no more than one drink. You won't need it."

"What does that mean?" The patrons chimed in near unison.

"You'll see. Rule Number Eleven—no requesting an 'I owe you.' Payment is due before you leave. No exceptions. Don't bother visiting us if you can't pay."

At their protests, Madam raised her voice. "Rule Number Twelve—you may not complain 'bout the poetry reading, card playing, chess games, or any other entertainment we've planned to begin the evenings. We work hard to prepare for your visits. I've plans to get a pianoforte, or a fiddle in the future for our presentations. For now, would be very rude to grumble, and we'll . . . we'll kick you out."

Fairbanks toppled his chair again and wagged his pointer finger at her. "I have been in these establishments for decades, and never heard of such nonsensical rules for clients."

"Madam Rose." Holly glided through the door in her red-silk dress, with the other costumed girls trailing her. "We counted to two hundred, to be certain the men were ready for us." She flashed her large, deep brown eyes at Fairbanks, and slowly maneuvered her body closer to his seat.

He plopped onto it, his jaw slack.

Madam heard a chuckle among the murmurs. *Murphy.* She grasped her feather from Cooley and swished it over the women like a wand. "Gentlemen, those were all the rules, and now, I'll introduce you to the glorious flowers of The Flower Garden. Holly, Violet, and Daisy."

Fairbanks scrutinized Holly's red gown. "Holly is a berry, not a flower."

Holly flicked his ear.

Madam growled. "She could be the flower on a holly bush."

Violet and Daisy curtsied during the hush, as Holly joined them up front. Madam backed up against the wall with Gal. She smiled with a nod to encourage her girls.

Holly pirouetted to her own humming, swaying and dipping, near Fairbanks' seat. The women spun in their purple, red, and gold ensembles which blended into a colorful and festive production. *Just as I planned.*

Daisy pranced around Cooley, while Violet glided over to Layton. Daisy's wide, ruffled skirt brushed against Cooley's legs. She squinted and bent near him, twirling her yellow and green parasol. She misjudged her proximity and whacked his forehead.

"Ow!" Layton rubbed the red splotch.

"Oh dear." She jumped back and poked the parasol's tip into Violet's arm as she sang in her sweet soprano to Layton.

"Daisy!" Violet grabbed her arm and twirled out of Daisy's reach, stepping onto Layton's stockinged foot. He howled, and Gal furiously barked.

Stunned, Holly halted her dance while she observed the shenanigans of her comrades, so Daisy plowed into her while avoiding Violet's flailing legs and knocked Holly onto Fairbanks.

The din from the yelling and screeches, accusations and name-calling were more than Madam Rose could handle. She plugged her ears to muffle Murphy's deep guffaws.

Daisy sat on irritated Cooley's legs apologizing, and inspected his face, while Violet tried to sooth Layton with her gentle strokes, fawning over his injured foot.

Fairbanks and Holly still snarled at each other, and it appeared they would break Rule Number Nine within a few seconds.

Madam Rose ducked her head, covered her eyes, and sank to the floor. The plume snapped beneath her rump. *Me dreams are shattered.* Her crown dipped over her eyebrow, and Gal sat on her lap, giving her a lick on her neck. "You understand me broken heart, don't you?"

Loud, slow clapping and growing cheers of "Bravo!" induced Madam to uncover her moist eyes, and Gal scrambled to his feet.

The group of three patrons stood near Madam Rose's three Flowers, clapping, and laughing. The "flowers" shot a peek at Madam, then curtsied.

"Thank you, that is all of our show for tonight." Violet massaged the red spot on her arm, and Layton claimed her with a bow.

Madam Rose patted her perspiring brow. "Didn't I tell you? 'Tis as it should be. The Flower Garden's entertainment is like no other business in town. Please tell your friends."

Murphy clapped again. "Oh, you can count on us spreading the word, Madam Rose, right men?"

CHAPTER 14

Her Men and Bears

Your eyes reveal a bit of a cunning devil, they do
Orla

*A*fter the couples cleared the room, Madam Rose leaned against the wall while Gal leaned against her leg. *What to do with Murphy?* He was unexpected and did not fit into her plans at all.

Murphy rose from the small chair. "Madam. This was the best evening I've had in years. You could charge a bag of gold for the show." He extended his crooked elbow.

Honestly? Chills spread up her arms. "Mayhap this hullaballoo was part of me scathing brilliance, don't you know?"

"Please keep Sir Gallant downstairs while we go up."

Brilliance destroyed.

"He stays with me, and don't dissent. You won't win. Gal, behind."

Madam Rose breathed in deep as she gracefully climbed the stairs. She hoped Murphy was a gentleman, and almost snorted. She floated as lightly as possible for a woman as tall as a tree down the hallway and through her bedroom door—her heart thudding a tune to an imaginary Irish jig. Her layered skirts swirled and swished around her long legs. Madam Rose concentrated on the feminine bedroom décor to calm her dancing heartbeat.

"Here we are. Gal, outside." The dog lay in the hallway. Madam Rose closed the door and was proud of her purchases of the lace curtains, red rose wallpaper, and luxurious scarlet quilt spread across her white iron bed.

"You like red."

She glanced over her shoulder at the dark man who towered over and hovered behind her. *I can do this.* She moved toward her windows to draw open the velvet panels. "I'll let in the moonlight."

Murphy pointed at her dresser. "I like candles. Light the candles."

"Don't you like moonlight?"

"Sometimes, but I like candlelight best. Especially on you. Your fair coloring will be striking in it."

"I like moonlight best." Madam Rose reached for the curtain sash and realized her hand shook.

"You're not much for pleasing the customer, are you, Orla?"

Orla jerked her hand back and faced Murphy. "Me name is Rose."

"No, it is not. I heard Mrs. Kincaid say your name. I am not calling you Rose. Like your wallpaper." Murphy cocked his head sideways. "Why do you all not use your given names?"

"We don't want to, that's why. 'Tis none of your business."

"Always arguing." Murphy grinned and shook his head. "Tell me the story, I want to know."

Orla sidled over to her long dresser, where her silver candelabra stood beside a porcelain wash basin. She kept Murphy in her sights as she reached for the lucifers. Did he value honesty? *Why should I have a care what he thinks . . . 'bout anything?* She lit the three candles. "The story? We don't use our given names with customers. Would create a false sense of . . . of a lover's attention, aye? What we do, has no relationship in it. Strictly for business dealings, 'tis sure."

"Makes sense."

"'Tis that glad I am you understand, aren't I?" She grappled with her irritation, curtsied, and folded her hands. Time to show him her cooperation and return to a better footing. "Would you like some tea?" His eyebrows shot up. "Or best yet, a whiskey?" She indicated the bottle and glasses near the lit candelabra, and the dainty rose tea set.

"No drink." Murphy shook his head and grinned, revealing his delightful dimples. "Just as I thought, the candlelight is glorious on you." He reclined on her bed and reached his hand out to her.

She gripped her hips. "Not yet. I got a routine to show you."

Murphy folded his arms behind his head. "I'm in no rush. Sounds intriguing."

"Supposed to, you dimwit." She huffed. *Why does me tongue run away with itself?*

"Ah, the real Orla emerges." Murphy laughed. "Does not put me off, you know. I like your spirit, or I would not have chosen you." His eyes sparkled with mischief.

"And your eyes reveal a bit of a cunning devil, they do." She flounced over to her hand-painted dressing screen she salvaged from a burnt home. "Give me a chance to get on with it and stop nattering on 'bout everything." She mumbled. "Must concentrate on me job."

"I will not stop you. You can count on it."

She kicked off her slippers behind the screen, unclipped a lace stocking, slid it down her leg, and smoothed it out. 'Tis trying me patience, you are. You still there?"

"Definitely."

She flipped the stocking over the room divider and hummed a bawdy Irish tune, *The Black Velvet Band*, to prepare her mood. "You're a handsome hunk of a man."

"Hoped you would think so."

She attempted to coo and slid the other stocking off to join the other. Her corset did not cooperate with her fingers. She yanked on the strings laced through the grommets. They held fast. No matter how deft she believed herself to be, she struggled with tiny knots without budging them. Madam repeated the tune, her voice jiggling with her efforts. She joggled and twisted while her lilting hum sank into a growl.

"May I help you?"

"No, you may not. I'm not a youngster, nor am I an old crone." She yanked on her stiff corset. "Holy heavens . . . get off, will you?" She puffed while she stamped her bare feet.

"Are you speaking to me? The heavy breathing is tantalizing, Orla."

"Stop calling me Orla. Me name is Madam Rose."

"You stated you did this before. What exactly am I paying for here?"

"Said what, didn't I?"

"I might have forgotten by now."

"All I ask, is for you to concentrate on what I'm doing." She ground her teeth.

"I will, if you will." Murphy chuckled.

"Having meself some troubles, is all. Glad you're amused by it." She jerked on her laces and twisted at the same time, knocking herself off balance with a crash against the wall and the edge of the screen. "No worries. Not injured." She waved above the wobbly screen.

The bedsprings creaked. "Glad to hear it. I am having troubles as well. My lower legs hang off the mattress, and I am at an uncomfortable angle here. Go ahead and give it up, Madam Rose, I appreciate your efforts."

"I don't ever give up. Never have, never will." She puffed, and managed to loosen her bodice laces enough to wriggle it looser. "Out of practice is all."

A deep sigh echoed around the bedroom. "No problem. I am yet hale and hearty. So, you do not use the name, Orla, because of your past? Is that it?"

She gasped and massaged her aching hands. Tears welled in her eyes and a clump of sheep's wool stuck inside her throat. She coughed to dislodge it, so she could speak. It did not budge.

"No retort, Orla?"

She shook her head. What should she say? She refused to speak of her choices for this line of work. *I'll lose a paying client from it.*

"Awfully quiet back there. Are you sure you want to do this?"

"Brilliant bear." She squeaked. "You figured out me feelings."

"I am happy you found your voice, as well."

"Aye." She whispered. "A good name, with painful memories attached to it. How could you ever understand?"

The bedsprings creaked again. "You would be surprised how. What are you mum—"

"You stay put. I'm not done yet." Orla stared at the ceiling. "Don't pay attention to me, will You, God? No one's watching from up in heaven, are they? Look away."

"Cannot see a thing, darling."

She pulled the pins from her piled hair, which fell waist length into shiny, peach-colored ringlets. Its warmth comforted her like Dr. Ross's gift of the wool blanket on the ship over the Atlantic. She tugged off her veil, took a deep breath, and stepped from behind the screen into the candlelit room. Her knees shook. "I'm guessing I do need your help."

Murphy's midnight eyes glinted, and a slow grin emphasized his deep dimples in the candlelight. "Oh, I do not know, it is more interesting all a kilter. A deviation from the typical. Makes for a unique memory." He joked, but his eyes held something somber, disturbing, almost near to pity. "You are a very beautiful woman."

"No one believes that." Orla straightened, as tall as she could, then fingered her cheek. "You must be unhinged to think so."

"Always complimenting your patrons, are you?" Murphy rolled onto his belly, stretched out on her lovely quilt, and reached for his jacket draped over the chair beside her bed. "Here is a gift for your business." He dug through his coat pocket and pulled out a small, dingy canvas bag with drawstrings, and dangled it toward her. "If you are sure I am safe, come take it. Only if you are certain."

"Course, I'm sure. Can't do this job without risk." She bit her tongue in time to avoid a complete business disaster. She approached Murphy, and he dropped the bag onto her outstretched palm. Orla stared at him, while amusement replaced the pity in his eyes. *'Tis a relief, that.* She did not know how to operate a business with pity from clients.

"Open it please, lovely lady." Murphy winked and braced his large frame on his elbow. "You can use it for whatever you need."

She gulped and forced her gaze to the heavy little bag nestled in her palm. *Just me luck.* Was he deranged? Or was this manipulation money? This bear's presence was intimidating to be sure. She wanted to like him a bit, but if he was as evil as the English officers, he could kiss her dog instead.

"Your room is idyllic for you. Roses everywhere, and the color is appealing."

What man ever cares about such things? "Are you an artist type, then?"

Murphy stood. "In a way. Can we go downstairs to your parlor or scullery? There is more room for me there."

She frowned. "And why would we do that? Are you already forgetting The House Rules? For Rule Number Seven specifically states to remain clothed in public areas."

"I recall the clothing rule. I heard no rule against talking. Let us get to know each other better after you slip your gown on."

"Talk? After I'm clothed?" She raised her brows to at least the ceiling. "You're the oddest man I've met, and that's saying something flabbergasting."

He chuckled. "I am certain that is true. Let us go below."

She donned her dress, and they entered the parlor together, Gal following, She indicated her latest piece of furniture in the room. Although slightly used, it was one of those happy finds in the local newspaper. He arranged himself on the ornate settee across from the stone fireplace. It creaked with his weight.

"Hope it holds." He winked.

Orla took a position on it furthest from the bear. "Did you have something you wished to say to me? Go on, now. Don't believe you'd want only and biscuits this evening."

He stretched his muscled arm across the back of the wood frame, and his hand almost reached her shoulder. He flashed a lopsided grin.

One dimple this time. "Why not? Cannot a man enjoy those? Must it be alcohol? I enjoy many things that maybe other men do not. How well do you know me after all?"

"'Bout as well as you know me, I'm thinking." Orla curled her lengthy legs onto the cushion between them to create some distance. Her toes tapped his hard thigh, and she quickly shifted her feet back onto the floor. Heat rose from her chest to her face. *Curse me pale complexion.*

Instead of laughing at her, Murphy resettled himself to give her more space. "Go ahead, get cozy. You can probably feel the chill on the floor through those slippers." He tipped his head to inspect them. "Hmm."

She tucked her legs onto the cushion again. "What do you wish to know?"

"How did you get your scar?"

She slammed her feet back onto the floor and stood. "Didn't expect that. Only rude creatures ask, and I never speak 'bout it."

He raised his hand. "Orla—"

"Hush." She rushed out of the parlor, and contemplated hiding upstairs when she arrived by the staircase. But Murphy the bear paid good money. *Holy heavens.* Gal stood beside her waiting for instructions. She must return. "Don't know what to do."

Orla swung around to find Murphy directly behind her. Gal had not warned her. "Traitor dog."

Murphy entered the scullery before she did and found the drink tray in the pantry, then he gathered and set out serving items on the scullery table. She sighed. *Considerate man. And those muscled arms.*

She eyed the kettle. "Looks like our Daisy accidentally left the kettle on the stove. Is there hot water in it?"

"Yes. Thanks to Daisy. My apologies, for prying, Madam Muldoon. Let us talk about business. Is that a satisfactory subject?" He carried the fully laden tray to the sideboard in the parlor.

She nodded. "Predictably, but you're not a predictable man, aye?"

"Some think not." He sat on the settee.

She busied herself at the sideboard with pouring and tucking the biscuits with the cups onto the fine porcelain saucers. She had never owned such a grand tea set. Her mother's set was not this fine. "Do you take cream or sugar?"

"No, thank you."

Orla carried their painted rose cups and saucers to the low table in front of the settee. It was the first time she used her new household additions. She smiled to herself. They were the evidence that some things go according to plan, and money is the key to a joyous life.

Murphy raised a cup with his pinky up in his bear paw nearly hiding it, and bit into a cinnamon biscuit. "Nicely done. Give the cook my compliments."

"Aye. 'Twas our Violet. Our best cook." She settled herself on the divan with the evening snack.

He slid a glance her way. "What caused you to decide to get into this particular occupation?"

"Are you asking because I'm a woman running a business? Or you'd ask a man that same question?" She dunked her biscuit into her coffee.

"I have met a few madams in my life, and none cared about their establishments like you do. Just curious why you do care. There must be a story behind it." He leaned back and sipped his drink.

"Like that Ma Brown I've heard 'bout?"

"Yes, for one. Beware of her. She is not one to cross. In fact, I met Holly there a year or so back."

She shrugged. "Don't care. Women alone must earn a living if they leave their family. I can't be a teacher, for I've no experience nor patience for that. Me face keeps me from working in a household for people of means who must needs hide me. Can't pay for higher learning. I wish to earn lots of money to pay for a grand life. 'Tis the quickest way."

"Ah, the desire for riches. Now we are getting better acquainted." He studied her as he nibbled a biscuit.

Orla considered the bear for a moment over her teacup's rim as she blew on the steaming surface.

He raised one brow.

"Do I detect disdain for those who desire riches?"

"Greed is what I object to. See? We are one step closer to being friends."

Orla scowled. "What's wrong with money? I've been without it for all me life. I can tell you poverty, well, 'tis not something to be desired. Those with money control the world and other people's fate in it. They're the oppressors, and there's nothing to admire 'bout being the oppressed at all."

Murphy set his empty cup in its saucer. "One moment." He headed to the sideboard to gather the entire plate of biscuits and returned with them, to place within reach on the low table.

"I agree with you about oppression often being from the rich. But you would be one of the benevolent rich people?" He popped another biscuit into his mouth.

"Aye. Nary a once would I oppress another person. I've been a victim of that. Cursed Crown rule." Orla drained her cup, and Murphy took it to the sideboard. "In Ireland, this occupation was tolerated, because the Crown cared naught for starving us. They welcomed it. Women without means, or alone with children, found 'twas the way to avoid what folks here call the Poor House." She shuddered.

He sat himself nearer to her this time and leaned his elbows on his knees. "Atrocious. Well, since that is a sad subject. I will lighten it up and call you by your given name. Mine is John."

"Don't understand why 'tis important to know it, but John's a fine Irish name." She attempted to scoot a little distance away from his disconcerting nearness, but the settee arm gouged her ribs. It was odd being this near to a man in a public room.

"Some Irish. A bit Scottish." The bear man showed his dimples. "Your turn to ask."

She pursed her lips for a moment. "No English?"

"No. I am safe, and your friend."

Orla snorted. "Friends? You're not me friend. Nuala's me friend."

"I will give it some time, then. How many siblings do you have?"

He returned his arm to the settee back, and his fingers reached her shoulder. He stroked it with his fingertips.

Chills ran up her neck. She trembled and resented it. *Ignore it.* "I've eight. Two died in childhood, but they were here on earth, so they count. One passed on the way over on the cursed ship. Down to four brothers, now."

"I had one brother. Now gone. What do your brothers do?"

She squirmed, but he continued to caress her shoulder, then her neck. "Well, me favorite is a priest, named John. Then there's Mick, who's a farmer turned railroad worker. He's the only one who'll speak to me or see me. Nonetheless, me Cousin Tarah writes me from Ireland. Rory stayed in Ireland caring for Mam and the farm. And me least favorite, Ed, wanders here and in Canada. He's a gambler."

Murphy chuckled. "Sounds like the start of a limerick. There once was a priest, two farmers, and a gambler . . ." His eyes glinted with amusement. He leaned closer, captivating her with his beautiful, manly face.

She held her breath and could not look away. Did she want to?

"I am getting to know you. I want you to know me. What do you say, Beautiful?"

"Umm." *Why's he so keen to know me better?* No man had ever requested this from her. She slowly nodded.

"Let us seal our agreement with a kiss, shall we?"

"In a lit room?"

He nodded and gently pressed her shoulders. He drew her to himself, and softly kissed her. Murphy repeated the feathery kisses. No grabbing and tugging. No avoiding her face. He intentionally kissed her scars.

And her toes never curled before. *This one's treacherous.* A sneaky grizzly bear dressed in men's clothing.

CHAPTER 15

Picking Her Poppy

A pretty Poppy missing a petal
—Orla

L ate Autumn

ONE WEEK LATER, Gallant scrambled to his feet and growled at the front door a moment before a soft tapping interrupted Orla's cash counting at her desk. His black hackles ruffled.

She glanced at the wall clock. "Near three o'clock. Not a man's knock, and they've all left. And who'd be out in this storm?" She grasped her shawl from the chair-back, wrapped it around her shoulders and long braid, and unlatched her door. A chill wind off the lake brushed over her, spattering raindrops onto her cheeks.

Huddled a few feet from the doorstep, stood a drenched girl. Her hair was so dirty and wet it disguised the color, and it stuck stubbornly to her head when the wind battered it. "Name's Colleen. Heard you were Irish. Like my parents were." Her teeth clattered as she shivered. "And I need a job, Madam Rose."

Orla jerked back and huffed. "Now? You come to me in this storm? Unbelievable, girl." She remembered to close her mouth after she spoke.

The girl straightened from her slump, shuddered fiercely, and pointed at the sign in Orla's window with a makeshift cane made from a chipped broom handle.

"Oh, me sign brought you here."

Colleen stared at Orla's uncovered scars, then shifted her gaze to the windows. "Yes, mam. I saw your sign. For help needed, aye?" She glanced through the door, past Orla to Sir Gallant, and backed up two steps, dragging her feet in an awkward pattern.

"Well, and another sign says only clean girls may apply." *This girl reeks. Nonetheless, pity is a virtue.*

The rain paused, and Orla glanced up. The wind scattered the clouds, and stars twinkled between them in the midnight sky.

"I wish . . . To be clean. . . I do." Colleen's voice trembled. "And dry. And warm. And eat." She fidgeted with her matted, unknown color hair, and kept her face turned away as though she could read the sign through the wall. "Clean girls must mean . . . you care about people. In some way. Somehow?" She peeked at Orla sideways. "Am I right, then?"

What do I do? "Me apologies for keeping you standing there, all soaked through to the skin." Orla stepped closer to Colleen, then wrinkled her nose when the breeze shifted. "Do you know 'bout this establishment? Have you done this sort of work before?" *Unbelievable that, but the world is surely a wicked place.*

"Might have. Not exactly?" Colleen turned her face away.

Was that a blush? Her skin was too dirty to tell for sure. Her lips had a bluish tint for sure. The trickles of water down her face made stripes on it like a tiger. Orla tugged a handkerchief from her dressing gown pocket. "Hoping this doesn't offend you." She covered her nose.

Colleen shook her head, and droplets flew out from her hair like a shaking dog. *Gallant had done that many a time.* "What's your age, girl?"

"Fourteen."

Orla caught her breath. "Well, holy angels. There's no way in God's heaven. Colleen, you must allow me to tell you the truth. The sort of work we do cannot be described as 'not exactly' done, don't you know? You either have or you haven't. Don't believe there's a halfway. If there is, I'd like to hear more 'bout it, because that's a valuable trick I'd surely like to learn."

Colleen burst into tears. When she wiped her face with her patched blanket and blew her nose with its edge, it left darker smudges on her cheeks. She straightened. "I'm sure that I can learn. I must have this job or starve."

Orla swallowed. She knew well that fear. "Or freeze yourself unto death." She could not turn this wretched girl away. What could Colleen do? How could she help? "Cook. Can you cook? We need a cook." Relief for a solution for this young girl's plight swept through her.

Colleen huddled and shivered beneath her dripping, filthy blanket and clenched her fists tight enough to turn her dirty fingers almost white. "You mean, I wouldn't have to?"

"Aye. You wouldn't have to."

"Then, I can cook. I can clean as well." Her face might have beamed.

Orla continued to inspect Colleen's smudged face. A dark spot jumped from Colleen's cheek to her chin. She flinched. "Holy heavens." *The girl has fleas.* She glanced down at Gallant and mumbled. "Forgive me for what suffering I may inflict upon you."

"Pardon?" Colleen limped a step nearer.

Had they not been discussing hiring a cook and a housekeeper earlier today? But this innocent, dirty waif? There must be some law against a brothel taking in an innocent. How could she protect

Colleen from unseemly things if she lived within a house of ill repute? God would surely strike her dead for that sin.

"Am considering." *Look at her*. Was it not more of a sin to leave her starving on the streets? Who knows what would happen to her.

Gallant tapped Orla with his muzzle then twisted his head back toward the stairway.

"Madam Rose. Who is that?" Holly stood behind Orla, but Gallant squeezed his head between them and growled. "Oh, no. It is the cripple I have seen around. She stinks." She pinched her perfect nostrils closed.

The cripple. Like people called her brother. "Rude girl. I'll throw you out, Holly, and keep her in your place if I must choose. She's our own sweet Poppy. I'm naming her after a California wildflower I heard 'bout. 'Tis strong and weathers many troubles. Call the other girls down. We've got a job to do. And get Violet onto heating up the water for the tub."

"This girl is worthless." Holly's dark blue eyes widened above her fingertips. "Are you sure, Madam Muldoon? No one else wanted her." Her nasal voice was worth something to lighten the moment.

Orla clenched her jaw. She would not take orders from an unstable and heartless woman like Holly. "Aye, you horrible creature, and get going. We all need our sleep at some point this morning."

Holly stomped away.

"Upstairs, Gal." She stroked Gallant's head then pointed to the staircase. "You'll be grateful for our bond of mutual protection. No miserable flea infestation for you, don't you know?"

The dog sniffed the air, and obeyed Orla's command.

She swung back to the pitiful girl on her doorstep. Everything lay in dark blue and gray shadows, except for the beam of light from her window. Orla leaned out the door and glanced up and down the wharf's surrounding area but detected no one else. She reached around the jamb, snatched the window sign, and tugged the nearest thick curtain closed. Orla waved Poppy up to the last step and stopped her.

Tears pooled on the poor shivering girl's lashes.

"You wish to live with us and work for me, aye? First, you must bathe. Leave your shawls, shoes, underthings—all your clothing outside. And that blanket. Nothing comes inside with you but your hair and cane once the Flowers come downstairs to help."

"What?"

After the Flower Garden's four women made a screen with some extra blankets, Orla firmly urged Poppy to strip out of her soaked, soiled clothing on the doorstep. They all promised not to look while they slowly shimmied with shuddering Poppy and her cane within their center into the scullery.

Violet prepared the galvanized tub with warm water, a bar of soap, and set a folded towel on the table.

Poppy shook with fright or cold. Maybe both. "I . . . thank you forever . . . I don't . . . you've warmed my heart with your kindness. I thought—"

"Kindness works both ways, girl." Violet coughed and gripped Poppy's thin arm. "Steady as you step in. Be kind in return by sitting in the tub. Grab the lavender soap and get going. The sooner you wash up, we can all return to bed."

Daisy dropped her blanket and yelled. "For the love of hotcakes, is that a flea on me?" She swiped at her arm.

The others, except Orla and Violet, threw their blankets and scrambled from the scullery with screams sure to awaken the neighbors.

How will she explain the ruckus tomorrow? Orla faced Poppy's back, suds dripping from her hair and arms. *Dear holy angels.* The scars on Poppy's young flesh were worse than her own face.

"I'm sorry." Poppy's lip quivered, and tears streamed down her cheeks, unless it was bathwater. She hung her head and sobbed.

"For what?" Orla made eye-contact with Violet, then grimaced and cringed while she raised one of the tossed blankets. "There, there, girl. You're safe and sound tonight. 'Tis best they've gone. You've more privacy."

Violet made a face at Orla and nodded. She mouthed, *I saw,* then patted Poppy's sudsy head. "Cheer up little one. You cannot help it.

Fleas do not scare me and Madam Rose away, do they? We have been round them before." She raised her brow at Orla.

"Oh, aye. Many a time. Don't mean we like them. It means we know 'tis best to be rid of them." She cleared her throat. "Violet, can you finish up with her hair? I must latch the door and finish counting our earnings. Almost forgot Poppy's wet clothes."

"Go ahead."

Orla grabbed Poppy's cane and headed back to the door. She swung it open further, glanced both ways, and nudged the pile of tattered soaking wet fabrics and worn shoes to the side with the stick. *Will burn those disgusting things tomorrow.*

The women upstairs finally settled in for the night from the silence that followed footsteps and scurrying above Orla's head. She closed her unfinished ledger and rose to join Violet back in the scullery.

Holly descended from the staircase as Orla passed it. "I cannot get back to sleep. Wish I could do so like Daisy."

Violet screened Poppy with a blanket as the girl carefully raised herself from the tub with Violet's aid.

"Finished up, are you?" Lavender aroma filled the room. "That's grand, now."

Violet wrapped Poppy in the blanket, and the girl's thin figure allowed it to be almost doubled. Violet turned to Orla. "What shall we dress her in Madam? She cannot wear this wet blanket to bed."

"True, that. And her hair is damp. Poppy needs a cot near the fire or stove." Orla tipped her head while she studied Poppy. "Violet, stoke the stove, and Holly, you look to be nearest to Poppy's size. Fetch her one of your gowns, and a set of under things with haste."

Holly scowled. "Me? Why not Daisy? I can get one of her gowns. She sleeps through everything. She will not notice what is missing in her closet because she does not wear her spectacles. I do notice." She stamped her foot. "They are my clothes, not for this . . ." she fluttered her fingers at Poppy, "this ragged thing."

"You are a sad, selfish person, Holly." Violet sneered. "I had not realized that about you until now."

Holly snatched a ladle off the wall and ran up to Violet swinging it at her. Violet ducked, and Poppy whimpered.

"You are a selfish person as well, Violet. Has anyone ever taken things from you that you did not want them to take?" Holly raised her weapon again. "We must lookout for ourselves because no one—"

Orla yanked the ladle from Holly and towered over her. "Stop it, girl, or get out of my house. Calm yourself. We aren't your enemies, nor are we thieves, aye? You're under me protection, same as Poppy."

"What is all the screaming for? Why are you all in the scullery?" Daisy squinted from the doorway. "It is still dark outside." She scrunched up her face as she stared at the window. "Or am I mistaken?"

Holly thrashed her arms in the air. "That is it. Now, we cannot take Daisy's clothes."

Daisy picked her flyaway, flaxen tendrils away from her eyes. "Take my clothes?"

"No, no. I feel bad to upset things." Poppy wrung her blanket's hem.

Orla turned to Daisy. "Daisy, we'll not take your clothes." She tapped Holly's shoulder. "Have some mercy on a bedraggled young woman and lend her some clothing, will you? Do you want her parading around our home without a stitch? I surely don't. The rest of us don't. I pledge to purchase you a new dress and a set of under-things in return for your begrudging generosity."

Daisy and Violet objected with why Orla could not also purchase something for them for helping the newcomer.

Orla clenched her hips. "Well, and I'm not a bank, now, am I? 'Tis a fair swap for Holly from giving her clothing to Poppy. May've taken a tantrum, a threat of violence, and a senseless argument, but there 'tis. Who owns this establishment, aye? As the owner, 'tis me own choice to reward who I will, yeah? Do you wish to keep your jobs? Do you?" She stared at each in turn.

"Yes, Madam Rose," they all mumbled together.

"That's settled then. Off to bed. Not you, Violet. Need you longer."

Holly glared at Poppy, before she turned toward the hall. *There'll be trouble from that ungrateful wretch.*

Daisy trembled, her stare glued to Poppy as she passed between her and Orla heading to the door. She whispered something that sounded like, "Keep away from me, you devil." *Holy heavens, the girl thinks Poppy's possessed.* Her words sounded exactly like her fanciful brother Mick's.

Someone pressed Orla's shoulder, and she turned to Violet at her eye-level.

"Madam Rose, will you promise me something? Between the two of us only. As friends?" Violet's purple irises darkened. "I may not have the right to ask this, but will you resist taking in any other women? We are bursting with conflict as it is. Managing a harem of sorts is not enjoyable."

Orla nodded. "Don't I know it? I do vow to make everyone get along if you'll help me lock up any weaponry. No more ladles, knives, nor anything heavy like pots."

"We have listening ears." Violet tipped her head at Poppy.

"That we do." Orla focused on the new girl, swaying beneath her blanket. "Poor thing. We must get you to bed." *Poppy shall be the keeper of the keys to all the doors.* That would be her power and match up with her cook's job.

Holly entered the room dragging a mattress with clothing draped over its edge. "Thought I would help out to thank you for forgiving my temper." She blinked at Orla. "Where do you want it?"

"Where'd you get it?"

"From the storage closet. I saw it once when I was looking for something." Holly busied herself with rearranging the clothing.

Suspicious, that. Had she not gotten rid of the old mattresses a while back? Maybe not this one. She would deal with it later.

Violet handed Holly's selected clothing to Poppy and laid the grubby mattress near the pipe stove. "Seems clean enough, but slightly musty and damp."

"But it's not dirt, nor sand, nor the cold, hard ground." Poppy hobbled near the stove. "It'll be fine."

Orla approached the pipe stove and hovered her palm over it. "There's still good warmth from the stove from Violet heating your bathwater." She removed the pocket watch from her pocket. "Half past four o'clock. A few hours of darkness left. Let's allow Poppy to change and we can get some winks."

Poppy smiled for the first time. "Thank you."

"Good night." Holly glanced back at Orla and Violet with their backs turned to Poppy while she dressed. She left them together.

"I'm dressed as can be."

"Now, 'tis time to fulfill me promise to Gal. Violet, grab the sewing scissors, wherever they may be."

"Your promise?" Violet slid her sewing basket out from the nearest cupboard, and carefully burrowed through the contents. She raised a shiny silver metal pair. "Got them."

Poppy clasped her wet strands. "Oh no. You mean to cut my hair because of the fleas, don't you now?"

Violet laid the blanket under a chair she slid out from beneath the table and carefully helped Poppy to sit. "I will cut your hair very fashionably. Like the ladies of Paris. I saw them in a magazine once. They style their hair after boy's cuts, and it is lovely. Besides, you can grow it out again if you do not like it."

"But I'm not a fashionable Parisian lady, aye? I'm a poor misfit." Poppy's chin trembled. Her voice rose with each loud snip. "Would you ever, in all your life cut your hair off, Madam Muldoon?"

"Never. 'Tis me one beauty since me face isn't." Orla caressed her scar while Violet snipped off a long clump which landed on the blanket.

"Oh merciful heavens." Poppy sniffed.

Orla tipped Poppy's chin up. "I see you clean up grand. A pretty Poppy missing a petal. Mayhap I can get you some customers after all. Or mayhap not."

Her Bear Named Murphy

What's the difficult thing 'bout House Rule Number Eleven?
—Orla

 *hiskey Row, Lake Superior*

SEVERAL DAYS LATER, it was time for Madam Rose to go visit The Swimming Mermaid Pub, number fifteen of twenty in the town. Her mission was to find her sneaky patron, Mr. Wally Sheffield, who was Daisy's debtor for his brother's birthday gift. Hunting down sneak-thieves who skipped payment to her establishment was another part of her business she loathed. "What's the difficult thing 'bout House Rule Number Eleven?" *'Tis as if I'm selling wares at market and must*

watch everyone's hands in the fruit baskets. Good thing she knew a thing or two about handling drunks in a pub. She yanked open the pub's heavy door against a stiff breeze.

Seated at a card table near the doorway, Mr. Murphy, her grizzly, flashed his dimples at her. She startled and tried to tamp down her racing heartbeat. She met and held his dark blue, fathomless gaze. He did not seem to mind her staring at him or her discomposure as he focused on her twisting her fingers. She tucked her hands behind her bustle.

Mr. Sheffield, who sat next to her grizzly, waggled his brow. "Well, and if it ain't Madam Rose, fellas. What brings you in tonight? Not enough customers?" The other men at the table guffawed. "Unbelievable you'd have troubles getting your girls customers, or is it?"

"Bite your tongue, Wally." She pinched his arm. "Or you won't be allowed inside anymore. You know what I came here for. Sir Gallant is waiting outside, as well. Won't bother me at all to call for him." She tapped her foot.

The other men jeered and whistled, except for the blue-eyed, grizzly. His expression was unreadable. She swung a long curl over her shoulder.

"Who names their guard dog after a knight?" Wally rubbed the back of his arm, stood and bowed. "I beg your pardon, Madam. Forgot that you like respect."

"Sir Gallant means he earned his knighthood from earnestly guarding me and me castle."

Wally reached into his dirty jacket's pocket, pulled out some money, and contrived to slip it into Orla's palm. The men at the table murmured.

"Count it aloud, if you please."

He followed Orla's unwavering stare. "Oh, ho. I suspect you haven't been properly introduced. This is Mr. Murphy, from Duluth. He's the supervisor of an ore barge team. This here is Madam Rose of the Flower Garden establishment a few doors down."

Murphy stood and tipped his head. His eyes twinkled with his pretense. "Madam."

Orla tipped her chin up to its limit and stared up his nostrils. "Sir."

His smile revealed sparkling white teeth, none missing, and that glorious cleft chin peeking from behind his black stubble which tempted her caresses. She studied the money in her palm instead.

Rustling skirts and soft footsteps shuffled behind Orla. She glanced over her shoulder. The Flower Garden's three working girls lined up behind their Madam and peered around her taller figure. "You couldn't stay home as I asked?" Orla sighed and turned back to the substantial size of Murphy.

He raised one brow. "Do you have an opening in your calendar tonight?"

Orla slowly nodded, and her heart ran for cover as fast as a galloping horse from a wildfire.

From her girls' nervous whispering, Orla knew he would be her client again tonight. "Certainly, 'tis always good for business. You can follow us over, Mr. Murphy, after I've collected what I'm owed."

Wally slid from his chair toward the door and the girls, but Holly and Violet blocked his exit.

She scowled at him. "Do you believe me threat to you, or are you a simpleton as well as a thief trying to cheat me? I'm a businesswoman and I do me numbers very well. Plant your boots over here whilst I double-check what you paid me."

Wally turned his attention to Daisy and Murphy frowning beside Orla and shifted his weight to fumble for more of his pocket money. "All's well. Just having you on. Let me know if I miss counted."

Daisy harrumphed. "I do not believe you can count. Why, I seem to recall you having difficulty with your numbers and—"

"Never you mind Daisy, he's paid in full. Nonetheless, you're only welcome back to my establishment if you pay beforehand, Mr. Sheffield. Let's go Murphy, and girls."

Madam Rose might have a mutiny on her hands if she allowed too many patrons to skip out on payment and then welcome them back. She glimpsed her reflection in the pub's window and straightened her posture. "You girls do understand why I invited Sheffield to return, aye?"

Violet cleared her throat. "It will take some time to build up our list of patrons?"

"You've hit the bullseye. We must cater to unmannerly men. For now."

The girls shimmied through the Flower Garden's door as soon as Orla widened it one foot. Where they disappeared to was anybody's guess, until hushed voices in the dim candlelight hinted at their whereabouts in the shadow beneath the staircase.

Orla removed her dark green wrap. "Daisy, since your behavior forced me to collect for you this night, you'll do the honors of signing in our guests and manning the entrance. Please come to your post."

After a hesitation, a dainty, yellow slipper, and a yellow satin skirt slid into the light, followed by Daisy's slight figure. Her green eyes widened. "Yes, Madam Rose."

"Mr. Murphy, please follow me." Orla did not glance at him, turned, and climbed the stairs. She was careful to hold correct posture and concentrated on each polished step.

Gal trailed the couple. Orla heard him panting. He always knew his duties with minimal commands. He would follow them to her door and lay down to block the entrance after they entered. She could count on his obedience.

Orla turned in time to catch Murphy enter her room, and gasped when he filled the entire doorway. He was just able to miss colliding with the top of the door by ducking. He did not turn sideways to enter. She was grateful for that and released her breath. *'Tis why I call him grizzly.*

Murphy waited, and his intent gaze followed Sir Gallant.

Instead of the dog's usual challenging behavior, he kept his stare on Murphy, then sat.

"Lay down." Orla gave the hand command as well.

Her obedient guard dog refused. He licked his muzzle, and flipped over, whining at Murphy. Gal panted and froze his unbecoming posture.

Murphy approached the dog.

Orla reached toward Murphy's arm. "Don't. He's likely to—"

"Be my friend?" He bent far down and rubbed Gallant's belly. "Good boy. You are a good boy, are you not?"

Orla clenched her fists. "What in the world is this? He's never done such a thing."

"He recognizes the master." Murphy continued to croon and stroke her dog. "I was raised with sled dogs. Spent years with teams. You have an intelligent breed, and he recognizes the leader." Murphy glanced up at her. "He will still protect you, if he feels the need. Not to worry."

"If you say so. Nevertheless, what good is a guard dog like this?" She huffed. "By the looks of it, he's fallen in love with you."

Murphy stood. "He subjects himself to me, but he does not love me. He loves you." He pointed at the double bed. "That is still your bed?"

"Well. Aye. 'Tis not the dog's, is it?" Her heart pounded again, and she twisted her fingers.

"Hm." He paced around it once. "Is this all you have?"

Orla scrunched her nose. "What else would I have? Are you a numbskull?"

"Still mocking your patrons with your wit? Well, the size is all wrong. Thought you were getting another." He ran his fingers through his dark waves, making him appear much like a large, sleepy boy. But she knew better.

She forced her tension away with a long exhale. "All me others are smaller." She ground her teeth and shook her head. "Your height. You tower over most men, don't you know? There's a rug, but it doesn't appeal to me."

Murphy took two steps past her and stopped. "It has been . . . interesting. I will be sure to tell Ma Brown how fine your establishment is, and I will return in a few weeks. Can you accommodate me by then? If so, you have my continued business." He removed a roll of bills from his vest and handed them to her with a lopsided grin.

Orla slowly grasped the roll. "What's this for? You owe me nothing for nothing."

"Not true. Something happened." He bowed and opened the door. "Good evening and until next time."

"Doubt there'll be a next time." *Whoever paid money for nothing?*

* * *

FOURTEEN EVENINGS LATER, when everyone else was busy, Orla sat on the chair in front of her bedroom window staring at the lake. The almost windless surface shimmered silver with the full moon's reflection. Murphy hadn't arrived as he promised.

Her pet loon sounded a mournful hoot. Its tune did not startle Orla anymore as it did before. She had yet to see the creepy bird with red eyes she had only heard from these past months. She hurried to tug on her burgundy dress, boots, and matching jacket while Gal curiously watched her don her outfit.

"Well, Gal, 'tis a grand opportunity to find the creature. I mustn't take you with me, for you'll be sure to spook the loon away before I shall catch sight of it. I wish to see this *'lóma mór'* for meself. You know, don't you, that I named it *'aingeal dubh,'* as if it were me own pet? Well, and the idea to name it Black Angel was to make it less terrifying." She shivered anyway.

Gal tipped his head sideways.

"Don't try to give me the willies with your amber stare. I'll be finding out if Angel's more frightening than you, aye? Your unbecoming posture with the bear gave me some doubts. Watch out for me at the window, won't you?"

Although lantern light may scare off the loon, it gladdened Orla to have it with her as she stepped over cumbersome or partially hidden stones down the slope to the shore. "'Tis darker out here than it looked to be from inside."

The dramatic sunset glowed red, orange, and gold higher above the sun's reflection against the clouds, and blue with lavender near the Great Lake's horizon. She stopped to appreciate its magnificence. A chill breeze off the water tickled her face with tendrils of her loose hair. She brushed them away and checked the pins holding her hat to her piled locks.

How often did she venture outside at night? Business took place inside most evenings. This was the path she chose. A lady of the evening. It was supposed to be a lonely living, one way for women to get rich, and here she had been deluged by misfits. However, they accepted her as no others, except for Mick. She sighed. Her crew of girlies turned out to be a balm for her wounded soul. *The unexpected benefit of other women.*

Orla raised her lantern and turned in a circle. This lovely setting, and often perilous as well, was where she chose to plant herself. Or maybe it chose her. She awaited the darkness tonight for had she not always belonged to it?

Nearby, lay a large piece of driftwood. She stepped easier along the sandy soil close to the lake's edge. "'Tis a good seat for observing and waiting for me Angel. May you come tonight." Orla set the lantern on a sandy spot a little away from the wood. She lifted her skirts, adjusted her bustle, and situated herself into a comfortable position by leaning against the thickest vertical branch. *Shall do grand for a chair.* She yawned.

A haunting call sounded from a distance. Orla opened her eyes and straightened. *Must've dozed off.* She scanned the water's surface in the twilight as a full moon rose behind the trees.

Water lapped at the shore, and she squinted at a black floating object drawing closer to her position. Its size was not yet discernable, although she did not need any spectacles like Daisy did. She murmured. "There 'tis. Me Black Angel."

Another wail urged Orla to her feet. She broke off a branch to protect herself for only God knew how big her Angel was. Should she run for cover? *It eats fish, they said.* Humans are meat as well. Chills spread up her neck into her scalp.

The black waterfowl ducked below the silver surface. *Preparing for a sneak attack?* Orla craned her neck and searched the beach in case it jumped out of the water and headed for her. Geese were known to attack people. Was this bird anything like them? Daisy had insisted they were not dangerous. Orla's branch was ready should she need it.

It popped to the top of the water and closer to Orla. The black fowl was smaller than she had imagined. Its red eyes were as frightening as they should be. But it did not seem interested in attacking her. *Holly won the bet.* Orla unclenched her fist and lowered her branch as the bird continued to float past. It ducked underneath the surface a few more times.

After the loon disappeared from her sight in the growing shadows of night, Orla took her makeshift seat again. In the stillness, Orla listened to waves hitting the shore, and the buzzing of night insects. This was an unfamiliar setting yet soothing somehow.

"Fool. Frightened of a small water bird. Angel had no hostile reaction to me presence." Nor any repulsion or attraction. How many other things had frightened her in her life before they vanished into the mist? Nothing to be dreaded at all.

Orla studied the round, bright moon now hovering over the water, while painting a trail of light from its glow, and joining the parting clouds of heaven. The unveiled stars twinkled their tiny lights with all their might. *Uncovered at last.* She knew how that felt, and sighed.

The wind chilled further, and she wrapped her arms over her coat to keep out the cold. Her piteous branch was not much of a defense, but she must always find something to wield to guard herself.

Orla picked at the branch's bark. She had endured people's expressions of horror, revulsion, and often judgement accompanied by bullying or abuse. She then learned to avoid most of it by covering up. Many of her beliefs or expectations were from her deep-set dread of how people would react to her, even before she had scarred her own face.

"Didn't plan to mull over me past tonight." Should she pray? What for? "Me girlies reacted oddly when they first saw me face." No horror then. Next, they showed her respect and devotion. *Murphy calls me beautiful. He probably doesn't mean it.* Could she release the injuries from previous people's judgements and embrace herself the way others did in Whiskey Row?

She dropped her branch and surveyed the sky again. Clouds scuttled away, leaving the stars to shine brighter. God created it all, as the church told everyone. What about God's love for her? He was perfect. She was not. Jesus had a lot of misfits as friends. Did He truly like her? She could ask Nuala about it later. *She seems to understand God well enough.*

"Must be time to head home." She reached for her lantern. A tall shadow swayed behind her, and she nearly screamed, until she recognized him. "Bear. Ah. Murphy."

"Good evening, Orla. You can call me Bear if you wish." His hands were in his pockets, and his eyes sparkled in the lantern light. He did not appear evil in the yellow light that highlighted his face, only intimidating.

"Holy heavens, nonetheless, I'll not call you Bear in front of others. How'd you find me here?"

He indicated her lantern and grinned. "Yours is the only light on the beach."

"Aye. So 'tis." Heat scampered up her neck to her face.

He aimed his shoes toward her establishment. "Were you about to go inside? If not, I am in no hurry. We can walk along the sand and talk." He offered her his elbow.

This man was attached in an unnatural way to talking. "'Bout what shall we chat this time? Never mind, tell me how you knew to come down here." The sand shifted beneath her boots, and she slowed her pace. Murphy's muscled arm was too easy to depend upon.

"I had business to attend to earlier after we docked. When I arrived back at The Flower Garden, Violet ushered me to your room. We found it empty. But Gal stood at the window with his front paws on the windowsill and staring outside. I peered out and saw what I assumed to be your lantern."

"Good Gal. Did as I told him. Makes me proud."

"He is superb. So, Beautiful, how is business?"

Orla took a deep breath. Should she tell him about something being amiss? Why? What could he do about it? Men do not know more than women. She could figure it out.

He pressed her arm. "Madam Rose? Out with it."

"Why do you always think you know everything 'bout me? You don't. Nor do I wish you to know me business—"

"While it is true that I am prying, you will eventually learn to trust me." He guided her around a large rock.

"Not that you can do anything helpful 'bout it, but there're some odd goings on, aye. Lately, there's been money unaccounted for, missing hosiery, hair combs, and a reticule. Even food stuffs from the pantry. I'm afraid they've been scuppered by someone I oughtn't trust. Was hoping the first missing item was a prank but me suspicions grew with the third. Nevertheless, I refuse to believe 'tis me precious new housekeeper, Poppy. Holly blames her. You've yet to meet me Poppy. I can't believe any of me girlies would steal. I'm plain flummoxed."

"It must be one of them, Beautiful. Who else has access to those items?"

"The men, you dolt. Our customers."

Murphy halted their walk by tugging her arm. He took her hand between his like her warm, cozy mittens on a chilly day, and stared into her eyes. "Facing and dealing with betrayal from a friend is a terrible necessity, Orla. Whether it be personal or in business."

She yanked her hand out of his clasp. "Of course you'd say 'twas the women. Always protect the other men. Why can't a man steal? You're all no better than us."

"While true, we are not worse as well. Most of us. No, maybe we are worse . . . With your brilliant mind, figure out how a man could take those things, hide them on his person, get past Gal, and escape with them. Are the men always supervised? What about your girls? Who has the most opportunity to get around the house undiscovered?"

Orla clenched her hips. "You mean a sneak thief in our midst, aye?"

Murphy slowly nodded. "Aye. Consider the motive behind it. Are these items valuable? Can they be sold for a substantial amount of money? If not, then the thief is most likely not an intruder. Gal would not allow it. He does not allow much to get past him, does he?"

"What you say makes sense. Surprisingly." She slid her gaze away. "Holy heavens."

He offered his arm again. "Shall we go home?"

"'Tis me own home, not yours. Who invited you anyway?"

"Your window sign did. A long time ago, Beautiful." He winked.

They entered The Flower Garden through the lakeside, rear door. "Glad the lamp is lit for us. Didn't relish entering a dark room." Especially with her bear.

Poppy dropped the book in her hands onto the tabletop by the lantern. She scrambled to stand. "Pardon me, I didn't expect anyone to come into the scullery. Where shall I go, Madam?"

"'Tis the first time I've realized you need a room of your own, me girlie."

Murphy bent to pick up her book for her. "Our apologies for disturbing you. I suggested to Madam Rose that we come here." *Now, he calls me that.*

"Contrarian. We can go into the parlor, me girlie. Stay warm and comfortable here as you were. Would you please bring us some . . ." Orla looked to Murphy.

"Coffee. Coffee or tea. I am not a drinker of alcohol." Something dark shifted in his magnificent eyes. *There's a story there.*

"Aye, then. Poppy, hot tea and some of your delicious biscuits. Follow me."

"I intended to."

"Was speaking to Gal, you nitwit." Orla trounced to the doorway, turned toward him, and tapped her not dainty foot.

He chuckled. "Do you hear how she speaks to me, Poppy? Such a shame."

"Yessir." Poppy leaned on her cane and curtsied. *Odd, that.*

Murphy flushed. "No need to address me so properly. I am a barge crew supervisor. Nothing special." He approached Orla and slid his hand through his wavy hair. "She is a mannerly young miss, is she not? Lead the way."

"Aye. Poppy girl, ring the bell when the tea tray is ready. I'll fetch it."

Thankfully, Poppy had thought of lighting the lamps and the hearth in the parlor as well, she never would have come downstairs to do it herself. "Lay down, Gal." *Smart dog chose the warmest spot in front of the fire.*

Her bear waited in the center of the parlor for Orla. "What shall we do? Any ideas?"

Run for me life? Say I've taken ill? Kiss him for all he's worth?

The bell jingled from the scullery.

"There it is, Madam Rose. No need to decide. Our refreshments are first."

CHAPTER 17

Troubles in Her Garden

I'll not be complaining 'bout me own childhood again
Orla

The following morning, Orla flipped over for the eighth resettle and scrambled her quilt into a wad. The dawn could not rise quick enough, as she stared at her window curtains praying for the slightest light to seep through the slit. *Mercy me. What's the time? May as well get up.* Her eyes stung with sleeplessness. She sat up anyway and pushed the wad of warm material away before her feet hit the icy floorboards. "Almost makes me wish to get back into bed, Gal."

In the shadows, Gal's warmth leaned against her lower leg, and she smothered her squeal as he licked her toes. *Good thing I expected that.*

She donned her silky dressing gown hanging over the cast iron filigree at the foot of her bed, and arose, heading to the silver pocket watch on her dresser that Murphy had left behind. "Always wanted one of these. He'll be returning for it to be sure, aye? For now, 'tis mine." Its smooth, metal back enticed her to caress it with her thumb. She turned its face toward the window, but the dawn light was too dim to discern it.

Woof!

"Me being vertical doesn't mean 'tis time to feed you, don't you know? 'Tis rude to beg." She drew closer to the opaque curtains and parted one, revealing the transparent red liner between her and the world below. Faint peach hues tinged the lake, docks, and nearby roofs. It was light enough to reveal the watch face. "Nearing six o'clock." She slipped the timepiece into her robe's pocket.

Sir Gallant awaited at her feet.

"Since you're minding your manners with patience, let's go down." Her slippers engulfed her chilly toes, and warmed her tired, frustrated spirit. "Shall sneak some bread and jam before breakfast." She opened the door, stopped to listen for hushed sounds, then crept downstairs with Gal close behind.

A stair creaked, and she slowed her pace, avoiding the center of steps seven and three by keeping to the right side, nearest the banister. The pair made it down and turned toward the scullery when a hushed *clink* halted their progress. "Holy heavens. Wished to gather me thoughts in peace."

Rustling fabric and a soft humming confirmed Orla's guess she would not be alone. She chewed her lip. *What to do?*

Sir Gallant broke protocol and trotted into the scullery, setting whoever it was on alert.

"Gal, come." She raised her hands above her shoulders and shook her head. "Your loyalty disappears with your hunger, then? Ah, well. Nothing to be done 'bout it." She scurried to the doorway.

Poppy stood leaning against the sink. Her long auburn braid hung down her back. Her brown eyes widened as Gal approached, but he did not growl at her.

The dog sniffed Poppy's bedding and mattress, then around the room's edges with his ears perked forward on the alert.

"Gal, by me." Orla patted her leg, and the dog circled back to her side. "No need to be frightened of him when he's with me, me girlie. He doesn't like many people. Sure, and he has good reasons."

"Oh, I'm not afraid. I like animals. Better than people." Poppy smiled and studied the dog.

Orla fluttered her hand at the room. "Didn't expect to find you here. Thought we may have frightened you away last night, what with all the tiffs and bad will bandied 'bout all the missing items."

"They won't scare me off with any accusations."

Madam Rose tugged her dressing gown's belt. "Truth to tell, I don't know these women all that well. Most haven't been with me long and I never expected you upon me doorstep, or some to treat you with contempt."

"I'm happy Violet lent me her old nightgown." Poppy shook the voluminous white fabric that trailed over her feet, then turned her face toward the window above the basin. "Besides, Madam Rose, it looks to be time for snow. Did you see the sky? Without a doubt, they're snow clouds."

"Snow's part of life on the Lakes."

Poppy shifted awkwardly and faced Orla. "I'm very grateful for a warm home and a place to rest these past weeks." She indicated her sleeping cot near the stove for the winter months.

"Aye, I can imagine."

"No more living on the streets and hiding from thieves or others with more horrible things in mind, which is exhausting."

"Well, and I'd never let something terrible happen to you, me girlie, aye?" A lump gripped Orla's throat, threatening to choke some logic into her groggy brain. *Here I thought she might be the troublesome one.* What should she do with Holly's rude behavior toward Poppy?

She bent over to pat Gallant and gather her composure. "When you put your thoughts so clearly, I'm glad to have you. I'm that grateful to you that you're cooking for us. Violet was our best cook, but she's got other things . . . to do." How could she keep Poppy at a distance from her girls' work in her new abode? *I can't.* There was not a perfect way.

Poppy slapped her forehead and suddenly pushed off from the sink. She nearly toppled. "My goodness. I'm your cook. And I haven't put the water on yet. You don't usually rise so early." She scanned the scullery. "Are there coffee beans or tea in your pantry? I must take stock of your goods."

"Rise early? Almost never. 'Tis a fluke." Orla chuckled. "Aye, to the right of the rear door in the pantry, you'll find beans since Daisy shopped yesterday. We voted to switch from tea just before you arrived after having it at me friend Nuala's. Coffee does a better job of getting us going. You know your way round a scullery, don't you?"

Poppy grabbed her broomstick cane and hobbled to the pantry door and turned sideways to enter. "At the orphanage," her voice was muffled as she searched for the coffee beans, "we all learned where and when to find the food. Us weaker and smaller ones got our rations stolen off our plates."

"Tragic."

"There's not much in here to work with, Madam Rose." She clinked some items deep inside the narrow cavity. "I found the beans, though."

"Should be plenty of food. Daisy and I filled it last week." Orla fumbled with her own braid. The foodstuffs had been disappearing too quickly. Something was amiss there as well.

"Some children in the orphanage learned to pick the door locks. Hunger is a powerful motivator for thievery. I braved the attacks to fill myself. I was hungry most of the time there." Poppy limped toward Orla with a small bag of coffee beans, carrying it beneath her free arm. "The assaults were from—"

"Stop. Holy heavens." Shudders ran up Orla's body. "Me imagination's always been too keen." How could anyone do the things she envisioned to a defenseless child?

Poppy halted. "I'm sorry. I talk without thinking what it must sound like. Older children were the bullies, more often than the adults."

"No, no, speaking the truth can help us. I always thought orphanages were safe places run by the churches to care for children, not hellholes of mistreatment and despair." Orla stepped toward Poppy and cupped her shoulders. She embraced the girl. "Terrible life you've had. I'll not be complaining 'bout me own childhood again."

"Does anyone have a good childhood?"

Gallant pawed Orla's foot and barked.

Orla released Poppy. "The girlies here surely didn't. Most of me own troubles were from other children, as well." Scarring herself was one outcome. She reached into the pantry with trembling fingers for Gal's fish tin and vegetable box.

"Children are not always little angels, are they?"

"Devils more like. Been making poor Gal wait for his breakfast. Haven't I, pet?" Orla dumped his food onto his plate in front of the back door. Tiny orange wheels of sliced carrots rolled onto the floor.

Poppy had shuffled a few steps from the pantry almost to where the counter held the coffee bean grinder. She reached down to move the carrots but froze at Sir Gallant's low growl.

"Ho! I'll do that. The coffee can wait a minute, me girlie. Wasn't thinking 'bout your limp there. Since you can't hurry to leave the scullery, best to stay still. Gal doesn't like anyone near his food. Thinks we'll steal it, aye?"

Gallant guzzled down his food and did not glance again in Poppy's direction.

"I know what hunger is like and guarding one's food, poor thing." Poppy studied Gal as he ate.

"Odd that." Orla frowned. "He must be awful hungry to pay you no mind. He often lunges at the girls, mostly Holly, if they're in the room with me whilst he eats. He's 'bout done." *Does he sense that Poppy's fragile and no threat?*

The Shepherd raised his head, focused past Orla, and growled low in his throat.

Holly stood inside the doorway clenching her hips with both

hands. "I have been standing here listening to you. Why is he perfectly fine with her in the scullery? She is a stranger. He should be accustomed to me by now. I have never done anything to him. Look at what he does when I step forward." She stepped one foot over the threshold into the room.

He growled.

Holly stepped back, and he stopped. She stepped in again, and Gal growled. "He is like some sort of alarm going off. Should I just ignore him?"

"I wouldn't." Orla gave a hand signal for Gal to sit. He sat. What is the trouble between him and Holly?

"You are both up early. Did the cripple not sleep well on the smelly mattress? Poor little thing." Holly's snide tone grated on Orla's nerves.

Poppy ducked her head and shuffled the last few feet to the counter to set the beans down beside the grinder. "I slept grand, thank you."

Orla shook her finger at Holly. "Keep a civil tongue in your head, you rude creature. You're not irreplaceable."

"Yes, Madam. I did not mean to injure her tender feelings. Well, I might as well return to bed since we have a . . . a cook of sorts. That will give us working girls more time to rest, will it not?"

Wish our Holly's beauty beamed from the inside out. "Well, now, Poppy. Do you wish for me to help you with breakfast before I finish up me ledger?"

Gold light now lit the scullery through the eastern facing windows. It warmed the room with color although the temperature was chilly. Poppy followed Orla's stare and peered over her shoulder on her way back to the pantry. "I just love sunrises. They mean another day to hope for the best. God might be at work on our troubles. Don't you think so?"

Orla shrugged. "Hadn't given much thought 'bout sunrises being a hopeful sign. Or God doing much for me. Mayhap you're right. I'm fiercely hoping me numbers balance in me ledger. Been having troubles with that. Never have before in me entire life."

"I'll pray they work out then. Must get on with breakfast, and no, I don't need your help, Madam. I'll get to grinding the coffee beans next. Everyone will surely want their morning cups." Poppy slowly made her uneven trek to the stove with a bowl in one hand. "I found four eggs. They'll do for a scramble."

"Odd, that. We'd six eggs yesterday."

Poppy laughed. "Maybe a raccoon made its way into the pantry. They're sneaky creatures with their tiny hands. But shoo. You do your work, and I'll do mine." She turned her back to Orla and removed the blue striped apron from its hook.

"That thing will wrap twice around you, me girlie. And don't burn yourself on me stove. Breakfast isn't worth that tragedy." Orla headed to her desk and the unusually difficult task of figuring out her business book. Had her mind slipped with aging? But she was yet only thirty-five.

The pungent aroma of brewing coffee cheered Orla's mood until angst increased in her soul. She scribbled, struggled, and calculated to balance her accounts receivable and expenditures. How could her income be so low? Numbers do not lie. Something was terribly amiss. She started over and unlocked the green metal cashbox again. The lock jiggled. Was it not latching correctly? After half an hour, Orla still could not balance the books. She gave in to the aroma of perking coffee and her growling tummy, then scraped her chair back.

"Breakfast is ready, ladies." Poppy leaned through the scullery door.

Violet and Daisy exited the parlor together, and Holly glided down the last steps of the stairway. "Oh goody, we get to taste our new cook's latest offering." *Her vile tone comes from a gloomy heart.*

Orla carried her ledgers and cashbox into the scullery. She was not letting it out of her sight until she had this mess resolved. "I'm glad to sample cooking other than yours, Holly. Was your turn, aye?" She set her items on the floor beneath her chair.

"I am happy about that, too. What is it?" Daisy squinted at the platter in the middle of the table.

Holly scoffed. "You would know if you would wear your spectacles."

Violet unfolded her napkin and placed it in her lap. "No more cooking for you, Daisy. You must be relieved. I know I am. You burned yourself too many times."

"I will bet you five dollars I am more relieved than either of you." Holly snorted.

Daisy shrugged. "Say what you will about my cooking. At least I am not a mean, nasty woman to everyone around me."

Holly jumped to her feet. "You take that back, you wretched girl."

"Girlies. Stifle it." Orla motioned Holly to sit. "If you can't be civil to each other, then return upstairs, and skip the meal. No one wishes to listen to squabbles whilst trying to enjoy their food, aye?"

Holly sat and snapped her napkin like a mouse trap. She reached for a biscuit from the platter.

"May we say grace first, Madam Rose?" Poppy steepled her fingers. "We ought to thank the good Lord for providing for us, don't you think?"

Holly guffawed. "You little innocent. As if God gives us anything in this den of iniquity. You can thank Him for yourself and leave me out of it."

"Well, I think it is a nice idea, Poppy." Violet stroked Poppy's braid.

"Seeing 'tis me own home I purchased with me own money, and you all agreed to stay here, 'tis me own word you must abide by. I say aye." Orla glared at Holly. "Should you ever have a place of your own, you can make the rules, aye?"

Holly folded her arms and sulked. "Yes, Madam Rose."

Orla looked to Poppy. "Go on." She crossed herself.

Poppy did the same and bowed her head. "Bless us, O Lord, for these Thy gifts, for which we are about to receive. Through Christ, our Lord. Amen."

"Didn't realize you're Catholic as well, Poppy. You said 'orphanage' and that could mean anything." Orla scooped some eggs from the rose patterned platter, then butter onto her plate and handed the little crock to Violet.

"We haven't had time to talk about everything." Poppy lifted the jar of jam and passed it to Orla. She forked a bit of egg onto her plate. "Oh, I forgot the plate of sausages."

Violet rose. "I will get them. Stay put."

Holly scoffed. "Forgot you cooked them? I mean, does anyone do that?"

Orla slapped the tabletop, and her fork slid off her plate. "Holly. One more rude remark to Poppy, and you ought to depart this house for Ma Brown's establishment. Do you grasp me meaning?"

Poppy gasped, and Holly bit her lip. "Yes, Madam Rose. Wait. How do you know about Ma Brown's? I ran away from her and came here, but I never told you that."

"Murphy and Nuala mentioned her."

Violet returned with the sausages, and nudged Daisy. "We know terrible things about that place, do we not? It is much better to be on the street." She grimaced.

Daisy spoke around her mouthful of sausage and waved her fork. "Oh, yes. We worked there. But when we arrived, the girls told us to run for our lives before Ma Brown saw us. They said she beats them, keeps their money, and makes them endure all sorts of evil treatment from the men. We stayed for a little while anyway, then left after a few months. Maybe she has a gun. Do you think that is true? They should have all pounced on her and locked her in the basement. Although someone could have gotten a broken leg. Or messed up their faces in the fight, then that would have done in their careers. Do you think they did not because she—"

"Stop that, Daisy. We'd be guessing at the goings on over there." Orla turned to Holly. "You would know, aye? Any of that true?"

Holly squirmed in her seat and shrugged. "Ma Brown is not a nice woman, but Daisy, you make her sound positively dreadful from your ramblings. I ran away for other reasons."

"It takes terrible things to make people run away from their homes." Poppy wagged her head.

Daisy poked Holly. "But her girls said those things to us, and why would they?"

Violet tapped her plate. "Speaking of not nice things. My new reticule is missing. Has anyone seen it lying around?"

"You, too?" Daisy leaned over the table to snatch the jam. "My pearl hair combs are lost. They were on my dresser, and now they are not."

Holly snorted. "You do not have pearl anything. Those were fake."

Daisy gasped. "You are what is fake. Acting as if you like Madam Rose, when you—"

"Girls." Orla rubbed her temples. "A cruel enough thing's been the morning after a sleepless night without these squabbles added to it. Nonetheless, I do wonder, where're all these missing valuables, aye? If a prank, 'tisn't funny."

Daisy giggled. "They grew legs and ran off like Holly."

"More childish insults." Holly pointed at Poppy. "Could be the new girl we barely know anything about."

Poppy dropped her teacup and spilled her coffee. The dark liquid spread across the tabletop, and everyone jumped up to avoid its advance in all directions. "I'm so sorry."

"I think that was a diversion." Holly scowled.

"You accused Poppy before. Why would she do that after finding a safe place, then get thrown out?" Violet snatched the apron, Orla grabbed a towel sack, and they daubed at the coffee while the others moved the dripping crockery to the sink.

After the brouhaha settled, Orla shooed the girls out, and hugged Poppy. "I'll not believe 'twas you are the cause of our angst. Some thievery, if that's what 'tis, began before you arrived, aye. Hoping 'tis a prank that'll end soon."

"I do, too. I'd never do such things to you." Poppy awkwardly rose with her cane.

Orla wiped her chair and sat. Poppy's shuffling around and clearing the scullery soothed her enough to help her think. Should she carry the cashbox around with her? No, store her cash in her room from now on. *Under the bed.* Gal would protect it.

She studied the pantry door. Should she order Gal to stay in the scullery all day? Or get another dog to guard the pantry? Gal would not like that. Have Poppy stand sentry by the pantry? *A bit cruel.* Put a lock on the pantry door. All the doors. *That'd do the trick.* Check if Poppy's cot will fit inside it and give her all the door keys as the official housekeeper. *That'll shut up Holly.* For nothing else would go missing or it should stop the prankster.

That afternoon, Orla stood in Nuala's mudroom. "Isn't it woefully unbelievable there could be disloyalty in me own home?"

"'Tis awful, me friend. Nevertheless, you've received your warnings. You aren't naïve 'bout the situation." Nuala patted her arm.

She sniffed. "True, and I'm thankful for this delightful distraction of another clothing barrel, nonetheless. 'Tis the third, aye? How many theatre troupes are going out of business these days?" Orla bent closer to the crumpled stash packed inside the wooden container. "Poor women. Hope they aren't being kicked out of vaudeville."

"You don't know anyone in vaudeville, do you? Why should you care?" Nuala selected a purple silk something and tugged.

Orla sniffed at a red lacy scarf, or sash. She was unsure. "I wonder at women having monumental dreams of being in vaudeville. Making their living. Mayhap I should've, aye? I'm drawn to these fancy gowns."

Nuala shook her head. "These aren't from vaudeville me thinks. For 'tis Father Furmanski himself who gives me these barrels. Donated by families, the theater, and various other businesses, he says."

A priest. At a church? No priest she ever knew got involved with such things as vaudeville or the theater. *Or a bordello. Could be the flabbergasting truth.* She snorted, and tossed a rather smelly, nasty undergarment on the floor. "Does he know that you give these clothes to me, a Madam?"

"Aye. Orla, help me drag the worktable into more light, aye? I'm having troubles seeing if these're wearable or old toss aways someone wished to be rid of." Nuala gripped the edge of the table and Orla helped drag it closer into the window light.

She straightened, and tipped the barrel while Nuala scooped out the garments. They spread the pile to the edges of the tabletop. "Let's sort it by type, aye?"

Nuala retrieved a few items that missed the table and landed on the floor. "Well, and Father Furmanski, says he takes what's needed from the donations, and a theater's rejections to distribute. I get the leftovers. The unsuitable ones. He doesn't care to know what you do with them. He trusts me with the gifting."

Orla held a dark green velvet gown against herself with one hand and smoothed it with her other. Such a lush fabric. No alterations needed that she could tell. "Would you look at this, now? Seems to be unworn. There're usually a few holes to patch."

"It's perfect for you, me friend. Would swallow me up. Too generous in the bosom." Nuala fingered the crushed material and frowned. "And why would a velvet dress be in a donations barrel? Seems nonsensical to me, aye?"

"Too good to be true, 'tis sure. Yet here it is. Up against me height with the perfect length to wear it as if I'd made it for meself." Joy bubbled inside her, and she grinned. "Such a lovely thing has never happened to me."

Nuala matched a pair of stockings and laughed. "See the color? 'Tis an early Christmas gift for sure."

"And from whom would it be? Not the priest." Orla twirled, watching the light play on the dark green velvet skirt as it flew. She giggled.

"Why 'twas God Himself, to be sure. Only He could do such a thing for you. He's got your exact size from creating you." Nuala dug through the pile on the table and squinted at a glittery piece of silver material. "What's this?"

Orla gently draped the sleeveless velvet gown over her arm. "Wish I could think of God the way that you do, me friend. He's never paid me any good attention for me entire life."

"Who else could do this for you?" Nuala shook out a slightly worn brown coat of an indeterminate size. "Is this a man's or a woman's?"

Was the pretty gown intentional? *Couldn't be.* There must be a worthy reason for believing in coincidences.

She shrugged and spread a blue ruffled bonnet on top of the stack to inspect it. "Nah, can't think of a whom. The girls will squeal when they see some of these boas and hats for sure. Oh, you gave me a brilliant idea. I'm wrapping these accessories up for Christmas gifts." Orla snagged a gold color veil for Daisy with green trim. "Let's make haste to set the prettiest things aside before the girls return from the market, shall we?"

Nuala clapped. "We shall. Clever me. I'll help you to hide them inside your wardrobe. Don't you just love Christmastime?"

CHAPTER 18

Cultivating Her Flowers

If we sneak, we'll mayhap catch someone up to no good
—Orla

he Flower Garden
December

CHRISTMAS MORNING ARRIVED A WEEK LATER, and after their usual daily rest, all the women donned their new items from the donation's barrel. *Didn't they sparkle and shine like multi-colored Christmas stars?* Red for Holly, gold for Daisy, blue for Poppy, and purple for Violet. More like precious Christmas gems. *And I'm the emerald.*

"Aren't you glad, girls, we agreed upon beautifying ourselves to welcome Christmas? Won't Nuala be surprised? She may jump from shock right out of her own frock when she sees us."

Daisy and Poppy giggled. But Holly sneered and curled her lip.

"Why should we care what Nuala thinks of us? She does not pay us anything for looking pretty. We missed our rest time. I do not see the reasoning to dress up in our finery and trudge through the snow and cold just to visit for afternoon and evening. That is what we are doing, right?"

Violet gave Holly a brief hug. "Don't spoil this for us with your prickly ways."

Holly shrugged off Violet's arm from her shoulders. "I am not. What time are we to arrive? Two o'clock, correct?" She twisted to inspect her skirt and picked at flecks only she noticed.

"Nuala is me best friend, and nothing's changed. Same time as I told you." Something was amiss about Holly lately. She was always tetchy, but she acted oddly when she was with everyone as well. *Why's that?* "You seem ungrateful for a chance to wear your Christmas gift."

"That is not it. I prefer to wait and wear it for the men." Allure altered Holly's expression, and she pursed her full lips.

Violet returned from staring at the sky through the front window. "Only clouds now, Madam. Friends are just as important as the men, Holly. Mrs. Kincaid has been very good to us. She had Janeen send Daisy and me here to The Flower Garden from off the streets and has given us food and clothing. You should also be thankful for a place to belong and celebrate. Especially at Christmastime."

Orla nodded. "'Tis the season of goodwill. Get your wraps and mittens, girls. Let's away."

They traipsed on the frozen street from The Flower Garden up to The White Feather with Daisy in last place behind them. She had yet to go near Poppy. *Time may change that.*

Although the wind was chill, it had blown a gap between storms, and any new snow held off its assault on the women. Orla wound her scarf tighter over her face. It was strange to not cover herself in public as in past times but memories of being ashamed came with the scarf's material against her scarred skin. "Me best gift this year was when you girls didn't think anything evil of me scars or me odd eyes. 'Tis the freest I've ever been in me entire life."

Holly huffed. "And the attentions of Murphy have not hurt you either. I have heard rumors about him in town. Some say he is an outlaw in hiding, or an escaped convict. No one knows much about him. He keeps secrets."

"You always have to ruin everything with your snide remarks." Violet patted Orla's arm. "Pay no attention to any rumors about him, Madam Muldoon."

Orla bent over with laughter. "Since the gossip mongers are all spreading their opinions, I'd think the law would be onto him. Besides, there's often a bit of truth to rumors."

Holly tipped up her nose and turned her face away.

Poppy stopped her slow struggle with her two new canes to adjust her too big, brown mittens Orla had lent to her. "The many rumors 'bout our orphanage were mostly true. Wished someone would've paid heed to them."

"'Tis an awful shame, that. Just where was this orphanage?"

"St. Paul."

Violet slowed her pace to match Poppy's. "Go ahead, we will catch up."

The White Feather wore dark green garlands on its porch rails, and a holly wreath on its front door. "So, the house expects us, and I expect your best behavior towards our hostess." Orla eyed Holly while she held the picket gate open for the girls. A few snowflakes drifted onto the ground.

"Of course." Holly shot her a quick glance as she passed.

There's not an of course hovering anywhere round that woman. Orla crossed the porch and awkwardly tapped Nuala's new, brass lion knocker with her bulky red mittens. "I hear footsteps. Look lively and appreciative."

The door swung open. *Murphy?*

The women froze in silence, along with Orla.

"Merry Christmas, ladies. Please enter." Murphy stepped aside and Nuala rushed up to the group wiping her hands on her cooking apron. Tantalizing aromas of turkey, potatoes, and gravy filled the entryway. Pumpkin pie spices alerted Orla that dessert was sure to follow.

"'Tis a happy surprise for you, me friend, aye?" Nuala's smile had doubt written across it.

"Aye. For you told me you'd no guests for Christmas." Orla stomped off snow, then swiped her booted feet against the wooden boot brush, and the girls followed her example. She slid her glance up to Murphy as she entered the house. His grin appeared mischievous. He always had the black stubble, but without it, he would resemble a gigantic innocent boy caught sneaking a piece of that pie from the windowsill.

Violet curtsied, Holly sneered, and Daisy stepped into the entry keeping her distance from Poppy. Everyone hung their wraps on the metal wall hooks in the entryway that The White Feather provided for the guests. Except, there were no other guests.

Dread, elation, and resolve swirled inside Orla's mind. *What trickery is Nuala up to?* "What's happened here?"

Nuala bit her lip. "He purchased all the rooms until New Year's Day. As you know, winter doesn't bring in many guests, if at all. I couldn't say no, aye? And why would I to such a lovely idea?"

Murphy waved the women further into the boardinghouse. "We've been planning this surprise for some time, haven't we, Nuala?"

"Aye." Nuala linked her arm through Orla's, and she squeezed it against herself. "I couldn't tell you. He made me swear upon me mam's grave."

He did? A collective gasp joined Orla's and filled the air around them, then an outburst of excited chatter from her girls.

Just inside the parlor, sat a highly polished pianoforte with a large, and wide red ribbon bow atop it.

"Nuala, what have you done?" Orla snapped her mouth shut, and her body quivered with overwhelm from such delight.

"Not your friend, beautiful. It is from me. You recall you said you wanted one on opening night for your business's entertainment?" Murphy grinned so wide she thought his gleaming, white teeth would fall out. "Here it is. I expect to see jolly evenings and much more dancing from now on."

Orla released Nuala's grip and reached for the nearest chair to lower her quaking body onto. "'Tis beyond anything I'd ever ask for, Murphy. I don't understand your reasoning for renting all The White Feather's rooms or for such an expensive gift."

Murphy winked. "Do you not? I will give you some time."

Holly smiled tightly and sauntered over to Orla. She bent beside her ear. "He was a scoundrel at Ma Brown's. Maybe he really is a bank robber." She turned her gaze to the joyous scene of the pianoforte inspection. "Such a happy day you will long remember, Madam Muldoon, when an outlaw fell in love with you."

* * *

A FEW MORE ITEMS DISAPPEARED IN the following months, without a clue as to who or where. *Nuala's warning could be valid.* Ma Brown may be the one behind all the thieveries in Orla's home, although it sounded outlandish. Nuala said Brown was in love with Murphy, from the rumors her friend overheard in town. Did Murphy return Ma Brown's affections?

She bit her lip. With her suspicions about a sneak thief in the house, and Holly's accusations against Poppy, she must devise a way to form some unity and sisterhood between her girls. Then they could withstand any attacks from Ma Brown. But what? "We'll not survive this tumult. Shall I not take care of this, Gal?"

With his head on her lap, she scratched her companion between his pointed ears, and he whined.

"I know what time 'tis. You're an eager creature this morning. The sun's not yet above the horizon. Give me a few moments to think before we head down to the scullery." She braced her back against the iron headboard and placed her elbows on her bent knees. What could she possibly do with the girls to get them to trust and lookout for each other? Especially the most vulnerable one. *Sweet Poppy.*

The Shepherd climbed onto the bed beside her, with his eyes fixed on her face.

"Ah. No, you don't. Off. You're not allowed up here. Down. Now, sit, Gal. So, mayhap you can tell me this. What makes you want to be close to me, eh? To protect me? The food?"

Gal tipped his head sideways and licked his chops.

"That's aye to the food. How 'bout the warm lodgings?"

His ears twitched, and he huffed.

"Another aye. Well, the girls have all these things from me as well, aye? There's too much bickering amongst them. And pilfering. They must need something more." What else is there? She had Cousin Tarah back home, who was already family, and they had been close since young girls. Could she foster in her girlies how she had felt toward her friend Allana during their garrison work? That friendship formed by ministering to each other's deeper emotional needs for survival in a perilous man's world.

Gal brushed his front paw against her quilt and whined.

"You're saying I've thought enough, aye? Let's away then." She scooted off the mattress and slipped her blue robe on over her night-dress. Once her slippers fit snuggly, she met Gal at the bedroom door. "Hold. We must listen."

The house lay hushed. She cracked open the door, and a faint metallic sound clinked from downstairs. "With me, Gal. We'll go quietly. We'll mayhap catch someone up to no good."

They slowly stepped together out of her room, to the top of the stairs, then down each step. She halted at creaky step number seven and stepped over it. Gal's weight didn't budge it, and halted at step three for the same reason and avoided that. Another muted sound echoed from within the scullery. *Hoping 'tis Poppy fixing us an early breakfast.*

She gave Gal the hand signal to lie down with her palm faced down and tiptoed to the scullery's entrance. Orla kept out of sight to the side of it and peered around the wall. "Holly?"

Holly startled and dropped whatever was in her hand onto the table. It clattered to the floor. She bent to retrieve it. "Oh, my. Madam Rose, you gave me a fright." She held her empty hand over her heart and slid the object into her skirt's pocket with the other.

"Aye. Saw your fright and more. Tis sure you're surprised to see me. What's all this?" Orla studied the items spread out on a flour sack on the tabletop while she drew nearer. A knife, a measuring cup, a silver spoon, two candles, and a bag of coffee beans.

Holly's hands shook. She hid them behind her back, then shrugged. "I was helping Poppy. With her inventory. Thought I could make it up to her for injuring her feelings earlier. You always tell me I am prickly with her."

She would believe Holly if she was not a selfish sort. Holly would do nothing that did not benefit her in some way, would she? "And where's the household ledger to check her list? Don't see it here." Orla supported her point by twisting around and surveying the room.

"Must have carelessly left it on your desk. Silly me." Holly's red nightgown swished with her hurried steps across the scullery, and she sidestepped the dog to fetch the ledger. Gal growled as she passed him.

He's certainly a clever dog. Senses things I never do. "Gal, by me." From Holly's stony expression, when she returned to the table of items with the ledger and a pencil, Orla knew she would not get more information. She would bide her time. There would be a better way to deal with Holly someday.

"Here." Holly scribbled on the list while Orla studied her. Holly gathered her composure enough behind her wall of snobbishness mortared with her air of superiority. Her chin raised, her eyes flashed a challenge at Orla, and her movements were quick when she snapped the pencil down. She crossed her arms.

Orla sniffed. "Poppy shall surely appreciate your hard work on her behalf. Well, now—"

"I heard my name. Is everything alright? Did I oversleep?" Poppy poked her auburn head out of the pantry where her small sleeping cot barely fit, and she yawned. "I was so tired from going to the market yesterday. I'm sorry."

Holly snickered, then slid a side glance at Orla. "We all get tired sometimes."

"Morning, Poppy. Holly here had a thought in her head to be helpful to you and make amends for her rude behavior by doing some inventory. See? So considerate, aye?" Orla selected the measuring cup and inspected it.

"Yes, it is. But I don't need my utensils counted. And there're only two bags of beans. All the same, thank you. Your help is nice."

Orla glanced up at Holly. "Wasn't it? Was very sisterly. I like that."

Poppy smiled and blinked at them. "Well, I'd best get to making the coffee, and cooking us some eggs. Is anyone else awake?" She hobbled to the stove with her two canes.

"Only the three of us." Orla plunked the cup back in its place on the flour sack. "Holly volunteered to crack the eggs for you. She wants to help you, she said. Such a surprise, aye? When the others are up, I'm calling a meeting. Got some things to discuss 'bout our pasts and futures here at The Flower Garden."

A fleeting flash of apprehension in Holly's eyes convinced Orla she was rightly suspicious of her. Holly lowered her gaze to the floor. *Now, how to catch the little minx.*

With breakfast cooked and served, their plates emptied, and cleanup completed, Orla scooted her chair and stood. *Time to toss me idea into the waters.* "Well, now, as I told Holly and Poppy before you all came downstairs, I've a few thoughts for how we shall become a family. I don't wish to have a cold, hard business only earning our coin. Let's warm up our world with sisterly affection and protection."

Holly coughed or choked, Poppy smiled widely, while Daisy and Violet blinked rapidly with their eyebrows lifted.

Violet slid her chair back and went around the table to hug Orla. "Thank you for that, Madam Rose. I think this is a positively wonderful idea. I would love to think of us as a family. We are already working and living together, are we not? Bravo."

Poppy glanced around the table and giggled. "I'd love for you all to be my family. I've never had one, and you can show me what it's like."

"Silly girl. Families are not always a nice thing to have." Holly scowled but quickly changed her expression. "I mean, they can be . . . disappointing and have many problems that never get ironed out."

Daisy squinted at Orla. "I wonder what made you decide this thing, Madam Rose. You do not want us to be a business anymore? Is it not going well?"

"Not wearing your spectacles also affects your hearing, hazy Daisy. She just said why. To cling together in a man's world." Holly smirked. "As if it would help us."

Violet returned to her chair. "I think it is a splendid idea. We are not in competition here. We all have our own customers, agreed? But we could share everything else."

"I do not get it." Daisy frowned. "I have nothing to share. No one can wear my gowns or my slippers. Holly is too thin, and Violet, you are too tall. My bosom is too big for all of you, except Madam Rose, and I have dainty feet. Oh, I guess I could share my feather boa and hair ribbons. And jewelry. But not my hats. Jane at Quigley's Pub told me you can get lice from other people's hats, and I do not know about you, but that is not something—"

"Not what I was referring to by sharing, Daisy, me girlie." Orla shook her head and chuckled.

"Then what do you mean?"

"Follow me into the parlor. We'll take a few moments to plan our teaching courses." Madam Rose led them to the more comfortable seating area.

Everyone chose their places and settled with a variety of expressions on their faces. Holly was the one Orla monitored. She daily challenged Madam Rose the most and was the most guarded. Maybe her behavior would belie her words?

"Well, now." Madam Rose shifted on the settee. "Here's me thought. We can teach each other some skills to better ourselves. We can meet once per week, on Monday."

"My goodness. Will this be like your House Rules, Madam Rose?

You had so many I finally had to write them down to remember them all." Daisy clamped her hands over her pale blonde head. "Gave me quite a headache, I assure you."

Poppy giggled.

"What is so funny? You and your customers do not have to abide by them. Oh, my apologies. You have no customers." Daisy looked to Madam Rose with a confused expression.

Madam Rose sighed and drummed her fingertips on the back of the settee. "Nah, Daisy, and to the rest of you. Not like me House Rules. These things will be for our own enjoyment and betterment. Not to keep unruly men in check. Holly, you appear to be unconvinced 'bout me plan. You got a question for me?"

Holly curled her upper lip. "Really, Madam, I see no use for this sort of thing. I am not interested in creating a happy family here. It is the work I want. Nothing more."

"I see. Forgot to tell you girlies. This is not up for negotiation. If you wish to remain here with me, you'll be doing our tasks together. Meant to mention this as well, that we'll be sharing bits of our pasts on Monday afternoons to better understand each other. I'm sure there's plenty we don't know, aye?" Madam Rose impaled Holly with her stare.

* * *

ON A MONDAY AFTERNOON IN MID-APRIL, Violet laid out supplies on the dining table to show them how to make paper doll chains to decorate their bedrooms. She insisted it was a sisterly thing to do.

Orla frowned. "Never did this with me sister, nevertheless, as you wish." She monitored how Violet cut a piece of smaller paper and folded it like an accordion before she cut the shape of a girl.

Daisy hunched over her newspaper, scrunching up her face to better see her pencil mark, then cut her folded layers of paper. She snipped her fingertip. "Ow!"

Violet quickly grabbed a flour sack towel and dampened it with water. "Here, hold it against your wound. Then go get your spectacles,

Daisy. This kind of work takes good eyesight. You must wear them when I teach everyone sewing basics as well."

"She is too vain." Holly snorted.

"My spectacles worked at first, but not anymore. They are useless at doing anything like sewing or reading. My friend Penny says—"

"I'm very excited to learn to sew. Oh, look. How lovely." Poppy's face beamed as she raised her doll and carefully tugged it open to reveal girls holding hands. "I'll keep it in my pantry. Thank you, sister Violet. I'm so glad you showed us how to do this."

Holly tossed her dolls to the side. "Not bad."

Orla studied her prickly girlie. Still no new clues from Holly. Nothing had gone missing for a few weeks now. There must be more behind the thefts. "Girlies, when Daisy returns, meet me in the parlor for our visit. Gal, with me."

He shadowed her as she left the scullery.

"You're me best friend and comfort, Gal. These girls only have each other, for I have you, aye?"

The girls filed into the room a few minutes later and chose their seats. They did not appear eager, although Holly, being typically churlish, dragged her feet and rolled her eyes. *Not a surprise.* Neither was Gal's low growl as Holly entered the room.

Madam Rose smiled at her girlies. "Well, today went grand, aye? Violet taught you something you hadn't done beforehand. She's asked permission to teach the simple basics of sewing as well. Me mam taught me and me sister, Kathleen, God rest her soul." She crossed herself.

Daisy sucked on her injured finger. "May I skip learning to sew, Madam Rose? It does not interest me at all. Neither does wearing my spectacles." She shot a glance at Holly.

"Hm. To continue abiding here in me home, you must learn a sisterly task. Anyone have a suggestion for Daisy?"

Poppy perked up. "I know, I can teach everyone some basic cooking, if you don't already know how. What do you think, Daisy?"

Daisy shook her head. "I know that already. Madam said to learn something new. Right, Madam Rose? It must be something we do not have a skill for yet?"

Holly flipped her long, freshly washed black locks behind her back, and leaned against her chair's cushion. "You surely do not know how to dance. My toes still throb from several nights ago."

"That's the thing, then. Holly, you'll teach Daisy to dance." Madam Rose almost laughed at Holly's incredulous expression. "And whoever wishes to learn that skill. Dancing with Holly is next for us, then some cooking with Poppy, and we'll sew or craft with Violet. Glad that's all set. Now to have a chat 'bout our pasts."

Everyone groaned but Poppy. She had already told her horrifying story.

Holly sneered and picked at her fingernail. "I would like to know why you are in this trade, Violet, if you can sew expertly? Would not a seamstress be a good fit for you?"

'Tis always a snide comment from that creature. "That's a very fine question to begin our sisterly exploration into our pasts. What say you to that, Violet?" Madam Rose nodded.

Violet inhaled deeply and focused her attention on the floor. "I actually was an assistant seamstress, before certain things happened that upheaved my life. Those things were part of my own making several years ago. You see, I was seventeen and naïve. A charming married man promised to leave his wife for me. He was a friend of my father's and lied about me seducing him. It was unwise for me to believe the man and devastating for so many others. I have two younger sisters and a brother, but my family disowned me and threw me out on the street." She swiped at a tear.

Orla clenched her jaw. "I know a thing or two 'bout family disowning their own. Only me brother, Mick, speaks to me. Others turned against me, and don't answer me letters. Anyone else suffering from this?"

Daisy gave Violet a sorrowful expression, then shook her head.

"Then tell us your story, Holly." Madam Rose leaned sideways to face her directly.

Holly shrugged. "What do you want to know?"

"How did you come to be in the trade? I promise to tell you me own past afterwards."

"My story is not like Poppy's or Violet's. I do not know yours and Daisy's yet." She stared into the distance. "When I was thirteen, I discovered men take what they desire. Saying no does not stop them. Later, I recognized the power I had over men, and I make them pay for what they want. That is it. Men are easily manipulated. Women are easily fooled."

Orla's ears rang with the silence in the room. What should she say to this horrible story and this cynical, wounded woman? Had she not felt the same with her dragon lieutenant?

Daisy clucked her tongue. "My goodness. That is a sad way to look at the world. So far, I have the best story. I simply enjoy my work. It pays well. I do not need to worry about wearing my spectacles, and I do not have to read. I could not be a teacher or a nurse with my poor eyesight. Someone may want to marry me, but I do not know if that will happen. You may be right, Holly, because Betty said that men usually want to use women and not marry—"

"Ho there, girlie. You can't count on something other working girls say. Betty's only speaking from her own experience. Having our dreams to keep us going in a cruel world is a hope we all need. Aye?" Madam Rose stood and paced the parlor.

Holly guffawed. "Wait. Madam Rose, you dream of marrying? You really do? That is the funniest thing. You think Murphy would marry you—a madam in the trade? Ma Brown was right. You are in love with him." She laughed so hard she bent over and landed on the settee.

"That is not unusual, Holly." Gentle Violet nearly yelled at her. "You are being quite rude to Madam Rose. Ruder than normal for you."

Ma Brown? A painful sword of betrayal pierced Orla's soul. Was that Holly creature in her home as a spy and a thief? *Worse, am I in love with Murphy?*

Daisy stood and stroked Orla's shoulder. "We all have dreams, Madam. Mine is to have my own place of business one day. Jane says it is a good idea—"

"I understand that dream, girlie." Madam Rose swallowed hard. "Time to get on with the rest of our day. Gal, with me. What'll the rest of you be doing?"

Holly dabbed at her cheeks. "I have an errand to do."

"I will go with you." Daisy turned toward the entryway.

"Not this time. It is a private matter. Maybe the next time?" Holly sidled past Madam Rose and Daisy and glanced back at Poppy. "Although, you can count me for supper."

What are you up to, sly Holly?

CHAPTER 19

Her Impossible Problem

I'll not tolerate you berating me dog
Orla

The front door shut behind Holly, and Madam Rose peered into the parlor entrance. She hurried to the window and wiped the condensation from it to be certain Holly travelled into town. She cupped her icy hands to blow warm breath on them and spun to the other girlies as they approached together. "Make haste. Go upstairs to Holly's room."

"Why?" Violet grasped the banister railing as she turned to Madam Rose.

"We've got some searching to do, that's what." Orla turned to Poppy. "We'll get you a chair to block the bottom of the staircase and you be our lookout, aye? Should our Holly return before we're back downstairs, yell a hallo to her so that we can hear you, aye? Gal, by Poppy."

Poppy nodded, and Gal sat beside her feet waiting. "I could polish the rails. Someone bring me a cloth?"

Daisy carried a chair from the scullery and a rag then placed the seat in position for Poppy. "I cannot imagine what you want us to look for in Holly's room, Madam Rose. That is her private space, after all. Are we not to respect—"

"You'll get your answer why when we find what I'm looking for. Let's make haste."

The women searched through Holly's wardrobe and dresser but found none of the missing items.

Orla chewed on her lower lip. "Did anyone look under her bed?"

"I will." Violet got down on her hands and knees. "Daisy, can you please fetch one of Poppy's canes for me? I see something in the shadows, but it is too far back against the wall."

With Poppy's cane, Violet prodded and grunted, until she tugged out three large and full flour sacks from beneath Holly's bed. She stared up at Orla. "Oh dear, Madam Muldoon."

"Open them." Orla's heart raced. She did not wish to be right about this.

While Violet opened each sack, Daisy drew close to see their contents. "Everything is here, Madam. Even I can see that. The now spoiled food, and our things. What will you do?"

"That's the question." Orla sat on Holly's bed.

"What are you all doing in my room?" Holly screeched and rushed inside her room. "You . . . you have found . . . my—"

"Ours. Our belongings, you mean, aye?" Madam Muldoon scowled and stood, gripping her waist. "I want, nay, I demand, your explanation. I've guessed much of the goings on. Nevertheless, why did Ma Brown send you, and what've you told her? There's no escaping me wrath, or your room until you confess."

Holly knelt on the floor beside her stolen stash. "I did not do this. Someone must have hidden these things beneath my bed. Why would I behave in such a vulgar way?"

"You can't deny your activities with this evidence before us. Can she, girlies?"

They agreed. Violet shook her head, and her violet-blue eyes sparkled with tears. "We trusted you, Holly. We thought it was a thief from outside our family."

Holly scoffed and scrambled to her feet. "We have called this . . . group of misfits a family for two weeks, and now it is suddenly true?"

Daisy slid behind Violet. "Why did you do it, Holly? We have been good to you.'

"I said it was not me." Holly screamed until her face reddened.

Gal growled and barked at her.

"And that dog. That horrible dog—"

"Enough, Holly. I'll not tolerate you berating me dog. Don't you dare. He's known who you are this entire time, and I've not accepted it. Know this. I'll find out the truth, whatever you may say, or I may not be called Madam Rose Muldoon any longer." Orla stood chest to face with her nemesis.

Holly crumpled to the floor and sobbed. "She forced me. She owed me money. From the days I was in her employ. She kept it. I need it. Do you understand?"

Violet frowned and tugged Daisy from behind her back. "We understand. She is a terrible person. But Holly, you became no better than her by betraying us and Madam Muldoon. We are taken good care of here, and you took advantage of her good heart. That is very shameful. I think you should leave."

Holly sniffed and grabbed the stolen scarf to wipe her face and blow her nose.

"Hey, that is mine. Oh, do not do that." Daisy huffed. "I also think you should leave. Why Penny told me how a working girl burned her madam's house to the ground, because—"

"Please do not throw me out." Holly wrung Daisy's scarf.

Only Holly would look prettier with tears. "What do you think, me girlies? 'Tis America. Let's take a vote. Ah, we need our Poppy. She's our sister as well." Madam Rose Muldoon headed out of Holly's room to the landing at the top of the staircase and bent over the balustrade to check on Poppy.

"Dearest Poppy, are you awake? Holly came up. She got past you somehow."

She leaned back and stared up at Orla. "Oh my goodness. I did fall asleep and awoke when Gal growled, but I didn't know it was because of Holly. He wouldn't leave my side, but I'm so sorry, Madam." Poppy collected her canes.

"Never mind that. We need your vote, so give a listen. Holly's been the thief in our midst. Shall we throw her out or keep her in our family?" Madam Muldoon turned around at the footsteps behind her. The girls waited at the balustrade, except for Holly.

"Come stand before your judges, girl. Give your plea and what you have to say, for we determine your future, aye?" Madam Muldoon gazed at Violet and Daisy as they huddled and whispered together.

Holly slowly emerged disheveled and contrite. She stood by her doorway with folded hands. "All I can say is . . . I allowed myself to be under Ma Brown's influence for selfish reasons. Please let me stay . . . I promise to never steal from you again." She wiped her cheeks with the back of her hand and bowed her head.

Madam Muldoon pursed her lips. Having been caught, would that creature dare to lie now? "Was your vile behavior only to do with stealing, or did you pass messages to her as well? What's her plan?"

"I think she wants to put you out of business. You, we, have become her competition—"

"Ha! There're at least twenty other brothels in town. She's in Duluth. Try telling me the truth again, or you're out on your rump." Madam Muldoon stepped toward Holly.

Daisy clung to Violet's arm, and Violet scowled. "Dear me, we have a chance to save you right now. Better give us the true story, Holly. It is your only chance. Unless you wish to return to Ma Brown?"

Holly recoiled, then tipped her chin up. "No. I never want to go back. Please Madam Rose, it might not make sense to you but the only truth I know is how Ma Brown feels about you, which is threatened. She asked me to report back to her how many times Murphy visits here. If I were to guess, without her saying so, I believe she wants him for herself. She must."

"Murphy? She sees meself as competition for him and not me business? Well, I like that. 'Tis insulting." Madam Muldoon kicked at the doorframe with her toes, then turned to face her girlies.

Poppy called out from below. "I could hear all that Holly said. Are we voting yet?"

Daisy released Violet's arm. "You have not said you are sorry for any of it, Holly. Being defiant does not help your cause. You stole several things from me. My ribbons, my scarf—"

"Yes, yes, Daisy. I am very sorry. To all of you. I only did what Ma forced me to. I will not do it again." Holly faced Madam Muldoon. "Madam Rose, since you all found me out, I have lost my money. She cannot make me do anything for her again. Do you see?"

Madam Muldoon stared at Violet. "What're your thoughts? Shall we throw her out? I've a mind to do so, nonetheless, you know how that feels. You've more of a good heart than me."

Violet slowly wagged her head, then studied Holly. "No one should suffer that degrading harm of being thrown out for doing something they are forced to do by another. I vote no."

"I vote with Violet that Holly stays." Daisy smiled slightly in Holly's direction.

"How do you vote, my dear Poppy? You're the one Holly accused of thievery. You've the deciding yeah or nay in this. I trust you and the other girlies to do what's right." Madam Muldoon scrutinized Holly's expression for signs deception. Fear was foremost.

Scraping sounds echoed from below, then a few thumps on the stairs. Poppy climbed up to poke her auburn head and delicate face above the landing. She puffed out a few breaths. "It's only right to address Holly when I say this. You made me so upset when you told everyone I stole from them, especially from our dear Madam Rose. Nevertheless, forgiveness is what God would want. I vote with Violet, because she's the wisest person I know. Our Madam Rose Muldoon has a right to feel as she does about you. But you've a chance to stay with us and change your ways."

Madam Muldoon turned to Holly. "There we have it. You're staying. I'm watching you, nevertheless. One more thing like lying to me, and I don't care what the girls think, you're out of me home, aye? Now, I'm away to visit Nuala and process what this kerfuffle."

The three girls murmured together, as Orla descended the steps toward Poppy. "Need some aid, there? Getting down is worse than up." Orla slid her arms under the girl's armpits and helped her to the bottom of the staircase. Flashes of helping her auntie Mary tugged at her heart.

At the base of the stairs, Poppy raised her face to Orla. "I hope you aren't upset by my vote, Madam Rose. I just don't wish the streets on anyone, and God forgives us so many things—"

"Nah." Orla stroked Poppy's hair. "I expected no less than mercy from you. Rest awhile. The girlies are busy upstairs, and I'm away to Nuala's for a breath of air."

A large cart was parked outside of The White Feather. She should turn back home. "Hm. Nevertheless, I must speak to Nuala 'bout the happenings." She strolled ahead and tapped the knocker.

Footsteps, then the door swung open. "Orla, good gracious. I didn't expect you. 'Tis fortuitous for you to visit today. Come in."

Orla wiped her shoes on the mat and entered. "Desperate to get away. Why is it fortuitous?" Low voices murmured from the dining area.

"Well, the boarders have just finished a late luncheon, and Father Furmanski is here from Duluth. He was called away to see a local parishioner but shall return later. Would you like a cup of tea?" Nuala entered the scullery, and situated two chairs for them as she usually did for their visits. She checked the kettle and added more water to it.

"Never met him yet. All those clothes he's given us. Shall he wish to meet someone like me?" Orla selected a chair.

"He's met someone like you. Me." Nuala laughed and sat across from her friend.

Orla smirked. "Not exactly."

Nuala leaned onto her elbows. "Very similar. You're subdued today. What's amiss?"

"Well, it began as a grand day. Ended with a vote on whether to throw Holly out on her backside or let her stay. She's the one who's been thieving." Orla rubbed her face and sighed.

"What? One of your own girlies? Never say so." Nuala squeezed Orla's arm.

"Now that I'm here, I can't find it within meself to speak more of it. Do you have any news for me?" Orla rested her hands on the low counter.

"I do. Me own Janeen and a regular boarder from way back have fallen in love. They're to be married. Isn't that such a tender thing?"

Orla's heart constricted. "Ah. Good news. Marriage. Who's the man?"

Nuala smiled. "'Tisn't your Murphy, me friend. He's the widower who owns the mercantile, Mr. Savage." She rose to attend to the whistling kettle, then gathered two cups, and a plate of fresh biscuits.

"We're settling in for a coze, then?" Orla added milk to her coffee and stirred. "Well, 'bout the subject of marriage, that's one thing to discuss, aye. It came up today. Holly said Ma Brown is jealous of meself. Ha! Not of me thriving business, but of me link to Murphy and his visits. Don't know what to think of that."

"'Bout marriage? Or Ma Brown, or Murphy?" Nuala blew on her steaming tea.

"All of it. Unexpected news. Confused me altogether. The events of the day threw me head into a spin, so I came here to think it over." Orla selected a biscuit and dunked it, splashing coffee into the saucer.

Nuala blew out a long breath. "Mayhap 'tis time to face yourself. What do you wish to have happen? What worries you the most? Ma Brown's vile angst, or Murphy rejecting you, or betrayal by your Holly? Begin with that."

Muffled sounds came from near the entry door, then a tap with the knocker. "Pardon me a moment, me friend. I like to keep the door locked." She hurried away. "Ah, Father Furmanski, you're in time for coffee with us."

'Tis all me day needs. To meet a priest. Orla shoved her chair back and

readied to make her escape while the door was open. She could slip out quickly and avoid more conflict.

Nuala and the priest met her in the entryway. "Orla, where are you away to? You've only just arrived, and Father has—"

"Sad, I know, nonetheless, I recalled something I must do." *Hide.*

"I insist you stay for a moment. Father Furmanski has brought another barrel of clothes from Duluth. We can sort through it as always, and you can take what you wish back home. 'Tis good luck all around. An answer to me prayers." Nuala grinned widely and her eyes sparkled. *Must remember to tell her not to pray for me.*

"Miss Muldoon, I am happy to meet you. Your friend has told me many things about you." He smiled and nodded toward Nuala. *Holy angels, must I go to Confession?*

Another clack of the knocker, and Nuala unlatched the lock to answer. "Good heavens. 'Tis like a train station here today. Oh, what fun is this? Your girlies are here, Orla."

In stepped Violet, Daisy, and Holly herself. Their smiles disappeared with the shock of seeing a priest in their midst. Orla could not restrain her chuckle at their discomfort. At least she was not alone in her unease.

Nuala clapped her hands, then headed to the scullery. "Well, now, everyone, go to the dining room where there're more chairs for all of us, and we'll partake of afternoon coffee together. Give me a moment."

"Ladies." Father Furmanski bowed and waved them ahead. *Never been called a 'lady' before, especially be a priest.* This curious event may be worth the time and highly entertaining after all.

They filed into the dining room and selected their seats.

Orla took the one furthest from the priest, but he suddenly stopped to gaze out the front window through the wide doorframe of the dining area. "Ah, I see help has arrived." He returned to the entry and exited The White Feather.

She followed and stared outside. Two young men she vaguely recognized from The Swimming Mermaid greeted the priest beside the cart and helped unload two barrels. They rolled them toward

Nuala's door. Orla scurried to the dining table to avoid being caught spying.

Violet raised her brows. "Madam Rose—"

Orla vehemently wagged her head. "Don't call me that in front of the priest, for heaven's sake."

Daisy's mouth hung open. "What are we supposed to call you? Will 'Rose' work? Or does he know your name is Orla? You are the only person I know with three names. I think we should always—"

"Miss Muldoon. He knows me by that. Now, why're you all here? Has something happened to Poppy? Nah, you're all too calm for that."

Holly cleared her throat. "We—I, *er* all of us, are concerned for you. From all that we had to endure earlier. About me."

Nuala carried the tray of drink items and set it in the center between the women. "Serve yourself whilst I check on the men. Isn't it exciting? We'll go through the clothing donations all together." She hurried out of the dining room.

"'Tis 'bout as exciting as Christmas, no doubt. You're here at the exact moment of discovery that Nuala and I share each time we open a delivery. Now 'tis your turn to enjoy it." She scanned her girlies' confused expressions. "The barrels of costumes."

They chimed their excitement and finished serving themselves.

Deep voices drew nearer, with thumps of the rolling barrels. Father Furmanski asked Nuala where to place them.

When the girlies started to rise, Orla waved them back. "Hold your curiosity until they've delivered and left. Manners dictate you take your afternoon coffee from our hostess before opening the barrels of clothes. Aye?"

The priest led the two men into the dining room. "We've situated your containers where you said to, Mrs. Kincaid. These men are Mr. Joe Flanagan, and Mr. Joe Black. I hitched passage on a barge from Duluth."

"Thank you for bringing these to us. I know Father has a few parishioners in town who required his aid as well. And would you take coffee with us?" Nuala reached for the tray.

Joe Black, the one with a smashed and crooked nose, stepped back.

"Nay to that. I have someone to meet later." He flicked his dark gaze at Orla, then to Holly, and flushed. *What's this 'bout?*

Mr. Flanagan grinned and shook his head. "Aye, we've elsewhere to drink. Father, we'll take the cart and await you at The Swimming Mermaid, for 'tis the nearest pub to The White Feather. I'm needing to leave within the hour, if you will accompany me then." He bowed.

"Meet up with you soon, Mr. Flanagan." Father nodded.

Nuala escorted the two men to her front door, then latched it again. "Well, now, I'm thinking our coffee is cold. Is it?" She took her seat and cupped the pot. "Seems warm enough."

Orla gathered her courage. "Oh, Father Furmanski, Mr. Black seemed familiar. Should I know him? He doesn't live in town, does he?"

The priest returned his cup back into its saucer. "He is from Duluth. He has been in a few boxing matches here on a Friday evening, although I doubt you have attended those." *Not I.*

Daisy leaned forward over the tabletop. "Is that why his nose is all mashed and misshapen? I knew a boxer once, and his was nearly flat. He also had whirly things for ears—"

Violet elbowed her. "Daisy, drink your tea."

Father Furmanski chuckled. "Boxing is a brutal sport. An Irish friend of mine once said, 'Many a man's nose is broken by his mouth.' A man does not need to be a boxer for that to happen."

"Oh, did you read that in the Bible?" Daisy's eyes widened. "Did Jesus say that? I heard He is very wise."

"Not in the Bible, Miss. Although, it could be for the truth of it. It is an old Irish proverb."

Keep him talking, Daisy. Turn his attention away from meself. She might survive this encounter with a man of God after all. Orla slowly drank her tea.

Daisy turned to Holly. "I have not seen him before, but Mr. Black seemed to know you. Has he visited us, and I missed seeing him? I can understand how that could happen with Violet's, or mine, plus your customers traipsing back and forth all over the—"

Holly must have kicked Daisy because she jumped in her seat and dropped her half-eaten biscuit. "Do not bore the priest, Daisy, with your ramblings. And no, I do not know him."

Nuala stood. "Our coffee was lukewarm. Can I get anyone more that's hot this go round?"

"Not for me, Mrs. Kincaid. No need to fuss. I shall head to the Mermaid. Hope to see you young women on another delivery trip. One day soon, the Church may build one on Whiskey Row, and I will expect to see you in attendance." He wiggled his eyebrows as he rose from his seat. *Witty fella.*

"Farewell Father Furmanski." Violet and Daisy spoke together.

"I will see you the next time." The priest bowed and smiled at everyone.

"Let me escort you." Nuala joined him as he departed.

After Nuala returned, Orla and her girls helped clear the tea items to place in the scullery, and ready the wide worktable for the clothing selection. Nuala took an apron off its hook and handed another to Orla. "Time to open the barrels and sort through the clothes."

The girls giggled. They shoved the chairs aside from the table and chattered about who got the first pick. They agreed Violet earned it because of her wisdom regarding Holly.

Nuala used a small crowbar as always to pop open the first barrel. Orla gripped the edge to tip the barrel halfway over, when something sprang out of it toward her hand, barely missing it as she jerked it away. The barrel clunked against the floorboards and rolled to the side. A snake slithered out onto the floor, and aimed its triangular head at her, but she snatched a chair to defend herself. It struck the chair leg with its fangs. "Holy heavens. Save me!"

Her girls' terrified screams gave her an earache, but she focused on the snake's whereabouts. It slithered underneath the spilled clothing. Then she noticed several gray critters scattering across Nuala's floor. "Mice."

If the screams were loud enough before to shake down the roof, they grew deafening as the women scrambled to get out of the dreadful invaders' reach and onto the furniture.

Orla climbed on top of her chair.

Someone pounded on the front door. The girls clung to each other, and Nuala yelled she could not answer it.

"Aye, everyone, stay above the floor. Don't get down. Nuala, keep an eye on the snake." Orla was nearest the scullery counter beneath the window. She stretched out and scrambled onto it to peer outside. Lake. Trees. Someone rushed past toward the rear door. "Father, wait!"

The rear door unlatched, and it swung outward.

"Stay back, Father, there's a viper in the scullery." Orla's heart raced and perspiration dripped down her neck. *Keep the man of God safe.*

Nuala yelled. "Grab the shovel, Father! Under the window. Grab It."

He shut the door, appeared in view of the rear window, and disappeared again. The door slowly swung open. Furmanski raised the shovel above his head. "Where is it, do you know?"

"There." Nuala pointed at a mound of shifting clothes. *Holy angels.*

Furmanski whacked the mound with two powerful swings, and everyone screamed again. The mound stilled, but several mice skittered past the priest's feet and outside. "What was that? You have mice as well?"

Holly sobbed, covered her face, and sank flat onto the tabletop.

A chill ran up Orla's neck. *This is bad.* Did Holly play a part in this ruckus?

Father Furmanski pushed the mound of clothes aside with the shovel's tip and revealed the smashed snake beneath it. He scratched his head. "Dead now. It is a puzzling affair. I am certain that snakes hibernate, and it is not warm enough yet. Am I right? How did it get inside Miss Orphelia Black's barrel? And the mice? It is the first time I accepted a barrel from her. I feel terrible that your clothing is ruined, and that unbeknownst to me, I brought danger into your home, Mrs. Kincaid."

Orla slid from the counter and glared at Holly. "Mayhap 'twas unbeknownst to yourself, nonetheless, wasn't a surprise to everyone here. Father, you go on your errand, aye? We'll take care of the rest of this hullaballoo."

Holly sniffed, and wiped her face, while she waited for Furmanski to depart. "Madam Rose, you need to know that Orphelia Black is Ma Brown. One and the same. Joe Black is her son. I recall seeing him a few times when I worked for her, but I swear I knew nothing about this terrible scheme. Do you believe me?"

"Belief is difficult enough, nonetheless, trust is a more fragile thing." Would believing Holly's story make her, Madam Rose Muldoon, as naïve as a child? Could she keep this ragtag family together with her own trust in them? *Well, now this would be a perfect time for an omniscient, omnipotent, and omnipresent God to show up and say something.*

CHAPTER 20

Vanquishing Her Bullies

Survival is our fiercest battle
Orla

 he White Feather

ORLA TURNED TO NUALA. "May we sit once again? We girlies need to chat 'bout this horrific affair."

"You may all stay, 'tis sure." She chewed her thumb and scanned her scullery. "Nevertheless, I'm more than a bit concerned 'bout those little creatures hidden away inside me establishment. If only I could be sure they all ran outside. None of me guests wish to be stepping upon them or hearing them crunching inside the walls, aye? Mr.

Baylor next door has a good mouser tabby, and I'm away to fetch her on loan for a while."

Holly, Daisy, and Violet scampered onto the table again at the mention of mice. Orla sighed. "Mice are nothing compared to the rats we had in Ireland. All the same, feel free to put your plump fannies atop Nuala's fine dining table where food is served, aye?"

They slowly climbed down, then sat on Nuala's counter. *Holy heavens.*

Orla waved her hands in surrender and blew out a breath. "Now, Holly, you've broken much of our trust. Mayhap, if you'll tell me 'bout me unknown enemy, Ma Brown, it'll go far in repairing it. Do you agree girlies? I'm desperate to know what I—we are up against here. Go on, then."

With the near-death event, the drastic threats, and revelations of the day over, exhaustion overcame Orla when she arrived home. Then, dawned a brilliant idea while she climbed the stairs with her Sir Gallant watchdog. *Pray to God for help, for heaven's sake.*

"Only thing left to do. It's come down to this." They entered her room, and she left her door halfway open. "Stay, Gal. Think we'll be safe enough? You rush out me door quick if anything bad happens. Got it?"

The Shepherd lay in front of her doorway, his amber eyes intently focused on her face.

Orla dug through her wooden chest. "Here 'tis." She covered her head with her old travel bonnet for a veil. She tugged out Kathleen's rosary from her gown's deep pocket, knelt, and folded her hands. "Our Father who art in Heaven, hallowed be Thy name. . ." At the end of the prayer, she paused and glanced around her room. God had not rained fire down from heaven. The ceiling did not cave in. No thunder and lightning crackled outside. She hugged herself.

Gal whined and laid his head on his paws.

"Think I'll skip the Hail Mary for now. I'm not confessing exactly. I'm going to pray like me brother, Mick—not to the Saints, and bypass them. Did I get Your attention, God Almighty? 'Tis sure You know what I do by now, which makes me frightened to ask for things."

Gal whined, and she hushed him.

She scrunched her eyes tight. "Nevertheless, I want it bad enough to approach You. Haven't prayed much since I was fifteen. You're holy, or so I'm told, and I'm far from that. 'Tis a wide valley of difference between us, aye? If I remember me catechism—You're pure as the freshly fallen snow, whilst me own heart and body are impure."

Orla opened her eyes and scanned the shadows in her room created by her kerosene lamp. "Sorry 'bout me choices, and many times I've regrets. There're reasons, and I don't blame You for making me ugly . . . well, I suppose I truthfully do. I know if I lie to You, I surely won't get anything. Hang on, there's more."

She shifted her kneeling position and her skirts. "'Tis what Nuala had. That's what I wish for. You gave it to her, she assured me, so You can give it to me as well? I want a good woman's life. I'm daring to hope for it after hearing of Ma Brown's fears. Mayhap she knows something 'bout Murphy and me. I'll spell it out clear, aye?"

Footsteps passed her door, she glanced over her shoulder, as they faded, then she cleared her throat. Gallant lifted his head, ears forward. "I'd like to have a husband, and me own children. That's it. I got the dog. Gal, don't you know 'tis easier to pray the more I go on?"

The shepherd tipped his head sideways.

"You haven't struck me dead, God, 'tis a good sign. Getting to the worse part, but I must bring it up. I'm getting a bit old to have children. If You feel alright granting me this prayer, shall You make haste? I'll know 'twas You. No other way it shall happen. It shall go a far distance to help me believe You do care for me. And I'll apologize for me unbelief."

Gallant *woofed*.

Orla crossed her chest. "In the name of the Father, the Son—ah, I forgot to tell You something else. I'm warning You beforehand, I shall ask You this every night, until You give it to me. You know I'm persistent. Me promise to You is I'll never return to me profession, which shall make You the gladdest of all."

She arose, and stepped downstairs to her desk and ledger, and scribbled numbers with Sir Gallant settling beneath her chair.

Numbers are fixed things one may grasp and understand. Not like God. Or praying.

Violet approached her with a piece of rhubarb pie. "It is freshly baked. I was going to deliver it hot to you after supper, but I heard you praying to God. Poppy wanted me to bring it up to you to cheer you up. Are you in the doldrums?"

"Hm." She took the plate and fork. "Nah, only wondering some things."

Poppy shuffled over to join them. "What was that about Madam Rose?"

"What I shall say to God to force Him to listen to me when I pray."

Both girls' jaws dropped, and their eyes widened as they slid glances at each other.

Orla chuckled. "Suppose that sounded terribly odd coming from me, aye? There must be a time when people arrive at a point of such desperation that they beg God for things. Have you ever done it? Does begging work? Gal does it to get something."

Poppy nodded. "I've done it more times than I can count. Isn't prayer much like begging? We ask God because He's the only One who can do something sometimes. Right?" She looked up at Violet.

Violet puffed out her cheeks and scratched her neck. "I do not know . . . what to say. You pray all the time, Poppy. You tell us, does it work?"

"It's not a magic potion. You don't just say a prayer and poof, something happens." She shifted her slight weight against her cane. "What is it you want, Madam Rose?"

Orla swallowed her bite of pie. "Shan't tell anyone. If it happens, it's from God."

Poppy and Violet slid side glances at each other again. Shafts of sunlight beamed through the front window and highlighted their heads.

"There 'tis. That. You've got halos." Orla aimed her fork at them. "Me brother would say 'tis a sign."

"Halos? Or sunlight?" Violet turned with Poppy, and surveyed the window and the shaft of sun, then swung back to Madam Rose. "You think the sunshine is a sign? It happens every day."

"The way it shone at the exact moment we're speaking 'bout prayer." Orla relished the sweet and sour flavors of her pie, and she licked the fork. "I never put much faith in signs. Nevertheless, I've asked God for one, so I'll know what to do."

"You have asked God for a sign?" Daisy stepped down onto the floor from the last stair. "I did that once. Let me tell you, it was truly strange. I wanted to have fun with my cousin, but it was a stormy day during our community's picnic. I asked God to make it sunny, and the sun came out. Our fathers told us no when we asked to ride on the tractor's wagon. They would not say more to us except the weather looked bad, and they told us to go down into the cellar. The sky looked fine to us. Our fathers were being mean. I wanted to scream, but did not want to get in trouble. So, instead of going into the cellar, we climbed a tree where they could not see us. We grumbled to each other and watched the tractor and wagon. Just as it came back around to the house, some fast moving clouds started to hail, and the wind blew hard, then the enormous tree next to us fell over and crashed onto the wagon. Everyone died. All eight of them. I have never been so glad to ignore a sign from God since then."

Violet gasped. "What? Daisy, that is terrible."

"I know, is not it?" Daisy shuddered. "I have never trusted Him since."

Poppy frowned at her. "That's tragic, but God didn't do that. The weather did."

Daisy smirked. "Well, I heard God controls the weather and—"

"That's enough 'bout that, methinks." *Just when I thought I had me answer of what to do.* Orla stood. "Stay, Gal." She went into the scullery to return her plate, or maybe get a second helping of the piece of pure delight.

Holly had snuck past them into the room and sat eating her own serving of pie. "I am relieved that Poppy knows how to cook and has taught Violet. The meals and sweets here are much improved. We will have gentlemen callers tonight, yes, Madam Rose? I have a new gown to wear."

"Aye to both."

"I overheard your conversation about God. I am surprised by what you said. Does Murphy know you pray to God? He may like that."

Murphy had not been around for a visit for over two weeks. Orla clattered her fork and empty dish into the basin and turned to Holly with clenched fists. "Are you saying you know him better than meself? And if so, how do you?"

"No. No, that is not it. I sometimes overhear things—"

"Because you sneak 'bout and listen to things that're not any of your business."

Holly slowly set her plate into the basin beside Orla's and stared out the window. "To be very clear to you, Madam Muldoon, I want to pay back your kindness to me. And the girls for voting that I can stay. Ma Brown is a schemer. She is vicious and vile. When I lived in her bordello, to keep out of her way and not be her victim, I always did her bidding."

Madam Muldoon snorted.

Holly faced her. "Surviving at all costs is what I am accustomed to. You understand, I think. Right? From your life's story you told us when we talked about our pasts."

Orla sagged into a chair at the table. "Aye. Survival is our fiercest impulse."

Holly sat on the chair beside her. "Madam, you must be very careful since you thwarted her scheme to injure or kill you. She does not give up. Ma Brown finds ways to get revenge, to harm, or even to destroy. She spoke her confidences to me because she believed I was like her. She is also the one who mentioned Murphy was raised in the church and wondered if she should get baptized to secure him."

"When was that?" Orla's heart squeezed. Surely, it had jumped out of her breast and splattered onto the wooden floor. She searched for it for a second.

"Last year. Before I left her place."

"You're saying she'd go to that degree of deception to ensnare him?

Girlie, this all makes no sense. If he was or is her client, she doesn't need to secure him, aye?"

"I agree, Madam Muldoon. That is why I believe she is in love with him. Like you are." Holly patted Orla's arm. "I have told no one, and I promise not to. Certainly not Ma Brown."

Madam Muldoon startled. "Holy heavens. You think I'm in love with him?"

Holly giggled. "Of course I do. Denial will not get you to change my sharp eyesight. Be careful. Always be watchful and aware. But I hope you are the one to secure him and not that horrible woman."

A chill spread up Orla's neck. Was it because of the dire warning or the possibility that Murphy was as observant as Holly? *Mayhap both.*

* * *

LAUGHTER AND MERRIMENT from the men and girls filled The Flower Garden's parlor, but it didn't reach Madam Rose's soul. Murphy hadn't shown again for the third week in a row.

Orla rose and called Gal to join her. Maybe there was something to tempt her appetite in the pantry. Poppy had made some fresh molasses cookies earlier.

They reached the scullery, and Poppy smiled as they entered. "Ah, so I'm to have company tonight. I like that. Hey, Gal, hey there." She reached out as the dog approached, and he leaned against her chair for a good scratch on his back.

"'Tis absolutely astonishing how he's taken up with you, me girlie. Thinking he's fond of your gentle ways and voice. You've a friend for life. Are there any cookies leftover? Nah, I'll check, you keep resting."

"Thank you. Check the pantry for the tin. Last I saw, Daisy was down here nibbling on one. Hopefully, she left a few behind." Poppy cooed to Gal, then yawned. "Who's a good doggie now, huh?"

Orla stepped around Gal's makeshift bed and Poppy's cot to unlock the narrow door. "'Tis a wonder you can coax Gal to sleep with you occasionally, aye?" She spied the cookie tin and carried it to the table.

Poppy yawned widely. "Sorry, Madam Rose. Gal must be in the mood to stay with me. Think I'll let him out for his nightly business and then get some sleep."

"All grand by me. I'm heading up to me room. Lock the backdoor, and send Gal up when he's finished, aye?"

The parlor was empty, and all the cheerful chatter came from upstairs now. Orla dragged her heavy feet and heart up each step. Loneliness hadn't been her visitor in many years. She still found it abysmal.

After settling atop her bed wrapped in her blanket, Orla munched three molasses cookies and had replaced the tin's lid, when a strange sound seized her attention. Then ferocious barking. Orla flew off the bed before a muffled scream came from downstairs. *Poppy!*

Sir Gallant barked feverishly, and Orla skipped a few steps in her rush to the scullery. A man, Joe Black, lay against Poppy's body, her arms beneath his elbows, and pinned against the floor. He cupped her mouth shut with both hands. Her gown was up around her waist, her canes were to the side, and Gal was locked inside the pantry. Black had not seen Orla yet, being so intent on his assault of her precious Poppy.

Orla snatched the burner lid from the pipe stove and struck Black on the back of his head. He slumped to Poppy's side and lay still. With all her strength, she kicked his body further away from her Poppy. "Despicable. Abominable."

Sir Gallant growled through the door, and Poppy lay gasping and pale. Her gown was all askew, and her eyes were glazed with shock. Her lovely Poppy. *Sweetest girlie.* "Poppy. Did he injure you? Can you rise? We must get you away from him. Give me your hands."

"You got him in time." Poppy whispered and raised her hands for Orla to tug her to standing. She held Poppy with one arm and moved her from the scullery to the side of the staircase. She straightened Poppy's clothing and ran to retrieve the canes to return to her. "Sit on the step and don't move. There's business for me to finish. Hallo, everyone upstairs! Quickly. Help us. Something terrible has happened."

Moaning and groaning came from the scullery and set Gal to barking again. He scratched against the pantry door to get out.

Orla sprinted into the scullery.

Black had pulled himself to standing at the sink. He swayed to one side, clutching the back of his head. She hurried to the pantry and fumbled with her set of keys to unlock the door as the burly man stumbled toward her.

The door unlatched and Sir Gallant sprang out of the tiny room intent on the intruder. Black yelled loud enough to shake the roof when Gal's fangs sank into his arm and the dog shook the wicked man off his feet onto his knees.

Orla hurled herself at the rear door and tugged, glad it was unlocked. "Out, Gal, take him outside."

Everyone upstairs arrived at the scene at the same time in various states, talking all at once. She could barely hear them over Black's raging cries and Sir Gallant's vicious growls as he dragged him to the rear door facing the lake. One voice stood above the cacophony— Murphy's. "Orla, what madness is this?"

Madam Muldoon reached down and yanked on Black's legs as he thrashed back and forth with Sir Gallant clamped on his shoulder. She the dog to drag the abuser's legs halfway out the door. "Black. Attacked. Poppy. Get away girls."

The women scrambled out of the room, and the men rushed to Orla's aid. She caught her breath enough to direct the watchdog. "Gal, drop it. Sit."

The shepherd didn't sit, but he released Black. He barked again, fangs revealed, slobbering. Orla loved her dog, yet he was terrifying even to her.

Murphy, Cooley, Layton, and Fairbanks grasped the struggling Black by his arms. Murphy stared at her. "Where do you want him, Madam Muldoon?"

"The lake. Toss him in."

"You got it."

The men hauled Black down the hill to the lake. All his protesting that he could not swim, the water was too cold, and they would get arrested was all for naught. They shoved him in, and a noisy splash followed.

Madam screamed her rage at the man thrashing about in the water. "Keep your pants buttoned, and your hands to yourself around children!" Nausea swept through her and she retched.

Sir Gallant sat calmly by Murphy's leg. The dog stared at the proceedings with his aggression against the attacker in check.

"Gal," Orla gasped, "how do you turn it off? I desire with all me being to drown that horrid man. Never knew I'd so much violence inside of meself." She battled more nausea.

"What you witnessed should never happen. Ever." Murphy ran his palm over his disheveled hair. "Shall we leave him to find his footing, men?"

"The water is not that deep where we threw him in. Too near the dock pilings. He will be fine. Sadly." Fairbanks shook his head.

Murphy helped Orla to get her balance on the stones and the shifting sand after she straightened from retching. "Do you have any idea why Black would come here to do this, Madam Muldoon? Had he ever seen Poppy? She is not one of your working girls."

Madam took a deep breath. "Holly's been telling me that Black is Ma Brown's son."

"That is why he seemed familiar, but he is older. I frequented her place several years ago. Before I met you."

Orla hugged herself to warm up her body. She could not reach her icy soul. "Well now. What's happened whilst you were away from us for so long was Ma Brown sent me a viper in a barrel of clothing, then sent her son to attack me own girlie. Holly warned me to be watchful and aware because Ma Brown is persistently wicked."

"I do not get it. Why is she singling you out? She is up the lake in Duluth."

Here 'tis. Nervousness grew in the pit of her stomach. "Because of you, I'm told. She wants you and thinks I caught you." *I'll never see him again. Dearest Murphy.*

He threw back his head and burst out laughing in near hysterics. *Holy heavens. Me heart belongs to a madman.*

Orla clenched her jaw to restrain herself from clenching her hands around his throat or stomping on his foot. *Doesn't the fella understand anything?*

The men wanted to know what was so funny at a horrible time like this, and Madam could not think of an answer. Not at all.

Daisy and Holly joined the group on the shore, awaiting Murphy's answer to the men's question and the outcome of the villain who could not swim. Daisy scrunched her nose. "Who knew when we met him back at Nuala's that he would return to town to viciously attack Poppy?"

Holly whispered into Madam Muldoon's ear. "This attack was nastier than anything I imagined Ma Brown doing. Did I mention she is spiteful? You thwarted her a second time. Keep Gal alert every moment, Madam Rose, because her actions here tonight do not bode well for you. Or for the rest of us."

CHAPTER 21

Her Purifying Fire

Not a peep from Heaven
Orla

$\mathcal{L}$ake Superior, Whiskey Row
June 1884

POPPY'S close call with tragedy at The Flower Garden back in early May urged Madam Muldoon to frequently rethink her goals. She had added prayers every night. Now, she considered what to do with her life while she strolled with Nuala to the lake. The sunset over the gray-blue water cast gold, orange, and scarlet edges on the clouds hovering above it. *Wonder if me Black Angel will be out tonight.*

"Look at that glorious sunset, me friend."

"We've the best view of it, aye? Nuala, shall you abide here forever? It's become threatening lately. 'Tis sure, we've experienced Whiskey Row's lawlessness since settling here. The gambling dens, and bars benefited our earnings from the men, nevertheless, do they outweigh what's turned perilous? Or what's missing? We've no law and order to control everyone, or no church with good intentions to pry into our lives. You're a church woman."

"I've Father Furmanski's services on Saturdays when he's in town to visit good Catholics. Don't know for sure 'bout staying here forever. Wished to make me a living and finish raising up me own Janeen, aye? Now that she's grown and married, I'm a bit lost. You?"

Boisterous voices and out of tune music echoed from Whiskey Row's dirty and busy streets above the shore. "Sounds like another fight, 'tis sure. Seemed grand enough here for a few years, aye? Now with Duluth sending us their ore, and the Iron Range Railroad work-ers, 'tis become wilder. More perilous. After Poppy's attack, I can't go into me own scullery without seeing her pinned down by that wretched Black." She shivered.

Nuala linked elbows with Orla. "That must've been terrible for you to witness that. Yet so fortuitous that you stopped him. God made sure to interrupt that evil fella."

"Was Gal's barking that stopped him first, by sounding the alarm for me. And since God made dogs, I shall agree with you. 'Tis sure, both Poppy and Gal were rejected strays, nonetheless, they became me greatest blessings in many years." Tears choked her throat.

"Aye, 'twas your Gal. At some point, Orla, you must give more credit to God. You've been wondering 'bout His involvement. He's been taking care of you, and you've not always seen it."

Orla scoffed. "Well, and aren't you the wise one? Been praying for a sign, don't you know? Been begging God for something I want with all of me heart, and nothing. Not a peep from Heaven. Me heart is desolate within me."

"It will all work out, you'll see. I wonder at you not bringing Gal with you for company."

"Gal's watching over Poppy. She'll be safe from harm that way."

Nuala gave her a side hug. "You're on the right path, chum. Prayer takes patience. Sundown is near, so I must be away. Are you heading back with me?"

"Nah. Murphy hasn't been around since that repulsive night with that horrible fella. Thinking he's done with me and The White Flower." She blew out a breath. "Don't wish to be involved with tonight's merriment at home that's sure to arise with everyone dancing and all. The only good thing coming out of Holly's deceitful ways is Violet's new friendship with her. She's an understanding and compassionate woman."

"Aye. Later, then, me friend. Don't stay out late here alone. Tell me what happens with your prayers, aye?" Nuala raised her skirts and turned to climb up the hill into town.

Orla switched her gaze to await the full moonrise sure to silhouette the point of high rocks and tall pines. This night reminded her of the time Murphy found her with her lantern watching for the loon. *Aingeal dubh.* Black Angel. *Was two years ago, wasn't it?*

With the darkness growing around her before the moonrise, she bent and lit the lantern she always brought with her when visiting the shore. She would remain for a few more minutes in her peaceful place. Her life changed significantly since coming to Whiskey Row. Shame for certain things remained, but she also found freedom. She no longer wore a veil covering her face. She had a new family and a dear friend. The worst change was the restlessness growing deep inside her bones ever since discovering Murphy may be interested in Ma Brown. *Face it, girl. You love him.*

Heavy footsteps crushed and slid in the gravel and sand behind her.

She swung around and almost plowed herself and the lantern into Murphy.

"Woah, there." He stepped back. "It is only me, seeking you. When you were not inside the parlor, I knew to find you here. How are you, Beautiful?" His teeth glowed white in the lantern light. The cleft in his chin and his dimples deepened, and his unshaven jaw emphasized the shadows.

I'm lost. How dare he look so well and unbothered? "I see that."

"Surprised you came down to the shore alone after Holly's dire warnings."

"Nevertheless, I wanted to think, and left Gal with Poppy. She needs his comfort the most. Didn't expect to ever see your superior face here again or get a scolding. Should've left me lantern unlit."

He chuckled. "Superior face at Lake—never mind. And quite a how do you do and welcome for your missing man. The fire in your eyes is not from that lantern's reflection you have there. You came down to think?" He surveyed the lakeshore. "Aha, and watch the moonrise. Have you seen your Black Angel yet?"

"Nah. And I won't ever, with you yelling and making noise."

He smiled his slow, melting smile. "There she is. I knew you were in there somewhere, Beautiful."

Orla flopped onto her favorite log and focused on the midnight blue and silver landscape across the lake. How could she seriously chat with a man who was so obtuse, lighthearted, and a scoundrel?

Murphy sat beside her. A bit too close.

She scooted away as far as she could until a large knotty branch poked her backside.

He chuckled. "Have you settled yourself yet? I take your hint. You are not in the mood for company. No matter. I will enjoy the moonlight with you in silence."

She ground her teeth. *Relax. Let the beauty engulf you.* Water lapped at the sandy shore, for the crashing waves of winter had calmed, and night insects sang their tunes to whomever would listen. Why was she trying to escape his presence? He never did anything to frighten her. It was fear from within herself. Her fright came from risking vulnerability with her heart.

Gravel crunched beneath Murphy's boots as he shifted his long legs and crossed them at the ankles. He folded his arms and stared up at the millions of tiny lights in the sky. Even his profile was magnificent. Everything about the man was exceptional. *He'd never, ever love someone like me. And why does he call me beautiful?* There was no need to flirt with the likes of Madam Muldoon.

Black Angel called from somewhere beyond the foremost lakeshore point. The clever creature knew just what note to hit that would echo its loneliness within her own soul.

"Your angel knows you are here, Orla. What is it saying to you? Hm?" His whisper caressed her neck and ear. "I am keeping my loud voice low so as not to frighten him away. Is it working?"

She slowly turned her face toward his voice, and he kissed her with kisses as soft as a downy feather. His gorgeous eyes sparkled in the full moon's light. Orla closed her own and gave herself over to the tender moment until it intensified. She scrambled away from him. How could she keep doing this when her heart wanted more from him?

"I apologize, Beautiful. I misread the situation. I have not frightened you before—"

She covered her face but could not cover her sobs.

"Orla. What do you want me to do? I want to hold you." He stood beside her.

She violently shook her head. "No. Don't."

"I will go—"

"No. Don't." She took in a huge gulp of air and wiped her cheeks with her shaking hands. "I've . . . some questions. Shall you sit again? 'Tis a . . . good time to ask. Need a moment."

He sat on the log gripping his knees, and she hurried down from him to the beach to collect herself. *Be brave, girl. You know how.* What else could she do?

Black Angel floated past them in the middle of the harbor's inlet, and directly into the silver reflection of the moon on its surface. Out of the darkness. Was this her sign? *Go into the light.*

She swung around to face Murphy. "Methinks Angel gave me a sign to speak up. I asked for a sign. Do you think I'm a madwoman?"

He steepled his fingers beneath his chin and studied her. "What I think is that there is something bothering your brilliant brain, and you need someone to speak to about it. Did you choose me for a personal reason? Or am I the one that happens to be on hand?"

"Well, you don't pay me to harass you with me thoughts, do you?"

"No, I do not. Do you think I pay you for my presence?"

Orla twirled around to again calm her racing heart with the serenity of the lake. *Speak up now, girl.* She inhaled deeply a few times, strode back to the log, and sat beside him. If she avoided his eyes, she could speak from her heart.

"Pay. Aye, pay is good. Money solves much of the ills of the world and creates many evils as well. Me plan's always been to earn all that I can and set meself up in business. I succeeded. Grateful to you for that help as well." She swallowed hard.

He scoffed. "Money is everything to everyone. But I have another take on money and the link to evil. Women marry for it—men are stingy with it. Men control women and others with their income. Greed causes the evils of money and what it is used for. Greedy women use their wiles to secure the hearts of wealthy men—"

"You're saying I'm greedy. Is that it?" She stood and faced him. "Men are never greedy, aye? Only controlling? I've used men to create me wealth, such as it is. You think me heart is grasping for what isn't mine—to claw meself out of poverty with the tricks I play on men?"

He raised his palm. "That is not it. Do you truly believe I think that about you, Orla? You do not know?" He reached for her hand.

"Madam Muldoon!" Holly scrambled and slid down the hill. "Come quick, it is Poppy. Nightmares. She is inconsolable. Calling for you."

Murphy stood and handed Orla the lantern. "Let us go, and we will talk later." He took each woman by their arm and helped them navigate the rocky hill as quickly as possible to The Flower Garden.

They hurriedly entered the scullery to find Poppy sobbing at the table, Gal sitting beside her chair, and Daisy and Violet trying to comfort her with gentle words and embraces. The male customers glanced at each other and hesitated outside the doorway. Murphy joined them.

Orla knelt in front of Poppy. "Sweet girlie. I'm back. Was down at the lakeshore. Tell me what happened, aye? Are you hurt?"

"It was him again. I couldn't escape."

"What? He's not here, aye?" Orla scanned the room. "Wasn't real though, aye? Only a terrible dream or memory."

"But it was real in my dream. Like that night. He won't come back, will he?" Poppy frantically slid her gaze around the scullery.

"Nah, he dares not." Orla raised her brow at Murphy. She must ask for his help. She had no one else to trust with her girlie. Dizziness enveloped her, and she gripped a chair back. *Deep breaths. Be strong for her.*

Murphy stepped forward with his arms out. "Come here, Poppy, and you can stay with Madam Muldoon and Gal tonight. That will comfort you."

"I can't climb the stairs." She rubbed her eyes.

"Right. I will carry you up. Put your arms around my neck. There you go. That is the way." Murphy turned to Orla and tipped his head toward the hallway.

Everyone in the area stepped aside and murmured reassurances as the threesome passed them to the staircase.

Once inside Orla's bedroom, Murphy lowered Poppy onto the bed and stepped back for Orla and Gal to surround her. "Will you be fine, Madam Muldoon, to get her downstairs in the morning?"

"Aye. Down is easier. Thank you for your kindness."

"I will be on my way and return tomorrow for our unfinished discussion, Orla. Maybe I will surprise you. Good night." He winked and left. Her room grew starkly empty without him. *Desperately wished to hear more of his thoughts.* Or did she?

Poppy sniffled. "He called you 'Orla.' Does he always do that?"

Orla waved away her question. "Ah, me girlie, let's get you comfortable for the night. Shall it please you to tell me 'bout your nightmare? Mayhap it shall help to erase it." She sat beside her youngest, frailest girlie and enfolded her within her arms. *Shall this event never fade from her mind?* Her own nightmares had not.

In the morning, Gal growled low in his throat. The room was bright with sunshine alerting Orla it was past sunup, then there was a knock on her door. "Madam Muldoon?" Holly's voice was muffled. "It is after eight o'clock. Are you alright?"

"Aye. We're only now awakening." Poppy had tossed about and kicked against her all night, and Orla's poor eyes were gritty with exhaustion. She shook Poppy's arm. "Me girlie, the day has begun. You've come out safe from the night terrors, aye?"

Poppy twisted around and blinked in the brightness. "It's morning, then, and all is well. I'd best get downstairs and make the coffee and the—"

"No need, Poppy." Holly swung the door inward and entered wearing her pink robe wrapped tightly around her slim body. "Violet made us the coffee, and Daisy attempted the pancakes. They wanted to let you rest. We should all survive just fine after drinking a cup and eating our breakfast. I have come to help you down below."

After Orla and Holly successfully maneuvered Poppy down the steps, Holly hurried away to fetch Poppy's canes from the scullery. Daisy and Violet peered around the corner doorway.

"A message came for you, Madam Rose." Daisy hurried to her with a folded piece of paper.

Dread swirled in her mind. Messages often communicated something confrontational. "A dire warning from me nemesis?" She quickly unfolded the letter and read the script aloud. "Please come to The White Feather tonight at nine o'clock. Dress nicely and bring your girls. I have a surprise awaiting you. It was Murphy's idea. Warmest regards, Nuala."

Daisy gave a little hop. "I adore surprises. It has been so long since the last one. I mean good surprises. There can be bad surprises as well, like the—"

"Sh." Holly peeked over Orla's shoulder. "Do you recognize the writing, Madam?"

Orla shrugged. "Don't know. Nuala hasn't written me a post before. We stroll to each other's establishments and chat when we wish to. Murphy's idea, aye?" She flipped the paper over to the blank backside. It made no sense to get a note. Would Nuala not have come to invite them? *Mayhap not. Mayhap no time.* What was she doing? Cooking a huge feast?

Violet set two cups of coffee on the table and frowned. "Something seems strange. Does it sound like Nuala? The wording, I mean. And why would she send a note and not come in person?"

Orla's head throbbed and her eyes burned from lack of sleep. "Me thoughts as well. She has a house full of railroad men awaiting the ore shipment to begin passing through. Did a messenger bring this, Violet?"

She shrugged. "I do not know. It was slipped through the letter holder onto the entry floor."

"Methinks we'll be grand. Poppy, me girlie, do you wish to go with us?"

Poppy shook her head.

"We shall leave you with Gal for a short time and lock the doors, then. Mayhap half an hour. Gal won't allow mischief to happen. Nonetheless, I'd rather you go. You can borrow one of Holly's—"

"No."

"Yes, Poppy, please." Holly nodded. "Really, you fit easily into my gowns. I will let you borrow my green one. It will bring out the green tints in your amber eyes."

Poppy bit her lip. "I don't know."

"It will be fun, Poppy." Daisy squeezed her shoulder. "You need a nice surprise like anyone else. Do you want to miss out? I know I never would. There was one Christmas when my ma was so angry with me—"

"Daisy, hush." Violet sat beside Poppy. "I will stay here with you if you prefer not to go. Madam Rose can share the surprise with us both when they return. How is that?"

"Can I think about what I want to do?" Poppy stared up at Orla.

"Oh, aye, aye. Nevertheless, tell us in time to get you ready, then." Orla handed Poppy the plate of surprisingly lovely blueberry pancakes, and the tub of salted butter. "Tasty aroma, Daisy."

Daisy grinned. "They are. And I wore my spectacles. You should have seen Holly's face. She almost fainted."

Madam Rose Muldoon and her girls did not require the lantern's aid to progress to The White Feather that evening, because the lanterns hanging in front of the town's bars and gambling dens adequately lit the dirt street. She glanced back for a last look at The Flower Garden before she and the girls rounded the corner. "Me heart thinks Poppy'll be grand with Gal, nonetheless, I wish she would've come with us. We must make haste to get there and back again without seeming unappreciative of Nuala's surprise."

Violet sniffed. "My wish is that Poppy would have agreed to my staying with her. She became so upset when I insisted that I gave in. She is always concerned with the feelings of others. To her own detriment, I might add. Daisy, one of your locks is coming loose. Hold up." She checked the hairpins.

"Well, and I've stout door locks, girlies. And you heard me tell her not to answer the door for anyone, aye? Gal will stay by her side. If Black did return, Gal would smell the vile fella and attack him again."

Holly glanced over her shoulder. "We are only a few minutes away, Madam Muldoon. We can run back home, if necessary. We wore our boots just in case. Right, girls?"

This cautionary discussion gave Orla chills. She dragged her feet, then rallied. "All will be well, no doubt."

They approached The White Feather and its rose arbor highlighted by the bright glow emanating from inside. All the window curtains were open, and piano music played a lively tune.

"She invited us to a large party?" Violet frowned. "Why would she add us to the mix? Are we not competitors of a sort?"

Orla craned her neck to peek through the tall front windows. "Those men aren't our customers. I assure you girlies, we don't have a competition going for patrons. Nuala feeds them and boards them. 'Tis not our specialty, is it? There're enough men in town for everyone. Nevertheless, 'tis confusing."

Daisy headed up the steps and onto the porch. "I was promised a party, and I am going to attend it with or without you. The last party I ever went to was when I was ten. It was a birthday party for Clara Fredrickson, and I nearly talked my ma into letting me go—oh dear— is that smoke?" She squinted over the women's heads. "I think those are flames. Look there."

A chill slithered up Orla's neck. The women twisted around in unison and gasped. An orange and gold glow lit the only low hanging pine branches left in the town. The few pines that grew behind The Flower Garden.

"Our Poppy!" Orla screamed and ran until she could not breathe anymore and dared not halt until she got home. *Dear God in heaven. Protect Poppy. Don't let it be our home.* How could this happen? The hearth and flue were cleaned recently.

"I am with you, Madam Rose." Violet matched her stride.

"Run! Fast as you can, Violet. This can't be."

The fire's flames were at the rear of The Flower Garden and spreading across the roof to the building beside it. Smoke billowed from upstairs. Orla made it to the locked front door and pounded on it with all her might. "Poppy!"

Violet shoved her aside and thrust her own key into the lock. "The door. It is hot. Watch out."

Orla and Violet burst into the smoky building. "Get down and crawl, Violet. We must find her and Gal with haste. She could be passed out. Go right. I'll go left." Her palms pressed against the floor. Hot smoke seared her lungs. Sweat dripped down her face and neck.

Something dark moved ahead. Gal licked her nose and mouth. "Gal, outside. Get out. Poppy. Where are you?" Violet joined her in calling out.

They both choked in earnest. The smoke increased. The fire's roar grew louder, warning them to escape. Orla refused. Not without her girlie.

A moan came from somewhere nearby. Where was she? Where were they? "Poppy, call out again." To her right. She dragged herself that direction and coughed more. She tried to ignore the burning in her throat.

"I have her. Madam. Go to the door." Violet yelled, then had a choking fit.

Part of the ceiling collapsed behind her. Sparks flew in all directions. *Where am I?* She blinked hard and squinted her stinging eyes to find a way out.

Holly screamed. "Here! Over here. The door is open. Please get out. Please, please. Come this way. There is more smoke. More flames. Madam!"

"Keep calling!" Her violent coughing halted her speech. She crawled on her elbows and knees toward Holly's voice, then Daisy's screams as well. Gal barked frantically.

Smoke billowed around her. The threatening gray-brown river of smoke flowed like a waterfall trapped inside her home. It surged overhead in search of its own escape. She followed its direction and there stood the open door. Her girlies voices calling to them increased in volume over the roar of the hungry, rushing fire.

Something hit her foot. "Go. We . . . are here." Violet choked and rasped. "Grab Poppy."

Orla stopped. She tightly clutched the fabric and the arms her hands landed upon in the murky, suffocating air. She tugged hard with her considerable strength. "Got her."

The women hauled each other together until they arrived at the doorframe, at the same time as the window glass burst above them. Shards hit the floor in front of them. Orla ignored the sharp pains on her elbows, knees, then her palms as she struggled to escape. *Keep going.*

Rescuers must have snatched her and the girls and carried them away from the fire, because sometime later, she lay on her back staring up at the moon and stars dulled by the smoky clouds. Men yelled instructions to each other.

Orla could not concentrate on their words. All she could do was choke, and retch, while the relief of being snatched out of the fire engulfed her mind. Her throat and lungs burned.

"Madam." Violet clasped her arm.

"Poppy?"

Holly's face hovered in the haze close above her. "She is safe. You are all safe. The men are doing a bucket brigade from the lake. It does not look good. I am so sorry. I think somehow my presence has brought all these catastrophes down upon us." She sobbed hysterically.

"Nah." *More like wicked Ma Brown's schemes.*

CHAPTER 22

Embodying Her Claddagh

You'd think a fella would notice
Orla

*W*hiskey Row
The Flower Garden's Ruins

THE NEW CLADDAGH RING. *How fortuitous of Colleen to write about it before the fire.* The symbols gave Orla a lovely hope and focus on friendship, love and loyalty. But what should she do now? Should she rebuild or regroup with another plan? Although it was two days after the fire, she coughed for the hundredth time. "Think I've lost me dearest hopes for the future with me good lungs."

The Flower Garden girls, except for Poppy, picked with sticks and shovels for hours through the rubble of their former home. Madam Muldoon's business and her house were not the only buildings destroyed—seven structures in total offered up their black, skeletal remains with lighter gray smoke. *When one structure catches fire, the rest light up like matches in a matchbox.* Why was it her own business? Was it a plot? The only person who considered her a threat was Ma Brown.

Orla bent over and tried to catch her breath. *Be strong for the girls. What shall I do?* Her money was in ashes except for any coin she had saved inside her bodice or could dig out of the rubble. *Would never be enough to rebuild.* Father Furmanski might offer her more charity. She gulped hard but her dry throat resisted. *Breathe deep. Imagine the green hills of Ireland.*

"Madam Rose, I can tell you are terribly upset as you should be." Daisy rubbed her nostrils. "This ash gets everywhere. I think it went up my nose and clogged my brain. Well, we all desperately need some hope. Why only last week, Katherine told me about how her grand-mother was supposed to die, but when she refused to because of her grandson's upcoming wedding, that old lady held on for months and months waiting—"

"Stop talking about death, Daisy." Holly shuddered. "Madam Muldoon had a near escape from it, along with Violet and Poppy."

Daisy poked at a smoldering pine branch with flickering coals buried beneath charred bricks of the chimney. "It is a mercy there were not many trees to catch on fire. With all the woods newly cleared away from near the shore to make room for more docks and the rail expansion, it stopped the spread around the whole town. It could have cooked us all to crisps. Can you imagine if—"

"Let us not, if you please." Violet stood on top of a slight heap of what resembled a mattress with charred springs. The design of the iron bedframe helped identify it as Orla's bed.

"And I'm glad I wasn't sleeping in that thing when it caught aflame." Orla squinted at the singed metal.

Holly kicked a partially melted tin bucket over and found only ashes heaped under it. "I heard merchants went to Duluth for supplies to rebuild today. Will you do so as well, Madam Muldoon? You have not said a word about that."

"'Tis sure I should make plans for us. Nevertheless, me brain isn't feeling brilliant enough to figure out me next step. 'Tis fogged up entirely with smoke, like our Daisy said 'bout hers." Orla used her shovel to balance while she reached down to tug on a shiny object. Beads expanded into a string and a crucifix. *Kathleen's rosary.* She had pretended not to take it all those years ago on the S.S. *Mona*, yet she had. She could not part with it by having her only sister take it down with her into the depths of the sea. It had survived yet another catastrophe. Fingering the rosary gritty with ash transported her to Ireland. Her childhood. Praying in church. Kathleen's gentleness and faith. The way she brightened each day no matter how dreary. What would Lamb say about her prized rosary buried in the ashes of a hateful act against her own sister's bordello? *A sign from God to hold onto hope?* But what new life could a bawdy Madam hope for? Tears trickled down her cheeks and she swiped at them with the back of her hand.

"What is that in your fingers?" Daisy scrunched her nose and eyes and took a few steps nearer to Orla.

"Me sister's rosary. Wouldn't you know 'twould survive a fire? Nevertheless, me mam's satchel it was within did not."

The girls slowly stepped over and around the heaps of destroyed furniture, or fragments of their belongings to gather around Madam Muldoon and get a glimpse of a survivor from the fire. Madam looped it around her neck to display it better and stepped back. Something crunched beneath her boot, and she turned to satisfy their exclamations of curiosity. She lifted her foot and discovered Murphy's timepiece hidden under the mess. "Aha. Another thing that truly isn't mine. Forgot to return it to him."

Violet bent and used her stick to flick off the ashes before she picked it up. "It feels a little warm still. Do you want to finish cleaning it? It might still work."

Orla flattened her empty palm, then raised the timepiece Violet dropped onto it. She held it against her ear. "Ticking, 'tis faint, nevertheless there. Don't know if Murphy's been missing this. You'd think a fella would notice." She slid it into her pocket.

"Morning, ladies. Here to help search for anything salvageable." Nuala joined the women with a voluminous grain sack, handed each woman a smaller sack, and poked a worn broom missing some straw at the piles of soot. "The grand thing 'bout doing this search now? 'Tis the dampness suppressing the ash, aye. Stinks to high heaven, none-theless. Sticky as taffy." She wrinkled her nose and tugged a scarf from her pocket.

Holly sneezed. "Damp soot or not, I cannot imagine doing this for much longer. Mrs. Kincaid, we are all grateful to you for taking us into your boarding house. The railroad men that still live with you as they wait for more housing seem curious about us being there. Although they have not asked me questions about the fire. Have they spoken to you?"

"Me pleasure to have you. One fella was asking for you, Orla. He's got questions. Made me a bit uneasy—can't say why."

"Good morning, ladies." Father Furmanski strode up to Madam Muldoon's demolished Flower Garden, his black robe swaying, and extended his hand to her. "Miss Muldoon, such sorry news to hear of this tragedy, and now see to it for myself. Let me offer my condo-lences on the loss of your home."

"And me livelihood." Orla swallowed a gulp of indescribable grief and nodded as she switched her shovel into her left hand and shook his with her other.

"How did you hear of the tragic news of the fire so quickly, Father?" Nuala picked her way back to a level open area nearer to him.

Furmanski crossed his arms. "The news captured everyone's atten-tion all around Duluth yesterday and spread further with a few of Whiskey Row's merchants. They told the dramatic tale to any who would listen after they arrived in town to get supplies for a rebuild. But you did not go with them, Miss Muldoon?"

"Me heart's not in it just yet, Father. I'm still a bit numb." Orla blew out a shaky breath.

He gave a nod. "Not surprising. Well, I brought a small cart lent to me by a Mr. Roth at the docks filled with a few supplies from my parishioners. Went to The White Feather to ask after you, Mrs. Kincaid. Thought you might be with your friend here." He pointed over his shoulder. "Your boarder over there hitched a ride with me. His name is Sanderson, Miss Muldoon, and he wishes to have a few words alone with you."

Nuala shaded her eyes. "That's the fella I spoke of Orla."

Orla frowned. The man sat in the horse cart staring at them. His dark hat shadowed his facial features. She felt exposed for an indiscernible reason and rubbed her arms. "Don't know him. But I shall in a moment, 'tis sure."

Furmanski smiled at the other women. "Such a terrible job to do. May I be of help in some way? There are some shovels in the cart, and I can fetch more of the townsmen to aid us. Would you like that?"

"Sure, and thank you for your kindness, Father. Best to go face Mr. Sanderson head on." Orla raised her brown skirt and carefully trod over objects to return to the street and the man in the cart awaiting her. She did not believe the priest would bring her someone dangerous, but tingles ran down her neck and shoulders.

Sanderson climbed out of the cart backwards, then faced her. His brown eyes glinted. Not with malice, but more like intelligence. He tipped his black hat back from his blond hair and settled it again. He gave a slight bow. "Miss Muldoon, Mr. Murphy sent me to find you."

"Holy heavens. Why would he do that ?" Had she heard correctly?

Sanderson grinned lopsidedly. "Murphy is one of my clients. I am an investigator. I work occasionally for him when requested to and am compensated for it. He also warned me that my presence would shock you. He did not say why it would."

Say something, girl. She had no words. A blank mind. *Think.* Ask him something. "I don't get it. Why would a barge worker hire an investigator, never minding how he could pay for such a thing? And how did Murphy to send someone so promptly to our lawless Whiskey Row after this disaster?"

Mr. Sanderson shifted his feet. "He sent me several days ago, before the fire, to investigate the incident with a girl named Poppy and a Mr. Black at The Flower Garden."

"He did that, did he?" Her jaw slackened.

"Yes. I have been asking around town and following the rumors about Black before approaching you. My boss wanted discretion. If I heard enough to then notify you, I was to then ask you for more details. The day of the fire, I was otherwise occupied, and that night—with someone. We can keep that between us, if you please. So you see, Mr. Murphy did not send me to investigate the fire. I have not wired him about that yet. You and I could discover if there is a connection to both incidents since they took place at The Flower Garden."

So much viciousness aimed at her and poor Poppy from just one woman. Orla's knees shook. Was this fire truly another plot by Ma Brown? She nearly toppled over, and Sanderson grabbed her arm. She tensed. Should she be wary of him? His presence, and Murphy's actions in hiring him, made no sense. "Where'd you come from, Mr. Sanderson? Duluth?"

"From St. Paul."

"What? I'm more confused."

"My apologies, Miss Muldoon, but Mr. Murphy instructed me to only ask you questions, and not to tell you any personal details of his life. He wishes to do that himself. Since he is the one who pays me, I do as he says. Can we stroll for a few minutes while you answer?"

"Aye."

"Perhaps I should also ask you about this fire while I am here. They could be linked." He turned toward the lakeshore. "It will not take long, then I can leave you to return to your cleanup."

Orla called back to the group. "I'm going with Mr. Sanderson to the lake. I'll return shortly."

"Shall I go with you?" Nuala straightened and took a step.

"Nah. We'll be grand." *I've a shovel, if not.* She slid a glance at the stranger beside her.

Mr. Sanderson lowered his hat brim against the sun when they turned west along the shore.

When they had gone several yards, she stopped and leaned on the shovel's handle to study the rear side of the burned shops and a bar on the row nearest to her own destroyed home. She wiped the perspiration from her forehead with her forearm. Smoke still twirled upward in narrow tendrils from certain spots. The buildings were all roofless. "This town is misfortunate, indeed. Seeing this calamity from here makes me wonder where the fire started. So, me place seemed to be the first to catch fire? I don't like this at all."

He tucked his hands into his pockets. "That is a clever observation. I will be direct with you, and it will make our conversation quick. Mr. Murphy believes you are the target of a hostile scheme. A crime or crimes. I am here to discover any evidence of that."

She bit her lip. Had she not suspected the same thing? *Not coincidences.* Her knees weakened, but there was no place to sit. A spell of nausea swept through her gut. *Don't despair. Get through this, Orla. God, will you help me?*

Sanderson removed a small notepad and pencil from inside his vest. "Tell me what you recall about the night of the attack."

"The first or second attack? I'm now convinced in me own mind they're both from the malicious heart of the same person." She ground her teeth and fisted her hands.

"Too coincidental? It seems to be so. Will you please start with the first?"

Orla hesitated. Could this fella also be another ploy by Ma Brown? "Do you have a badge of some kind? Or a note from Murphy, explaining why I ought to trust you, and why he wishes me to speak with you?"

Sanderson grinned. "You are a clever lady. I do have his request with me." He tugged an envelope from inside his vest pocket, opened it, and unfolded the letter before handing it to her.

She scanned the paper. The signature was unreadable. It mentioned 'Orla Muldoon' not Madam Rose Muldoon. Had she not protected her given name from most of the town's knowledge? Except for Mr. Flint, the viper house estate agent, Nuala, her girls, and Murphy. *Mayhap Ma Brown heard it. But it must be Murphy's signature.*

Several hours later, after Orla and Sanderson parted, and the bedraggled and exhausted women finished searching through the muck, they returned to The White Feather. Three townsmen had joined with Father Furmanski in sifting through the remnants of The Flower Garden, yet the responsibility for keeping or tossing the recovered items landed upon their own shoulders. The girls' sacks were only half full of their salvageable treasures.

Nuala shooed away the few remaining railroad workers from her boarding house to keep themselves occupied elsewhere, then set up a tub for bathing again after their grimy search. "Girls, Orla and I shall unpack Father's parishioner donations for you and shall lay them upon the table whilst the bathwater heats. Choose the order of who gets to bathe first, aye? You'd all best toss your filthy clothes. No amount of washing will remove the soot and stink of smoke off them."

Orla gathered a blanket from Nuala's linen cupboard in the hallway to hang over the indoor laundry line positioned to one side of the scullery. "A bit of privacy never hurt. Nuala has a metal burn-barrel out back. Pile your soiled clothing by the back door, and I'll light it up. Who's first, then?"

The girls stripped and wrapped themselves in Nuala's extra sheets while Orla transferred their pieces of clothing to the burn barrel after she stoked the coals. Would she never escape the repeated sight of nasty smoke, ashes, and flames? She would not view a hearth the same in the future, because fire was not always a cozy thing on a chilly, damp day. Sometimes a fire is from a mouth of a dragon or in the form of a woman. *Monstrous Ma Brown.*

She stuffed the last scraps of the girls' soiled clothing into the smoldering ashes with an iron poker and wiped her palms on her skirt. It did not help to clean her palms with soap. It added more grime to them. "Holy heavens. What good comes from battling that wretched woman? She's a female dragon."

Must she do battle with evil monsters all her life? This one was not her own inner dragon. This one, she did not earn money from. This one, she stole a man from. *So she thinks.* If that were the truth, was this fight worth winning at all costs? What about for her own heart?

Without Nuala's loving friendship, she would never have made it thus far. But Nuala cannot help her forever.

Tears swam in her eyes, then sobs of grief and heartbreak from loss and longing flooded her being. She dropped the poker, collapsed onto the ground beside the burn barrel, and allowed the disastrous situation to overwhelm her.

"Me friend. Hush, now. I'm here with you." Nuala wrapped her arms around Orla. "You'll recover. God is with us. Let it out, then."

Orla lost track of time, but when she opened her eyes and wiped her face with Nuala's kerchief, the sun hovered low above the lake. *It must be nearing suppertime.* She straightened to a sitting position, and Nuala released her hand. "Ah, me chum. I'm grateful for your love and kindness. Your hospitality. Your generous nature. You're nothing like me Maeve, in New York City, who claimed to be me friend. Nevertheless, you must be away to fix our supper, aye?"

"Glad to not be her, for you told me the stories, but you must get your bath, first, aye?" Nuala smiled.

With Orla bathed and redressed from the priest's newly delivered donations, her spirits improved. If only the shirt buttons connected with the button openings. Nuala's own lightweight blue scarf worked to cover her bosom by tucking it into the gaping bodice. "Don't wish to present me chest to all and sundry at the supper table, do I? A pixy must've worn this dress." She chuckled at how the short skirt hung over her long legs. It covered her calves but missed her ankles. Stockings would help. *Does Father have any of those with him?*

The clanking of dishes and clatter of silverware emanated from the dining room area. Someone dragged chairs, and cheerful chatter further proved dining preparations were underway and that a few boarders gathered for a meal.

Father Furmanski laugh and voice carried into the scullery. "No, no. I will tell you more stories when we sit down to eat. I rarely have such an appreciative audience. I wish to speak to Mr. Murphy here, for a moment."

What? Murphy's here? "Holy heavens." Her heartbeat raced. Her mouth dried. The weight of her longing for Bear burst free in her giddiness and flew up to the ceiling. *God does answer prayers, after all.* If only she had a mirror. What was she thinking? She avoided mirrors. She patted her damp hair, fluffed it with her fingers, and straightened her too tight clothing.

Nuala knocked on the doorframe. "Orla, are you presentable? I must get into the scullery to collect our supper and heat up a few dishes. And I've news for you."

"Aye. Let me help you, if I can." Orla's hands shook when she gathered the blanket from the clothesline across the bathing tub. *Holy heavens.* Her heart pounded but she hoped it would slow by the time she saw Bear. She would keep busy for a while first with emptying the tub and helping her friend.

"You just leave everything be and put that man out there out of his misery. Ever since I told him you were cleaning up, he can barely keep his eyes off the scullery door. Send me Violet and Poppy, for they've a wish to help. Go on, now." Nuala flicked her hand toward the other room.

"You're one of the hands and crown of the *Claddagh*. A true friend, and loyal, aye."

"Go on with you."

The nearer she drew to the dining room Murphy's voice increased in volume. By the sounds of the conversation, he addressed Father Furmanski. Her view was Bear's own handsome profile. She hesitated to catch her breath in the entry while he finished speaking. And collect her thoughts.

"I heard about the fire from the Whiskey Row merchants when we crossed paths on the docks in Duluth. They were returning with supplies to rebuild their various shops. They also mentioned you had been asking about it, Father. Rather fortuitous for you to be there."

"Yes, it was near the time I typically deliver donated goods from my parish. Look who is here, now." From the other side of the table, Furmanski smiled at Orla and took a seat beside Violet.

Murphy turned. His expression brightened, then changed into something near passion. *Methinks.* He gave a slight bow. "Madam Rose. I am happy to see you are uninjured."

Rascal. Why must he always mock her with gentlemanly behavior? "Glad to hear that you care. I heard as well, what brought you here. Your man, Sanderson, kept to his part of the bargain. He told me little. Said you'd tell me. What do you have to say for yourself, I'd like to know?"

Orla's rising volume scattered everyone in the room as they excused themselves for various reasons. It was laughable, but her frustration and pent-up angst restrained her amusement. What could this man say that would make one bit of difference to her? Secrets were little foxes. Destroying lovely gardens.

Murphy pursed his lips. His eyes roamed over her unusual outfit and stopped at her bare feet. "Have you chosen a new fashion style? I have not seen that before."

She stomped her foot, then rubbed it, hopping on her other.

Murphy's eyes twinkled. "My apologies for attempting to add humor. Shall we talk somewhere before supper?" He bent his elbow toward her.

The only place available was Nuala's room. Her wet hair and bare feet excluded a walk on the shore. Could they trust themselves upstairs? Holly stood at the farthest window gazing outside at something interesting. "Holly, we'll return in a few moments. Call upstairs if we don't."

"Of course."

Once inside the shared bedroom, Gal nearly melted into the floorboards with Murphy's greeting, and strokes on his belly. Orla shoved aside clothing from a chair for Murphy to sit in and plopped on the bed to face him. Her efforts to calm herself failed. She clenched her hands. "Explain yourself, please."

He deliberated a moment. "Sanderson, or my absence?"

"You're a grown fella, you figure it out."

Murphy narrowed his eyes. "First, you do not require rescuing. Nor did Poppy because of you and Gal. I am the one who wanted some answers as to what happened that night. After hearing details from Holly, she convinced me Ma Brown was behind the terrible actions of her son, Black. Should I continue? I have a man on retainer,

Mr. Sanderson, and I sent him. I am to meet up with him later this evening. There is more to tell you, but this is not the best time or place to explain."

"True, that. There are people downstairs I may frighten away if I yell out what's on me mind."

"Supper." Holly's voice echoed up the staircase. "You told me to tell you when."

Orla rose, and Murphy reached for her. "We will talk later, then. One embrace. One?"

Why not? She nodded, and the solace of his physical strength reached deep into her heart and soul. He was one man whom she nearly trusted. *May his presence anchor me in this moment.* But a man who would never want her. Why did she cross paths with him? How could she keep from crying? She must.

"My beautiful Miss Orla Muldoon. You are trembling." He mumbled above her head.

In truth who is this fella? Not who she thought. Orla broke free from his arms and rushed downstairs, with his footsteps behind her. It would be unseemly to run out the front door, would it not?

Nuala had left two empty chairs at the table beside each other. *Thoughtful. Torturous.*

Murphy pulled one out for her and took the other. After they occupied them, he brushed his arm against hers. More than once.

Shivers skittered up Orla's arms. "Holy heavens. Even now."

"Now? Very well. Now is the time for the blessing." After Father Furmanski blessed the food, he addressed Orla. "I see that you ladies have put to good use my parishioner's gifts. They will be so pleased to have helped you with their clothing. Are you all equipped with what you need, now, or is there something missing? Do you need housing and food? They have said they will make room for the five of you, if you require it."

Is he jesting? "Father, aren't your parishioners aware of what type of business I ran? Why would they offer us food and housing within their own family's havens?"

Father Furmanski chuckled. "Have you not experienced authentic

Christian charity, Miss Muldoon? Not all of us believers are good, and not all of us are bad. There are plenty of good souls out there to give aid to others. Judgement is reserved for the perfect, and only One is that good."

"Perhaps I've been the judgmental one. Meself." She must think hard about this, along with other recent developments. *This priest is a strange fella. Nevertheless, he seems genuine enough.*

CHAPTER 23

Her Golden Rings

All that remains to complete the claddagh is love
Orla

hy was everyone so cheerful when her heart is shredded, her dreams destroyed, and her plans all in tatters? *Unfair, that.* The girls depended upon her, and she had no one to turn to other than Nuala. Plus, her friendship had already fulfilled the loyal segment of the *claddagh. All that remains to complete the claddagh is love.* Is it the priest's Christian love? She slid a sideways glance at Murphy. What about a man's love? Would that ever complete the ancient exquisite ring of life for her?

Between her last bites of roasted chicken, carrots, and potatoes, she uneasily observed Holly and Daisy, flirting with the railroad workers at their supper tables. Her face heated. *Have they no morals to behave in such a way before the priest?*

Nuala raised one eyebrow and shrugged.

Orla chewed her lip and studied Father Furmanski. He seemed unperturbed and chatted with Poppy who was seated beside him. She surveyed her two working girlies again. They slid occasional furtive peeks at the priest. *So, they do care. Nonetheless, how else shall they earn their living whilst staying here?* That was the immediate long-term problem for Orla to solve. *How to earn wretched money forevermore.*

"Madam Rose." Murphy leaned close to her and murmured. "May we sneak away to the shore now? It will be dark soon."

She set her fork down beside her plate and murmured back to him. "Hm. I wish to go, nonetheless I'm barefoot, I don't wish to talk with you ever again. I'm in a quandary."

He chuckled. "Your honesty is what has always beguiled me."

Honesty? She nearly cuffed his chin. *Beguiled?* Why must he mock her heart with tender words? "I'm sure me hair has turned from its lovely shade of peach to dark red with those comments of yours, aye? You best watch out for me Irish temper. Fair warning. You've lit it to high heaven."

Nuala paused her conversation with the priest, and everyone at the table halted their conversations to listen to the squabble. *Had she been screeching like her own mam?*

Bear stood behind her chair. "I expected no less. It seems we are at a crossroads and have much to clarify for each other." *Acting a gentleman for an audience. Imposter.*

Everyone at the table furtively glanced at Orla as she arose. She swished her entangled skirt away from the chair legs.

Nuala's dark brows furrowed. "Are you away somewhere tonight?"

"To the lake. Let Gal out to come after me, if we don't return within an hour, aye? This fella here is a stranger to me after all."

Murphy grinned. "She speaks truth. Better to heed her claims. Excuse us, please."

"Aye." Nuala rapidly blinked.

Orla gracefully sashayed to the entryway. Or maybe she stomped.

She must remain in control of her temper, until she received some straight answers from Bear. Even then, he may justifiably receive the brunt of her ire.

"Your barefeet, Orla." Murphy's whisper caressed her neck. "You will also need a coat." *Was that a chuckle I heard?*

Nuala's boots lay on the entry floor. Probably a size too small. She sat on the bench and shoved her foot into the first one. Her toes curled under, but they should suffice for a short walk. After she loosely laced them both on, Orla tested their comfort by taking a few steps. "A little squeeze, is all."

Murphy opened the front door after she borrowed Nuala's cape from its peg, but it barely covered her shoulders and ended at her hips. *Curse these dainty women in me life.* Murphy waited for her to pass through the doorway. He shut the door with his foot and raised his elbow for her to take.

"No need for that." She led the way down with her neck stiffened and gingerly managed the steps from the porch to the beloved white picket fence—the only one in town. And with the only lovely rose arbor. One day, she must have both. *That could be me new dream somehow, aye.* A costly dream without enough coins in her purse? Her completely charred purse. She sniffed back tears and stuck out her arms for better balance. *Like a ballerina.*

"You still do not wish for my help?" Murphy chortled from behind her.

"Holy heavens, and no I don't. 'Tis glad I am to listen to your merriment over your own cruel behavior." She clenched her jaw and tried hurrying to the shore despite the pain in her scrunched feet without luck.

"I beg your pardon."

"Well, and wouldn't you like to have that? We shall see."

They rounded the yard to follow the path down to the lake. The rocks made it trickier for her to step over and around in her friend's tight boots. Every pinch of her toes nearly sent her back to The White Feather, but avid curiosity would not allow that. She absolutely must hear Murphy's story. She slid her gaze to him. "Expecting you to tell me the truth. You shall now, aye?"

He gave her a lopsided grin. "Aye. It is beyond time to do that, I should say."

"You should." She hastily selected a boulder easy enough to sit on and get the pressure off her feet. "Can't make it to the log on the shore tonight. These boots shall give me the worst of blisters if I try. Aye, this'll do."

He sat beside her. They stared out at the harbor and the point of cedars bordering it. The water reflected in his wide beautiful eyes. *Still noticing his looks?* She tensed, crossed her arms snugly against her ribcage, and scooted another quarter inch away. Would screaming make her feel better? They had known each other a long while, yet his effect on her senses had not altered at all. This was all much too unfair to deal with for a brilliant businesswoman. He should remain only a customer, should he not? How did she allow him to pierce her defenses and into her heart? It hurt more than anything yet in her life. She pushed her fist against her chest.

He surveyed the lake in silence.

Their surroundings turned darker by the moment. She blew out a breath. "Shall this be a difficult explanation for you, then? Are we waiting until Christmas arrives? Or can you not recall your own life's details? Mayhap you've been deceiving everyone for so long that—"

"Orla." He slowly turned to face her. Sorrow or regret shimmered in his eyes. *Tears?*

She had been so focused on her ire with him and her tragic circumstances she had not given any thought about how this conversation might develop into sadness. *Could it be a farewell?* Her most feared and tragic thing in the entire world could befall her. Him, never loving her in return. Her, being so disappointed with him in his appalling deception. Orla's breath caught, and perspiration dripped down her back. "Murphy."

"You are right that I have been deceptive for many years. The time to confess is now. What you could not possibly guess, are my reasons why, without knowing my background. You will hear exactly who I am. Stop me if a question arises, please?" He still had not touched her, but his eyes met hers, and he gave her a slight smile.

"Hm. Aye. One moment." She shifted her backside on the chilly rock and folded her legs to reach her tight boots and loosen the laces to better concentrate without the pain. She tugged Nuala's boots off and situated her feet on top of the leather. "Ready."

He grinned and crossed his arms. "You always find a way to adjust to discomfort, Orla. Persistent. Resilient. A person who finds a new way to thrive. Three traits I admire for survival. That is who I am as well. A survivor who thrives."

"Me da said not to trust a flatterer. You're sounding like one."

"Your dad was wise, Beautiful." He leaned sideways against her for a second. "Although, it is not flattery to state the truth. I was born to an affluent family and raised in Chicago."

"Affluent?" Orla frowned. *Can he speak without a jest?*

He took a deep breath and slowly nodded. "I have been incognito here with my crew to put distance between my father, his relentless bullying and threats, until it was safe. He passed away recently. That is where I was. In Chicago settling his affairs as his oldest and moving my mother to Duluth and away from terrible memories."

"This is the truth?" Orla leaned away and inspected him head to toe. Should she believe him?

He tapped his chest. "So, this is John Finnegan beside you, an iron ore barge worker, who is now an owner of a working gold mine."

"Finnegan, you say. And you're a rich man, then? You've loads of gold?" At his nod, Orla nearly tumbled off the boulder from hysterical laughter. It was better and less embarrassing than bawling. Of all the things he could be, that was not what she expected. After all the time she wanted riches and discovered it is the people who cared about her that are the real riches. Next, a fire set by an enemy destroys her dreams and way of life, and she could not afford to resurrect her business. A near brush with death for herself, Violet, and Poppy due to a madwoman's jealousy. Then she discovers the man she loves is wealthy. Pure irony.

His shoulders and poise had relaxed with her reaction, and he grinned wide, deepening his dimples.

She dabbed at her tears. "Pardon me. I'd expected you to say you're a criminal of some sort hiding out. You're not. To be certain, aye?"

"Not to most. I wanted to avoid witnessing and defending my cruel father's treatment of my indomitable mother, and to control my destiny and identity until I was ready to embrace it. He pledged not to abuse her if I abandoned the household. She assured me she would contact me if he did not keep his promise. You see, mother and I threatened my father with exposure and arrest. His reputation as a businessman and pillar of our community was all he cared deeply about. Our threat if he lost his control was the line he would not cross. It kept him in check."

"Cruel men are something I understand, unfortunately."

"Well, I am relieved you took the news so well. I expected a good dunking in the lake. No?"

"You've redeemed yourself. Nevertheless, there's more to this story. You've been hiding from your destiny. And I'd embraced mine. Tell me 'bout avoiding your life and your mam and da."

He stood, stuffed his hands into his trouser pockets, and paced slowly in front of her. "Father was an angry, violent man. He beat us, 'to keep us under control' and remind us of who we answer to. Father could have disciplined me differently, but he seemed to enjoy the violence. He beat mother long before he ever turned on me. Her injuries are the evidence of it. She was to blame for her mistreatment —so he always told her. The fear he cultivated in Mother and her submissive determination to make excuses for him kept her there until she was exhausted from it. She blamed the alcohol. I blamed his selfishness. I think his violent childhood damaged his soul."

"Aye." Orla cringed, and her throat constricted. She cleared it and swallowed. "Seen this tragedy many a time in Ireland, so why would it be different here? 'Tis most distasteful to treat a child badly. Drunkards often do that. Not me brother, Mick. He drinks to stifle his pain, nonetheless, he's not a vicious man because of it."

"My mother's father drank heavily, and beat her and her brothers, so she thought nothing of men behaving that way at first. I do not tolerate violence from loved ones, or timidity. I admire the inner strength it took for her to finally face his rage and secure his promise to stop hurting her with dire consequences for him if he broke his vow."

"Ah. So, you hid your identity to keep your father from finding you?"

"Guessing where I was put more fear into him. He could not have me traced. I am happy you understand. Father Furmanski and I met and became friends, and he counsels me now. We often crossed paths in Duluth the last several years. I like and admire that priest. He is a good man. He is also persuasive—about many things. We discussed what to do about Mr. Black, and he advised me to come here after Sanderson delivered his findings." Her Finnegan Bear turned to face the opposite shoreline.

Orla chewed her lip and wrung her hands. Time to explain her newfound pathway to God and hopefully changing her life. "Finnegan, did Father Furmanski urge you to seek God in your life? He's persuaded me to, along with Nuala herself. I ask because of something I heard 'bout you. And if 'twas true, do you believe in God and attend church?"

He stopped pacing and drew near her. "You surprise me, but yes. I have a growing faith in God. How did you hear of this? Did Sanderson say something to you?"

The tension eased in her neck and shoulders. "That nosy fella we've yet to discuss. Nah. Holly heard it from Ma Brown. That wicked creature hoped to secure you with a ruse she'd found God. A trap she set for you."

"Ma Brown?" He lifted his brows and chuckled. "Nothing she could do or anything about her entices interest within me whatsoever. Never did. More like revulsion." He sat beside her again but pushed his thigh against hers.

His proximity comforted her this time. "If you please, tell me 'bout Sanderson, then. I gave him the answers he sought. What's your plan for her son, Black?"

Finnegan ran his fingers through his hair. "Of course you would like to know. Sanderson has turned over your testimony, along with Violet's, Holly's, and Poppy's to Duluth authorities. Their investigation into him revealed that Black has long had a penchant for young girls. Let us pray he will be locked away for years."

"Holy heavens. Wasn't all 'bout Poppy, then? But Finnegan—"

"Will you please call me John? My last name is reserved for my crew and people who work for me. We know each other more intimately."

"Aye. So, I no longer work for you?"

"Did you ever, Beautiful?"

She smirked. "I think you're daft to call me that. Yet you seem to think it. I humored you to keep your business, don't you know? Mostly, you wanted to talk. Walk and talk. No man ever does that. It confused me to no end, with you knowing what I am."

He laughed. "I know you are not a gentle mannered woman, if that is what you refer to."

"Doesn't say much for your taste in women."

"Does not say much about your self-worth."

Orla stared at her bare, freezing white toes in the twilight. "That comment stings a bit, nevertheless, me worth hasn't ever been good within me own eyes. I know 'tis been fragile at best. Made it difficult to believe God loves me. Struggling with that fact yet."

"Without cause, as far as I am concerned. You are loveable." He stroked her fingers folded on her lap.

Her heartbeat sped up. She withdrew her hands from his reach, although she did it reluctantly. There was more to discuss.

He leaned away and studied the shore. "What do you think? Will your Black Angel visit us tonight?"

Here 'tis. Time to speak up about the changes within her heart and desires. *Nevertheless, I'm unworthy of this wealthy fella.* Will her words about seeking God shock him?

John slid a glance in her direction.

She dreaded his response, and she regretted the choked tone of her voice as she hurried to explain. "Now, 'tis me turn. I must rebuild me heart, and me life after the fire. I've begun to pray lately meself, 'bout returning to God and forsaking me own dreams. Being raised in the church didn't tether me with following Him, aye? Been reluctant. 'Tis painstaking to force meself to return."

"Orla, good things are not always the easiest to do."

She cleared her throat and picked at her skirt. "Aye. Nevertheless, I've accomplished nothing without God in me life. Was all gone in one horrid flame. I placed me faith in meself and hard work and plans. All for naught. Me purse, savings, and home are in ashes. All that's left is what I stashed inside me bodice. Suitable to me profession, aye? But nevermore. John, I'm finished with it all."

John stood and extended his hands to her. "You fought many challenges since your arrival in Whiskey Row. The distress caught up with you. Did it take a fire to help you realize you need more than yourself to rely on? More than your brilliant mind?"

She stared at his outstretched hands. What did he expect from her? Sharing the deeper things in her heart? Did he understand? "Do you believe I wish to change? To not be Madam Rose any longer? To live a good woman's life? For I won't be staying here. I won't run a bordello any longer." Her voice hit that high pitch she had inherited from her mother.

He gently grasped her arms and tugged her to standing within a few inches from his chest. "Barefoot Miss Muldoon. Will this convince you I believe your wishes? If this is what you truly want, will you be my wife? I want to take you home to my mother." He flashed his glorious smile with dimples and gripped her hands.

Her knees buckled, and she was glad he held her. The leather boots jabbed into the soles of her feet. When his fists tightened around her hands, she climbed up onto the boulder, pulling him to the edge of it with her. "Mr. Finnegan, what courage you must have to wish to live with the likes of me forever. I can only admire that quality and say— aye, my own Bear." She wrapped her arms around his neck and shoulders. His chest rumbled, then he kissed her neck.

Bear stepped back and slid her slowly down, until her feet landed on top of his own. Their kiss began gentle and slow, with murmuring promises in between. Passion grew and he drew back. "Why Miss Muldoon, there is no rush. We have many years of kisses before us, don't you know?"

Orla sighed. "I do know that. Every day. With nothing hidden that can separate us ever again?"

He winked.

"Well then, I'm glad I agreed to this engagement. Knew you were fond of me. Thought you'd never love a Madam—"

He pushed his fingertip against her lips. "No doubts about us. Not ever. Agreed?"

She grinned. "Let's tell the others. But you must carry me, love. Get used to it."

John hoisted her onto his back. She giggled. "Nuala's boots."

He bent slowly underneath her weight, then handed them to her. "I am trying to imagine what circumstances would force me to do this for you in the future."

"Ah, what 'bout to keep me from tripping over all your gold? Could be a perilous adventure climbing over that mountain of treasure inside that dark cave." Although, this was a gentle dragon who would not injure her and would share everything with her.

"In the mine?" He puffed in earnest by the time they reached the top of the hill. Lowering her off his back, he wrapped his arm around her shoulders, then kissed the top of her head.

They entered The White Feather, and she dropped the boots where she had collected them. Laughter echoed from the dining area.

Orla hung Nuala's little cape on its peg. "Sounds like Daisy. What's she up to? Her and Holly were fluttering their wiles at the men earlier. Was the first time they embarrassed me."

John selected a peg for his jacket. "That is unusual for you. Did you consider, when you said yes to me, what they will do without you?"

Icy dread built within her soul and its chill bumps spread over her body. She restrained a sob of worry and clutched her throat. "That's what I've had no answer to in all me considerations. 'Tis sure the girlies shall come up with something, but Poppy? That one's me own responsibility. I wish to keep her with us, John, and Gal."

He smiled and nodded. "Of course. My home is a mansion with many rooms."

Orla gasped. "A mansion—"

"There you be." Nuala peered around the dining room's entry. "Glad you're back. We've more visitors and a cake. Shall you join us?"

Daisy stood beside a beaming Mr. Cooley in the dining area. She clapped her hands and curtsied to the diners. She also wore her spectacles which slid down her nose. Daisy adjusted them with her forefinger.

What's this? "Never thought I'd see the day you'd wear your spectacles in public."

Daisy shrugged. "Well, here we are. Mr. Cooley convinced me that I look very scholarly and beautiful with them on."

Cooley flushed and grinned at Daisy.

"Madam Rose, can you guess what happened while you were at the shore? You never will. Mr. Cooley, Bill, has asked me to marry him and go to California so he can teach children there. Is that not wonderful? Jenny, that jealous harpy, told me that I would probably never marry, and I cannot wait to tell her—"

"Me girlie. I couldn't be gladder for you." Tears gathered in Orla's eyes. *Again, holy miracles.* She had never had so many of them in one day. Orla gave Daisy a squeeze and shook Bill Cooley's hand. "Mr. Cooley, you've shown yourself to be a wise man in choosing Daisy. She'll brighten your days for all your life long."

Daisy hugged her back. "Do not cry, Madam Rose. I have never seen you do that. Well, maybe a time or two. Not very often. Unless those are happy tears? Then bawl all you want for me." She laughed.

Orla giggled through her tears and wiped her cheeks. "'Tis grand news." She turned her back and faced the wall to compose herself. Her body trembled. She must get a grip in front of all these people. What must they think of her?

John stroked her back lightly with his fingertips. "Everything will work out, and your girls will be fine. No need to worry. Do you see it?"

During all the well-wishing from people, John clasped Orla's fingers. "Do you want to wait to tell everyone?"

She raised her face to him. "Nah, 'tis a night of merriment after much tragedy. I'll tell the tale when we sit down for dessert."

Father Furmanski joined Orla and John before the others did. "What have you to say, Mr. Murphy?" He glanced back and forth between them. "Is it good news? The Church encourages marriage and family, yes?"

"You certainly do. And I have a private confession to make. My name is not Murphy."

His deception's gotten himself into a tricky spot with a man of God. She restrained her smirk, for she now knew the consequences of pretense.

Those within earshot of John's comment murmured together, and the priest's brows disappeared beneath his low, thick hairline. "Eh? What was that?"

John grimaced. "I promise to tell you privately before the night is over."

Orla elbowed him. "You should've waited to say that. Puts a damper on things, aye?" She headed for the dining room and settled in the chair John scooted out for her.

John and Orla took their seats again at the table and waited for Violet, Poppy, and Nuala to serve people as they gathered back together for their celebration.

When Orla and John took the opportunity to announce their own engagement, Orla studied Nuala, and the girls. The women seemed genuinely happy for her. She detected no angst, yet Poppy frowned slightly when she thought no one was paying attention. *Should've assured her of her place with us before announcing. Eejit.*

John mumbled to Orla. "Our eagerness to spill our plans to everyone caused some issues. Poppy looks uneasy, right? You can tell her she is invited to go with us. Put your favorite girl out of her misery."

Orla reached across the table between the plates and glasses. "Poppy, give a listen. You're to come with us, aye? Should you wish to, that is. What do you say?"

Poppy dropped her fork, clattering it onto her plate, and squealed. "Oh, Madam, I'd love to, above anything else! We'll have Gal with us as well, right?"

"Could never leave him behind."

The evening's celebrations and merriment continued past midnight. Orla was not ready to go to bed after John, Layton, and Father Furmanski departed for their lodgings. She and Nuala agreed to chat for a while in their bedroom in the glow from the candle on the dresser.

Alone with her trusted friend, Orla shared the doubts she harbored. "What happened with John tonight was something I never foresaw. Sure, and I prayed for it. Not much faith, aye? I pestered God with them night after night in my bedtime prayers. Nevertheless, I'm unworthy of a fella like John. This reminds me that I'm even more unworthy of God's love as well. He's holy. I'm not. The chasm between us is wide and deep. Am I a fool to think He'd want me to draw nearer to Him? You said He welcomes us."

Nuala covered Orla's hand with her own. "Me friend, we go to God just as we are. We can't completely clean up first. Aye, we should confess and turn from our old life, nonetheless. Who is holy enough to stand before God? Not I. Go to Him in whatever condition you're in and He's there to meet you."

"You helped me often see God at work in me life. And your words just now sounded like what Father Furmanski might say."

"Aye, for he helped me to see the truth 'bout me own sins and attainable change. We lay all of it before God to clean us up." She curled her legs up beneath her nightgown.

Orla smirked and shuddered. "Me own dear friend you'd redeem most of the Crown's sins against the Irish with your logic. I know those who'd not like that at all."

"We've all many sins, yet we only covet redemption for ourselves, aye? Not as a gift for others who've wronged us terribly. I entertained a long, hard think to accept that fact."

"You're a priceless gift to me, you are. Before you, I'd only Maeve. She's a mess. Before her I'd me cousin, Tarah. Their only thoughts were what to do each day to eat and survive. They spoke of no deep nor difficult truth. We were all trying to earn a living and live in a harsh world where what we do caused others to shun us."

"I know."

Orla squeezed Nuala's fingers. "You, Nuala, are me best friend. You encouraged me to hope. To think in a better way 'bout meself. You'd see God near and point it out to me, when I was blinded by me own sorrows."

"Me chum, 'tis been me pleasure to know you. Stop it now." Nuala sniffed and wiped her eyes.

"Listen. You did more than these things, for you invited me and the girlies into your home. We were in frightful need, aye? You didn't hesitate or blink before opening your door to us. We'd nothing to give in return, nevertheless, you filled our lack with your own belongings. This is what Father Furmanski meant by Christian love, and you've shone it like me lantern glowing on the dark lakeshore."

Nuala climbed off the bed to snuff out the candle. "Enough, now, 'tis late. I'll miss you, I will. One other thing. Do you think Poppy will be happy? And Sir Gallant?"

Orla snuggled against the pillow and headboard. "I want her with us, and John agrees to it. Me only concern is his mother. I've never met a fella's mother, and now to bring another young woman with canes into her household, and one who can't manage stairs as well? Did I mention it's a mansion, no less? John must know I'd bring Gal with me. There's sure to be a brouhaha in his mother's house for I'm even less certain a big dog is acceptable. Think his mother shall be flexible in her ideas?"

"I suppose you'll find out."

CHAPTER 24

Her Picket Fences

God can't expect me to be always good now, can He?
Orla

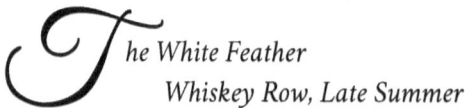he White Feather
Whiskey Row, Late Summer

TWINGES OF LONELINESS settled into Orla's soul when John took Sir Gallant back to Duluth with him to get accustomed to his new home and family. Then came Daisy's bittersweet departure with Cooley a few days ago. Today's farewell for Violet and Holly's plans to move to California completed this new phase of Orla's life. Her Flower Garden women took little with them on the ferry across Lake Superior. However, thanks to Father Furmanski's church donations, they packed a change of clothes in their bags, shoes to wear, and capes.

Orla and Nuala spoke with the kind priest. "I'll be glad to meet your people, Father. Never have met such a generous flock as yours. They give their clothing often to charity, aye? Nonetheless, the bit of coin they collected for the girlies to begin anew—well, 'twas surely unexpected."

"You may personally thank the parish on your wedding day. Do not worry, it is all set. My goodness, have they been following your love story like a *fascicle* in the newspaper. Never seen such an interest in church business. Officiating your wedding will be the hubbub of the church for months. Now, to escort your women to Duluth and return to my pressing responsibilities. Ready to say your fond farewells, ladies?" He waved back at Orla and Nuala and headed for the waiting horse cart.

Violet and Holly approached Orla with mixed expressions of sorrow and excitement. Violet quickly blinked her shiny violet eyes and swallowed with a half-smile. "If I could, I would not miss your wedding for anything, Madam Rose. You know that? We must return to work after so much time without it. And burdening poor Mrs. Kincaid as well. It was fortuitous that Mr. Layton had connections and investments to set up a business in California was it not? Unfortunately, we must hurry away from Duluth. I would rather attend your wedding more than anything in the world. Although, being penniless is terrifying."

"I agree." Holly bowed her head and dabbed her eyes.

Violet nodded at Nuala. "We thank you, Mrs. Kincaid, for absolutely everything. And Madam Rose, I have never met anyone like you. You seemed harsh at first and I was unsure how you would treat us."

Orla's jaw slackened. "Ah."

Violet fluttered her fingers. "My concerns were terribly unfounded, but I think you wanted us to see you as a tough business-woman. I will always remember you with a great fondness of heart. Making a new friend with Holly was nearly as big a surprise. We will write soon from San Francisco. Goodbye, and Godspeed." She kissed Orla's cheek, then dashed back to Father Furmanski.

Holly watched Violet until she reached the wagon, then twisted back to face Orla. "I believe at one time the trouble I caused outweighed my worth to you. No sense denying that. Your resilience and bravery were examples for me to emulate. I can do this. No one needs to tell me how to live or what to do. What I really hope now is that you know without one doubt that I came to respect and admire you. I am happy we made amends, Madam Muldoon."

Orla nodded. Tears swam in her vision. "You gave me sleepless nights and quite the tussles, aye. And kept me off-balance and on me toes. I learned much from you as well. I'm grateful for that. You now have a friend in Violet. Don't muddle it, prickly girl."

"Never thought you would be grateful for my presence." Holly pulled a face. "I do know not to mess up our new friendship. I will be mindful of that."

"You'll go far with that new attitude, then."

Holly sniffed and turned to Nuala. "Mrs. Kincaid, you nearly made a believer out of me by your charitable behavior. You surprised me with your kindness many times. Who knows? Perhaps one day, I will find it in my heart to seek out God. It could be possible. Once we settle into our new bordello, we shall write to you both with our address. May you have all the happiness in the world—the both of you. Fare thee well." The soles of her donated shoes scuffed along the gravel to the wagon.

After everyone settled in their places, the wagon's driver directed his horses down the hill toward the lake and the ferry. She and Nuala waited until the girls disappeared, then turned back toward The White Feather.

Orla dabbed at her wet cheeks. "How shall I ever adjust to being without them? 'Tis already too quiet in me life, Nuala. It once vexed me to no end to witness the frequent wearying kerfuffle they had with each other."

Nuala smiled. "Take heart. There's still your Poppy. She shall keep things lively for you. And Mr. Finnegan's mother. Has he told you much 'bout her? Is she timid, bossy, or motherly? She might be a bit of a challenge for you as well."

"Hm. He's told me little. His respect for her is solid. Mayhap me presence shall change that. Our Poppy brings out the best in everyone, aye?"

Nuala grimaced. "'Tis possible. Let's partake of some coffee with Poppy whilst we discuss your wedding plans, aye? Just think, another month, and you're a Mrs. Finnegan. Nevertheless, I've mixed feelings 'bout your desertion, leaving me with only the boarders once more."

Orla strolled to The White Feather's porch and turned. She chuckled. "Don't you know, I asked our Poppy if she'd wish to stay with you. To give her a choice. She's not having it. Truth be told, I need her delightful presence to help meself adjust to a rich man's world. Been having some nightmares 'bout entering that life, 'tis sure."

"There, now. Thought you'd been seeing your own worth these days, aye? What shall it take for you to believe it? Must you have a golden crown? I shall name you Queen Orla." Nuala looped her arm through her friend's, and ushered Orla inside and to their favorite spot by the window in the common room. "Will be only a moment."

Orla stretched her arms wide and cupped her palms behind her head. She raised her voice. "Wish me girlies could all be at me wedding, Nuala. They'd been too long without a means of working, then have that ride from Mr. Layton to San Francisco. Not difficult to understand, aye? Hoping all will be well for them. Heard that city is as wild as could be. Mayhap worse than Whiskey Row."

"Aye, the stories from that place curl one's toes. Our Poppy is dozing on her cot in the scullery. Shall I awaken her to join us?"

"Nah, me girlie needs her rest."

Nuala set the drink tray and blueberry biscuits in the center of the small table between their chairs. "I understand as well, don't you know, that the girlies must begin over. Couldn't keep you all here much longer. We've been stacked like corn cobs in a basket, and I needed me rooms to rent once more. Turning away lodgers couldn't go on, could it? 'Tis sorry I am 'bout that, me friend. 'Tis always 'bout the money in this world, aye?" She patted her tears with her apron hem.

"Money is how we survive, and you've done more for us while we were without it than I'd ever expected." Orla rose and embraced her friend. "You and Poppy shall be at me wedding as bridesmaids, and that's blessing enough to cheer me heart. You be glad, as well, aye?"

* * *

Once Orla and Poppy arrived and settled temporarily in Duluth, Orla wondered how she'd get through her long list of sins during confession the week before her wedding. "Nigh impossible, I'd say, Poppy."

"I've had trouble imagining confession as well, Madam—"

"Hey, now, you? What could you ever have done wrong? And you must stop calling me that. 'Tis Orla. I'm your sister. Repeat it within your mind, aye?" Orla inspected the newly constructed Catholic church highlighted by the sunrise on Duluth's outskirts. "Why did that fiancé of mine believe this to be the best place to confess?"

Poppy giggled. "You'll be just fine. As am I, snuggled tight inside this blanket. And no, for the thousandth time, I don't wish to accompany you inside. Climbing down from the wagon is more trouble for you. Go ahead. God already knows what we've done or didn't do anyway."

"Thinking on that makes me queasy, me girlie."

"You'll feel better soon. It'll go fast, you'll see. Before you can shake a lamb's tail like you say, you'll be a prepared bride, married, and we'll eventually be living in Duluth."

Beads of sweat pooled on Orla's brow. Her legs trembled, but she had set this whole thing in motion, had she not, by wanting to do her wedding right? *One confesses before one's wedding.* She tipped her head with her brand-new feathered hat at two passing women headed for the entry, just as the church bell chimed seven o'clock. How long had it been since she had heard the gong of church bells overhead? Not since Killarney. Her eardrums vibrated with each strike. *Is it a death-nell?*

Sunbeams flared around the steeple. Orla studied them for God's warning. Her behavior at St. Mary's Cathedral flitted through her mind on the day they had visited their brother. Had she not unashamedly announced she hid secrets from God?

"Best get it over with." Poppy called.

"Aye, don't I know it." She kicked a dirt clod and headed for the church steps. Her heart pounded, and her eyes had trouble adjusting to the dim interior. The hush of God's presence surrounded her. Soft echoes from people on the kneelers or their footsteps as they found a bench took her back to her childhood. The church was not yet full.

"Good morning. Welcome to St. Luke's." A young man near the door startled her. He was probably the greeter and stepped toward Orla. He spoke in a whisper. "Confession is about to begin. You can go in, for there is no waiting. I will follow."

"Name's Miss Muldoon." Nerves shook her hands, but she genuflected facing the altar by grasping the edge of a bench and grit her teeth as the confessional booth's threat increased in her mind. *Holy heavens. What am I doing?*

Fresh cut wood, varnish, and the fragrance of flowers before the altar assailed Orla's nostrils. She glanced around the interior noting the construction stage in its finishing touches.

A saw and sawhorse stood in the far corner with a pile of other tools stacked underneath them. The two women from earlier knelt in the second row of unvarnished pews. A man sat with his head bowed three rows behind the women. An altar boy behind the first altar polished a gold item, a *thurible*, with a cloth. The altar seemed to be missing some items, but she could not recall what. *Makes sense, for the church isn't truly completed.*

A movement coming out of the shadows on her right side halted her progress. An aged, white-haired priest with sallow cheeks and clutching a cane almost collided with her.

Where'd he come from? "I hear you're offering confession, Father."

The greeter mumbled behind her shoulder. "That is Father Doolin."

Father Doolin's head trembled to match his shaky voice. "Aye, making me way to it." The priest's purple lips parted in a wide smile over the teeth remaining in his mouth. He continued toward the booth, and she followed, glancing over her shoulder at the greeter. *Blocking me way of escape, is he?*

Father Doolin cleared his throat.

Orla turned and jarred against the priest, for they had arrived at the confessional. The priest used his cane to catch his balance. "Pardon me." He hobbled away and disappeared behind the booth's curtain.

The greeter waved her forward. "You'll find it a bit rough inside, Miss Muldoon. It's awaiting more sanding, varnishing, and finishing of the upholstery while Father Doolin conducts the sacraments. Mind the splinters when you kneel."

Orla paused. Could she remember what to say first? She did not trust her memory of something she had not done for decades. Her heart pounded. *Should've rehearsed at home.*

The confessional bench creaked from the other side of the wall. The priest was ready and expecting her confession. *I must go through with this to be married. Is it worth this risk of reminding God what I've done?* She took a step back and half turned away.

A loud cough sounded from within the booth. It mimicked her name. 'Muldoon.'

She hesitated until a flash of light from the rear of the church shone across the confessional's red curtain. Orla sprang to the booth and brushed through the curtain. Her brother, Mick, always spoke about keeping in God's angel's good esteem. Surely, He sent them to hold her to her desire to return to His flock. She carefully knelt on the unfinished bench below the screened window positioned between her and the priest. Her eyes slowly adjusted to the darkness.

Whoosh. The two-by-two square door slid open in its track, and the priest murmured through the wood screen. He whispered. "Would you like to make your confession, me child?"

Orla blew out her breath and shook her head. "Forgive me, Father, for I have sinned." *No lightning strikes yet.* "'Tis been too long, uh, decades since me last Confession." *Must I confess everything?*

Silence. *Did I recite it wrong?*

She folded her hands and spoke closer to the screen. "Father Doolin?"

A faint clicking noise carried through the screen. *Snoring?*

"Hallo, there." She spoke a little louder.

Silence. She could not believe her Irish luck had resurrected. *If he's asleep, I'll confess, and be done with it.* Orla listed every sin she recalled for the past thirty years and might have skipped a few.

Every so often, she stopped to listen for his snoring, and at the end of her list, she knocked loudly on the screen. "Father Doolin. I'm finished with me confession." With no response, she repeated her words and knocked louder.

"Eh? What?"

Orla cupped her hands around her mouth. "I'm thanking you for me confession and need me penance for *absolution.* Please, tell me how many Hail Mary's and Our Father's I must pray for that very long list of sins I've committed." *Is it another sin not to tell the priest he was napping? Forgive me, if so.*

"Well, now, as you say it was such a long list. Ten of the Hail Mary's and five Our Father's. Go and sin no more, me child." The bench creaked, something wooden banged against the wall, and Father Doolin mumbled. "Don't recall a thing she said."

Orla gathered her skirts to head for the pews and pray for her penance. She struggled because of her numb knees to gain her footing and shook the blood back into her legs. She was still alive. *I'm grateful to God for that.*

* * *

St. Mary's, Star of the Sea Catholic Church
Duluth, Minnesota
One week later, the momentous occasion was exactly how she had

imagined her wedding day to be, if it ever happened. *A girl always dreams, no matter her station in life.* Orla's reflection in the cheval mirror presented a tall bride adorned with her perfect wedding dress. The cream color suited her pale complexion as a beautiful backdrop to her peach hair. Its high, ruched collar's pleats filled in the deep, u-shaped neckline. The drapes of pearls woven throughout the ruffles on the bodice, and three-quarter length sleeves added the unique touches Orla coveted. "I'm dreaming, aye?"

Poppy giggled. "You're wide awake, M—Orla. Your long train is delightfully draped over all that lacy underskirt. I'm honored to carry it and to be part of your procession."

"Having you and Nuala with me are one of the best parts of me wedding day, 'tis sure."

Nuala blew her nose. "I'm reminded of me own lovely wedding to my handsome husband and glad me daughter wore me own wedding dress. I pray for grandchildren now."

"Sure, and I must begin with children. Mayhap God will answer that prayer next? And they will be beautiful like their father. Without scars." Strange, but tugging the veil over her face was not as crucial to her as it had been for most of her life. The mirror reflected the most statuesque bride to ever traverse a church's aisle. "Never seen so much of meself at once. Had I, mayhap I would've had a better impression, aye?"

Nuala and Poppy's reflections appeared behind her own when Nuala pushed Poppy closer to the mirror in her newly purchased wheelchair. *John is so considerate.* Orla's bouquet of red roses and green ferns trembled slightly. She slowly inhaled and exhaled to control her nerves and excitement. She must not care what people think of her being John's bride, or why he would choose a woman like her.

Poppy clapped her hands. "All the women will be so envious of you, Orla. I wish Holly could see you. And the others. I miss them."

"Me own thoughts for sure today." Orla breathed in deep. "What shall John look like, do you think?" *Handsome devil.* "He wouldn't look terrible in a pair of filthy overalls and barefoot."

Nuala peeked over Orla's shoulder and grinned at her reflection.

"Aye." She fingered the veil, and chuckled. "Can you breathe within that thing, me friend? Would be a tragedy to finally get you to the altar only to discover you'd been suffocated while strolling down the aisle, aye?"

"Doing just grand. Tip it back, all the same. No need for it now." Orla batted her darkened lashes and inspected her darkened eyebrows. She peered closer at her uncovered face. "Do me eyes appear more striking, or is it me own foolish desire with these enhancements?"

"Mrs. Finnegan's maid, the older Mrs. Finnegan, did a grand job painting you and doing up your hair. Shall you call Mrs. Finnegan 'mother' to keep it less confusing?" Nuala brushed down the rest of Orla's veil behind her back.

"Don't know. Shall ask her when we meet at the house. You know she stayed home because of her health, so she said. Hoping 'tis true. I suspect John hasn't told her every detail 'bout me, her new daughter-in-law."

Nuala grimaced. "Could be that. You'll be sharing a home, nevertheless."

"Aye, and a mansion, he said. Here." Orla handed the gorgeous bouquet with the delightful aroma to Poppy and shifted herself sideways to check her profile and the veil. The bustle created the illusion of a tinier waist. "Can't see clearly. All the buttons are latched, aye?"

A knock on the door stopped Orla's chatter but heightened her nerves. *What if he's changed his mind?* Her heartbeat raced. She really did not deserve such a man. "Enter."

Mrs. Finnegan's immaculate, petite, brunette maid, Maureen, gracefully slid through the doorway, then bobbed a curtsy. "Mam, I'm here to retrieve you."

Orla released her pent-up breath. "Orla's me name. If that's grand with you."

"As you say." The maid glanced at Poppy and dimpled. "Shall I push the chair?"

Nuala gripped the chair bars and shook her head. "No, thank you. I'll be taking her with me."

When the maid opened the door again, organ music floated around the wedding party. 'Tis truly happening, holy heavens." She closed her eyes. *God, only You could make it so, and I'm very grateful, I am.*

They trailed the maid, with Nuala pushing Poppy, gripping Orla's long train.

Orla restrained a chuckle at what this entourage must look like to any witnesses. She halted outside the open entrance into the sanctuary awaiting the music to change to the wedding march as the maid departed from them.

Nuala squeezed her fingers, lifted the wedding bouquet from Poppy's lap, then handed it her. She winked. "God loved you always, didn't He?"

The church bells tolled above the congregation. *Remember the cathedral in Killarney?* She had refused to enter it. "Isn't this interesting, girlies? God answered me prayer. Even as a soiled woman. And me not even a nun. He must've remembered I asked for this life, and then He gave it to me. I went to confession. I cleaned meself up. We're on good terms, now. Not expecting lightning strikes this time."

Poppy's brow furrowed. "Why would you think that?"

Before Orla stepped through the new arched door so like the other and older St. Mary's in Killarney, the wedding tune alerted the congregation. Orla peered at the colorful gothic stained-glass windows, and up at the matching carved, gothic shaped, golden archway over the altar. "Holy heavens. 'Tis 'bout to happen. He's watching."

Nuala laughed. "God does see you, Orla. He's been awaiting your homecoming for many a year."

"Thank you, friend. Now, I've returned."

$$* \; * \; *$$

LATE IN THE evening of their wedding day, Orla and John climbed down from his carriage after his men unloaded Poppy and set up her chair. Orla shook the last pieces of rice from her veil.

The newlyweds stood with Poppy seated comfortably in her chair in front of the Finnegan's enormous, red-brick mansion. Every window was lit in a welcoming manner and poured golden light against an encompassing wrought iron fence. *So much like Dr. Ross's home.*

Orla counted three stories, four tall brick chimneys, and a magnificently high brick arched portico. Her jaw dropped. She was going to live here. Her own home. She laughed until her sides ached.

"I enjoy hearing you laugh, even if it is about your new home." John's dimples deepened handsomely. "Although, darling, there is one thing I should tell you. My mother can be difficult to get along with. Flighty. Moody. Vague when it suits her. I do not expect you to like her, or keep quiet about things you object to, but can you be civil to her? That would be nice. Thoughts?"

A voice screeched from within the house. Its shrill was like a seagull. Not that of an invalid, as John led her to believe. "Stop that scruffy dog from pawing at the doors! Finnegan, is that my boy? Finally! My nerves are frazzled with worry. I suppose he went off and married that awful woman? Did he expect me to let her enter my home? What was he thinking, that ungrateful son?"

Orla massaged her cheeks. "John. You said she knew and didn't feel well enough to attend our wedding."

His eyes twinkled. "That is what she said. She forgets things. So, can you be civil? What do you think?"

Orla pursed her lips. *What do I think? God can't expect me to be always good now, can He? Surely not. He's given me another Mam.* She lifted a brow at her new husband. "I'm grateful, I am, to have a new mother that you're sharing with me."

He winked.

Poppy smiled up at John. "I've never had a mother. Are they always a bit rude? I'll still be happy to have one."

"I am glad you will be happy, poppet. Mother has a unique personality." He pushed Poppy forward to the steps, and two waiting male staff lifted Poppy and her new chair over the obstacle and opened the mansion's doors.

Gal shot outside quick as an archer's arrow headed for the bulls-eye. He landed on Orla with both front paws, nearly toppling her over. John braced her from behind while Gal jumped for joy and licked them both on their hands. His tail whacked Poppy's arm, and she giggled. The happy dog restrained his enthusiasm with Poppy and sniffed all around her wheelchair.

"He shall get accustomed to it in no time. Watch out for his paws when you roll it, Poppy girl." Orla raised the hem of her purple silk ensemble in her dampened lacy gloved hands as she climbed the steps toward the open door. A staunch and grim butler stared straight ahead and stood at stiff attention guarding the entry.

Gal bounded into the mansion through the open doors and back outside again. He sat by Orla.

"This is Hobbs, darling." John nodded at the butler from inside the doorway. "He has been with our family long before our home here was purchased. How is your family, Hobbs?"

"Very well, sir. Our best wishes, sir." His dark eyes glinted and darted to Orla.

"And has Mother adjusted to her new home? I should think so. She seemed relieved to leave Chicago."

Hobbs bowed slightly. "Yessir. However, the dog was more difficult. If I may add, a maid Greta, is familiar with the breed and speaks German to him. He seems to know it."

Orla chuckled with John. "Of course me Gal would understand the language." *Let's get to it.* She nodded. "'Tis grand to meet you Hobbs, and is that you in there at last, Mrs. Finnegan? You sound exactly like me own dear mother. I shall call you Mother Finnegan, I will. Won't you be liking that? We'll be a matching pair of doves, I know 'tis true."

John chuckled, and his warm palm heated her lower back. "We shall see."

No one answered her from inside, but Gal entered their new home ahead of her. Orla's eyes adjusted to the shadows in the foyer. She sucked in a quick breath at the surrounding magnificence that could shrink a statuesque woman within a few seconds. Then she noticed the staff lined up near the spiral staircase. *Holy heavens.*

A petite elderly woman in a black mourning dress with black gloves, sat in a chair much like Poppy's. Her thick, white hair was tidy in a braided bun yet revealed a terrible burn scar from her jawline and ear, and down her neck.

"A scar, John? Now I fathom why—"

"So, this is the little girl you brought to me, then?" Mother Finnegan's intense dark glare focused solely on Poppy while she brandished a large magnifying glass to inspect her without expression from head to toe. "Your name is Poppy, and my son invited you to live here with us?"

If this woman who's supposed to be me new mother says one rude thing to me Poppy, me marriage shall be over before it begins. Orla pressed her lips together.

Poppy folded her gloved hands and smiled gently. "Yes, Ma'am. I'm so happy to be part of your family." Gal joined Poppy and sniffed at her wheelchair again.

"Of course you are, and I have been waiting for a daughter for many years. I have only a son. Not much comfort to a mother in her need. I believe you and I will have many enjoyable hours together. Call me Mother. Do you play chess?"

"No, Ma'am, uh, Mother."

"I shall teach you. Race you to the game room." Fragile Mother Finnegan launched her chair forward with such force from her delicate hands and surprising speed that the staff leapt out of her way, and two maids scrambled after her. They squealed when Gal barked and dashed in circles around Poppy.

Poppy giggled, tugged off her gloves, and skimmed her hands on top of the wheels, gaining speed. She caught up with the group, with Gal sliding on the polished floors and nipping at her wheels.

Orla giggled with relief. "Gal shall get accustomed to the chair and not need to guard Poppy from it. Unsure if the maids shall adjust to the brouhaha. Some looked downright panicked. All's right with the world then. God blessed our dearest Poppy."

John caressed Orla's neck with his fingertips. "Are you blessed that you married me, darling? Mother fully ignored you. I am mortified—"

"Sh." Orla turned to him and placed her palms against his chest. "Don't be, darling Bear. If she lavishly loves on our Poppy, and makes her the daughter of the house, I shall be most content. We've each other forever, aye?"

He kissed her forehead. "Shall we join them in the game room? Do you like chess?"

"Hm. You've given me much to think 'bout. Shall your generous hospitality and imagination offer me anything else?"

The End

ABOUT THE AUTHOR

E. V. Sparrow is an emerging author of historical fiction. In <u>Those Resilient Muldoons</u> series, this is Sparrow's third book, and she wrote a prequel novella.

E. V. Sparrow is a short story writer turned novelist. Her readers encounter God's unexpected presence through her character's escapades. Her own adventures she wrote short stories about involved traveling in over twenty countries. Sparrow lived overseas for a year and hopped a freight train for a weekend.

A highlight for Sparrow is when Guideposts and Bethany House Publishers accepted four of her anthologized stories before she signed a 3-book historical fiction series contract with Celebrate Lit Publishing.

Her father's family's immigrated from Ireland, and saved their photos, letters and documents. Some family stories inspired her current 3-book historical fiction series.

In E.V.'s personal and church life, she ministered through prayer, worship, mission teams, and in Divorce Care and Singles. California native relocated to North Carolina. E.V. Sparrow and her husband enjoy family time with their grandchildren and exploring their new state. Sparrow never misses a day without coffee, chocolate, and feeding her birds, squirrels and chipmunks waiting outside her door in Sparrow Woods.

ACKNOWLEDGMENTS

I thank God for the call to write stories, and my mom for encouraging us to read books. Reading stack after stack of books increased my imagination. I'm grateful to my oldest brother, Ray, who told me a snippet of our grandfather's experience with his aunt, who I named Orla Muldoon. That vague and almost lost piece of family history piqued my curiosity about her, and readers wanted more. Now the world has *Madam Muldoon's Garden*.

My daughter, Hannah Hagen, is the only one who has read this entire book, my only other editor, and tireless researcher. Without my macushla's teamwork, there would be no entire books by me—only short stories.

Whenever I travel to Ireland, my spirit soars. I embrace the county and area where this branch of my family came from. I may never know why, but it embraces me in return.

ALSO BY E.V. SPARROW

Novella prequel, *Muldoon's Minnesota Darling, a novella, a prequel to the series* (2023).

Book 1, *Muldoon's Misfortunes* (2024) Bookfest, General Historical Fiction First-Place award-winner.

Book 2, *Madam Muldoon's Garden* (2025)

Book 3, *Rescuing the Muldoon Family* (2026)

*Published short stories in compilations:

Heaven's Sightings (2019) *Heavenly Hand*, a Bethany House Publishers' anthology

Miracles Do Happen (2019), *Jesus Made Me Feel Better, Miracle Among Friends,* and *Chill Alert*, a Guideposts' anthology

*Grace Publishing short story anthologies:

Short and Sweet, Too, *The Sword of Truth* (2017) https://grace-publishing. com/short-and-sweet-too/

Short and Sweet Goes Fourth, *Soles* (2018) https://grace-publishing.com/ short-sweet-goes-fourth/

Short and Sweet Takes the Fifth, *Chills* (2018) https://grace-publishing.com/ short-sweet-takes-fifth/

Celebrating Christmas, *Christmas in Bavaria* (2021) https://grace-publishing. com/1950-2/

*Inspire Writers short story anthologies:

Inspire Joy anthology, *Don't Bypass Joy, My Love* (2016)

Inspire Love anthology, *Ella's Heart* (2017)

Inspire Kindness anthology, *Stranded* (2018)

Inspire Grace anthology, *Unexpected Grace* (2019)

AUTHOR'S NOTES

My parents had me baptized and raised me in the Roman Catholic Church. The purpose of this novel isn't to promote or degrade my Irish Catholic heritage and faith, it is to include it for introducing me to faith in the Lord Jesus Christ and the Holy Trinity.

An unexpected thing happened when I wrote *Muldoon's Misfortunes*, Book 1 inspired by my great grandfather's life. My oldest brother told me about Mick's sister that immigrated with him from Ireland. Writing her as a secondary character in the book intrigued readers, and they wanted to know more of her story. The idea of *Madam Muldoon's Garden*, Book 2 was born.

My brother also told me the two stunning facts he'd heard about from our grandfather surrounding her life, and that was enough for me to start a novel.

You may already know that research is foundational for historical fiction. I dug through everything I had from my family in my possession after I spoke to my brother. Then, my researcher, Hannah, unearthed some gems via the internet, Irish history, and Ancestry.

Here's a list of documented facts, and/or family rumors about the character, Orla Muldoon.

The era is accurate, and the place names I used in Ireland were exact. I cited dates that are varied from actual to ballpark. When useful to Orla's story, I included the family structure, church culture, health, and legal systems within 1850s rural Ireland.

Orla's profession was true, and I focused on why it was needed for the survival of families. This story is from Orla's viewpoint on her situation. Of course this is one-sided as the characters are Irish, and many readers will already know about the terrible angst between the English and Irish with their hundreds of years history of war.

Whiskey Row was an actual area in a rowdy shipping town on Lake Superior north of Duluth, and exactly where my brother said our grandfather told him Orla had her bordello. The region of Agate Bay was settled by Thomas Sexton in 1856. Later, it developed with a focus on ore shipping and a railroad link to The Iron Ore Range on Lake Superior. Since 1907, it is called The City of Two Harbors. I read that locals are uncomfortable with Whiskey Row's wild history, but it intrigues me because of Orla.

See: https://mix108.com/5-things-you-might-not-know-about-two-harbors/

Rumor has it that Orla married and had children. We couldn't track down any definitive records, so I created a redemptive love story I hope you enjoy, because God even loves a Madam.

THE FLOWER GARDEN'S HOUSE RULES

Rule Number One—always be polite.

Rule Number Two—take a bath before visiting us.

Rule Number Three—no chewing tobacco.

Rule Four—no spitting on the floor.

Rule Five—no petting the dog.

Rule Number Six—no cursing or taking God's name in vain. No version of His name is acceptable.

Rule Seven—always remain clothed in public areas.

Rule Eight—no running down the hallways.

Rule Number Nine—no hitting, pushing, or kicking.

Rule Ten—no more than one drink.

Rule Number Eleven—no requesting an 'I owe you.' Payment is due before you leave.

Rule Number Twelve—you may not complain 'bout the poetry reading, chess games, or any other entertainment we've planned to start the evenings.